THE DEPUTY CORON. ... here were three or four people na ... s office, and she hadn't learned who was who ... ard had observed the body in the water, assisted with removal, and taken pictures. He seemed to consider his work done.

Callie turned back to the body, speaking over her shoulder. "Guess you need to get him back to the morgue before you know if this head wound was the cause of death."

"You're good, Chief."

Sarcastic bastard. He'd said less than a dozen words since stepping onto the boat. Quiet. Borderline rude. But he could simply be pissed he'd had to leave a good warm dinner on the table.

"Recognize the guy, Callie?" Yeargin asked.

Callie shook her head. "I take it you don't either."

"Nope. Hank's still in the water waiting for orders, Chief."

She kept feeling the pockets for clues.

"Wish you wouldn't," Richard-somebody said. "I should be the first line in the custody of evidence, and I don't like anything touched until we get back."

She ignored him. In her flashlight beam she counted over a hundred dollars in the deceased's money clip. A cloth handkerchief but no initials . . . old school without flare. Keys to a Nissan and most likely a residence. She felt around his waistband to his back.

Here we go. A small-of-the-back holster, clipped to his belt . . . empty.

Yeah, Richard-whoever. This is why she should search the body here.

"Tell them we're missing a handgun," she told Yeargin.

Praise for C. Hope Clark's Edisto Island Mysteries

"[*Echoes of Edisto*] delivers a riveting ride, with irrepressible characters."
—Rachel Gladstone, *Dish Magazine*

". . . a real page turner and I couldn't put it down until I found out who did it. Wonderful! . . ."
—NetGalley review for *Edisto Jinx*

"An engrossing mystery with a beautiful backdrop"
—For the Love of Books Review on *Echoes of Edisto*

The Novels of C. Hope Clark

The Carolina Slade Mysteries

Lowcountry Bribe

Tidewater Murder

Palmetto Poison

The Edisto Island Mysteries

Murder on Edisto

Edisto Jinx

Echoes of Edisto

Edisto Stranger

Edisto Stranger

Book Four: The Edisto Island Mysteries

by

C. Hope Clark

Bell Bridge Books

This is a work of fiction. Names, characters, places and incidents are either the products of the author's imagination or are used fictitiously. Any resemblance to actual persons (living or dead), events or locations is entirely coincidental.

Bell Bridge Books
PO BOX 300921
Memphis, TN 38130
Print ISBN: 978-1-61194-764-9

Bell Bridge Books is an Imprint of BelleBooks, Inc.

Published in the United States of America.

We at BelleBooks enjoy hearing from readers.
Visit our websites
BelleBooks.com
BellBridgeBooks.com
ImaJinnBooks.com

10 9 8 7 6 5 4 3 2 1

Cover design: Debra Dixon
Interior design: Hank Smith
Photo/Art credits:
Landscape (manipulated) © Dmitriy Karelin | Dreamstime.com
Foliage (manipulated) © C. Hope Clark

:Lser:01:

Dedication

To Mayor Jane Darby and the wonderful people who fought to rebuild our beautiful Edisto Beach after Hurricane Matthew . . . and continue to preserve its old soul.

Chapter 1

UNROLLING LAST month's police report in her hand, with two dozen residents assembled behind her, Police Chief Callie Morgan spoke to the Edisto Beach Town Council. Not the best way for a girl to spend a Saturday evening.

But this was a command performance. Even without the council meeting, her son Jeb being home for spring break prohibited her usual six o'clock routine. She hadn't had a drop of Bombay Sapphire in—what? Three days?

She read from her sheet—the council holding copies of their own—listing her tasks for the past month, her thoughts on the hurricane contingency plan, and the general performance of the force after receiving two additional officers the council so graciously approved for hire five months ago.

Thank God for the last one. Kept her from traffic duty. Kept her from people . . .

Finally, the end. *Smile for the camera.* She flashed a professional show of teeth at these five people who expected her to be beholden. Unfortunately, that included Councilman Brice LeGrand. Then she gave a nod to the mayor—who was nice to her face, neutral in public.

They'd made her the last item on the evening's agenda. Not that she was on trial, but she made certain her report included the accomplishments of her department, details the council seemed to take more interest in of late.

The report was complete. Competent. But her heart wasn't in it this evening. Her heart wasn't in much of anything anymore. Muscle memory, work ethic, and an office manager named Marie kept Callie running the Edisto Beach PD, but heart? That was asking too much. She left passion in a rainy ditch on Pine Landing Road last September. Everyone had seen Mike Seabrook as invincible, never thought he could die, but he did . . . attempting to save her.

"Well," Brice drawled at the front of the room, glancing at his casually dressed peers to his left, then his right. "She's obviously no Seabrook, but we can check off the police department."

The words slammed her like a mallet. A female gasp came from behind her in the audience. A councilwoman covered her mouth, and mumbles arose around the stuffy meeting room reeking of overcooked coffee, the confinement too tight for whispered words not to be heard.

Everyone watched Brice, the supporters and the opponents, both sides equally intimidated. "Y'all remember those jokes he'd tell? Mike could make these meetings more of a social. He'd bring donuts, Snickers bars, even sang his report that one time." Brice managed a hound-dog look of sadness while giving no condolences to the police chief at attention before him.

Blood rushed in Callie's ears. With an embarrassed board frozen before her, stunned citizens behind her, Callie stiffened in defense. "Excuse me?" She crushed the papers in her hand, but she wasn't sure she had the strength for Brice's challenge, or the focus to handle it properly. Not without getting fired on the spot . . . or being arrested for murder.

And God knows there'd been ample murder on the island.

She'd been exonerated by the South Carolina Law Enforcement Division in the shootout. But that fact paled in the shadow of Mike Seabrook's death. The community had adored him. And he'd been the man she'd professed to love just twenty-four hours before he succumbed to a bullet and a knife on a muddy, desolate, rained-out road.

The room had gone silent. Silent! How many people still held her accountable?

Did they expect her to brawl, retaliate? Surely they sensed she couldn't take a single breath without the memory.

Or was this a test as to what she could handle?

Then, Sophie Bianchi, wearing her more formal black yoga pants, leaped from her seat, jeweled hands on tiny hips, her black pixie hair shaking with rage and a hundred-dollar highlight job. "Well, I'll sure as hell say something if none of you will. What's wrong with you people? And Brice, you're a gold-plated jackass and do not represent the voices of everyone here, regardless how big and bad you think you are! Don't you remember the price this woman has paid for us?"

"How about the price we've paid?" he yelled. "Not all of us wanted her as chief!"

One councilman gave a soft "Yeah." The councilwoman nodded, then seemed to catch herself when Sophie gave her a glare. Grumblings traveled the room.

Callie was mortified. Were they doing this now? Formally, they couldn't launch into judgment of her without the issue being on the agenda, but the mention this month meant a formal discussion the next.

Her phone vibrated in her pocket. As Sophie continued dressing down the council despite Brice's hard, heavy-lidded, and challenging gaze, Callie peered at Jeb's caller ID. No message and no urgency. She refused it and turned her focus back to Sophie. Jeb had probably forgotten her town-council meeting obligation.

"This woman"—and the yoga mistress gripped Callie's hand—"has saved this beach more times that you've peed in the ocean, you pompous dolt."

Snickers rolled around the room. Brice's cheeks reddened.

A text came through Callie's phone. *911, Mom. Call me.*

Callie spun her back to the council and strode to the back of the room, redialing his number. He picked up after one ring.

"What's wrong? Where are you?" she whispered, a hand covering her other ear to hear better. Jeb had never cried wolf in his life. She glanced over at the government-issue wall clock. Quarter to eight.

"Chief Morgan," Brice said into a microphone the small room really didn't need.

She held up a stiff arm, finger pointed, indicating one moment.

"We're kayaking up Bay Creek," Jeb said, his voice quivering. "Oh my gosh, Mom. We were coming back and . . ." His words turned softer, his mouth away from the phone. "It's all right. Mom will take care of it."

"She's on the damn phone, Brice," Sophie scolded. "Probably an emergency. It's what you hired her to do."

Callie pressed her ear harder to hear better with the other. Was that Sprite crying? Instinctively, Callie glanced at Sprite's mother. Sophie was still giving what-for to Brice.

"Jeb?" Callie spun back, head tucked down. "Is Sprite okay?"

Panic still laced his tone. "She's fine. And I'm fine, but this floating body hung up in the grass isn't."

Callie stiffened, then held a hand in front of her mouth and whispered, "Give me one second." She scooted back up the aisle and patted Sophie's arm. "Gotta go. Police emergency."

The board deserved the yoga mistress's spitfire temper, and her ire would distract them from this new issue long enough for Callie to escape and reach her son.

Jeb's voice rose. "What do I do, Mom?"

Knocking a chair in passing, Callie barged toward the door to the hallway, heart pounding. "I'm moving to where I can hear you. Are y'all alone?"

Night insects chirped and called in the phone's background. "Yes, ma'am. We're the only ones out here."

That he could see.

As she passed the audience, some mumbled at her abrupt departure, but Jeb was the only person left in Callie's life who could keep her going. Humidity smacked her as she burst outside, praying the phone signal held. She barely heard Brice calling after her.

The fire of dusk heightened the tension of the what-ifs playing in her head. It would soon be dark. She heard Jeb soothe Sprite again.

"Okay," Callie said, reaching the parking lot streetlight. "Talk to me." She jogged toward her car, fobbed open the cruiser, her black shoes making divots in the sand and gravel lot.

"We found him a half mile north of the public dock near the state park."

She ran to her trunk, extracted a cap, flashlight, and windbreaker. The Zodiac rescue craft was ever ready for use, but she'd never called on it before. Firefighter Bobby Yeargin was the designated driver of the boat.

The thought of her son with a dead man chilled her to her core. "Are you sure he's dead?" She cranked up the engine and left.

"Trust me, there's no doubt about that."

"Do you know him?"

"Jesus, Mom, I'm not rolling him over to tell!" She heard him catch his breath. "And I thought that would be tampering with evidence."

Adrenaline coursed through her like a rain-swollen river. Was this a drowning, a slip in a boat, a drunk who fell in—too inebriated to find his way out? Jeb probably had the same thoughts, but what he might not think of was murder. And he wouldn't wonder if the murderer watched in hiding.

God, make this all an accident.

"Okay, listen to me, son." She forced a calm, steady tone to override his fear . . . and hers. "Does the scene appear safe?"

"What do you mean?"

Without being there, Callie had no idea if the body was fresh, old, just dumped. . . . Jeb and Sprite maybe having interrupted something at the hour of day when the grays of nightfall beckoned someone with equally dark plans. Jeb didn't need to touch the corpse to determine any of this, either. "Without upsetting Sprite, Son, scan the area. Look nearby first. Then do a three-sixty. See anyone?" She swallowed. "While you're doing that, I'm ordering the boat to come out there. Be right back."

As she turned left on Lybrand, she placed the emergency call on the radio, which would alert the first responders for water rescue. Clipped words, directions, and an order to meet her at the dock.

Then she returned to her son. "Jeb? See anyone?"

"No, ma'am."

She released half the breath she held. "Now, scour the distance, up and down the creek. Any boats? Anybody on the land watching? Any cars running? Look for lights."

More seconds, with water sounds against the fiberglass kayak telling her he moved to follow her directions. A thump from his oar. "No, Mom. Nobody."

Thank God. She tore past the Wyndham resort entrance and shot a small, desperate prayer up that the body wasn't a local, in spite of the fact a tourist could be worse.

As she moved her cell to the other ear, her fingers gave a slight tremble she wished hadn't surfaced. She fumbled the phone, but recovered it. "Damn it," she whispered before she caught herself.

"Mom, you okay?"

"I'm fine," she said, almost angry at him for asking the routine question he'd asked for every day of the four months leading up to his departure for college—and in every weekly phone call since. Synonymous with *Have you been drinking?*

Sure, she sometimes ended her days by smoothing the edges, but she hadn't today. You'd think he could tell the difference.

"Okay," she said, her cruiser making a small slide into the marina parking lot. "Stay there. Stay alert, and keep this call open. I don't care who tries to call in, don't hang up. I won't be long."

At the dock, she saw from a distance that someone already prepped the boat. Two divers, locals, readied another boat a few slips down. The emergency call also directed the coroner in Walterboro to send someone ASAP. By the book. Per the plan. Without fanfare or interruption of the council meeting in the administrative building she'd just left. It was April, spring break, and the last thing Edisto Beach needed was street talk about a death . . . or another of Brice's lectures, hammering her inability to keep Edisto safe. Again.

A gust tossed her hair and made its way across the bay, the tide incoming. She donned her cap.

"Chief? You ready?" hollered Yeargin.

She waved her okay and headed toward the watercraft. Calm settled over her. "Jeb, we're about to head your way. You'll see our lights. I'm hanging up now. We'll lose signal over the water."

She remained police chief of Edisto Beach because of her ability to manage trauma without spilling it onto everyone else. She'd been hired originally because she "walked the walk" due to her Boston detective experience and "talked the local talk" having been born and raised in these parts. But Officer Seabrook and Officer Francis's deaths last fall bit a huge chunk out of her self-assurance. She never wanted to pull a firearm again after she'd shot the killer that night, with relish and way more bullets than needed.

But this wasn't about the cop in her. It was about the mother. She'd find a way to do whatever needed to be done. Jeb had no idea of the ramifications of finding a body . . . particularly if he'd run across a body not meant to be found.

Chapter 2

JEB HAD FOUND the body hung up in the weedy marsh a few dozen yards north of the Edisto Interpretive Center in the state park, on the Colleton side of a water that changed width, depth, and character with each tide. Charleston County owned the other side, a magical line in the water dividing the counties. Jeb and Sprite still huddled in their kayaks against the marsh grass of the Colleton side, well out of the way of the dive operation.

As the two divers reached the boat's side, Callie braced herself against the Zodiac's rocking. She was still frustrated at how long it took the deputy coroner to arrive. He hadn't even apologized.

As divers laid the floater in the boat, a credential case slid out, smacking onto the deck like a dead fish. Yeargin and the coroner were focused more on the body, so, pushing back a dull headache, Callie shined her flashlight and one-handedly pried the wet leather open to identification and a badge. *Well, hell.*

She shifted to block Yeargin's view. The body's driver's license hid behind the creds, and with her hand covering the gold shield, she studied the dead man. Even bloated, the face fit the photographs close enough. "Bag it and put it away," she told the deputy coroner, who quickly slid the ID into an evidence bag, then into his case. Then at the coroner's disapproving grunt, Callie shifted her light, reaching farther into the victim's soggy pockets.

She restrained a small moan of her own, feeling somewhat relieved—and not the least bit guilty—at the corpse being a stranger. A dead federal agent meant federal company within hours. She just happened to be the poor uniform in charge of the tiny beachfront town where this guy chose to die. Her responsibility for one night, tops.

Soft water lapped against the inflated black boat, the briny odor of the disturbed pluff mud dominating that of a death too recent to have begun to rot. Chilly saltwater drained from the body to form puddles in the skid-proof bottom of the twenty-five-foot worn-looking Zodiac. The gray-haired dead man wasn't in much better shape—ocean denizens had commenced feeding on small sections of his eyelids, hands, ears. The sea recycled the dead pretty friggin' fast, but he hadn't been in long, she guessed, having fished a few out of the Charles and Merrimack Rivers back in Boston.

The young, lanky deputy coroner, Richard something, did a cursory study, and when his gloved hand touched the skull, he gave a quick glance at Callie. She touched lightly where he had. Something, or someone, had knocked the dead man hard on the right side of his head. As if rearing a bat and hitting for a homer.

She sat back on her haunches and scoured the close vicinity, then took her scan farther out. One upscale home shone north of their location before a bend where a few others would be. Only the wealthy could afford to front meandering Big Bay, where the smallest parcels of land ran upward of half a mil. Everywhere else she looked remained silent and pitch black.

This was a body dump. Too many obstacles for this body to have floated far. The deed happened here, or barely a stone's throw up the creek. *A stone's throw from where Jeb had been.*

Kayaks nestled amidst the grass, Jeb reached across to hold his girl's hand while his police chief mother did her thing.

In round halos of halogen lights, a couple of johnboats floated to the side of Callie's vessel, the emergency first responders numbering seven plus the coroner. Though loyal to the tiny South Carolina beach community, these scanning eyes belonged to people who didn't need to know much more than that they'd found a floater. News of a dead federal agent would explode like a virus once they made shore, faster than Callie could make the proper family notification . . . or reach the authority connected to that badge.

Just what everyone needed at the beginning of the season.

She couldn't get Brice's evening performance out of her head. The man would be even more driven to ruin her reputation since she walked out of his meeting without clearing it with him or playing Father-May-I. He would second-guess each of her moves—*like he didn't already*—and take the opportunity to misinterpret facts and spin scandal. Which made one thing certain . . . she'd keep the details of the night hidden from the councilman as long as possible.

Everyone's flashlights bounced off reeds and sawgrass, searching for the unusual, but the water barely moved now that the body had been extracted and secured in the boat.

"What you thinking, Chief?" asked the Edisto firefighter at the helm. Yeargin wasn't a native, but he had fifteen years under his belt. He bore responsibility for maintenance of the rescue boat because he fished these waters every chance he got. Her youngest officer, Thomas Gage, had been begging for Yeargin's responder slot for a year.

"We got ID, but not much else," she lied, not wanting to mention the badge, then reached a hand to the deck, a mild wave threatening to teeter her off balance. The night breeze flapped her windbreaker, and she fastened the bottom two snaps and tugged down the brim of her cap covering short brunette hair she trimmed herself. In spite of the recent warm spring days, she'd worn her more formal long-sleeved uniform for the town-council meeting. A shiver made her glad for the warmer apparel. Inside, a nervous freeway of anxiety zipped and zinged, seeking those old instincts that once served her so well on the street.

Unfortunately, this poor dead chump served as the first test of her ability to function since losing Seabrook.

The deputy coroner returned to his seat on the boat. There were three or four people named Richard in the coroner's office, and she hadn't learned in her ten-month tenure who was who yet. This Richard had observed the body in the water, helped remove it, and taken pictures. He seemed to consider his work done.

Callie turned back to the body, speaking over her shoulder. "Guess you need to get him back to the morgue before you know if this head wound was the cause of death."

"You're good, Chief."

Sarcastic bastard. He'd said less than a dozen words since stepping onto the boat. Quiet. Borderline rude. Resentment against her, or was she overthinking this? He could simply be pissed he'd had to leave a good warm dinner on the table.

"Recognize the guy, Callie?" Yeargin asked.

Callie shook her head. "I take it you don't either."

"Who is it?" shouted one of the other responders in another boat.

"Don't know yet," Yeargin hollered, then turned back to her. "Hank's still in the water waiting for orders, Chief."

She kept feeling the pockets for clues.

"Wish you wouldn't," Richard-somebody said. "I should be the first line in the custody of evidence, and I don't like anything touched until we get back."

She ignored him. In her flashlight beam she counted over a hundred dollars in the deceased's money clip. A cloth handkerchief but no initials . . . old school without flare. Keys to a Nissan and most likely a residence. She felt around his waistband to his back.

Here we go. A small-of-the-back holster, clipped to his belt . . . empty.

Yeah, Richard-whoever. This is why she *should* search the body here.

"Tell them we're missing a handgun," she told Yeargin, who again shouted to the two divers.

Finally, she dared shine the light deeper into cloudy eyes that used to be brown, widened with the shock of the unexpected. "Why were you on my beach?" she muttered. "Age, say late fifties. New khakis, new polo, mild sunburn already . . . not local. A vacationer but not an outdoorsy sort." She studied his hands. "Not blue collar. No ring. And most of all, no boat." Still crouched, she set down a knee. "How did you get out here?"

Unless this unarmed FBI agent fell off the closest dock and floated until he got hung up, a more sinister motive made the most sense. But Richard-something could make that determination.

The diver shouted. "Not finding anything, Chief, but depending on how many tides happened while he floated, that gun could be under six inches of mud by now. We can look again in the daylight, if you like."

"We can head home," she yelled back, already calculating that the man had been in the water for one tide cycle, max. The death happened that day. "I think we've found all we're going to find in the dark."

She nodded to the deputy coroner. "Help me zip him up, if you don't—"

In looking up at him, her gaze landed on her son and his date still huddled with a flashlight.

"Jeb? You and Sprite paddle over here."

Still shell-shocked, Sprite lifted her oar and plopped it into the water, Jeb protectively letting her lead. Her long raven curls piled on her head, the eighteen-year-old high school senior reached the marine response boat and gripped a rope.

With her oar resting lengthwise atop her craft, she made room for Jeb, who securely wedged her kayak against the boat. Their small waves kissed the rubber sides of the Zodiac.

The chivalry wasn't lost on his mother, a reminder of Jeb's father. Though proud of her blond, way-taller-than-her son, she recognized the fear, too. Keeping in mind the girl he liked to impress, Callie searched for the right words. The kids needed her strength, though she hated bodies worse than anyone present, regardless of her experience . . . because of her experience.

She and the coroner finished zipping the bag, then she leaned on the side of the Zodiac, her gloved hand slipping once on the edge, which was wet from when they lifted the body into the boat. "I'm sure this scared the bejeezus out of the two of you, and I'm proud of the way you handled it. However, until we identify this man, we can't afford for you, me, or any of these men to chat it up around the beach. Understood?"

"Yes, ma'am," Sprite said demurely, sweeping a curl blown loose behind her ear. Jeb nodded.

"And I hate to say this, but Sprite, you cannot tell your mother. Not yet. We can't have people freaking, going nuts calling, thinking this guy belongs to them. It shouldn't take long to find his name, and I should be the one to tell the family, not some gossip on the street. You hear? Let me explain it to Sophie, so she doesn't get mad at you."

"She's already tried to call me," Sprite said, holding up her phone.

"Text her you're on your way in, but if she presses for answers, tell her to call me." Callie'd have to tell Sophie something or she'd dig hard at these guys upon their return and spread the news as colorfully as she addressed the town council. Everyone loved Sophie, but the problem was she loved everyone back, which meant lots of loose conversation.

Callie shouted at the closest johnboat. "Hank? Can your boat tow the kids back?"

"Sure thing, Chief."

Sprite gave a nervous scoff. "Can't I just ride in the big boat? Hitting your oar on a dead body, that's just . . ."

Jeb pushed off, emboldened. "There are no more bodies. Come on. We'll just hook up behind them and coast."

Sprite hesitated, then paddled effortlessly like the young could, and moved out of the boat's path, catching up with Hank. He anchored them, then motored slow while the others took off to the marina.

"Get us home, too," Callie said, removing the gloves and taking her seat, acting as if they found waterlogged stiffs every week. But her mind churned.

"Been a while since I've seen one of those," Yeargin said, tilting his chin down at the black bag.

"Never long enough," she said.

"Got that right."

He focused on his steering, moving around Hank and the kids. Callie waved as she passed, then sat back and pretended to study the moonlit landscape since the deputy coroner still remained in his own world.

What the hell was a dead FBI agent doing in her neck of the woods?

In an area of the Lowcountry that nobody accidentally got lost in.

Edisto Beach existed at the end of the long highway known as 174, dead ending in the Atlantic. You either came here on purpose or you didn't come. The wind filled her jacket, and she hunkered down in her chair with her thoughts for the last half mile to the dock.

That first name on the creds was one not easily forgotten. Pinkerton. Like the detective agency, which was quirky. Last name Rhoades. She'd worked with many FBI agents in Boston. So had her deceased husband, a deputy US marshal. God, four years seemed so long ago.

"You're awful quiet," Yeargin yelled over the wind.

"Bodies tend to do that to me," she replied, knowing he'd hush at her response. Every administrative and government worker understood full well she had the most *body* experience of anyone on Edisto Beach, and had no desire to share the details.

They began to pass moored boats at private docks. Back at the marina, they'd load the poor guy in an ambulance and she'd escort him to Walterboro, calling the Charleston FBI office en route. She began to feel the first investigative itch she'd had since . . . well, in a while.

The agent wasn't dressed to be on the water, but had ventured armed. However, most law enforcement wore a piece, on duty or off.

Nobody had missed him yet. Unless nobody knew he was out here.

She instinctively reached for her phone. Seabrook would. . . . She withdrew her hand, trying to nonchalantly set an elbow on the arm of the seat, hoping Yeargin couldn't possibly have read her mental misstep.

She hadn't yet shed the reaction to call Seabrook's work cell, ask his thoughts, get him to ride along. And each time she almost dialed, she felt the unhealed hole in her heart crack and ooze.

He remained on her speed dial, and she caught herself rubbing her thumb over the number when she missed him. On the worst of evenings, she sat alone on the front porch of Chelsea Morning, her beach house, and called his voice mail.

Her office never questioned why Edisto still paid for that phone to remain active.

Along with her office manager, a chunk of the sympathetic community still handled Callie with kid gloves, and she let them. Her privacy was precious, plus, they couldn't see her sweat. They had to believe that the cop they hired could hold it together.

She could label the floater as a blessing, if one were prone to be so morbid. A reason to focus on something other than the huge hole in her life. An event to drag her back to law enforcement that consisted of more than the occasional rental break-in, or open–alcohol container tickets.

Or she could curse this incident as a chance for Brice to remove her for good.

She wasn't sure which was best.

Chapter 3

LIGHTS BLAZED AT the marina as Callie approached, unusual for almost eleven—the middle of the night around here. The one smaller boat had sped up to arrive moments earlier, as though eager to be the first to carry the news. At the dock also waited two EMTs and Thomas, her favorite officer these days at the ripe old age of twenty-eight. Callie smiled small at him. He stood feet spread, hands on his black leather utility belt, swelling himself as large as possible, then he tipped his head to his right.

A makeshift barricade of crime-scene tape, barrels, and pilings already kept about a dozen people at bay. Big group for this late, in this small a community, when nobody was supposed to know anything happened. Good man. Good thinking to put the barricade up instead of assuming the late hour would keep crowds away. This was just a transport scene and not an actual crime scene.

Several more people ran up, peppering those already there with questions. The temp had dropped to fifty-five, breezes irregular and sassy. The group instinctively huddled, swatting at no-see-ums nipping at their ears and necks. Spring and fall brought the tiny biting machines out en masse with miniature piranha teeth.

"Look at that crowd already," Yeargin said, slowing the engine, the boat catching the water's movement.

"He's bagged, so let them watch," Callie replied, holding on to the chair as she stood in preparation to disembark.

The gurney rolled out to the dock, and Callie stepped aside and let the EMTs and Yeargin do the heavy lifting, partly because she was chief, but mainly because she was ten inches shorter and eighty pounds lighter than most of them. They'd feel shamed if she hoisted weight in their presence. Sometimes playing the damsel just made the most sense. Not like they didn't know she'd offed her husband's murderer with a broken beer bottle, or sunk six rounds in the chest of her lover's killer.

The respect was there, with a subtle distance in place.

Then Jeb waved at her from beside a group of gawkers his age.

Callie's spirit lifted, so happy her son was home for spring break . . . a damn shame he had to be the one to find the body. Her son. The boy had seen too much death in his world, all thanks to her hand and the job that she swore made her whole. She waved in return, hating the distance between them. "Give me a sec," she told Yeargin. The mother in her needed to check on her son, but before she could part the men around her, Jeb turned and left, Sprite huddled at his side.

Like he didn't need his mom now that the crisis was over. A cool pain of disappointment squeezed her heart. Children grow up, but that didn't mean she had to like it.

She robotically returned to the business at hand. Ten minutes later, she cranked her patrol car and followed the ambulance and the coroner, no flashing lights. Time was not an issue, and once away from the marina, there'd be no traffic. The route from the island to Walterboro would be barren, and they'd have it all to themselves.

She dialed her office and left her office manager a voice mail with notice of her status.

"Marie? It's Callie. We had a floater tonight in the river . . . nobody we know . . . and it's"—she glanced at the dash clock—"eleven twenty. Headed to Walterboro. You know who's in charge until I get there. Oh . . . and thanks for that report. The council loved it."

In her late thirties, Marie had occupied her desk since high school graduation. A permanent fixture of Edisto PD. Most PDs would kill for that degree of inherent knowledge. She sure kept Callie collected . . . what Seabrook used to do.

Marie would appreciate the facetiousness about the report, and the office manager knew perfectly well who should assume the reins in Callie's absence: the senior officer on duty. But the trouble was that, since Seabrook died, Thomas assumed the favored-son status with Marie, maybe even edging out Deputy Don Raysor, the Colleton County deputy on semipermanent loan to the beach. Both had earned Callie's and Marie's trust a hundred times over. But experience trumped trust when the town hired two new officers in November—both seasoned gents from different parts of the Carolinas—putting Thomas down the list in years served.

Marie wasn't a lover of change, still mourned Seabrook, and had barely spoken to the new guys. Callie took her to lunch every couple of weeks, and Marie brought Callie oatmeal cookies, an unspoken sisterhood formed from the shared loss. Callie could understand Marie's preference for Thomas, but that couldn't change the hierarchy.

Since there was no asking the office manager to put a call through for her this late, Callie dialed one of the many inherited in-case-of-emergency numbers Seabrook gave her when she took office. She introduced herself to a way-too-ominous-sounding FBI voice mail. She asked for SSA Frank Stackhouse to call her back. The name sounded like a *Dragnet* character.

She pictured Sergeant Joe Friday, letting his fondly remembered one-liners distract her as Pine Landing approached on her left. She played the theme song in her head, sang it as her heart raced as she met the road, then passed it.

Five miles passed, and the road was dark as tar without the urban sophistication of streetlights. Edisto Island was about seventy square miles in size, and the residents preferred it remain as undeveloped as possible. But too many New York magazines labeled Charleston as the friendliest city, the best city to get married in, the best retirement city, which made non-Southerners flock to the Holy City. Some of that influx kept trying to spill into Edisto.

Just like crime spilled over tonight.

With the crime scene too fresh in her head, her concern for Jeb dosed heavy in the mix, she turned on the radio. Jeb had often accused her job of ripping their lives asunder, with Callie giving it too much priority. Blamed the job for enticing her to her moments of gin.

Jeb walking away with Sprite nudged at her again. Callie'd craved to hug him, ask how he was holding up, embarrass him with maternal affection in front of the crowd. And she'd hoped he'd wanted to check on her feelings, too. She'd been wrong.

Callie searched for a radio station that broadcast this far out this late. Static. Static. There, almost.

A fox darted out, and she let off the accelerator for a moment. She licked her bottom lip, picturing the blue Bombay bottle in her freezer, tasting that first cold, tangy bite of a drink.

Her phone rang. Caller ID unknown. "Edisto PD. Chief Morgan speaking."

"SSA Knox Kendrick here." Terse and businesslike. Probably disgruntled about his interrupted evening, too.

"I was expecting Agent Stackhouse," she said.

"He's no longer here. We don't get too many calls from police chiefs in the middle of the night, and you got me, so what's up?"

Boston *feebs* put someone on twenty-four-hour call like medical practices, so the callback didn't bother her. The rudeness, however, did.

Southern hospitality applied no matter who you were down here. "I'm sorry to inform you that we collected one of your guys out of a creek tonight."

"Shit." A sigh blew across the air waves, then a silent second as he gathered his thoughts. "Sorry. What's the name on the credentials?"

All she did was swallow, taking a second to get the name right in her head.

"Chief," he said harder. "The name?"

"Pinkerton," she said. "Rhoades. I'm escorting the body to the Colleton County coroner right now. I would appreciate if someone could come identify—"

"Where are you from again?"

"I'm from Edisto Beach, Agent Kendrick. About an hour south–"

"It'll be me. And Chief?"

"Yes?"

"Don't speak to anyone else about this. Your staff, your officers, anyone."

A bit late for that request. Two dozen onlookers—in addition to the first responders—were already home texting and making calls about the night's incident. Not that they had a name. Callie knew how Sprite must've felt when warned to remain silent. "Hadn't planned to, Agent Kendrick."

"You obviously didn't take a hard look at that badge."

"Moon wasn't particularly bright tonight, Kendrick." *Note to* self: *Check the creds the second she arrived in Walterboro.*

"I'll see you within the hour." And he hung up.

After checking the screen to see that the agent had truly disconnected the call, she laid the phone aside.

She continued following the ambulance, the deputy coroner between them, and reached the McKinley Washington Bridge as the old fingers of foreboding writhed up her spine. She shook it off and scanned the landscape instead. Beneath her, the Dawhoo River flowed to an ebbing tide. Moon glinting off their white backs, two herons spread wings wide, like dinosaur birds skirting the water. Callie wondered what predator roused them from their sleep.

The last six months had been a straight line of nothing but her trying to live without Seabrook, not to mention her dad. Her role was simple—writing golf cart speeding tickets and sanctioning beachcombers with dogs off leash. A job she'd have joked about in her detective days. She ought to crave a body and its change of pace . . . as much as she craved a damn drink right now.

The heel of her palm made its way to her chest and rubbed circles, pressing. In spite of the isolated, middle-of-the-night travel on a lightless two-lane, or maybe because of it, pressure built inside, cold pressure she thought she'd rid herself of a few months back. Sophie's yoga, runs on the beach, plenty Neil Diamond on the porch in the earlier days hadn't worked well after the funeral, so she later supplemented with gin, breaking her unspoken promise to Seabrook. Only the good stuff, though. Both of the beach's liquor stores carried her Bombay Sapphire, and she rotated which store she visited. Her days were often filled with nothing more than a simple effort to live through each twenty-four-hour increment.

And now a body shows up. A damn FBI body.

She didn't want a case right now, but neither did she want other law enforcement on her beach. The FBI never felt genuine to her, never seemed honest. And she wasn't ready to rally her force in this matter either, turning it into a beach event. If she'd learned anything from living in a tourist area, it's that you remain discreet about the bad stuff. Better she handle this alone.

No . . . better the FBI just take the damn case.

She tried to shut down her nagging investigative instincts and refocus. There might not be a need for much investigation. Tides, wildlife, and poor mariner skills led to mishaps. Even then the feds might want to wrap it up in a bow, walk on her turf. She was stuck in a vicious Catch-22 loop. Not only was her old self instinctively opposed to letting feds steal the show, but they'd practically killed her husband. They'd stolen the Russian mob leader from Boston PD back in the day, when the man who put a hit on her and her husband had succeeded in killing John.

She rubbed her chest hard once more and returned to ten and two on the steering wheel. Maybe these feds had more sense. Her more weathered soul nixed her shadow of an impulse to investigate, assassinating it with vivid images of the price she'd already paid for guts, daring, and way too much curiosity. This might not even be her case when the FBI arrived.

She was way too many months' worth of wrung-out-tired for this crap. Her father told her that Edisto was the type of setting to recuperate in, and for a few months she believed him. Then he was murdered. Then the Russian came to town. Then the Jinx. Then . . .

No. Edisto was as mythical as Brigadoon . . . appearing magical to only those who already believed in magic.

She sure as hell didn't.

Chapter 4

ARRIVING AT THE county coroner's facility in Walterboro, the ambulance turned right off Black Street through the open chain-linked gate, the orange sodium streetlights spotlighting unkempt confederate jasmine snaking the fence. The deputy coroner followed, with Callie's cruiser behind him. White oaks and a couple of pecan trees shaded the parking lot containing two cars and two trucks, none flaunting affluence. Rather, their style said, "small-town Southern conservative," with a taste of backwoods hunter in a couple of the vehicles according to the mud on the flaps and fenders.

Though she hadn't visited this facility before, Callie'd frequented others more times than she liked to recall. She would escort the body in, complete the paperwork, hope for some sort of preliminary analysis from the doc, then ask him to get back to her ASAP. In this instance, however, she expected the FBI to accept that role.

Some labs were fancier, but they operated with the same intent of assigning the who, what, when, where, and why to a person who'd passed on. Once inside, Callie entered a lobby area where an assistant type gave her a clipboard.

"I need to see that identification found on him," she said, filling out how she'd found Rhoades in the creek.

"You have to ask the coroner that," said the assistant as he accepted the clipboard and turned to leave. "He'll be out in a minute."

Body accounted for. Quickly done, sad for such a tragedy. She strode to one side of the room and studied the black-and-white photos that hung along a wall, showing the building's earlier days. Down a hall somewhere, a door closed with a soft *whump*.

A morgue was plenty eerie in the daylight, but in the late hours of night, the silence hung fatter and heavier for some reason, people preferring to pass without speaking, as if the effort wearied them. Tiled walls accented what little noise there was, but thick rubber soles made it easy for the deputy coroner to slip up on her.

"Sorry," he said, catching the flinch. "Contact you with the results?

Saw the FBI credentials."

"For now," she replied, finally learning from the embroidery on his white coat that "Richard" went with "Smith." "Mind if I hold those creds until the FBI rep shows up? I'd like to be the one to talk to them first, if you don't mind."

Richard shrugged, disappeared, and came back with the badge and identification inside the evidence bag, then made sure she signed off on the custody.

Richard showed Callie to the waiting area so he could go about his business with their dead agent. Callie doubted Colleton County dealt with much of a backlog.

Fifteen minutes passed. Being alone at home had become tolerable, but alone in a molded plastic chair with the hum of fluorescent lights and only a Bible to read sent her thoughts into ugly places she fought to avoid.

Both Seabrook and Francis had come through shiny metal doors like those, had been placed on those hard, frigid tables. She hadn't accompanied either, but had almost joined each on a gurney of her own. Eyes closed, Callie imagined each man alone in that cold, soulless room . . . and what happened to send them there. She could envision Seabrook's unclothed body. His ending here, under white sheets, amid the disinfecting air of science. She felt the pain of her inability to be there with him because she'd lain unconscious in a hospital, half dead from pneumonia she acquired trying to save Francis.

Francis. . . . He was probably visited here by his young sweetheart and his grandfather, who'd just lost his last blood relative. *Francis had planned to propose at Christmas.*

Callie smoothed creases out of her forehead, ordering herself to be the badge and not the girl. Shaking herself back to the present, she shifted her attention toward the FBI agent on his way. SSA Knox Kendrick. The name drew movie stars to mind. Like Rock Hudson or Bruce Willis. Three syllables with blue eyes. Average-sounding voice, though. Unless Kendrick broke all the speed laws, it would be over an hour before he covered the fifty miles of mainly two-lane road. There was no rush to study the credentials.

"I need a cup of coffee," she said to nobody, needing the noise as much as the caffeine . . . wishing it were more than caffeine.

The air-conditioner ran crisp, a few degrees cool for her taste, and she prayed they had a snack room with coffee less than two days old. It took her walking eight feet to see the tiny ten-by-ten room just around the corner to her left. It housed a chipped Formica-topped table, four vinyl-seated chairs, a refrigerator from the seventies, and a cheap sink . . . but no hot coffee. So, setting the evidence bag on the counter, she rummaged through prefab cabinets and found the means to make some fresh. Finally, she wrapped fingers around a stained ceramic cup that probably came with the fiftyish two-story pink brick facility. She returned to her seat in the lobby, facing the tile wall, and laid the transparent evidence bag across her lap.

Pinkerton H. Rhoades stared up at her. The photo seemed a few years younger than the body. While they weren't supposed to smile for credential pictures, she caught humor in his eyes, and tried to envision him shaking hands, chatting an introduction, smiling . . . instead of the stone-dead stare from the boat.

She dialed Jeb for diversion, and to be *the mom*. Whether he thought he needed her or not.

"Hey," he replied. "I'm at Sprite's house."

"I figured. Checking on how you're doing," she said.

"Are you kidding? Kinda hard to sleep after all that. But *I'm* doing fine," he answered, emphasis on the *I*.

"Meaning?"

"The boat towing us hit a piece of driftwood on the way back, and I think Sprite's about done with water sports for the next decade." Some silence filled in the moment. "We ran into Zeus at the house, who, um . . ."

"Had already heard about the body?" Zeus was Sprite's brother. Sophie Bianchi had used her New Age musings in naming her two children.

"Yeah, so Sprite spilled to him. Then Ms. Bianchi came in and . . . you can figure out the rest."

Callie took a sip of her fresh brew to feel warmer. "Well, you tried. Thanks for how you handled yourself out there. Sometimes the person finding the body is more trouble than the body itself."

He scoffed. "Those people didn't grow up with cops."

She beamed, happy with his aplomb, and his including his deceased father in the reference.

"How are you?" he asked. "You're at the morgue, right? That's what I heard. Find any kind of, um, nourishment in a place like that . . . I mean, that you can trust."

"Yes, at the morgue. Yes, found coffee. I'll be home—" She thought better of giving a time, and said, "—when you see me. Still waiting for someone to claim the body."

"Ah, good," he said. "Well, I'm about to head home. Just so you know."

After hanging up, she started to call Sophie to explain why she'd had to hear the news from the street rather than from Callie. Her neighbor and friend, and mother to Sprite, would not be thrilled at the bad juju under her roof. Tomorrow would be a sage day for sure.

As she heard quick footsteps on the hard floor, Callie paused before hitting speed dial, waiting to see who entered before making another call. A man blew in.

She checked the wall clock. At least a half hour earlier than she expected Kendrick, so she returned attention to her cell.

"Chief Morgan?" he asked.

She glanced back up, then stood. Damn, had to have used his blue light all the way. "Yes, I'm Morgan." The fast arrival, the harried, painful look. This death was personal to the man.

"Where is he?" he said, breathless.

She pointed down the short hall. "Through there, but—"

Instead of hearing her out, his long strides took him to those doors, his open palms smacking the metal as he parted them.

Following him, she caught up two rooms later to see a technician trying to explain just as Dr. Smith returned. She held back and let them talk, not wanting to violate their privacy. Instead of encroaching, she returned to the waiting room, intimately familiar with the need to give people a chance to accept the inevitable.

The phone voice hadn't painted the right picture. The man was her age. A jaw not nearly as chiseled as his name. Jet-black hair with enough of a wave to warrant attention in his grooming. Tall but under six foot. No suit, the standard federal dress code, but he'd probably been beckoned from his den, maybe dozing in his chair. He'd thrown on khakis and a maroon Henley, grabbed a windbreaker, and taken on a hard, embedded glower.

Maybe twenty minutes passed before Kendrick exited, his impatience drained. He approached with a card outstretched between two fingers. "SSA Knox Kendrick," he said. "May I see the credentials, please?"

First, she dug into her pocket and exchanged a card of her own, partially for identification, partly to focus the man on something other than the horrible images he'd just seen. "Edisto Beach Police Chief Callie Morgan. Wish we had met under more pleasant—"

He nodded with a hitch, silently telling her to get on with it, peering around the twenty-by-thirty room so as not to make eye contact. The dead man's credentials lay spread open in the sealed bag, and Callie lifted it reverently and handed it over.

Kendrick failed to control the sigh, hurt deep in his hazel eyes.

"I see he was retired," she said, having reexamined the creds. The badge noted it in tiny, pale print the average person wouldn't notice. A sort of pacifier since cops didn't retire easily. Her two years as a civilian between Boston and Edisto were proof of that.

Which also meant the FBI didn't have to be called. In the morning, maybe, as a simple courtesy, but not in the middle of the night.

The agent seemed fixated on the photo, his posture having lost its starch. "He was my training officer at my FOA in Atlanta." The accent was more Atlanta than Charleston.

First Office Assignment. A time an agent never forgot. Callie knew John's was Boston. He was one of the lucky ones allowed to remain in the city where he started. "I'm sorry for your loss. My husband was Marshals Service, so I understand."

Kendrick perked up at the federal connection and eyed her as if seeing her for the first time. "Retired?"

"Killed in the line of duty." Partially right. A Russian mobster had taken out his wrath for her on John, shooting him in the head then burning their home to the ground. The guilt at how they parted had lessened over the years, but sneaked back oppressive some nights, even more vivid since Seabrook died.

Kendrick's eyes softened, and he dipped his head in acknowledgment. "My condolences." He gave their conversation a moment, their bridge now clear. "So, how'd you find Pinky?"

She gave him a half smile to lighten the moment. "Love the nickname. A real gung ho, bust-down-the-doors moniker."

He smiled back. "He loves it, too. Says it throws adversaries off balance."

"Or he accepted it somewhere along the way with grace," she said, deliberately looking past his use of present tense. "Sit. Let's talk after I grab us some coffee."

She served them both, hers refreshed, his mug reading "1999 Rice Festival" on the side. He took the black coffee as if his norm, like she did.

Callie settled herself comfortably, which gave Kendrick permission to do the same. He left a chair between them. Without the ugly details of the body, she explained how she received the call, gathered her response team, waited for the deputy coroner, and collected Pinky Rhoades. The FBI ran more white-collar cases. Bodies were not a regular part of who they were. At least in most offices. The FBI wasn't nearly as tough as television depicted.

"So what was Rhoades doing on Edisto, Agent Kendrick?" she asked. "How long had he been retired?"

"Six unhappy months."

Wasn't happy about retirement, family, life in general? She wasn't sure of Kendrick's meaning, given his lack of qualifying details about the unhappiness.

"Where's his phone?" he asked.

"No sign of one," she said.

He frowned harder, annoyed.

"We'll keep looking," she continued, "but the tide, the mud . . ."

His mouth flat-lined.

"No weapon either, though he had one on him at one point from the holster at his waist."

He nodded to the metal doors. "They say they don't know anything yet. What do you think?"

"Well, we'll wait for cause of death to be sure, but he hit his head," she said, not quite ready to say *someone else* hit Pinky's head. "And we found no boat. We're hunting for his car, a Nissan from his keys. Any idea what model or color?"

"Green Sentra. Five or six years old."

Yes, he was personally connected. "You kept up with him, I take it?"

"I did," he said drawing the cup to drink, the move obviously to keep her from reading him, because his eyes were telling way more than those two words.

If she asked enough questions, maybe he'd catch the hint and tell her not to bother because he was there to take the reins. And as a courtesy, she'd let him. Happily. She'd finally made the decision that it was best to let this one go right now. "Did he have family?" she asked. "Do I need to be hunting a wife, a child, a girl- or . . . boyfriend? Somebody who might be waiting in a beach house for him to come back? I've clamped down on the news best I can, but in such a small community, with nine people at the scene, you can guess how quickly a story might spread."

"He wasn't there with anyone," was all he said.

"Okay, well, technically I have the investigation unless the FBI prefers otherwise?"

He cleared his throat, but said nothing.

"Would you like to notify his family?" she asked.

He hesitated. "Yeah. He had a grown daughter in Jacksonville. I'll call her."

"He retire local?" she asked, fishing for where the man was from.

"Yeah. Charleston."

Which meant Rhoades had most likely been visiting Edisto, since he lived only fifty miles up the road, but damn Kendrick and his tight-lipped answers. And why wasn't he using that authority of his to take the case from her?

One white-coated guy walked past in scrubs. Then a civilian. Callie finished the last of her coffee and set the cup on the table. "Agent Kendrick, it's apparent you're uncomfortable about more than just your agent dying. You're carefully steering your words like they have no place to land, leery of how much to tell me."

He cut her a hard look, probably more out of a hesitation to speak than frustration at being figured out.

She wanted to cross her arms as much for the chill as the gravity, but didn't care to give the impression they were at odds. So leaning elbows on her knees, she rubbed her hands and studied the room, though she'd already memorized everything there. "He wasn't the tourist type or you would've said. A retiree wouldn't be on a case. He could've been a private investigator, but I found no such credential. Frankly, I'm waiting for you to tell me this is none of my business, and that I'm done here," she summarized.

He just stared at Pinky's credentials.

"But you haven't, and you know any investigator would need answers to my questions," she said.

As if glancing up by mistake, his gaze returned to his cup. "I have your card," he said, then chugged the coffee to end the discussion.

It wasn't until he started to rise that she spoke up again, a little less empathetic. "Sit and let me tell you one more item before you go. No, two."

To her surprise, the agent complied, lacking the chutzpah and swagger of his peers, or at least the ones she'd met, making her wonder how long he'd been with the bureau. The age limit was thirty-seven for hiring, but they preferred new recruits in their twenties, so he had to have a few years under his belt.

She stood and moved in front of him, indicating she had to get back. "First, I have fifteen years as a Boston detective. Decorated more than once, if that sort of thing matters to you. So don't let the Edisto PD appearance erroneously lull you into thinking I don't know my business."

A brow raised, and surely that wasn't a smirk. "And number two?"

"Like I said, I have an investigation to run if you're not taking it, and—"

"Thought you said you found him in a creek," he interrupted. "Wouldn't that make it Colleton County's jurisdiction? I assume it's not in Charleston County since you had me meet you in Walterboro."

Well, what he lacked in swagger he made up for in smarts. "If you wanted to push it, yes, they could own it, but they often defer to me if it's close to town. Since we're standing in Walterboro, we can clarify that right now, if you like. Ride with me. I'm sure they'd get out of bed for our combined credentials."

She wasn't lying, but she wasn't completely truthful, either. If the FBI pressured, Colleton would keep it and ask for South Carolina Law Enforcement Division to get involved. But why wouldn't the FBI investigate Rhoades's death themselves, Kendrick claiming the case on their behalf? You'd think he'd want to do that last service for the victim. Investigative instincts that had been quiet for a time now began to sputter and fire back up.

Kendrick might tap-dance with her, but he'd have to put on a full-bore sideshow with SLED. Clearly, this man had been protecting Rhoades, and he had no earthly idea if the FBI wanted the case or not. What the hell had old Pinky been up to? She waited for Kendrick to make a decision.

A quiver started in her hand. Squeezing her fist, she then slid both hands into pockets.

But the agent saw, his gaze following her reflexive movement to compensate and cover. Their eyes met ever so briefly.

"Never mind. You do what you think's best," he finally said and sank back in his seat and waved aside her offer to visit the sheriff.

Callie dipped her chin and almost cocked some attitude, but this was a morgue. People acted irrational in morgues. "Tell you what," she said and tipped her head toward the double doors. "For now, just go say good-bye to your friend." *Like she hadn't been able to do with Seabrook or Francis.* Again, her gut shoved unexpected against her ribs at the memories, making her all the more eager to leave. "You have my card. If

I don't hear from you in twenty-four hours, I'll call your Charleston office and ask the basics about Agent Rhoades. In the meantime, I'll check the island for who knew him, saw him, spoke to him, trying to back into whatever happened." She took both their cups to clean up. "I'm sorry for your loss."

Dropping the cups in the breakroom, she walked past Kendrick with a nod and then poked her head through the double doors one last time, passing the credentials to the assistant.

She returned in no hurry to her patrol car, hoping he'd have second thoughts and pursue her. Snatch the case away.

Flopping in the front seat, she turned her mirror to reflect the morgue door. Nothing. Well hell, it looked like Pinky was hers.

She left Walterboro at one thirty in the morning, headed back on State Highway 64. In spite of the late night, Callie wasn't tired. Kendrick's behavior had heightened her interest. *Embarrassed* wasn't the word she would use for the guy, but he wasn't comfortable opening up to her even when they both knew her job was to find answers and seek closure. Or maybe he just didn't have the juice to take the case and intended to beg the FBI to take the case tomorrow, once the Assistant Special Agent in Charge strolled in. The ASAC. Maybe he'd have to call a SAC somewhere if Charleston was a smaller office? The ASAC and SAC might be in Columbia. She was familiar with the Boston's FBI hierarchy, but not of the one in South Carolina's Holy City.

She could hope he had plans to call someone, but in the meantime, she had a case.

Judging from his clothes, and his lack of calluses and tan, Callie knew the dead agent wasn't a beachcomber type. Her gut told her that if he wasn't combing the beach, he was pursuing someone, but her gut warranted validation. With a driver's license picture and general description, she'd start with the real estate agents, to rule out for sure that he rented at the beach. Then the restaurant workers, to see where he dined. The Bi-Lo to see where he grabbed cigarettes, beer, or snacks. Nobody hid on Edisto Beach. They might think they disappeared there, but the natives kept an invisible tally of the comers and goers, and especially the ones out of place.

Where are you staying? And if you couldn't recite the rental name, then, *Who are you visiting?* Friendly, casual . . . and observant. Some might say nosy. Callie viewed it as self-policing and appreciated the help.

It was after two in the morning as she recrossed the McKinley Washington Bridge. Even this late, the grapevine would be abuzz about the body found in Bay Creek. She would spend the day answering queries while capitalizing on the rumor mill for information.

People would watch her, compare her to Seabrook, maybe even remind her she was accountable for their loss of him.

Never considering she held herself far more accountable for his loss than they ever could.

Which is why she hewed her life these days to a different purpose. The two men she'd loved had died for her. Karma didn't have to knock any louder than that. No more room for a social life.

She embraced the responsibility to keep her tiny jurisdiction safe. It was all she did anymore. A robot on patrol. She served and protected, protected and served, then went home, locked the door, and had a drink. Some nights two. Some nights she ate.

God help her, if she had to deal with Pinky Rhoades, she preferred to take his killer down fast and neat . . . without a weapon, she added in an afterthought to her alter ego, who had killed two people in the last year. She'd weathered sufficient death at the hands of bad people.

She had two missions now. Finding Pinky Rhoades's killer and being Edisto's person guarding the wall. Brice would say the need for the first mission proved she wasn't doing the latter.

Ten miles to go. Shame South Carolina liquor stores were so damn regulated, closing at sundown. When she arrived home, Jeb would be in bed. She could almost taste the nightcap.

Chapter 5

DEAD BODY OR NOT, she had to rise at six, six fifteen at the latest, even if she hadn't gotten home until three. And an early morning phone call helpfully made sure she rose at five after six.

Pulling her fern-design comforter over her ears, she started not to check caller ID, squeezing out every last minute until her alarm dragged her into the day.

But this early, on her personal phone. . . . She was half awake now.

"Hello?" she answered.

"Chief Morgan, I was at the meeting last night."

Callie cleared a raspy throat, fighting the sound of sleep in her words. "And you are . . . ?"

"I'd rather not say, but watch your back. They spoke about you after you left. A lot of us really wish you hadn't run out like that. Didn't look good."

"There was an emergency." She croaked more than expected, and tried again. "Surely you heard—"

The caller hung up.

"Screw you, too," Callie whispered, dropping her phone on the covers before trying to slide back into unconsciousness.

Ten minutes of catnaps and traffic noises later, she gave it up. Stumbling to the shower, she rewarded herself with a long soaking, mostly over her head. She should've stopped at one nightcap. In a smaller glass.

Finally, wrapped in her chenille robe, Callie stood on Chelsea Morning's front porch cradling her hot black coffee in both hands, attempting to shed the throb in her head. Her mother named the place after a Neil Diamond song from her early years. Every beach house owned a name as well as an address, and in spite of Callie's disagreement with just about everything her mother stood for, she rather liked the name.

Gentle gusts clacked the stiff palmetto tree fronds, her sago dancing in its bed amid four dormant lantanas. A calm before the tempest—a metaphorical calm, because the sun shone sharp in the sky, the morning mist long burned off.

Today she would beat the pavement with a photo, seeking the purpose for Rhoades's presence on the island.

And Brice LeGrand waited coiled and eager for her to screw this up. She knew it. The police department knew it. The whole damn town knew it, with Seabrook no longer around to convince them they should feel lucky to have her or give her a chance.

She took another sip and appreciated the greenery once more, to lessen the image of a waterlogged body and to appreciate the early morning peace. Too many people would want to talk to her today. Most of them having no business in the case.

She retrieved the phone from her pocket and speed dialed Stan again. Her old Boston PD boss had appeared the day after Seabrook died. He knew what was going on in her head, her desire to stay in that abyss with her guilt and anger. He'd pulled her back. Or tried to.

Voice mail . . . again. She left no message this time, sliding the phone back in its hole. She'd already left three messages, each asking that he confirm his flight at eight tonight. Ten years Callie's senior, the striking man kept fit, his hair buzzed. They were tight. Real tight, and had almost crossed the friendship line ten months back, completely nude and on the brink before realizing they weren't that sort of friend to each other.

Still, he always understood when she needed him, and she'd never had to give him a reason to call her back before. After Seabrook's funeral, he'd relocated to Edisto, but divorce and retirement issues dragged him back to Boston recently.

What the hell was going on—and why wasn't he taking her calls? Or returning her messages? All questions she'd ask once he got home to his house on Pompano Street. After she told him about the floater.

Jeb whooshed by her in shorts, sneakers, and a College of Charleston T-shirt, totally recuperated from the shock of the night before. "Later! Oh, I told a couple guys they could stay for a few days in the upstairs bedroom," he shouted from the landing halfway down the two dozen stairs. "They left earlier. You were probably asleep."

Callie frowned and pulled her robe tighter around her and tried not to squeak her question. "They were here last night?" He reached the bottom of the stairs. "I don't know these kids," she hollered after him.

He leaped the last three steps to the gravel drive. "That's the way spring break rocks, Mom. Don't run background checks on them, either. Trust my judgment, please."

Finally, Jeb acted like the stereotypical teenager, shedding the protector mantle he'd worn too long taking care of her. He headed out to meet friends, natives and spring break visitors alike, with the latter mostly staying with the former. Guess that included her house.

Apparently her second highball had made her sleep through the fact they were even there—or they were atypically quiet for college guys.

Watching him jog between her house and Sophie's, Callie still couldn't wipe the grin off her face at the sight of him. Regardless of his uninvited guests, she was so glad to have her boy home.

Note to self: Throw a blanket over the cooler in the closet.

It hadn't been easy the first week he left, and the one lone bottle of gin hidden in the second shoebox on the right top shelf in her closet remained untouched. The only one Sophie hadn't found in her supposed covert sweep of the house months back. But two weeks later, Callie'd secured a new bottle and hid it under her mattress . . . her "backup," to avoid judgment for the occasions when she'd earned a mellow night. Before long, Sophie quit her not-so-stealthy sweeps of the house, and Callie upgraded from the inexpensive label to the Sapphire, promoting it to her freezer.

For spring break, however, Callie didn't want a fight with Jeb about her drinking. His naïve interpretation was that she couldn't control herself. Hers was that she was an adult with a lot of battle scars. She tired of assuaging her guilt. Best they just avoid the subject, and that meant moving the Sapphire to a cooler in her closet.

Abstinence had been easily promised while hugging him good-bye on the Charleston college campus, but his absence affected her deeply, adding to the isolation she'd felt after Seabrook's death. Why a mother should miss the oddest things, she couldn't say. But she did. His toilet flushing in the morning. Leaving his cereal bowl unwashed. That irritating pinging song when he played Mario on his Nintendo before he went to bed.

Sophie suspected her loneliness. . . . No, she read it fluent and crystal, but she'd tired of babysitting Callie, just as Callie had tired of her doing it, and the unspoken truce began. She was on her own, with Sophie making the occasional impromptu spot check. After Callie refused to answer the door, Sophie learned to call first. And Callie learned to exit discreetly out the back door and take long walks.

Alcohol was optional for her. Jeb didn't understand how it was, but out of love for him, she'd dial it back.

Crap, time had gotten away from her. Five minutes to get to work. Callie rushed inside, dressed, and set her security alarm, texting Jeb to remind him the system was activated. On her way to the office, Callie scanned the lithe, fit, spring-break bodies running helter-skelter. This type of Edisto policing experience was new to her, and she likened it to herding feral cats. Very young feral cats.

Her younger officers enjoyed this season, or so Marie said.

Callie rolled her window down, a breeze gushing into the car. The sixty-five-degree weather sent goose bumps across her flesh. Thanks to the huge scar on her right forearm, she preferred long sleeves. At least until summer temps. Her radio sputtered, then she saw Thomas's patrol car coming at her.

"Hearing the story all over the beach," he said.

She hit her button. "It's out, huh?"

"Like the score of a Clemson-Carolina game." His car passed hers, and she waved with her radio hand.

Thomas Gage. Her youngest officer had witnessed Callie at her best and her worst, saving her ass twice. Dark haired, tanned, average height, cute but not excessively so, he'd fast become the town's mascot after the loss of Francis and Seabrook.

Callie liked that. Thomas needed the attention. She didn't.

Her cell rang, caller ID reading *Mother Mayor*, aka Beverly Cantrell. "Hey, Mother," she answered, putting it on speaker.

"Who died?" she asked. "And I have to hear about it through my secretary?"

Callie couldn't even fathom the map of that gossip highway. She waved at the Ace Hardware store owner as he passed her cruiser. "Active investigation, and you understand what that means." Forty-five miles up the road in Middleton, her mother wielded her mayoral dignity like a Congressional Medal of Honor and papal ring rolled into one. The Cantrells had politically managed Middleton for five generations.

"This isn't dangerous again, is it?" her mother asked.

"No, Mother. Did you speak to Jeb today?"

"Chatted with him earlier in the week."

Excellent. Her son had kept his word to remain quiet about Rhoades. A thought occurred to her. Sprite, so different from Jeb, was her mother's daughter. The Bianchis couldn't spell *secret*, much less keep one. Precisely why Callie might be able to use Sophie to find out if Pinky Rhoades had been seen.

She was late to work and sped up to fifty on streets limited to twenty-five. "Got to go, Mother," and she hung up without giving her mother an opening for another topic.

In the light of day, after the adrenaline of the night before had ebbed, Callie wanted this case even less. She thought she'd welcome a return to something other than beat-cop work, but apprehension reared its scarred and ugly head in the midmorning sun. Brice was all she could handle right now.

Callie scanned the office parking lot. *Wonderful, just wonderful.* Cars and SUVs jammed the gravel area, every visitors' slot taken, some spilling onto the grass. Why hadn't Marie called?

Her phone rang. "I'm right outside, Marie." She glanced in her mirror, checking her eyes for redness. Acceptable.

Her lone admin staff spoke low, confounded. "It's stupid in here. Wanted to let you know."

"Thanks. Be right in." She popped a mint. Unusual for Marie to be off her game, which meant unique entertainment inside.

As she surveyed the lot for cars she knew, Callie played odds in her head as to who would meet her first. She won the lottery as the glass door opened. Bombastic and red-faced, Councilman Brice LeGrand huffed, his paunchy middle jerking from behind a woven belt. "We're getting calls about the man you found this morning. Was it an accident or not? Wives and girlfriends who haven't been able to contact their men are phoning . . . coming in." He inhaled with a lot of noise. "And you're late."

She turned sideways to move past him, so his close-up view of her was restricted. "Since it's not your job to identify bodies, guess you have an excuse not to have the answers, Brice. Excuse me, I'll take over now. I'll scoot down the hall and do your job next week to repay you."

His breathy grunt mixed with a huff.

Brice's revered daddy, a legend in the old origins of the beach, was practically canonized when he died. His middle-aged son coasted on the name and a Rolodex of buried skeletons, holding a death grip on his town-council position. The animosity toward Callie seemed to vomit up from a history between Brice and Callie's mother that Callie had no interest in knowing.

Five women hovered in the waiting area, each with a supportive someone at the elbow; one woman looked particularly irritated, with a tissue in each hand. Another paced, angry at the world.

"Ladies, may I have your attention?" Callie said, the small room making it easy to be heard. The eager attendees hushed. After a scan around the room, finding no cameras or recorders, Callie turned to Brice and two of his cronies. "And gentlemen."

Silence.

"The man's first name was Pinkerton."

Everyone looked solemnly at each other, as if the winner would jump up and wave her hand.

"No?"

Heads shook. "Is that the dead guy?" asked one.

"Yes, ma'am." Callie could say that much and not spill the identity until Kendrick notified next of kin.

Stress in the station dissolved like an unclogged drain. "Anyone meet a man named Pinkerton? Mid-fifties?"

Heads shook, and the room emptied of women who'd have to hunt for their men elsewhere. Brice mumbled something to his pals, who followed after the ladies.

When he lagged behind, her pulse sped up. Last night's public humiliation remained all too vivid.

"What can I do for you, Mr. LeGrand?" She reached around for the mail, and Marie handed it to her. "Sorry you got stuck with all that," she whispered to her office manager, hoping the mint still worked.

Marie scrunched her face in a no-problem move.

"I thought two new officers would make this place run better," Brice said, leaning in, sniffing. Allergies . . . or his attempt to pick up the amaretto in her coffee?

Sorry bastard.

Callie stopped flipping through envelopes. She dug deep and peered up at him, hand to her chest. "Gosh, Mr. LeGrand," she said, in full debutante mode. "I'll have to do better about stopping dead people from coming here and soiling our sand."

"Thought he was found in the water."

"Oh my Lord!" Callie exclaimed, letting the playacting drop. "Do I come to town-council meetings and point out the problems you haven't solved? We're public servants. There's no damn way we can keep all problems from happening. Sewers break on your end, and people get in trouble on ours. You handle your shit, and we'll handle ours."

Marie lifted the phone, played with buttons, and turned her back to the conversation, talking low.

Brice puffed, and his gaze darted to Marie, as if he wanted to hear her. "The police—"

"What else can I do to stop crime for you, Brice?" Callie held out her hands. "I've been sliced, stalked, and hospitalized for this beach. I've uncovered crime that slept under your nose for years. Now you want me to, what, go door to door and teach people how to behave? Hold night classes on civility?" She started to say she'd start with him, but she tired of the conversation.

He ventured closer, approaching the edge of her personal space. "We didn't know crime until you arrived. Look at the price we've paid."

Callie's cheeks flushed. Bracing, she waited for Brice to dare mention Seabrook again, ready to deliver a slicker quip than he could handle because, damn him, she'd paid the biggest price of anyone out here.

"Callie?" Marie said low, spinning her chair back to face them. "You have an *important* call I'm transferring to your office."

Their code phrase. A sentence sometimes used for no other reason than to cut short a long-winded visitor or interrupt before words strayed too far.

"Did you meet anyone named Pinkerton or Pinky?" she asked Brice. "You claim to know it all."

"No," he said, snapping the word. "But I might know something else."

Cocking a hip, Callie leaned one hand on Marie's desk. "Good. Great to learn from the knee of such a political genius."

"Callie," Marie reminded softly. "The caller?"

But Callie wanted to hear this.

Brice ignored the clerk. "We're considering an emergency council meeting to discuss the police department, Chief Morgan."

So he thought he had enough ammunition? "Wonderful," Callie said. "Am I invited, or is this closed door?"

A gurgle of a chuckle moved in Brice's meaty throat. "Uncertain yet. Wanted to be fair to you with the notice. If I'm anything, I'm fair."

Eyes wide, Callie bent forward. "Oh really? Letting me hear you *might* hold a meeting. Is that a threat?"

"Chief!" Marie interrupted again. "The important call."

"Is it really *important*?" Callie asked, knowing the code drill.

"Urgent."

"Then I best take it. See you, Mr. LeGrand." She turned without shaking his hand, entered her office, and shut the door in a genuine effort not to slam it. One day Brice was going to recognize how many urgent calls coincidentally came in when he did.

Hands shaking, she reached for her chair and flopped down. She instinctively reached into her bottom drawer for a quick sip. "What the hell is his problem?"

The chair on the other side of her desk creaked with the shift of someone's weight, and Callie left the bottle in place. "Doll, he struts," said Deputy Raysor. "It's his nature. You gotta let him roll off. Your mother spurned him, and you're the reminder."

She swept her arms out wide. "He owns this place."

"No, he doesn't," said her deputy on loan from Colleton County, his backside spread in the rolling chair. Deputy Don Raysor sat in it more than anyone, mostly in moments like this. Originally assigned as a liaison, then kept on when Edisto Beach got shorthanded, the deputy ultimately stayed on at the police chief's discretion. That had been ten years and four chiefs ago.

Callie took her cleansing breaths. All ten of them. A habit from her panic attack days.

"Here's the deal," she said, calmer. "The guy we pulled out of the water was Pinkerton Rhoades, retired FBI. Found him in the reeds past the interpretive center with his head caved in. Once we hear from the coroner as to time of death, and check the tides, we'll have a better idea of when and where he went in."

"Hate dealing with feds," Raysor said.

"Well, the FBI doesn't want the case, not yet anyway, so I need you to talk to Colleton and make sure they want us to keep it, then we need to check for any missing or found boats in the area. Because if there isn't one . . ."

"Got it. Someone dumped him."

She lolled back in her seat like Raysor draped in his. Their routine. He set the standard, and she would chill until she matched his level of relaxation, to include shoes on the desk. "I'll call our guys and give them some sketchy basics for now," she said, "but in the meantime, I want to find out why he was here. He's from Charleston, daughter in Florida, and the FBI guy I met last night is playing this close to his vest."

"They seriously don't want the case?" he asked.

"An agent is supposed to get back to me, but the dead guy's retired," she said with a sigh. "I don't want the damn thing, either." She stopped short of saying she didn't care, because any death mattered . . .

"You do, too."

She quit staring at the certificates on the wall and squinted on Raysor. "I do what?"

"Need this."

She snorted once. "The heck I do. Besides we were discussing 'want.'"

"Same difference. You mope too much."

"I have the right."

"Mike wouldn't like it. He'd tell you to lay off the bottle, too."

The mention of Seabrook and drinking stole her words, and she had no decent retort. "With my son being exposed to such a scene, I felt it my duty to pursue—"

"Bullshit."

Her cheeks warmed, hating that Raysor could see the flush. "I'm still your boss, you idiot."

"Trying to keep it that way, Doll. I sort of like you."

Raysor still wore a scar on his temple from the night Seabrook died, and Callie caught herself eyeing it on many occasions. Like this one. "You've been hanging around Stan too much," she said. Except Stan would've called her *Chicklet*, instead of *Doll.*

Raysor went back to rocking his chair, his belly looking larger than usual in the position. "I like your Stan. He handles your leash well."

"My leash?" She didn't challenge Stan being hers, because he sorta was, but the leash remark wasn't palatable. "Has he called you lately?"

"Yeah."

"So why the hell hasn't he called me?"

"That he hasn't said, and it's not my place to ask."

Thrumming fingertips on the arm of her chair, she recrossed her feet. "How about you let me pick him up from the airport tonight?"

"Sure."

A minute passed between them. "I miss him," she muttered.

The deputy's chair popped upright, and he stood, his boot heels striking the tile. "I ain't dealing with tears," he said, assuming she meant Seabrook.

Callie jerked to her feet as well. "And I'm not delivering any," she said. "Once Marie pulls me off a copy of Pinkerton's driver's license, I'm nosing around," she said. "I'd appreciate it if you did, too."

"What about the rest of the guys? Cover more ground that way."

No. If they did all the routine work, she'd be free to handle the floater. She'd be less judged. Less scrutinized, maybe. Less chance of comments made . . . and routed to Brice.

It had to be just her until she was certain she could handle the game. Her sleuthing reputation had taken a beating, and she needed to rebuild it.

Raysor shook his head with a couple of grunts. "I'll call Richard and get the cause of death. He's a second cousin."

"Everybody in Walterboro is your second cousin," she said, the humor a nice release.

"Nah." He rose and opened the door for her. "There's still two first cousins, but they're too embarrassing to talk about."

Marie glanced up as Callie and Raysor exited the private office. "Call the coroner," she said. "He's done with the autopsy."

Raysor held his arms out, palms up, like he'd accomplished his task by magic.

Smiling, Callie dialed the coroner from Marie's desk. "Hey, this is Chief Morgan from Edisto. What you got for me?"

The voice from last night spoke with a firmer gravity than at the morgue. "Toxicology will take a few days, but this man was hit with something cylindrical, about four inches in diameter."

The wound wasn't a surprise. The shape of the weapon was. "No accident?"

"Highly unlikely," he said. "The angle is such that it came from slightly above. No way he got this in a slip-and-fall. He'd been in the water maybe four or five hours."

Lips flat, Callie hiked a hip on the edge of the desk. "Can't say I'm surprised."

"Maybe not, but you will be at this."

Callie stiffened, dread wriggling down her back into her legs, and she stood to let it complete its course. "Tell me."

"There's bruising on the back of his neck and between his shoulders, his lungs full of water."

"Hit more than once?" she asked. "Making sure he was unconscious?"

"No," the coroner said. "Someone held him under to make sure the job was done right."

Chapter 6

CALLIE RETURNED to her inner office from the lobby. With the coroner confirming Pinky Rhoades's death as murder, she quickly informed her officers. Rhoades deserved respect and a thorough investigation. Still, her people would only know he drowned, and that Callie wished them to inquire around as to what he might be doing on Edisto. Who he'd seen. She'd keep the FBI connection under wraps.

Callie'd speak to Sophie about using her unrivaled grapevine. She'd already heard there'd been a body.

Old gears turned. Her intuition sparked and sputtered. Reluctantly, she let it feel good to be focused outward and not inward.

She also might not give Kendrick the twenty-four hours. If they wanted to investigate, the Bureau would've called. Her rusty gut instinct. But to reinforce that gut, she placed a call to an old FBI contact back in Boston.

SSA Mia McCarthy answered after two transfers from the main line. "Damn, Morgan, haven't heard from you since—well, for several years. Where've you been?"

"Hey, returned south after, you know."

"Yeah, I hear you."

Both women had once shared woman-in-a-man's-world stories over many a coffee at a sports bar/diner, either about frustrations or about pride at besting the boys. But after the FBI inserted itself in Callie's case, she and Mia sort of lost touch, the Bureau leaving a rather acrid aftertaste in Callie's mouth.

"Need your advice, Mia. I'm chief in a coastal town now."

"Sweet being on the shore." Then Mia gave a humph. "As for the job, um, congratulations?"

"It's good," Callie . . . lied. No need to discuss Brice . . . or Seabrook. "Had a retired feeb die here under questionable circumstances. Keep in mind we don't get that sort of thing here." *Another lie.* "Would your people want to get involved?"

"Depends on why he died. Was it from his working days?"

"Not sure yet. Not getting much help from your office down here, either."

"Hmm." Callie heard the agent sip something. "If it were up to me, but we both know how that goes up here," she added, a nod to their past gossip about management issues, "but if it were one of ours, I'd be curious and feel I owed him. Could be an act of payback."

"But if it were you, you'd be official, right?"

"On the book? Of course. The FBI doesn't like its agents going rogue. Probably wouldn't like its retirees doing it either, not that they can do anything about it."

Callie recalled Stan raking her over the coals for pursuing her husband's killer on the side.

"Want me to make a call?" the agent asked.

"No," Callie said, uncertain of Kendrick's motive, wanting to keep her suspicions to herself. "I'll handle it. Just wanted a read."

"I'm sure you will. Call more often, Detective."

Callie hung up and decided to give the Bureau a couple more hours, tops.

One more personal item now that the coroner's report was in, then she'd start canvassing her beach with Rhoades's picture. Leaning forward in her desk chair, Callie held the phone close, her head resting on the other hand. Jeb answered on the second ring. Bless him, he was good at picking up when she called.

"Hey, Mom, what's up?"

"Nothing but the aftermath from last night, which means it's all I'm doing."

He remained silent to the point Callie almost thought she'd dropped the call.

"Don't tell me," he said. "You think this guy was murdered, and you'd like me on text lockdown."

This was how she handled the strains of the job. Compartmentalize family, set rules, and face the crisis. He'd been kidnapped once. Without a doubt he'd never follow in his parents' crime-fighting footsteps, but she had rules. "I'd feel better if you stayed in touch," she said, avoiding the mention of murder.

"Mom." And he sighed. "I get that, but you freak out too much about me. You've got to get a grip on reality. I'm an adult. You can't make me do this."

"I can't what?" He surely did not say that. "I'm not freaking. I'm taking precautions. Not worrying about you lets me concentrate."

"I *totally* disagree," Jeb said, his emphasis hard and annoyed. "Crap, this is like you used to do when we first moved here. You don't do this when I'm at school. And you pull this crap when you're not in control."

Callie took a pen to the desk blotter, bolding designs, filling in blocks. She hadn't freaked out in ages. Actually, she hadn't felt much of anything in months. This urge to find Rhoades's killer was akin to shaking dust off a sheet covering an antique piano, and tapping the keys to see if they still played. "Maybe I can't force you to keep in touch, but humor me and text on the hour." She paused, waiting, then inserted a little whine. "Please. I need to know."

Yeah, she'd played the *I-might-drink-if-I-worry* card. He was terrified she'd return to the bottle, but if the threat worked, so be it.

A girl called Jeb's name mockingly in the background. Then another before the two giggled in harmony. Callie checked the office clock. One p.m. "Are y'all drinking?"

"You're asking *me* that?"

Her jaw dropped at the arrogance. "Yes, sir, I most certainly am."

"Whatever."

"That's it. I'm sending someone over."

"God, I hate being related to a cop." He blew hard into the phone. "No, ma'am. I-am-not-drinking. Please don't send a car. Don't mess things up for me."

But he still hadn't told her where he was. "Where's here?"

He went silent.

"Is Sprite with you? She's barely eighteen." Wait, wasn't Sprite in high school this week?

Still silence.

"You can't win this fight, Jeb."

"Geez, we're at Fantasea. It's the house right down the road—"

"From our place." Thanks to safety checks and jogging, she knew all the houses by name. This one had a year-round family in it, but nobody she'd met. Rentals commanded more attention. "Until I say otherwise, keep me apprised of where you are. No argument."

"I'm nineteen," he said, suddenly whispering.

"Jeb?" A young singsong tone called from what sounded like a few yards away.

"Come on, Jeb," said another one even closer. "We're waiting on you."

Wrestling noises came through the phone. Callie suspected someone was grabbing for the phone. "Jeb, let me talk to one of them."

"No, I'll do what you ask," he said, leaving off the word *Mom.*

"Ooh, Jeb," cooed the girl. "I'll do what you ask, too."

"Gotta go," he said, and the line clicked off.

Callie didn't want to imagine what was going on at Fantasea, but she was pretty sure parents weren't involved.

And she'd thought calling Jeb would let her check him off her worry list. *Not.*

She phoned Thomas next.

He picked up and, from the background roar of traffic, was driving close to the water. Long straight Palmetto Boulevard bordered the sand and coaxed the fastest drivers. Thomas enjoyed traffic stops, often winding up with more friends than disgruntled violators. And winks with the girls. "I'm here, Chief," he answered.

"I just sent our dead guy's photo to your phone. Casually ask around if anyone's met him. Downplay it, please. The last thing we need is Brice and the mayor ruffled about tourism."

"Gotcha. Who was this guy?"

"A man named Pinkerton Rhoades, retired FBI. Went by Pinky. And let's keep the FBI part on the down low." The less Brice knew the better. "Did he stay with someone, dine at certain restaurants?"

"How do you know that?" he asked.

"Know what?"

"His nickname was Pinky," he said.

A distant *Hey, Thomas* from a young female ebbed and flowed away, as if passing by.

"I'll explain later." Or not. "Oh, and Thomas?"

"Yeah, Chief."

"Cruise by Fantasea, if you don't mind."

"Casual, like I'm on my way someplace else?" he asked.

"You got it," she replied. "Jeb's there with a bunch of others, but I promised we wouldn't drop in."

Thomas chuckled. "I'd hate having you as *my* momma."

Callie hung up, feeling quite matronly and a tinge old. She stepped out of her inner office into the main part of the station. "Don?"

Marie looked up from editing the website for all the government offices. A Jill-of-all-trades. "He left, Callie. Said call him if you need him. Took the Rhoades picture and said he'd check in later."

The deputy had read her mind. Damn, she liked that man. Amazing how they'd hated each other the first few weeks they'd met, him thinking her crooked and her thinking him a 1950s throwback and dense as a concrete wall.

"I'll be out and about, Marie. Radio if you need me." Then Callie spun around on the brink of a fresh thought. "Who owns Fantasea? You know, on—"

"Jungle Shores?" Marie answered. "That would be the Wilkersons. We've never had to deal with them. Not sure I'd know 'em if I saw them."

Callie nodded. "Thanks." She turned and left the station, noting to query Marie more often.

She headed out, the new distraction having veiled Seabrook from her mind for a moment, inviting instincts to come out and hopefully play.

Unsure whether her momentary lapse in mourning warranted guilt, she backed out of her parking space, trying to avoid that psychological analysis. She headed up Murray. Wainwright Realty was two miles down, with Fantasea only a one-block sidestep.

Jeb surely hadn't been gone long enough to morph into someone so insolent. An angel that morning, yet such an arrogant persona in the presence of girls.

She'd already told Thomas to check . . .

But she was in the neighborhood.

She had passed the pretty two-story house often enough. The backside of it faced Yacht Basin, a deep branch off Scott Creek, and the sunsets ranked on the level of multicolor phenomenal. The turn was just ahead.

What was she thinking?

She had to trust Jeb would behave . . . had to. His core was solid. And Thomas would already be discreetly cruising by, more discreet than she would be. She let the turn go by, an urgency peaking as she did, but it faded with distance. If there was a problem, Sophie would ring her. She could see the place from her back porch.

She soon veered left and nosed into the island's largest real estate office parking lot, gravel with old palmetto logs marking the spots.

She missed the summer's flamboyant yellow and red flowers on the chartreuse-hued bushes that welcomed visitors along the walkway, but this was April and a bit too cool for blooms. Even during the hottest months of the year, the scents of sweet rose and lemony lantana carried on the salty gusts.

Callie climbed the standard two dozen stairs that raised most beach buildings out of storm surge reach. After querying Janet Wainwright's staff of one, she'd try McConkey's, then Bi-Lo, then the two other realties on Palmetto. At the top of the steps, broker Janet Wainwright opened the front door before Callie could knock, and stood fast in front of the threshold, vigilant and defending. Odd.

The Marine preferred to place people across from her mahogany desk, in a chair positioned about four inches lower than hers. With intimidation being her tool of choice, everyone used her to sell their homes.

Her white close-cropped hair popped in contrast to her tan. In her midsixties, sinewy, and tough as iron, the woman had retired to Edisto from her drill-sergeant role on Parris Island Marine Corps Recruit Depot. She'd single-handedly raised the property values of Edisto homes. In her own way she'd stormed the beach, planted her flag, and seized it.

"What brings you here?" Janet asked, in a civil, easy voice not matching the body containing it.

Wary, Callie couldn't read the change in behavior. Unnatural. Like a grizzly bear acting sweet, inviting you to approach. The fine hairs on Callie's neck rose in warning as she handed the photo to the real estate mogul. "We're trying to identify this man, to see if he's staying on the beach. Does he look familiar? Maybe rented a house from you?" Stroke that military ego. "I'm starting with you, because you have your finger on the pulse of everything."

Janet took the picture, frowned a deeper scowl than she normally sported, and handed it back. "I haven't rented to him."

Accepting the photo back, Callie continued holding it out. Janet held confidences close . . . unless she didn't like you. "Are you sure?" Callie asked.

"Am I ever not?"

"Fine, but I would like to talk to your receptionist, too." Callie moved forward, and Janet shifted in a dance-like standoff, blocking access.

Callie took a step back. "She may have seen him someplace, not necessarily in your office, but out and about. Maybe lunch or Bi-Lo."

Janet glanced back over her shoulder, guarding access into the real estate fortress.

Or maybe she had a quasi-famous client. They appeared at random on Edisto, avoiding the more high-profile beaches at Myrtle, Hilton Head, or Jekyll Island. Callie could respect that, but felt a little insulted that the woman didn't trust the chief of police to maintain a confidence.

"Ann's too busy at the moment. Come back later," the commando said.

"Won't take two minutes."

"Not when she's on my nickel."

Callie's temper climbed a notch, and she tried to peek inside. Too many corners. "Janet, I—"

Footfalls approached from within the building, and the door opened wider. "Chief Morgan?"

Callie recognized the male voice before she saw the face. A man pulled back the door and joined them on the porch. "Kendrick?"

He wore jeans, a button-up shirt, and windbreaker. Great! Maybe they were taking this damned investigation after all.

So why hadn't they looped her in before putting boots on *her* ground?

"You two have met, then, I take it?" Janet said. "And may I suggest we move indoors to avoid the inquisitive ninnies driving by?"

"Good call, Janet," Kendrick said, and led the way back inside.

Callie followed, marveling that Kendrick had called the broker *Janet*, and she'd welcomed it. Wainwright shut the door after scouting the landscape. No doubt the Marine ate up this *covert* activity—like a groupie allowed to go backstage and have a drink with the band.

The receptionist stared a hole in her computer screen, knowing not to open her mouth or show interest in anything but that screen.

Callie forced herself to wait for Kendrick's immediate explanation as to why he was on Edisto, and a personal sabbatical wouldn't cut it.

But as Janet entered her office, Kendrick pivoted and drew the real estate broker up short. "I appreciate all you've done for me, Janet, but could I borrow your office and grab about ten minutes with Chief Morgan? She's part of the reason I came, and, well, it's rather personal."

The woman's white brows arched at the word *personal*, or at being asked to sacrifice her inner sanctum; Callie was unsure which.

Kendrick closed the door, leaving Janet outside in reception. Kendrick motioned for Callie to take the second chair in front of Janet's desk, as if the space were his. Then he sat, the room filled with quiet at the uncertainty between them.

"Why are you here?" Callie asked.

"To help," he replied, almost apologetically.

Callie peered over at Janet's desk, lifted the receiver, and ensured the intercom was off. Then she slid to the edge of her seat, speaking low, fearing Janet might be listening through the door. "I have an investigation to pursue unless you're here to take it. If so, no explanation necessary and apology accepted." She rested one forearm on her knee, the other hand gripping the chair's arm. "So, which is it?"

He remained steady and tranquil, but a hint of melancholy still leaked through that Callie tried to ignore. "I'm here on my own time," he said. "Two weeks. Janet helped me find a place to stay."

His posture was less crisp, his jeans giving him a much humbler appearance. "Management is not pursuing Pinky's death. To their knowledge, there was no conduit between his active duty and retirement."

"So why are *you* here?" she asked, guessing the answer and not liking it.

He didn't react to her jab. "I have resources you don't, and nobody wants Pinky's murder solved more than I do. He treated me like a son. I'm an extra man on the job and it won't cost you a dime."

Callie sat back, willing to open a dialogue but fully aware she'd be taking a lot on faith. Kendrick could be on active duty, not leave. Or the FBI could have been fully aware of what their retired agent pursued because the unofficial case tethered back to them. Or Kendrick simply had a personal agenda.

"I take it you spoke to the coroner," she said.

Kendrick nodded, lips pressed hard, his eyes pained. "Ask me anything." He stood and extended his hand. "Let me work for you."

Sort of like Mia said she'd do, only Kendrick seemed more clandestine. Callie didn't know enough about the man to consider his offer of assistance a detriment or an asset. She had officers but no detectives, and had intended to rely some on Stan upon his return. But murder was her forte, and she wasn't sure of Kendrick's experience. The FBI wasn't God's gift to law enforcement like they touted on cable, but damn if they didn't have the resources, gadgets, and tools. Even if he was unofficially looking into this.

She rose and shook his hand minus a smile, a tentative acceptance of his presence.

Kendrick smiled. "I appreciate it." Then he walked to the door and swung it open. "Janet? Thanks for letting us use your office. Anything else I need to sign to get those keys?"

Janet magically appeared as if no more than a step away. She opened her hand and dangled two keys on a circle with a plastic tag. "Nope, you're good to go. You have our number if you need anything." Then leaning in slightly, she lowered her voice. "And as promised, we'll tell no one about who you are." The broker stiffened back up, a snapped, sharp glance at Callie, then back to Kendrick.

He took the keys and motioned for Callie to lead the way out front, and they left Janet standing inside, eyeing their exit. "I'd rather not show myself at your station if I can help it, Chief. A low profile is probably best until we have a better handle on things."

"So why tell Janet?" Callie asked.

His forehead furrowed, then smoothed with a grin. "Oh." He dropped a wink. "I'm rich and on a secretive vacation."

Explained Janet's aim to protect his identity, and Callie agreed with his discretion. She was the go-to for the rich and famous, and someone had advised him correctly to go through her. He might even prove convenient if he could keep himself camouflaged, his real purpose known only to her. They needed to talk, of course . . . in depth. He had information about Rhoades that she didn't. Not hard since she basically had nothing.

Outside, he shifted neatly behind a pillar, his back to the road, and jingled the keys. "Well, I have a house. How about you come to my place? Restaurants might be too obvious."

Edisto was too small for her to eat dinner in public with a strange man, and Jeb was home for break with friends. She'd be nuts inviting a stranger into her office at the administrative complex. With the police department, fire department, utilities, town council, and mayoral offices under the same roof, not to mention Marie, the place was the nexus for burgeoning buzz. Guess a private dinner worked best.

"Doesn't leave us much option, does it?" she said. "Which house are you renting?"

He flipped the key tag front to back, which listed only a number, so he unfolded his paperwork and studied the print. "I think it's called Windswept. You probably recognize every name of every house . . ."

But she'd quit listening. Her heart seized, her breath catching at the name.

"Chief Morgan?"

Of course she knew the house. Visions of a dark, low-rumbling storm flashed back to mind. An evening on a red porch swing, barefoot, sharing shrimp and sucking on a beer just to make a point she could handle alcohol.

Windswept was Mike Seabrook's house. It hadn't been occupied since the day he died, since she'd spent that morning with him in his bed.

Chapter 7

AGENT KENDRICK'S hand seemed alien holding those keys. Breezes chasing across Wainwright Realty's porch shifted Callie's internal vision to a day six months ago with a storm blowing in. "That house belonged to one of my deceased officers," she finally said.

All she wanted to say. She wasn't up to discussing her personal life with a stranger who had no business knowing.

"And . . . you have a problem with me renting it?"

Damn right she did. "No. Not my place, not my call," she tried to say as if her words were only a fact.

He could rent the place, but Callie wasn't entering Seabrook's house for the first time since . . . to talk with some FBI agent stranger and pretend what happened with Seabrook hadn't.

She moved into the shade of the porch, against the wall. The visitors and natives of Edisto motored up and down the road as if this were just another day. Meanwhile Callie shoved down a twinge of panic and a tsunami wave of memories, fighting hard not to look like an idiot.

Kendrick misread her reservation. "We can sit on the porch—"

Oh God, seriously? "No," she said too harsh, then tempered herself. "No, it's not that."

His mouth fell open to ask another question, but then it closed. Her opinion of him rose a tiny bit. Obviously, his curiosity at what he'd done or said wrong had been tamped down by his better judgment. He wouldn't press her. She was his obstacle to investigating Rhoades's death, or his opportunity. With her holding the case and his employer's refusal of it, Kendrick's best option was to join forces with her.

Truth be told, probably neither of them really wanted the other, but teamwork might be necessary to solve the case given her manpower issues.

"Um," she started, grasping for suitable explanations for her refusal to meet him at his place—explanations that wouldn't embarrass either of them. "I have some appointments in relation to Rhoades's situation." She shifted her shirt into place, though nothing had been done to disturb it. "How about you get moved in, and I'll touch base with you once I'm done."

"How long?" he asked.

Forever. And anyplace other than here. She had to find a different *where.* "Two hours?"

"Good," he said. "I'll grab some groceries while you're doing that. Give me your phone."

"Pardon?"

He gave her a silly expression as if she were joking. "Your phone. So I can give you my number."

She pulled out her cell. "Just tell me."

"Bad day?" he asked.

"You have no idea."

"Just lost my friend, if you remember," he replied. Then he recited his number to her.

She logged in his number, clicked off her phone, and tucked it away.

Offering his hand, he acted like they'd agreed on something. Like they were allies. She felt none of the camaraderie the man seemed to think they'd built. It was odd he showed up unexpectedly. If she hadn't run across him, just when would he have made contact with her? She would've known instantly when a light appeared in Windswept, but he didn't know that.

She returned his handshake like her father had taught her to do. "I'll be in touch."

He slid on his sunglasses, taking the stairs down to the sidewalk in a light, physically fit trot, then got into a gray Toyota. Plain and austere.

Callie pivoted and marched inside toward the Marine's office.

"Janet?" she called loud, though the office size didn't warrant the decibels.

The receptionist darted from around her desk. "Chief Morgan, let me get her for you. She might—"

"Damnation, what the hell is it, Morgan?" Janet appeared in her office doorway. "People'll hear you all the way down to Savannah."

As the receptionist disappeared, Callie turned around and whispered with a tight jaw, "You rented him Seabrook's house?"

"The father listed it." Janet stared at her, patronizing. "You think I'm refusing a rental?"

Mr. Seabrook had asked Callie to keep an eye on the place, and she had. Two to three days a week she took those steps, tested the doors, checked for the rare chance of vandalism. Then she sat on the red swing and remembered Mike. Never went inside.

Mr. Seabrook never discussed plans for the house, not that she had a say in the matter. Emotionally she felt she deserved some notice, but rationally she knew the father wouldn't be very familiar with her brief relationship with Mike. Would he?

Regardless, Janet would. Any native on Edisto would.

Callie took a breath. "I wasn't notified—"

"And why would you be?"

She knew why, damn it.

Janet waited, her stare parental, as if waiting for Callie to see the point.

It was no longer Seabrook's place, and Callie needed to move on. Marie had. Thomas had.

But they hadn't been there . . .

"Brice came by, by the way," said the broker

Callie raised a brow.

"This morning," the broker added.

"Am I allowed to ask what about?"

"You." Janet arched a brow, her alto voice lowering. "Watch your back, soldier," she said, then returned to her office and closed the door.

That was it. Nobody ever knew whose side Janet fell on when it came to issues of Edisto, but one could sure bet she'd fall on the side that made herself the most money. But the Marine's warning fell outside her normal behavior. This might not be a declaration for Team Callie . . . but Janet certainly didn't seem to be in lockstep behind Brice.

The broker was not her enemy right now, nor a part of this equation, and Callie had to start getting in front of things, stop being surprised, and grab command of herself.

In the parking lot, she fell into her cruiser's seat. Why was her heart pounding? Investigating should be like eating ice cream to her, but stepping back into the role gave her an almost neurotic sensation.

A text came through.

Jeb checking in, as ordered, underlined in sarcasm. She rubbed the creases in her forehead, moving down to knead her temples.

She texted Jeb back and reduced his reporting in to several times a day, his choice as to when, then dropped the phone on her seat, as if easing off Jeb made her more reasonable.

The dash clock read two. In a couple hours, Kendrick expected her at Windswept. Damn it, she needed a better place. She couldn't park the cruiser over there with a renter in residence or the sight would pique the interest of everyone on the island. Already this evening the residents would be buzzing about the strange man there, and if Callie showed up, well . . .

She dialed Kendrick, wishing Stan were already here. She'd give him the case facts, let him chew on them while she put her head on straight. Even at the peak of her prowess back in Beantown, he made her good better.

Wait. . . . What about his place? He leased a place on Pompano Street. She texted Stan again. *Can I use your house to meet someone? Duty related. Will update you after you come in tonight.*

Kendrick was such a big unknown to her, and an uneasiness stirred as she called him.

"Well, that was fast," he answered on the second ring.

"I want to search Rhoades's residence. Come with me to Charleston. We'll talk on the way. You'd planned to go there anyway, I assume, and I have his keys."

He didn't say anything for a few seconds, so she added, "I have his driver's license, unless that address is wrong."

"Okay, yeah, stupid of me. When and where do you want me to pick you up?" he finally said.

He sounded slightly off. The residence ought to be one of the first places to check out after the murder scene. "20A Jungle Road. Otherwise known as Chelsea Morning. Give me a half hour to shed the uniform, and we can head to Charleston." Dressing in civvies would keep her less memorable, and they could pick up Stan and chat on the way back. Do some serious ice-breaking. "But you can only drive if you don't mind going by the airport. My old captain arrives around eight, and I wanted to pick him up."

"Humph," he said.

"What's the problem?" she asked. "He's retired. It's only a ride home."

"Oh, then sure. Be seeing you in a few minutes. I look forward to meeting him."

Why didn't she believe him?

CALLIE ENTERED her house and noted the lack of set alarm. "Jeb? You home?"

Jeb rounded the bottom of the stairs, his bare feet slapping the hardwood floors, boys behind him.

"So, these are my house guests?"

A shy hand went up from one, half-dollar-sized eyes heavy lidded and charming.

The other kid reached out to shake Callie's hand, his grip not the least bit demure. "Nice to meet you, Mrs. Morgan. Or is it Chief?"

She squeezed harder, sniffed for signs of alcohol, and enjoyed the lack of evidence. "Whatever you like."

More outgoing, the heavy hand shaker sized Callie up in jest, his height a good ten inches over hers, a small gap between his front teeth adding character. "Dang. I feel like I could toss you like a sack of flour or something," he said. "How does the height-challenged thing work for you when you're facing down some perp? Isn't that what you call them?"

"Dude." Jeb backhanded the guy's shoulder. "Don't mess with her." He flashed a look of apology to his mom. "Met this mouthy one at school. He"—and he elbowed his friend—"and Yancy met at Fantasea earlier today. They're practically an old married couple."

The friend rolled his eyes. "No idea what you're talking about." Then he mouthed *hot babe* and waved a hand as if scorched.

Callie could barely suppress the grin.

"This other dude is a friend of his. They're staying the week."

She loved the support in front of friends, and she especially liked him making new friends. "Any of these *dudes* have names?"

The shy one came forth. "Sammy Blackstone, ma'am."

"Ma'am. I like that," she replied, then laid a humorous gaze on the tall one, the talker. "And who might you be?"

"Just call me Nolan," he said. "And I'll call you ma'am if you like. No offense on the size thing."

Look at this kid oozing charisma. She teasingly waved him off. "None taken." But time was ticking. "I'm headed to Charleston, Jeb. You know how to reach me."

He held up his phone, then with a subtle move, mouthed *thanks.* A warmth melted through her at having performed well as a mom.

"When you coming back?" he asked. "Stan home yet?"

"Part of my trip is to get him from the airport. Be back tonight, but when depends on whether we grab a bite to eat." She headed toward her bedroom, fifteen minutes already eaten through her half-hour notice to Kendrick. "Going with someone else, so leaving my car here. Call the station if you can't get me."

She shut herself in her bedroom before Jeb could ask with whom, and shed equipment and uniform with each step, hearing through the door a few of the impressed comments of Jeb's new friends about his mother's gun, job, and badge.

In jeans, tank, and a long-sleeve denim shirt folded up two turns at the sleeves, she tucked her service weapon into a paddle holster on her back hip. She made sure Rhoades's keys were in her canvas purse, alongside her creds, keys, and phone.

"Now that's a better 'mom look,'" Nolan stated as she passed the kitchen.

"It's called undercover," she replied, and opened the front door.

"No shit?" the kid exclaimed.

Jeb's laughter bounced off the walls, and, with a grin, Callie locked the door behind her. Nobody entered or exited Chelsea Morning without locking the doors. Except Sophie, who didn't believe in locks, period.

Kendrick hadn't arrived, so Callie perched in one of her porch rockers and phoned Raysor. "I have to run to Charleston for the Rhoades case, but I'll still get Stan. An FBI agent's come to the beach wanting to assist on the case, and I'm taking him with me. For your ears only, by the way."

"Still our case?"

"That's what he says."

"Hmm," he grumbled. "Stan texted me, Doll. Asked about you. I told him about the body and he called."

Why didn't he call me instead of you? But Callie caught herself. "Is he all right?"

"Oh yeah. He's not coming in tonight, though."

Her heart fell. "What's wrong?"

"Didn't say, but he sounded good," he said. "Also told me to let you know. Just hung up with him."

Hasn't texted me either. Which meant he probably wouldn't respond if she texted him now. Kendrick would arrive any second anyway.

"I appreciate it, Don."

He let out a clipped laugh. "You don't sound like you do. It's his business, Doll. Papers to sign, property to sell. Man's drastically changing his life."

Stan had remained on Edisto for six weeks after Seabrook's death, tending to her. Just like he'd been there for her after her husband died two years earlier. Their channel had always been unconditional, a twenty-four-seven open line. His shoulder broad, wide, and ever available.

This was the first time the shoulder hadn't been there for her.

The first time he'd relayed instead of delivering a message himself.

Second thoughts about divorce or retirement? Had to be. A pinch of concern pricked at her. He'd been her bellwether for years, but for whatever reason, he was avoiding her.

Especially now. With a murder, with Brice in the wings, with the FBI's weird response.

Raysor was loyal but not quite the same as Stan. She couldn't imagine pouring out her insecurities to the man. Plus she was his boss.

Movement caught Callie's eye. Sophie must've seen her through the blinds, because the neighbor fluttered out and skittered across the thirty yards between their properties and up the stairs. Nothing reserved about her friend, including that bright yellow skirt and tangerine tank.

"Girl, you and I need to talk." Sophie spoke loud enough to be heard across the distance, taking steps in a flurry, ignoring Callie's being on the phone.

"Gotta go, Don." Callie hung up to focus on the human hummingbird. "Leaving in five minutes, Sophie, so I hope it's quick. Sit?"

"No, I need to move." The yoga lady paced six steps one way then back, then again, the earrings and skirt swinging with each pivot, her Italian heritage audible in her irritated mumbling about "men" and "boys" and "her baby bambina."

"Four minutes now, Soph. What's wrong?"

Sophie hiked herself onto the wooden railing, balance perfect, her gold, beaded sandals woven in the slats to keep from toppling eighteen feet to the drive. "Your son is cheating on my daughter."

Callie rocked back. "What?"

"He's in there right now," she said, pointing to the door, "probably with a new girl."

Callie stared, perplexed. "He's in there with two guys spending the week with us. Friends from college."

"Bet there were girls earlier."

Callie stiffened. "In my house? Don't think so."

Sophie's eyes rolled around. "Like he'd tell you."

Wow, her friend was wound tight. And it was unlike Jeb to have girls over without Sprite being present. "Soph," she said, but not without thinking about the girly voices earlier, teasing Jeb off the phone. "Why not tell Sprite to come over. She's home, right?"

Sophie's tiny nose jerked up for emphasis. "Crying her eyes out."

Callie bit her tongue. She had no patience for teenage angst, and Jeb hadn't mentioned a word about any trouble in his world. "Let them iron it out. They seemed close last night."

Her sheer, gossamer skirt flapping in a sudden breeze from the water side of the beach, Sophie tucked the sides under her thighs. "Speaking of last night, I only caught part of what happened. You should've called me about my baby girl seeing a body. I was not happy about that."

Shells cracked and popped under tires as Kendrick pulled into the drive. Callie stood and held up a finger in his direction, indicating one moment. "Yes, the kids found a body while kayaking. I asked them to keep it quiet. You know how the powers-that-be overreact about issues affecting tourism, and Brice is being wildly belligerent these days. I want to ask your help on the case, but we'll have to talk later, okay?" She moved to the stairs. "Be proud how the kids handled themselves last night. We're raising great children."

Sophie hopped off the railing and held out a stiff finger. "I'm warning you. He better not hurt my baby."

Callie tried not to chuckle at the fairy-looking woman attempting to bully her. "Come on, what will you do, hex him?"

But her friend stared back cold. "Oh, honey, you have no idea."

Mojo or hoodoo, Sophie believed she possessed low-level spiritual powers, and she was pissed. "I knew he shouldn't have gone to college."

Callie squinted at her friend's oddball priorities. "So this is really about Jeb dating other girls?"

Her eyes owl-wide, Sophie gasped. "He's dating *several* girls?"

"Good Lord, no, that's not what I said." Callie sucked in through her teeth. "I have no idea what his dating habits are . . . other than Sprite."

Sophie crossed her tiny muscular arms. "Well, we have a potential tragedy."

Stooping down, Callie laid a hand on Sophie's knee. "No, we don't. At least not with the kids." Callie stood. "Hon, our children found a dead man, and I'm the person who has to determine what happened. Let me go, please."

Callie glanced over the railing to see Kendrick's head out the window, staring back.

"Go on," her neighbor spouted. "Pay attention to some new man over your son."

Oh good Lord. "He's not a new man."

Sophie raised her chin smugly.

Callie almost took the bait and then settled herself.

Sophie overreacted.

Sprite overreacted.

And if Callie thought too hard, *she'd* overreact about Stan's absence.

No. That didn't need to happen. At the moment a murder needed closure, and there was nothing overreactive about making sure Pinky Rhoades could rest in peace.

Chapter 8

NO SOONER HAD Callie buckled into Kendrick's Toyota and traveled one short block from home than she received a text from Sophie: *So . . . who's the guy? Is he a hunk? Do I know him?*

She typed, *It's work related*, and left it at that.

Then another. *Why won't Jeb answer the stupid door?*

Callie sighed, envisioning Jeb peering at Sophie from behind the blinds. *No idea, Soph.*

And from Jeb*: WTF, Mrs. Bianchi is banging on the door. What do I do?*

Up to you, she replied, sensing an unspoken undercurrent and a tale untold. She hit "send" and paused. Since when did Jeb use *WTF*? With her?

Kendrick glanced over.

Sophie needed to quit orchestrating teenagers, and Jeb had to learn how to manage his life. Good grief, if Sprite would enter the fray of kids celebrating spring break once she got home from high school, life would be so much simpler for them. Callie relished being mom of a boy instead of a girl . . . then a pang reminded her she once had a daughter, even if for only a few months.

She slid her phone in her purse, compartmentalizing, staring out the side window.

The Toyota headed up Jungle Road. "No offense," Kendrick said, "but I wouldn't think a place as small as Edisto could keep a chief so busy."

She turned around, an elbow on the door armrest, and measured the feeb. "Small?" she asked, ruffled at the subtle derogatory. "Don't underestimate it. A lot of bucks stop on my desk, because it's the only desk. We're a six-man crew plus a borrowed deputy from Colleton. Progressive enough to have a woman in charge. There are three eight-hour shifts in a day and seven days in a week. Sometimes we eat. The math isn't hard. The job can be. *Small* does not equate to *easy*."

His expression said, *Spare me,* but his words came out as "Sorry. Again, no offense."

Was he doing this on purpose? "None taken. Or not much."

Kendrick passed McConkey's Jungle Shack, and out of habit Callie studied the parking lot for familiar cars. She recognized a few people on the outside patio area, including the teenage waiter who had always lit up when Seabrook walked in.

Son of a biscuit. Brice was seated with Janet Wainwright. Now Callie really wondered which side she was on.

"Looking for someone?" Kendrick asked.

"Just habit," she said, realizing she'd never seen those two blowhards together before.

Kendrick took the left to Highway 174. Thomas's patrol car honked late in passing, probably at first not recognizing Callie in the strange Toyota.

Her whereabouts were public information, a concept Seabrook had warned her about. Yet another reason not to be seen at Windswept. Her personal life practically belonged to the town council.

When she accepted the job, she had proclaimed she'd use the public image to her advantage. She expected to learn every face, remember each resident's name, spot who was tourist and who was not. She lost the urge after Pine Landing happened, and she couldn't help but wonder if she would've recognized Rhoades or his killer as strangers to watch, if she'd been more vigilant.

She positioned her purse on the center console between them and settled in for the hour drive, relieved to cross the causeway and escape that life-in-a-bubble world for a while. "What part of Charleston did Pinky live in?" she asked, trying to estimate their schedule, fishing to see if he knew, and using the nickname Kendrick liked in order to bridge the gap between them.

"West Ashley. Thought you had his address."

"I do, but you're just so damn knowledgeable."

Probably a little too sarcastic a response, but something about this guy brushed her nerves. She was reminded of her pledge not to overreact. She refocused on the case and understanding Kendrick. While West Ashley was the closest side of Charleston to Edisto, she still had time for discussion . . . for discovery. He glanced over his shoulder to pass a car, and she caught a mild whiff of something he wore. "You're not officially here on behalf of the FBI. But you still want to hang tight and make sure I do this right. Interesting."

He frowned. "No, not it at all."

"Then explain why you're running around all black ops behind my back."

His mouth turned up. "A bit dramatic, don't you think? I'd planned to find you once I checked in."

"Sure you did. And the phone towers didn't work before you arrived."

Kendrick glanced over at her. "How long you been chief on Edisto?" he said, and she recognized the effort to smooth over the rough spots in their association.

They crossed the big bridge, where everyone officially left the island. With the tide out, the pluff mud made a grander appearance between the water and reeds. "Six months."

"What happened in Boston to send you out here?"

That question caught her by surprise. It felt weird to be around someone who had no idea whatsoever of her past. Weirder being around an agent who could read people. "Who says anything had to happen?"

"You know . . . marriage? Parents that needed tending? Opting for a change?"

"None of the above," she said.

"Hmm, I sense a story."

The blunt attention bugged her even more. Here sat a complete stranger, with her knowing little more than who his employer was because few people lied about working for the FBI. Too easy to check . . . too illegal to get away with. Still, she didn't know crap about this agent, his reputation, his abilities, who he was as a person. "You married?" she asked.

His deadpan expression watched the road. "No. Why? Interested?"

"Not in the least."

"Ouch, Chief."

"You're almighty FBI, Kendrick. You should've read my social inclinations the instant you met me at the morgue." She almost felt guilty about hurling such a fast and flat denial of interest. "Hmm. . . . Never really got a good look at your badge."

His mouth did a *whatever* maneuver, and Jeb's sarcasm skirted across her mind. But Kendrick leaned sideways, one hand on the wheel, and withdrew the black billfold from his pocket, and passed it over.

She looked. *Yeah, legit.* She gave it back.

She took a moment to profile the agent harder. With his age close to hers, then allowing him a master's degree just because she envisioned him as grad-student material, she had him entering the FBI around age twenty-three or twenty-four.

"Your history with the Bureau," she started. "My guess is . . . fifteen years. Most of it in South Carolina."

"Fourteen," he said. "Twelve in the state."

Squinting, she rubbed her chin, exaggerating. "You went to University of Georgia, both degrees, and grew up somewhere in the northern part of the state."

"Wow, genius guess," he scoffed. "I already told you my FOA was Atlanta. And I was a deputy in Conyers for two before making it into Quantico."

Two years as a uniform, which usually made for better agents unless all he did was walk a beat to check parking. "Turn here," she said, pointing at the Highway 164 turn in Adams Run. "It'll lead into 162 and take you to the edge of West Ashley. Saves you a few miles." The man might know Charleston proper, but he probably didn't know these rural parts. These were not commonly traveled roads, and white-collar crime didn't make it out this far.

He spoke more about his personal side. By the time they reached the entrance to a middle-class apartment complex, a redbrick pseudo–old Charleston with plantation shutters and wrought-iron décor, Kendrick had spilled his ex-wife's name, his brother's employment with the DEA in DC, and his sister's role as a parole officer in Chattanooga.

He could be spinning a cover, but surely he wasn't that stupid, because she could check. A test of her maybe?

Once they'd parked, Kendrick walked past the office and straight to apartment 4J. Callie scurried to catch up and handed him the keys, wondering because of his familiarity with the place if he already had a set of his own. A real friend would've already searched the place. She'd have done the same.

He had appeared mildly surprised about Callie's need to come to here. A thin barrier stood between them that he pretended didn't exist, but she couldn't afford to ignore anyone who inserted themselves into a case. She wasn't sure how hard he had fought for the FBI to pursue Rhoades's killer . . . or if he'd talked them out of it. Or if they knew at all.

The residence had one common lock with a deadbolt. No alarm, a surprise, but then not everyone barricaded their home like she did. She scanned for cams, finding none.

The day was aging, and Kendrick elbowed a light switch, which illuminated the living room. They both donned latex gloves that Kendrick produced from his pocket.

The interior exemplified a taste level she would label as Early American Single Male, complete with a brown sectional sofa sagging in the two cushions near the armrests. A well-worn leather recliner the color of November pecans had long lost its heady aroma, its scent now approaching that of old-man aftershave.

The curtains probably came with the apartment—a beige duck cloth–looking material with grommets. Someone must've felt sorry for the guy's decorating along the way, because they tossed 1980-ish Waverly floral pillows on the sofa in lieu of taking them to Goodwill.

She'd have donated the coffee table, too, the legs marred from vacuum-cleaner collisions. Dust coated the furniture, but no worse than her place at its worst.

Kendrick went straight for an old table desk in the corner and pulled out its only front drawer, shuffling the contents. He rifled through the stacks atop the desk. A pen rolled onto the carpet, and he ignored it. Rising, hands to his hips, he did a one-eighty scan of the room.

"What exactly are we hunting?" Callie asked. "Papers or photos? Flash drive or hard drive? If Rhoades worked a case, he'd preserve records of a time line, names, dates, phone numbers, interviews, public record notations, maybe copies, and a calendar, minimum. But what's his medium of choice? You knew him."

"Paper, folders. He was rather old school, but he may have used a flash drive."

Callie's guess, based on the simplicity of the place, was he kept nothing here, and instead maybe kept the information on his person, or close by. She hadn't found a safety deposit key. No file cabinet. The place looked dated, but barely lived in.

Kendrick flipped the light switch to the hallway. "Look for any sort of file or notes on missing persons. You finish this room and the kitchen, and I'll handle the bedroom."

Files? Who was missing? "He did PI work?" she asked to his back, recalling no such license on the body.

"Who knows?"

"You should know," she hollered when he disappeared down the hall. "He was *your* so-called friend."

After no answer, and muttering her go-to string of expletives, Callie peered under cushions, in the coat closet, and rummaged kitchen cabinets pitifully absent of the basics while Kendrick pilfered the master. Yeah, he was concerned, and almost as mystified as she was. Almost.

She also smelled depression in this place. Stale and dusty. This address could be where he got his mail, his real residence someplace else. While FBI made good money for law enforcement types—with enough years in—affording two residences would stretch a pocketbook. She didn't have the facts to form a conclusion on the two-residence possibility.

She met Kendrick in the second bedroom, a ten-by-ten with a twin bed, no dresser, and an empty closet.

"Sad," she said, remaking the bed after they'd checked the pillows and mattress. "No feminine touch. No social life. Heck, he barely stayed home. A LEO with no security."

"If you don't expect to be a victim, you don't take precautions," he grumbled, reaching under the mattress, then lifting the box springs, undoing what she'd neatened up.

She repeated making the bed. "Or you don't take them and become one. Sort of why we're here, isn't it?"

She exited to the hall with him staring at her. She couldn't help the comebacks even if he judged her for them.

She returned to the desk, reached under it, and ran a hand in, under, and around the drawer. Kendrick knew Rhoades hated retirement but didn't know if the guy was a PI? Suspected a missing persons case, but couldn't be specific what to hunt for?

The place seemed too benign. She lifted the keyboard, felt behind the boxy monitor, ran fingers down the wires to behind and around the tower. Nothing.

The room seemed lifeless, already recognizing its tenant gone.

Callie glanced at the air vents . . . and wondered. No. Not a one of the cheap chairs would've held Rhoades's weight to stash anything overhead. She made another round anyway, just studying the vents. Dust and a lack of smudges negated that suspicion. "Did he have another place?" she asked. Except for a file for utilities and another for his Visa and American Express, Rhoades had no interesting records. "An ex-wife or girlfriend?"

Kendrick shook his head. "Papers could be in his car."

Callie halted in the middle of the living room. "What damn papers, Kendrick?"

"Any damned papers. Just look."

She did, but she also resolved that they'd have a long talk about "any damned papers" pretty damned soon. He knew something.

The Nissan remained elusive as had the missing boat that left Rhoades in the reeds, not that Edisto PD had searched sufficiently for either. Callie's officers had just been briefed this morning. Boats didn't just disappear in the Lowcountry, and Rhoades didn't walk to the beach from West Ashley. "Let's take a look around here for his vehicle," she said. "You beelined it straight to the apartment, and it might be parked here."

"Probably driven to Edisto then the killer disposed of it."

Good Lord, if this guy doesn't love his quantum leaps. Stan wouldn't like this guy. "Or it's hidden here because he rode with someone else like I did. We really haven't canvassed the apartment complex, Kendrick. Is this how you handle an investigation?"

His pause showed he recognized the missing gap in logic, that he'd been operating on emotion instead of sense. Callie suspected lack of experience for murder. His tenure could've been behind a desk, on computer fraud, too distant from simple, old-fashioned sleuthing.

The microwave read quarter to eight. She would've been picking up Stan from the airport about now.

Damn this day. Jeb stupid over girls. Kendrick giving her just enough to get himself into the investigation and not enough to earn her trust. Stan's silence. She didn't want to think about Brice.

She was long overdue for an evening drink for balance.

"I'll grab the papers on the desk," she said. "You grab the computer tower. Don't you FBI types have all sorts of techie geeks? Maybe he kept his notes on his hard drive." She straightened the desk, took a moment to glance once more in the pockets of two windbreakers in the coat closet, then the junk drawer in the kitchen.

With a perpetual forehead crease, Kendrick looked agonized to leave. Or was that faked? He moved down the hall once more, peering in each room, behind doors, in the medicine cabinet.

And she watched him. For God's sake, she needed to halt this tap-dance routine around half information and half-truths. The trail to Pinky's murderer grew colder by the second. She had no tolerance for secrets, and limited patience for unearthing why Kendrick harbored them.

Chapter 9

CALLIE EXITED THE apartment with growing impatience and a dose of doubt about Kendrick's true intentions, and his connection to Pinky Rhoades. "Let's go," she said. "In the car, you can explain what the hell's really going on here."

"Nothing makes sense," he said under his breath, ignoring Callie's effort to challenge. He moved outside to the concrete landing joining the four apartment units.

Having found a grocery bag under the sink, Callie shoved the limited paperwork into it. "Let's take a spin around the complex to hunt for the Nissan."

With the light waning, they walked toward the front of the complex and Kendrick's Toyota, but then he veered, making an abrupt right, breaking into a trot. Callie spotted the man's target. In a recessed area of the residents' parking lot, around the side of a dumpster, the panel of a green sedan showed from behind some straggly bushes.

Wondering whether Pinky or the killer would hide the car, Callie rushed over. He'd already carefully popped the trunk and opened the doors, accessing another set of rubber gloves he retrieved from a box Rhoades kept on the floor in the backseat.

Flushed, the agent scoured seats, console, glove box, and trunk like a man on fire. Callie assisted, but jumped out of his way when he crossed her path, once brushing her into a door. When he retrieved a screwdriver from the trunk and made to peel back the interior of the doors, she grabbed his wrist.

Callie flicked on the flashlight on her cellphone. "What the hell are you doing? It's time to start talking. Did Rhoades mule drugs or something?"

"No . . . of course not." He breathed heavy, wielding the screwdriver like a weapon.

She held out her palms calmly, lowering her tone, not sure how to read the emotional urgency of the man. "Knox," she said. "What aren't you telling me?"

A heavyset woman in her midthirties watched from thirty yards away. A couple of tenants stood on their landings, one on a balcony.

"Would he be this covert to hide his car like this?" Callie continued, eyeing the crowd. "And if he hid his car, that means he rode with someone else to Edisto. That's a clue. He was a smart agent, right? Look at me."

He lowered the screwdriver. "Don't patronize me, Chief."

"Then don't go all novice on me. Get your heart out of your head. You're not a rookie."

"I'm not—It's just that Pinky . . ." But he couldn't finish that sentence either. Kendrick saw what he'd temporarily become in that instant. He inhaled deep and tried to hide the exhale.

She studied him. This surge of emotion and lack of controlled thinking spoke of a real obligation to the dead man. That was one of her questions answered.

"Pinky was an intelligent agent," he said.

"So either the perp was even more clever, or it's someone so close he never saw them coming," she added, recalling the Middleton reporter who had weaseled into her mother's business in order to create an opportunity to move in and kill Seabrook.

"Well, let me help you comb the car, then we'll lock it up and head back to the beach," she said. "Let your mind digest on the way. I'll do the same. Tomorrow I have a friend I want to call and run this by—"

He whirled. "No! We tell no one."

"I'm lead, Kendrick. Had you already inspected the apartment?"

Kendrick lowered the screwdriver. "Only briefly, this morning, on the way to the beach."

"Did you find anything? Was that search back there a pretense for my benefit?"

"I didn't find anything."

"Well, you obviously didn't search the car. Now, let's do it right, without that thing," she said, pointing to the screwdriver.

He returned the tool where he found it, steadier, but not as shored up as Callie would have wanted. They fell into an old-fashioned search of the interior, with Callie having an old-fashioned wary sense of her temporary partner's motives.

She fished around maps in pockets behind the seats, under the seats amid candy wrappers, dehydrated fries, and a drink straw. In the glove box, she nudged around registration, insurance, and a handful of sticky cough drops. Then in the trunk she lifted a sandy, sour-smelling carpet, methodically peeking here and there . . . when something beige caught her attention through one of the spare wheel's bolt holes.

"Here, help me get this tire out," she said, attempting to turn the wing nut.

Kendrick eagerly took over, and together they lifted the spare, but Callie left him holding the weight of the task so she could nab the papers first.

Not one folder but two. No FBI insignia or official *hands-off* verbiage but two simple generic Office Depot files. One contained a dozen or more pages. The other, however, was an inch thick and worn.

"This what you're looking for?" she asked.

"Yes," he replied, then let loose a breath. He dropped the tire back in place, not bothering with the bolts.

Here wasn't the place to fan through the papers and decode Rhoades's mission. "Were you working on this with him?"

Locking up the car, he started to pocket the keys, but she held out her hand. He dropped them in her palm and peered over her shoulder at the gawkers. "No. I fed him information on occasion, but let's take this elsewhere."

They'd leave the Nissan parked as they found it, the vehicle giving them no indication of having been involved in Rhoades's disappearance.

As they left, the woman who'd watched them intently from the sidewalk lifted a half wave, and Callie veered over to her, motioning for Kendrick to stay where he was. "Hey, I'm Edisto Beach Police Chief Callie Morgan. That's FBI Agent Knox Kendrick over near the car. Do you know Mr. Pinkerton Rhoades?" she asked the woman.

"Is this a drug bust? Oh my gosh, he's not missing, is he? I mean, I have to think about the complex . . . the tenants. I'm the assistant manager. Oh, God, do I need to call the manager?" The chunky woman stared through wide eyes, her contained nerves now spilling over into hugging herself.

"No. We're just checking his whereabouts," Callie said.

The manager deflated. "Oh. Thank heaven."

"Do you see him often?"

The lady's eyes tracked up to the left before answering; she didn't pull back, most likely speaking the truth. "Lemme see, maybe once a month? Never saw him coming or going like he had a job or anything, no friends in and out, but then, I've only been in charge for nine months."

Not much help. Callie wondered if it was worth the trouble of contacting the manager.

"He wasn't supposed to be parking in the dumpster area," she said. "We were forever telling him to move it."

By drawing out her badge and a business card, Callie silently reiterated her authority. "The rent's paid? Because the car's evidence in a possible crime and must remain as is."

"Yes, ma'am. Two months in advance." She took Callie's card, studying it as if it were alien in origin. The streetlights of the complex started popping on. "So, what do I do?"

Reaching out, Callie took the lady's hand in both of hers. "Just keep an eye on who might come and go, and let me know if the car moves. Don't mess with it, and keep out of his apartment. You seem like someone I can trust, am I right?"

"Absolutely, yes, ma'am."

Callie patted her hand, thanked her, and returned to where Kendrick waited. He said nothing. She, however, had a lot to ask him, but she'd wait for the confines of the Toyota.

Rush-hour traffic around Charleston moved like a slug, but that was three hours past. Callie flipped through the grocery sack to find zero-interest credit-card offers, bills, and ads for weekends in the North Carolina mountains. Surprise. . . . Rhoades still received bank statements via snail mail. Heck, online banking was way more secure than mailing one's business through the post office. She found a monthly federal deposit from the Office of Personnel Management. Assorted debits. Three random large four-figure deposits. But she needed more bank statements to see how far back these large deposits went. Hell, he could've actually been a private investigator.

She caught herself squinting in the dying light harder. No phone bill. She wanted to find that rather than wait on a records request.

Night was almost upon them, so she opened the smaller file to catch what she could in the dying light.

"That the boy's file?" Kendrick asked.

"Well, it's a file on *a* boy." She turned her phone flashlight on and flipped a second page. Lucas Estes. Five years old. Bound and drowned in 2003 like two others the year before per a note in the file. "Why this one?" she asked. "Why not an interest in the other two boys as well?"

"The mother," he said. "Mothers tore him up. They never found a thing on the grabber, and he never asked for a ransom. I was a rookie in Atlanta and not involved, but about four months ago, Pinky asked me for copies of the file."

She flipped pages. "Don't think he got very far. Not many notes."

"It's a dead end. You'd be amazed at how many of these situations go unsolved."

"No, I wouldn't," she whispered. A lot of bad people escaped law enforcement. She'd seen it, even lost to it.

"Have you studied these files very hard, Kendrick?" she asked, still distrustful of the man, his motives, and his actions.

"No," he said, and pulled off the highway and parked in an Asian fusion-type restaurant. "This work for dinner?"

She stared at him, like redirecting her from the conversation would be that easy. But she missed her evening drink more at the moment, and a girl had to eat. "Sure." Callie hated sushi but loved saki, and every Asian place had a bar.

Unwilling to leave the files, Callie carried them in, motioning toward a more secluded booth in the back of the restaurant. There were only three other couples in the house.

The waitress approached with menus.

Callie accepted hers. "Gin and tonic, please."

The waitress turned to Kendrick. "Water, thanks."

Upon the waitress's return, Callie ordered her second, along with General Tso's chicken. Kendrick went with a sushi and sashimi platter, and returned their menus.

"So gin's your drink of choice?" He shook his napkin in his lap.

"Raised on it," she said. Her mother indeed introduced her to French gin martinis at age eighteen, not that Callie had the woman's steady, heavy thirst. She lowered her glass. "Hope that didn't sound like I think it did, though my tolerance runs pretty high."

"I just hear that you like gin," he said, his brow giving a quick arch. "I'm a whiskey man, myself."

Moving the Estes file beneath the other, she opened the thicker one. "Hmm," she said. Scribbles everywhere. A few photos. Nothing appeared to be on Edisto. "He had more success with this one." Or seemed more fanatical.

Kendrick leaned across the table. "Mind if I move to see better?"

Callie shrugged, and he slid out and over to her side.

A girl stolen from her bedroom at age two almost seventeen years ago. A sizable ransom paid . . . with no results.

Callie tried to hide a chill at her unexpected substitution of her baby daughter for this girl. She took a huge sip. Bonnie would be four if Callie hadn't lost her to SIDS at six months old, but to have a stranger snatch her . . . a mother would feel the life force of that baby girl someplace, worried if she was fed, bathed, molested . . . probably refusing to accept the child was a cold body in a shallow grave or crammed in a suitcase in a county landfill.

Callie hunted past an old photo of a dated sedan and a partial plate, a man holding his arm out for his child to hop in the backseat. Callie licked her finger, changing papers, sliding past driver's license photos.

She had to see what the girl looked like.

There it was. Callie sucked in. A tow-headed, cherub-cheeked toddler, mouth open in a giggle, tiny baby teeth pretty and white, a small space between the front two, hands out as if asking to be picked up . . . punching a hole in Callie's heart.

She steadied herself. "This one predates you, too."

"Emma? Yeah." Kendrick held up the photo. "That one kept him up at night. He tried not to retire because of it, but the Bureau has a mandatory retirement age."

"He keep you updated?" she asked.

He shook his head. "Remained quiet to give me plausible deniability, he said. The Bureau had no idea, but he was excited whenever we spoke. Said he might be getting close to serious crumbs."

A thoughtful pause fell between them. He pretended to center his water glass on a coaster. She caught a whiff of a subtle cologne.

"Sorry," she said when the void grew heavy. "Again, my condolences about Pinky. It's pretty obvious you were close."

"Yeah, thanks."

This was better between them. They fell silent, moving papers, and surprisingly Callie's pulse quickened, bringing the rush of an almost foreign sensation after so long of feeling nothing. The unspoken, random trail of data and events hinted that either the girl or the abductor had led Rhoades to Edisto.

Totally unheard of. The odds were—"By the way," Kendrick said. "The mother drove Pinky's actions, too, so don't get any rose-colored ideas. A bored retiree and a desperate mother might've been unable to let it go. The Bureau's pretty sure that girl's dead."

One would think. The return and rescue of Jaycee Lee Dugard and Elizabeth Smart after years of captivity were so off-the-charts rare.

Then dinner arrived. "Mind if I have another?" Callie asked, holding up her empty and two discreet fingers.

"I'm driving," he said, still on water. The waitress disappeared and returned with the double, and Callie found the meal so much more enjoyable.

Afterward, over coffee and Callie's fourth, they talked about what Pinky was really like. A single guy. Loved M&Ms. Rarely drank, but was hooked on Diet Coke. Hated suits. Enjoyed cheap sci-fi movies. But to Callie the information seemed dated, as if Kendrick drew upon history, not current events.

An hour and a half later, as they drove through Adams Run toward Edisto, Callie continued to ponder her new partner. Kendrick possibly knew more than he said, but Callie had also spotted that he knew way less than he thought he should. A personal battle of sorts.

Rhoades's computer tower made a mild thump in the trunk as they took a turn. She expected little on the machine. Pinky didn't seem too techie.

The quarter moon didn't light up much, but Callie still stared at the black Lowcountry jungle passing by. Kendrick believed that Pinky held a seventeen-year-old obsession, and that the FBI didn't give a damn about either the case or the dead retired agent.

Maybe they thought Pinky a nutjob.

Night shadows flickered softly, and her phone grew sweaty in her palm. She'd never run a case without touching base with Stan, and she'd appreciate his take on Kendrick. Stan had more experience with the feebs. He had a way of helping her focus.

Stan coaxed her through the robberies last year, the ones connected to Papa Beach's death. He reinforced her efforts when a Twitter war introduced her to a serial killer. He grounded her professionally, answered her queries . . . finishing with a gruff good-bye and her nickname, Chicklet. He was familiar and safe. Something she could use more of these days.

"Waiting for a call?" Kendrick asked.

Yes. "No, why?"

"The death grip on the phone."

She slid it into her purse. "I *am* chief of police. This isn't all I have on my agenda."

"Any ideas you want to run by me? I'm right here."

Not really. He was a stranger despite their time together. And she had a suspicion or two about the lay of the land with this guy.

"You're concealing your involvement from your ASAC." She wasn't fluent in FBI, but she understood that an Assistant Special Agent in Charge would hold a finger on where his agents were, and what case they worked.

He maintained his stare on the highway. "I took leave."

Hah! Meaning yes. "That alone makes me trust you about as far as I can shot put your ass."

"The Bureau isn't interested. I am. Get over it," he said firmly.

"I'm trying to sort fact from fiction. The way you trashed that Nissan wasn't my first clue that you knew more than you said."

"I haven't lied."

"You've been damn cloudy, though."

Silence thick between them, Callie all but heard the agent sorting out an excuse.

"I think we started out wrong," he said.

"You just seeing that? First, I decide whether you're trustworthy enough to be involved," she replied. "Or if you bring sufficient substance to the table."

He jeered. "After four drinks? Five counting the double. Let's save decision making until you're sober."

Callie stiffened. "I beg your pardon?"

"Who else you going to use?" he shot back. "Doubt your people have the skills."

With heat flaring in her cheeks, Callie held up a stiff finger. "You have no idea what my people can do."

He blew out in jest. "You know I'm right."

"Whatever," she said, mocking him. "Let's say I hand this over to SLED. They take it over your head. Instant transparency, and less work for me."

But she'd have to listen to Brice broadcast how she couldn't cut it as a cop anymore if she did that.

The wheels hummed a quarter mile on the black asphalt, the midline reflectors the only detail in the night.

Fact was, her police force could run some cases, but they weren't detectives. Raysor served as her lieutenant, but he thought too linearly with a career limited to small-town politics.

No Seabrook. No Stan. Kendrick wasn't wrong about her lack of people with skills at the moment.

"Listen," she started, then stopped, uncertain how much to trust the FBI. No, not *the* FBI.

This FBI. She was already convinced he was too close to the case to be unbiased.

"I'm waiting," Kendrick said.

"When we meet, we meet at Sea Saw on Pompano Street," she replied, softening the attitude, Stan's house the only address she could think of off the cuff.

"Your rental or something?"

"No, but don't worry about it."

The causeway appeared a hundred yards ahead. "So, this is how it goes? Partners? The two of us solving this murder?"

"No, not partners. Question is can I trust you, because I'll do this thing alone if you aren't ready to put everything on the table and work for me. Can you do that?"

Kendrick entered the city limits and pulled into the nearest easy parking lot at Bi-Lo, leaving the engine running. He twisted to face her head on, the store lights giving them monotone views of each other in the night. "I'm FBI," he said.

"That's an employer, not experience or an agreement that you work for me on this."

His tension rippled the air between them. "This shit is what we do."

"Well, you're seventeen years slow on solving Pinky's old case, Dick Tracy."

He leaned an elbow on the console between them. "Now you're just trying to piss me off. Testing me?"

"No more than you've done me." She narrowed the space between them. "Just taking stock of what I have to work with. Hoping you aren't a mistake."

"After watching you drink tonight, right back at you." Kendrick, stiff and stoic, put the transmission back in drive and left the parking lot.

Stunned, Callie fought to control her breathing and had no easy words of rebuttal. Instead, with her arms crossed, the car's interior warm from their ire, Callie rode silent and wasted no seconds exiting the car at Chelsea Morning.

Ten thirty. Clouds covered the moon, making her stairs difficult to see. Once at the top, she set down the bag of papers and pulled out her keys, leaning on the dew-laden door frame when a small wave of tipsy met her. She let it pass, inhaling, smelling the moist air full of shellfish, salt, and marsh. Clicking noises sounded from the road behind the house. Raccoon, probably.

As she wiped her hand on her jeans, she caught light flickering through the front door window from the television. Jeb's video games, most likely. He'd be preoccupied . . .

But the door opened. "Mom?"

"Thanks, son." She reached down for her bag, the angle handing her a brief dose of the woozies. She rose back up for them to settle, before giving it another try.

"You are shittin' me," he whispered.

Searching around herself and Jeb, Callie sought the cause for concern, then his greeting hit her. "Since when do you talk like that?"

Taking the bag, her son spoke under his breath. "When my mother comes home drunk, I can talk any damn way I want." He touched her elbow. "Shut up and follow me to your bedroom. I don't want the guys to see my police chief mom wasted."

Jerking her arm from him, she backed out onto the porch. "I'm not wasted. And God forbid I embarrass you. They don't have to see me. I'll just sit out here and *sober up*." She gave him air quotes with her fingers.

"No," he said, and reached for her.

"Yes," she said louder, making him look back at his friends.

"Fine. Sit out here all night, for all I care."

Funny how his nostrils flared. She'd never seen them so big.

She grew weary, and the rattan chair creaked as she sat.

"I'll check on you later," he said. "Try not to fall out on the floor." He shut the door.

She listened for the click, disappointed at not hearing it. "Again, you don't lock up," she said to the night air, then hands on her knees, she rose, checked for her steadiness, and sucked in deep breaths. A woozy second, but she attributed it to a blood-pressure spike, drop, whatever. Her head felt fine. She took the stairs back down, hand on the rail, her balance passable. "And I'm not being relegated to my own porch by my son."

Time for her evening drive.

Chapter 10

HEADING DOWN A cross street, Callie drove to Palmetto. Since Jeb left for college, she'd developed a late-night vigil of driving down to Yacht Club Road and Bay Point, turning and cruising east along Docksite Road. Fewer people. Less judgment. Her patrol would eventually take her along every side street and secondary road as she slowly watched Edisto drift off to sleep. The routine gave her a slow, lazy peace to think.

Only twenty-four hours since she'd plucked Pinky out of the creek. Barely twelve since Kendrick had arrived. Her life had been funky enough before all this extra.

Stan should've been at dinner, helping her sort out Kendrick, the overconfident FBI jackass. Stan had taught her to study the duality in everyone. The good and bad. The cunning and the stupid. The fake and the real. Knox Kendrick owned gobs of *duality*.

One part of her was growing to enjoy this case, but she almost feared it becoming a rabbit hole. Reinvestigating the kidnapped Emma Flagg might lead them to Rhoades's murderer, but possibly steer them away, too. Wrong turns destroyed precious time . . . let bad guys slip into the mist, kill people.

Three college boys darted across the street. Callie slammed her brakes. They didn't seem to notice.

What if Stan had an accident and couldn't call? No, he had spoken to Raysor.

Her phone vibrated, so she drifted toward the curb on the 800 block of Palmetto. Crap, how had she silenced her phone? She overcompensated the braking, her head rocking forward then back as her tires made a notable bump.

Five texts. One from Marie with end-of-the-day updates. One from her mother asking Callie to appear at a political event in Middleton again, like *that* would happen. The third came from Jeb, informing her of his refusal for the same event.

Thomas let her know he'd written five tickets along the beach, noted no serious activity at the Fantasea beach house, and was taking Ike's shift tonight. One of the new officers, who was not quite the employee his résumé professed. A task for another day.

Then came the last, twenty minutes old. From Stan.

Damn it. She changed the ring setting and quickly typed, *I'm still up. Call. Need your advice.* Then she bothered to take in his original message. *Quit with the messages. Up to my ass in alligators and don't have time.*

Don't have time? What the hell?

A tap sounded on her window, a light glaring at her. She rolled down the window, hand in front of her eyes.

"Hey, Chief."

"Thomas, what's wrong?" Callie couldn't see his face for the glare.

"Um, have you been drinking?" he asked.

She laughed. "Is it that quiet out tonight?"

"Ma'am . . . it's just . . . well, the way you ran into the curb."

Ma'am? She almost said, *Is there a problem officer?* "I parked to check phone calls."

"Well, your tire scrubbed that curb for a good six feet, Chief. That and your son called me. Have you been drinking?"

Jeb called Thomas to run her down. Shame filled her at the realization her personal life had just collided with her job. Unless Jeb did it out of anger, or spite. In that case, she was shamed and crushed.

"I went to West Ashley on a lead earlier and had drinks with dinner."

"Come on out, Chief," he said, reaching for the door handle.

Her heart leaped into her throat. "What? Are we seriously taking a test?" She exited as asked, scanning the street for onlookers, particularly anyone she knew.

"No, ma'am. And be glad it's me."

Again with the damn ma'am.

"Hand me the keys," he added. "I'm taking you home. I'll walk back and retrieve your cruiser."

Embarrassment flew up her neck as she worried what to say. Thomas was one of her good ones, loyal, his humor a bright spot of her day. He should be trusting her. She was totally in control.

He locked up her vehicle, escorted her to his. Silent, sorely abashed, she sat rubbing her right temple, elbow on the armrest, while her youngest uniform walked around and entered the driver's side.

He was young, plus Jeb probably embellished the call to him. She damn well knew how to have a drink with a meal and not lose her edge.

"Thomas—" she started.

Turning in his seat, he left the lights off. "Chief. I'm on your side. Always will be. Nobody gets it better than me that life has doled you out a solid, stinking stockpile of shit. After we lost Mike, I wondered if you were done . . . not that anyone would've blamed you for cashing it in. Then you gave that speech at the funeral. Goddamn it, but you had me bawling like a brat."

Those words had just rolled out of her mouth that day, her notes forgotten, embracing a sea of uniforms from across the state. For weeks after, emails poured in. People who weren't there, had heard it second- or thirdhand, and wanted a copy of a speech she couldn't possibly remember. So many atta-girls about the example she set, and the stimulating words of wisdom she'd poured over the people saying good-bye to Francis and Mike.

Like she was the strong one.

Tears puddled in her eyes. She coughed, tried to clear her way to speak . . . but couldn't.

Thomas coughed once, too. "But me, Raysor, and your buddy Stan decided to take a wait-and-see attitude. Stan warned us there might be a delayed reaction . . ."

What the hell was he trying to say?

He seemed to give up, and donned his seat belt.

"Oh, no," she said. "We're finishing this. Y'all have been discussing me?"

"No, we've been worried about you. There's a difference." Thomas pulled away, taking an immediate right to a side street to Jungle Road. Only five minutes to Chelsea Morning, the stun choking Callie all the way.

Thomas let her out with a solemn "'Night, Chief," then parked his patrol car in her drive.

When he got out, however, she met him, the sodium vapor streetlight casting an orangish-noir array of shadows around them. He needed to feel okay at doing his job. She had to make peace with this piece of edge he now had on her.

"It's been over two hours since dinner," she said. "My head was clear, Thomas, but I understand you were doing your duty."

"Ma'am—"

"Don't call me *ma'am*. You never did before."

He peered down at his shoes, then, as if reminding himself he was the officer at the helm, he raised his gaze on her and held it. "Don't,

Chief. I can look at you and tell you'd blow point one or higher."

She really didn't want to argue this with him. "Have you even seen me intoxicated?"

He closed his eyes and inhaled, exhaled, then returned a hard focus on Callie. "I have seen you hungover. I've seen you buzzed. Probably when you weren't aware."

Almost about to ask when and where, Callie stopped herself. She wasn't sure she wanted to hear the answers.

"Never witnessed you drunk until tonight," he said.

"I'm not—"

"You're drunk. You drink. Often. Next time it won't be me who catches you, and even if it is, I'll have to take you in."

Such a knife to her gut. "Thomas."

He held up a hand. "Ain't right, Chief, and you know it." He turned and commenced his walk to retrieve her cruiser.

She watched until he disappeared around the corner, feeling ripped wide open. As she turned back to the house and began to climb the steps, a briny breeze gently rocked the fern hanging on the end of the porch. At the top she reached the chair she was supposed to still be occupying for Jeb. A humid coolness had settled in the night air.

Lowering herself back into that chair, Callie decided to wait for Thomas. Talk again. It'd been four drinks but atop plenty of food. She hadn't driven home, and plenty hours had passed for the alcohol to dissipate into her system. Having grown up with her parents' open bars, social soirees, and political fundraisers, she honestly saw herself as more tolerant to drink than most.

But Thomas's remarks. . . . She clenched her eyes. God, she felt like a damn fool, regardless of the level of alcohol.

She opened her phone once more, the glare of her text screen making her squint. Or was it the tears? *Please at least text*, she typed to Stan. Then, her head back against the house's siding, she closed her lids, sadder than she could remember.

While crickets and frogs slowly quit singing, she sat for ten minutes, stymied how to be Thomas's boss with this new secret between them. Praying his words were true, that he was loyal, and therefore not obliged to the town council . . . and Brice.

Shame sank deeper in her soul, and she tried to stave it off. She wasn't drunk.

Her phone rang. She groped and juggled the phone to answer,

wiping an errant tear that leaked out when she blinked. "Hello? Stan? Thank God."

"What's wrong?" he said, groggy.

She hadn't the nerve to tell him about Thomas. So she mentioned finding Rhoades, then with nary a breath launched into concerns of Kendrick, but before she could start in about the cold-case files, he stopped her.

"This is your emergency?" he asked.

Emergency? "Didn't say it was an emergency. You haven't returned my calls. I had to throw out a Hail Mary text to get your attention. Sorry, I didn't look at the clock and now I see it's late, but what the hell is going on with you?"

He growled. She loved hearing him growl. It was better than silence.

"Just a sec," she said when Thomas showed and parked her patrol car on the other side of the drive. He jogged up the stairs. "No more joyriding tonight, Chief. Here are your keys. See you tomorrow." He gave her a two-fingered salute in the darkness and returned to his shift.

God Almighty, bless his heart.

"Can you talk?" she asked. "Or will tomorrow—"

"Who was that?" Stan asked.

"Thomas. He brought me home."

"Have you been drinking?" He didn't bark, but the censure came through.

She couldn't lie to him. Never had. "At dinner," she said, using the excuse given to Thomas.

"How many? Two, three? More?"

This wasn't how this call was supposed to go. "Three," she lied.

"Lay off the booze, Callie. You'll make an idiot out of yourself."

He didn't call her Chicklet.

And he hung up on her.

Had Raysor told him she'd been drinking? That Brice was on her ass? That unknown people called her at stupid, way-too-early morning hours and warned her that people were beginning to talk?

Now she was vexed. Jumping up, she snatched the pillow from her chair, only it remained tied in the back. The chair tipped and fell across her feet. Then with a deep grunt, Callie kicked the rattan piece, bouncing it off the front-porch wall.

She was *not* calling him back. She was *not* leaving him any more texts. She would not pick him up at the airport, assuming he *ever* came back.

Which meant not using See Saw for her meet with Kendrick. In for a pound . . . out for a . . . whatever.

Callie repositioned her chair and prepared herself to face Jeb. She tried the door, jolted at the impasse. Locked. A first since he'd come home. Done to respect her need for security? Or to teach her a lesson?

She used her key and peered through the glass before entering. She should've eaten a mint. No, Jeb might notice that more.

Jeb and his two buddies remained awake but sprawled across furniture like octopi, long legs and arms draped every which way.

She entered, locked the door behind her, and tried to gingerly cross the chasm to her bedroom, wanting to say no more than *good night.* Bare feet, sun-kissed faces, and faded T-shirts. Someone had taken a recent shower, from the shampoo smell.

No girls . . . and no Sprite. Good at first instinct. Sad thinking of Jeb possibly dodging his girl.

"Go on to bed," Jeb said pensively, not taking his eyes off the screen, his hands methodical in keeping his avatar alive.

The other two boys didn't seem to care, showing no knowledge of what went down earlier between she and Jeb . . . with Thomas.

She felt almost as isolated as she did with Jeb gone to school.

Callie wasn't used to this side of her son, using his entertaining hours to be with guys. Ignoring her. Ignoring his girl after being enamored of Sprite for so long. The wrath of Sprite's mother on the porch better understood.

"Everything okay between you and Ms. Bianchi?" she asked, seeking a common topic.

Jeb flopped back in his spot on the sofa. "You mean Sprite?"

"One and the same if you don't do right by her."

His nose scrunched as if this girl he used to worship was a fleeting whim. "She's fine." He returned his attention to the screen.

She cleared her throat, half-paralyzed at this bungled struggle with a disillusioned son. "Can I speak to you a moment?" She moved into the kitchen.

Hesitating, he stepped over Sammy's legs and in four long strides met her at the refrigerator. "What?"

Opening the appliance door, she pretended to rummage. "I'm going in a little early in the morning. That body you found is going to keep me occupied for a while."

"Could've told me that in the living room," he said.

No questions about Thomas? "Where's Sprite?" she asked.

"At home. It's kinda late, Mom. She has school in the morning."

Right. Callie knew that. God, she was ruining this. "Did you explain to her mother about . . . things?"

Twisting his mouth, Jeb acted perturbed. "I told her what she wanted to hear, if that's what you're asking."

Callie stood still with a water bottle in hand. "No, that's not what I'm asking. And what does that even mean?"

"Mom," he said with a loud huff. "My relationship is none of her business . . . or yours." He leaned in. "And don't you ever embarrass me like that again."

The retort smacked her like a fish in the face. He acted almost unrelated, and six years older. "Jeb," she started, then reined herself in. "Date who you like, but whoever it is, treat her right."

The boys whooped in the living room at a virtual explosion. "I'm heading to bed," she said, her body yearning a mattress and four aspirin. "Take the decibels down a notch, if you don't mind."

"Guys?" Jeb yelled. "Turn down the game."

She winced, but the crashes and explosions muted.

"Oh." She turned back. "About the body you found? It's getting complicated. Don't be surprised if I feel the need to call and check on you."

His eyes went cold. "No, we're not doing the hourly text thing again. Just go to bed."

The demand hurt, then aggravated her. "Pardon me? I think I'm perfectly entitled to—"

"Hey, I saw that dead guy, by the way." The voice came from the living room, and the boys had paused the game, their ears having totally engaged the kitchen conversation with the volume lowered. "I mean, when he was still breathing."

Moving to the doorway, Callie leaned on the frame, trying not to act irritated at the eavesdropping, or buzzed. "Which one of you? Sammy?"

"Yes, ma'am," the boy answered. "Lots of talk about it this afternoon. The dude was watching the girls."

"Yeah," Jeb said. "I didn't see him, but a few of the other kids did. They're talking it up all over the place, especially once I found a body."

"A real perv," Nolan added.

Callie squinted. "What makes you call him a perv? And why didn't anyone come tell me or one of my officers?"

Nolan gave a twisted facial expression to Sammy, who rolled his eyes.

The guys carried themselves into the kitchen, as though the conversation gave them momentum to keep going and pilfer the fridge. Jeb shrugged. "Guess it's a nonissue anyway, huh? Perv or not, he's fish food. Or was."

This coarse and brazen, almost condescending side of her son wasn't sitting well with her. Various phases of childhood came with their pros and cons, but this provoked her.

The boys' remarks about Pinky, however . . . damn. Maybe this kind of behavior was what made Kendrick so secretive. Maybe he held more of Pinky's behavior secret.

Thanks to these kids, suddenly Rhoades was a dark horse, no longer the white knight carrying a torch. And Kendrick seemed a deeper well.

Chapter 11

CALLIE SLEPT LIKE the dead, dreamless for a change, like she liked, but awoke with a start to the alarm, wet drool on her pillow. A headache drummed behind her hairline, and she eased under the spread and cool sheets.

But rise she must. She shoved aside the covers. *Oh crap*—last night. Thomas.

She fell back on the bed, her headache rolling through her brain at the motion. There wasn't enough aspirin in the state of South Carolina to fix this. She wouldn't be able to look at anyone in the office without wondering if the normally discreet Thomas had let something slip.

Yeah, you should've seen the chief! Wasted!

Would he do that to her? Would he be so careless?

She wasn't wasted, though.

But she'd sure ticketed plenty who'd said the same to her.

Stop. Priorities. Get them straight. Put the emotional stuff about Thomas and Stan . . . aw, damn! Stan.

She dropped her legs over the edge of the bed. *You're an idiot! Stay in bed. Resign, for God's sake. It's not like you don't have sufficient money to get by. Thank you for that, Daddy.*

Daddy. She was almost glad he wasn't here to see what she'd become in these last few months.

Lifting her heavy head, she remembered him standing in her doorway the day she moved into Chelsea Morning less than a year ago, breaking up a spat between her and her mother. *Enough*, he always said. One word, and everyone understood to get over themselves.

She stared at her dangling legs as she tried to figure what this day should be about. Focus on the case, and the day's agenda, the public's concern . . . first things first, which meant haul her butt into the station. Delegate her guys to cover everywhere Brice might be watching, forewarn them about the pudgy, bourbon-sucking human drone striving to ax their reputations. Bashing the Chief was a shot at them all.

Meet Kendrick at eleven. Well, crap again. They were scheduled for

Stan's place, but that hadn't been okayed last night, because she got pissed, forgot to ask, and hung up. No. . . . He hung up on her.

Note to self: Run down a different meeting place before eleven. God help her, but she might have to call Janet. Mashing her lids hard, Callie held back rising desperation. She reached over to the nightstand and texted Kendrick to wait till noon.

Crap again . . . and to bring the computer to the station. Another text to him.

He'd probably think she was hungover.

Callie left the bed and turned on the hot water in the shower, her head still cotton stuffed from the night before. Today, the dead man would be a huge topic, because even without Brice fueling the gossip mill, the populace would wonder what the police had done to solve the crime so they could sleep easy. Ensuring people felt safe in their homes was one of the main reasons she became a cop.

When Callie arrived in the office, the computer was already on Marie's desk, signed for by Thomas. Score one for Kendrick. Not five minutes later, a lady railed at Marie about why the police let a body happen on Edisto. Marie told Callie she could handle the calls, assuring her boss that she handled worse in August when heat made folks crazier than this. But five calls later, Callie heard a man's cursing all the way across the small office. "What the fuck are you doing about this body?"

From that point forward, Callie fielded the calls, letting Marie check out Rhoades's computer. A couple hours later, Callie had consoled twelve people, grateful that Brice didn't call, or worse, barge in and demand results like the day before. Her two officers of the day had hit the beat at eight. Finally, around a quarter to eleven, with the hubbub less chaotic, Callie stood outside Stan's rental. These files needed serious study, and she'd wasted last night. But she really didn't have Stan's permission to be in See Saw, and she lost her nerve to ask Janet about an empty rental.

Screw it. She texted Kendrick, *Change of plans to my place.*

Two minutes later, she decoded the alarm at Chelsea Morning and entered the front door. "Jeb?" she called. No response. Good. She carried the two abduction files to her kitchen table and sat in her usual chair.

This was more like it.

While she hated that a murder woke her up and that a man died, picking at clues until the right ones bled was an old thrill she still relished.

And a double thrill at that. A murder and a cold-case abduction.

She would work the murder from the crime scene out, expanding from center point. The coroner had proven murder. No sign of robbery, which made her label the situation personal. They searched the residence, found the vehicle, and retrieved hidden files that somehow sent the victim to Edisto. Now to study what Rhoades studied, and put herself in his shoes.

She reopened the smaller file, in size, not tragedy. A missing boy found dead. Holding the beautiful school photo of the Estes boy, Callie gazed a long second, then laid it down. The case was full of dead ends, nothing to trigger a renewed mission.

The FBI was so large, they weren't used to lone individuals following all leads on a case. When they needed information, they shopped it out. A good and bad thing. Less emotional involvement, she guessed. More attention on sorting the pieces someone lower ranking gathered. If she were Rhoades, she'd double check everything anyone else had done. Reinterview people.

She closed the Estes file and opened the one for Emma Flagg. Rhoades had been way more keen here. The girl was abducted from Charleston. Rhoades pulled at threads here and there for years, with Emma Flagg's mother working with him, maybe pressuring him to keep his guilt alive, but no telling what the agent knew that wasn't written in the file, since his work as a retiree held him to no standard. She'd study Rhoades's notes, then compare notes with Kendrick, since he seemed close to the man, then interview the Flagg mother.

"Assuming the abducted girl isn't long dead," Callie mumbled.

Unless the kidnapped child was locked in a basement, having miscarriages and babies, a thin, malnourished girl serving as some man's toy.

Assuming the cold case had anything to do with Rhoades's murder, but how could she ignore the possibility?

Callie spread out the papers, repositioning one whose corner caught on the edge of her fruit bowl. She unclipped a photo, laying it atop the pile. The girl would be nineteen years old and appeared to be Rhoades's focus. Unfortunately, somebody became mighty unhappy about that . . . unfortunately on Callie's beach.

Too cool for air-conditioning, Callie opened her kitchen window a few inches. A soft breeze filtered through the screen, bringing with it Edisto's lively traffic noises. At half past noon, Kendrick knocked, dressed in a pale blue polo.

Callie let him in. Red-faced, Kendrick set a bag and two Styrofoam cups of tea on the table. "I swear, where do you find a drive-through here? Had to wait in line on a porch for this. The Sea*Cow*?"

Callie's stomach stirred at the thought of food beyond aspirins and coffee. "What's in the bag?" she asked, reaching.

"A shrimp salad burrito thing and a Reuben." Kendrick shrugged. "Figured I was safe getting you seafood. Beer-batter fries were a no-brainer."

"Funny man," she said. "I'm allergic to seafood."

He didn't miss a beat. "No problem. Eat the Reuben."

She took the shrimp, enjoying Kendrick being smart.

The guy actually found a great place to eat, too, and if he stayed more than a day or two, he'd learn breakfast was their pièce de résistance.

Kendrick rapped the table. "Let's get on with this. We should've met earlier."

She tossed his wrapped sandwich on his side of the table, forgoing a plate. "Yeah, well, some of us aren't on leave."

Callie's brain soon felt fed and capable. She was glad they'd waited for daylight to dive into the case. Last night had been sort of . . . off sync. "I've been thinking, Kendrick . . ."

"Call me Knox. I'll call you Callie. Now, what were you saying?"

It was only the exchange of names, but the agreement felt sort of . . . concessional. He was trying to get along.

The man held a wealth of snark, too, but he was on a quest. His friend died, and he probably possessed enough Quantico skills to offer solid assistance. She'd use him . . . as she suspected he was using her.

"Fine . . . it's Knox," she ultimately said.

"Wow, you had to think too damn hard about that. Didn't realize I was such a hard sell." Kendrick shoved the wrappings aside. "So, the case . . ."

"One," she listed "we focus on Emma Flagg. Rhoades thought she was alive."

Knox shoved briskly through papers. "Where does it say that?"

"Thought he would've told you."

"No. He didn't." His expression froze, stunned, as if his memory stalled, but then his gaze navigated his old friend's handwriting, darting around the spread pages.

Guess he wasn't as close to the guy as she thought. Kendrick searched for answers, too.

Callie moved the touching, all-too-sweet photo of the two-year-old under the stack and passed to him the synopsized, chronological notes she'd started.

"Seen these?" she asked, pulling out other pictures.

Recently developed from the color quality and four-by-six dimensions, but the images showed clothing and hair styles of two decades ago.

"No." He sounded surprised and took them from her. The car picture with a father happily ushering his family into an old vehicle. Two mothers talking in a park, their hands hovering, waiting for their children's swings to come back to be pushed again. A close up of a shy two-year-old Emma at play. A dozen pictures at some park possibly taken by the mom, except for the swing photo, since she wasn't in any others. The names David and Joan Metts with the scribblings *"they'd be fifty now."*

"Already had Marie attempt to pull up current driver's licenses of the Metts couple, but they expired ten years ago," she said. "You haven't worked this file at all, have you?"

"No," he said.

Rhoades had also utilized a facial recognition program, and a fabricated older version of Emma stared back cold, without much character. Age fourteen, per the note at the bottom, created five years ago while Rhoades still had access to FBI resources. The image rang no bells.

Both of them shuffled through the file, taking papers and photos from each other. His impatience showed on occasion as he grabbed things from her, as if she was taking too long. But nothing clued them to the girl's whereabouts. Nothing said explicitly that she was alive. Just the effort Rhoades was making told them he felt there was a chance.

She most likely died soon after being kidnapped, or was sold to some desperate well-heeled childless couple. Or was taken to horrible surroundings until she reached the age of prostitution . . . in Thailand, Singapore, or some other trafficking hellhole.

The odds of *that* child reaching nineteen were beyond calculation and off-the-wall crazy.

Any clues not in the file died with Rhoades in the marsh.

Callie revisited a scribbled list. "Want you to look at this. Rhoades visited the Colleton County courthouse." She held up a list of deed numbers, names, streets—some circled, then crossed through with a Sharpie, as if he'd ruled out possibilities. Most of the results were illegible.

She squinted at notes on another piece of yellow paper, ripped off from a pad, perforated across the top. "Phone calls where he tried talking to the College of Charleston and Charleston Southern University. From the *X*s I'm assuming they stonewalled him. Again, lots of *X*s and cross-throughs pressing hard into the paper."

Knox barely blinked, reading. "He sought the girl pretty damn hard. Almost as if years hadn't passed."

"Yes," Callie replied. "The Flagg mother is mentioned a lot. A son Theodore two years older than Emma. Daddy Flagg, first name Raymond, died three years ago, and it wasn't long after he passed that the mother seemed to rekindle a hotter search." Callie peered up at him across their research. "Sorry, but he kept the crappiest notes of any investigator I've ever seen."

Knox slapped the table. "But he had a nose, Callie. Trust me, he had a nose. And he never forgot a thing."

A lot of good that did them.

The agent took a breath and reached around to scratch the nape of his neck. "I recall the mother reconnecting, and the father dying of cancer. She called Pinky and set him on fire, but I was in the field. We didn't work together much his last few years." He retrieved the child's photo, laying it front and center. "What if he was just pacifying the mother in little increments, helping to keep her daughter's memory alive?"

"Not very humane," Callie said. She fought not to fall into the toddler's sweet, soft eyes. The loss of such young innocence wove sympathetic tentacles through her. "But I spoke to some boys last night who saw Rhoades watching the college girls here on school break. Unless he was a pervert, like one of the boys assumed . . . I mean, a fifty-something-year-old man watching teenage bikinis sort of paints that picture . . . we can hope he was imagining who Emma might be."

The flash of irritation swept across the agent's face. "Last night? You drink like that and hit the streets to investigate?"

And his snark returns.

"Give it a rest," Callie said. "For now, we're giving Pinky the benefit of the doubt. Just like I'll forgive your comment, and you'll forget last night."

He returned to reading, like he didn't hear. Or didn't care.

"Be glad the boys noticed," she continued, "because their observation and the college inquiries are the only hints we have that Rhoades thought the girl was alive. Otherwise, he only chased a kidnapper. In either case, the question is what led him *here*. The boys' sighting of him also places him alive on Edisto, not just a body dump from another location."

"Yeah," he said, the facts of their discussion not brightening his disposition.

She straightened papers, hiding the photo again. "Unfortunately, he could've been totally off the mark, too. Obsessed, with nothing else in his life to occupy his days. However, I can't help but give him some credit and analyze his work"—she paused, then said—"because he died."

"No," Knox said. "Because he was murdered."

Chatter came in on her radio, Marie's voice calling her name.

"Go, Marie. What is it?"

"A ruckus at Fantasea, Chief. Some fighting, some parental involvement. Spilled onto Jungle Shores. Raysor took the call."

Callie clicked to respond. "Okay. He ought to be able to handle it."

"Um, he told me to tell you Jeb's there."

Damn it, Jeb, please don't be involved. I seriously don't have time for whatever identity crisis is brewing with you.

"Hey, Marie, wait a sec," she asked. "Find anything on the computer?" She walked to her back window. Jungle Shores ran behind Chelsea Morning, with Fantasea being three doors to her left down on the marsh side. Too difficult to see from her vantage.

Marie came back. "He liked games, Chief. Had a Gmail account, but it's clogged with spam. Guy must've used his phone for most of his activity. I'll keep trying, but seriously, don't know why he even owned the machine."

"All right, thanks." Callie hung up and moved back to the kitchen, quickly shoving papers into their folders. "I've got to go. I'm taking these files with me since we don't have copies. Rather not have the information floating around. So . . . Knox, we really need Rhoades's phone history."

Knox stood. "I don't want to use the Bureau."

Callie tucked the files under her arm, still uncertain about Knox's reluctance to pull in his connections.

His head tilted. "But you don't need the FBI for this. Rhoades was old school, right?"

"You tell me," she said.

"So, I'll pretend to be him and open online access to his account. If he has one, then I'll say I forgot the password and get another."

Finally, headway. "The phone company hasn't learned he's deceased yet. Good deal. Have you contacted his daughter?"

"Yeah, but I told her not to hurry since the body would be held for this investigation at least a week or so."

Callie needed to get to Fantasea. "I know that call wasn't easy, but you bought us time."

"Time we don't really have, do we?" He leaned on the table's edge. "We're sitting here trying to séance what Pinky was doing, and you leave to break up kids from a beach party."

"Séance wasn't working," she replied. She *could* skip the call, let Raysor handle it, but this was Jeb's crowd, and barely a twenty-minute detour from the job at hand. But staring at the same information waiting for inspiration to strike was foolishness.

Knox's voice dropped then, turned hard as he shoved his chair up to the table. "They *bashed* his head. They held him under until he drowned."

"I know," she said. "Pinky was close to you and that skews your rationale. Infuriates you for the loss you weren't there to prevent. But we're not dragging our feet, Knox. We're doing this right."

Knox remained at the table. "I want to catch the son of a bitch who killed a good man."

"So do I." Callie moved toward the door, realizing she agreed with him more than she'd realized. "But we have kids spread all over Edisto this week, and Rhoades's murderer could be among them, working on his tan. I'm still chief out here. I've got to go."

If Stan were here, he'd add, *Callie knows what she's doing. Hell, I trained her.*

She didn't realize how inherent his support was until she'd lost it, but now she needed to function 100 percent without it. "I'm headed to the Colleton County courthouse with Deputy Raysor later this afternoon," she said. "He's related to everybody with a Walterboro phone prefix, so he'll help me check Edisto Beach deeds. Rhoades left that task undone, so I might as well finish it and pray it means something."

The agent shrugged. "And I'm stuck playing with the phone account."

"Where I'm going doesn't need your talent. Plus, you're calling Mrs. Flagg." Callie headed to the door, pulling her keys out, anxious to see if Jeb was no more than a bystander in the Fantasea fracas. "Your phone discovery might also dictate what we do this evening, but if you find yourself bored, go out and play like a tourist. You don't look as much like a perv."

She received a resigned half grin from Knox. "Any guy over thirty checking out teens looks like a perv."

"Then be more discreet than Rhoades." On the back porch landing, she stopped and waited for Knox to follow her out before locking the door.

Taking the stairs to the shell drive, Knox got into his Toyota and headed toward Windswept. Callie locked the files in her cruiser then walked out to Jungle Shores Drive, unaccustomed to worrying about Jeb being an overzealous teen . . . worried about how to collect him without him reminding her of last night.

Chapter 12

CALLIE STARED toward the crowd gathered in the front of Fantasea, not sixty yards away. A little after one in the afternoon, the day was as hot as it was going to get for April. Just to be sure, she phoned Jeb.

"What, Mom? I can see you coming, you know."

"And you'll be speaking with me in a second."

Voices yelled in the background, but this close she could hear them herself.

"This is private property!"

"We're not hurting anybody!"

"Mind your own business!"

She hung up, trying to reserve judgment. If Jeb wasn't trying to break up the feud, she'd be highly disappointed. If he were part of the problem, she'd be pissed.

A few young people hung on the porch and stairs, but a dozen clustered in the yard. Nobody shoved, no weapons, little more than barefooted stomps in the silted road. White-collar teens who wouldn't know what to do in a fight if their lives depended on it.

But she didn't see many adults. Didn't Marie say there was parental involvement? As she scanned, Callie couldn't help but study each girl. Emma would be nineteen now, and so were about eight of these young things. Bathing suit tops and cutoffs, cargo shorts and tanks, just kids, pretending they weren't.

"You kids are horrible!" The shrill voice caught Callie's attention.

On the street edge of Fantasea's oyster shell drive, Sophie was obvious in a lime-green, off-the-shoulder top over white Bermudas, her gold-bangled wrists going to town on a jabbing arm as she made some point lost in a chorus of defiant voices.

To Sophie's right was a lady Callie knew mostly by reputation, Parker Bender. "Come on, y'all. What would your mommas think?" Age sixty, she had a strawberry-blond, chin-length bob, and was about as tall as Callie, but twice as fluffy in the middle.

Where were all the so-called parents raising hell with the kids?

An outdoorsy type of sweetheart known for her positive attitude and Edisto Bookstore baseball cap, the Bender woman affectionately patted teens on the arm, trying to defuse this altercation. Each child took a second to respect her, but returned to arguing after she passed. Callie'd met her when she'd been sworn in as police chief . . . and at the funeral.

The woman nodded in unison with Raysor and briefly frowned when Sophie hollered again. There Sophie was in all her hippie, health-food-preaching fury, the main instigator of this minor rumble.

She'd probably watched out her window when the teens gathered, and she strutted over when she laid eyes on Jeb. "You kids are trouble!" she yelled, totally opposite from her namaste yoga voice.

Amid the reverberating retort, Raysor bellowed once for command, earning only a brief pause in the mayhem. Tempers flared too hot at Sophie to die easy. Parker Bender wasn't being heard at all.

Jeb tried to yell over the group, explaining to Raysor, looking so much like part of the problem. *Oh good Lord.*

Nodding at Raysor to manage the kids, Callie waded into the horde and gently encircled Sophie's tanned arm to ease her aside.

"You're drinking," Sophie shouted, stabbing the air. Callie caught herself, ready to defend her honor as she thought for a second Sophie castigated her.

But the yoga maven's ire was aimed at the kids. "You've hurt my daughter's feelings. She lives here just like you, Yancy Wilkerson. And you, Bea Wilkerson." The second girl at the end of Sophie's pointed finger slid shyly behind the one who had to be her sister.

"Everyone take it down a notch," Callie shouted. "Hear me?"

"Listen to the chief!" Raysor echoed.

The clamor lessened. The majority sulked, some hiding drinks behind their backs. One kid poured his in a bush.

With a jerk, Sophie tugged from Callie's grip as they moved away from the group. Sophie almost spat her words as she took aim at Jeb over her shoulder. "I'm ashamed of you, Jeb Morgan." Apparently first and last names carried more venom. "You wait until Sprite's in school then slip down here to playboy yourself with girls that don't mean a damn thing other than a sassy piece of—"

"Enough, Sophie." Callie shifted around to block her friend's view. "What's going on?"

Breezing off the marsh behind Fantasea, short winds whipped the yoga lady's pixie hair as if her heated disposition made it boil atop her head. "I told you Jeb was up to no good," Sophie said. "I came down here to check out their shenanigans and found boys and girls all over each other in plain public. You need to control your son."

Callie allowed the parental barb to pass by and whispered. "You're making a fool of yourself."

"That's not what we were doing, either, Mom," Jeb said, appearing from behind Callie.

"Don't you lie to your mother," Sophie ordered.

Red-cheeked from sun and vexation, Jeb gritted his teeth. "We were having fun, just talking . . ." He reared back as his mother leaned forward into his personal space. "What are you doing?"

The yeast aroma filled the air, so Callie sniffed again. "I don't smell it on you, but somebody's wearing eau-de-beer. And settle yourself down."

He blew through his teeth. "Some of the guys brought their own beer, what of it?" His glare of warning silently referenced her last night's binge, but Callie wasn't being blackmailed, by Jeb of all people.

"At least when I drink, it's legal," she said in his ear.

"Not when you drive," he grumbled back.

Sophie's nervous energy jingled her bracelets. "College has ruined that boy."

Jeb's tone spiked again. "College is corrupting me?"

Callie strived to keep their conversation up close and controlled. "Sophie, the serious partiers are at Myrtle and Folly. There's nothing for these kids to do but house hop. Be glad they're not raising serious hell at bars elsewhere."

The group had actually settled down, with Sophie pulled aside. But ignoring Callie's explanation, Sophie's hair danced again in reply, intent on making her point. "Sprite agrees with me. Zeus, too."

"No, he doesn't," Jeb said. "Zeus isn't here because he's working. Otherwise he'd be enjoying the hell out of himself with us. Sprite's in school or she'd be here, too." Jeb's cheeks flushed deeper in a mixture of anger and the effort to respect an adult. The former was winning. "And how about Sprite and I handle our own relationship, if you don't mind?"

With a hand decked with three rings, Sophie poked Jeb's chest, but Jeb resisted the smaller woman's touch, shading her with his six-foot height. Sophie still didn't back down. "I'll have you know . . ."

"Good Lord, you two!" Callie'd give them two hours in lock up, if she had a jail. She sandwiched herself between them, eye-to-eye with Sophie, but a hand on Jeb's chest. "Son, chill. Sophie, hush."

Jeb stepped back, shaking his mom's hand off. Sophie pouted.

"Ms. Bender witnessed it all," he said, as though the woman's word carried serious weight.

"And Deputy Raysor will talk to her." Callie glimpsed up at the house, surprised the owners hadn't come out. "The Wilkersons, right? And those are their daughters?"

As soon as Jeb curled a finger toward the two girls, they scooted over. They were even in height, about the same age. One sported a tight, short, chopped hair style, bright blue streaks coloring the longer bleached platinum tresses on top. She stood tall and confident, while the other hung back, more coy, her long auburn hair in a single braid down to her waist over a blue baby doll cotton gauze top. A sort of soft hippy so unlike the louder sister.

Raysor had a lecture going on, a half dozen kids glowering as he emptied their cups into the drive. Jeb's friend Nolan sidled over and held out his hand for a shake. "Hey again, Chief. How's the weather down there?"

"The line was old the first time someone used it on me," Callie said.

"I'll work on fresh material," he replied.

Covering her mouth, the long braided sister's gaze caught Callie's name tag and her eyes widened with a revelation, but blue hair did the speaking as if the twins were on the same wavelength. "Are you Jeb's mom?"

Already riled, Jeb rolled around on her. "Got a problem with that?"

"You don't come across as a cop's kid, is all."

His face clouded more. "What's a cop's kid supposed to act like?"

"Stop it, Jeb." Callie cared little about the girls' reactions to the badge, more interested in diluting the Sophie issue. "Any of you been drinking?" The question went to her son, mainly, but she studied each of the others in the process. None of them seemed loopy . . . except maybe Nolan, but his behavior rode a fine line between personality and a two-beer buzz.

"I haven't," Jeb answered, and the twins echoed in kind, but Nolan arched his brows playfully. "It's the beach, we're doing a lot of running around, so we sweat it out. No big deal."

Callie leaned in closer to Nolan. "You twenty-one?"

"Twenty and change, Chief. Not a month away."

"Well, until you can buy it, don't let me see you with alcohol in your hand, my man. Especially with you sleeping under my roof. Got it?"

With a playful salute, Nolan snapped his feet together.

Callie suddenly felt more parental about Jeb's guests. "It's not even one in the afternoon, people. When did all this drinking begin?"

Jeb's expression darkened. "There is no *all this drinking*, and we just . . . meet. We don't exactly send out invitations."

"Where's your other friend?"

"Sammy's with that girl," Nolan said, sliding the last word with a sense of bawdiness. "Lissa. They're, um, becoming acquainted."

An elbow in the ribs from the blue-haired girl doubled him over. "Shut up, Nolan. Lissa isn't *that* easy."

With a sarcastic shake of himself, Nolan raised his voice an octave. "*Lissa isn't that easy*. Well, she was yesterday. And Sammy hung back in hopes of tasting more."

The quiet sister nudged the other, but Miss Blue Hair was already all over this. "Lissa turned you down, you idiot. She's introverted, so lay off her."

"Name of the house they're at?" Callie asked.

"Crab Walk."

"Does Lissa have a last name?"

"Pasternak," Jeb replied when the others wouldn't.

"The girl's bait, I'm telling you," Nolan said under his breath. "I've seen her around campus. And she catches lots of . . . fish."

Jeb shook his head at his friend, a hand wave across his neck. The dominant sister, however, lit into Nolan with a lecture about male arrogance, too many heads to think with, and a threat. "Y'all shut the hell up about Lissa, or I promise to make you hate the day you set foot on this island, and my word is my damn bond. You're nothing but a visitor."

Whoa, temper. Callie held out a palm. "Stop."

So Lissa went to C of C? Callie added the girl to the top of the list to compare to the pictures. God, she saw every girl in her path as Emma.

She needed to wrap this up, but she'd learned ages ago if a cop asked your name, you thought they engraved it permanently on their minds. "All of you from College of Charleston? Apparently Lissa's popular. I already know about three of the boys. Which one are you?"

"Yancy. And all of us go to C of C," the girl said. "Our spring break is different this year than Clemson's and Carolina's."

Callie counted her blessings for that. She'd have a talk with the two liquor store owners and Bi-Lo concerning alcohol sales.

Raysor seemed done. In matronly fashion, Ms. Bender stood smiling, hands on hips, pleased and cooing at the dispersing crowd. Then she walked back to her house next door, squeezing through bushes. The remaining cluster of kids draped around the bottom of the Wilkerson steps.

Yancy acted like she waited for orders, though surely not one to quickly jump when asked. "Where are your parents?" Callie asked. "They've got to be careful with underage kids on their property."

"My parents would kill us if we drank," Yancy replied. "A few brought their cups with them, and there's nothing you can do about that."

"Actually there *is* something I can do, but I won't." Callie looked under the house at the carport. "Where are your folks?"

"Dad went to Charleston. Mom's running errands. I'm sort of left in charge."

"The fox in the henhouse," Sophie said.

"Just stay responsible," Callie said. "I may speak to your parents later. Have fun, just not too much, okay?"

"Yes, ma'am."

The kids moved to join their friends, but Callie tagged Jeb's T-shirt, holding him back. "We need to talk later, son."

He resisted, and Callie threw him a tight, firm glare. "I'm still your mother."

"Yes'm," he said, and returned to the group headed up the stairs, the carefree joy of their day dampened.

Callie pulled Sophie a few yards in the opposite direction, hissing in her ear. "What the hell is wrong with you? Leave these kids alone. You act like you're some jealous middle-school cheerleader . . . or her freakish mother."

"I was *never* a cheerleader." Sophie spun and strutted home, elbows pumping, sandals kicking up the silted road back to Hatha Heaven.

Callie thought the world of Sophie—under most conditions. The little yoga mistress loved the universe. But this feverish side of her motherhood did not flatter her, and if she meddled this much with her eighteen-year-old daughter's social life, God help the boy Sprite married. Maybe Jeb needed to play the field after all.

Jeb had changed. Sophie saw it, Sprite apparently was distraught over it, and Callie'd never experienced such retaliatory language from him. College indeed changed him. And it saddened her.

Raysor strolled over to Callie, his bulk under the dark uniform making him appear humongous. "Some of these teens migrated here from Looney Dunes. Might get Thomas or one of the new guys to patrol a little tighter."

Sliding her sunglasses back on, Callie searched her mind. "Where is Looney Dunes?"

"Osceola Street," he said. "Two houses back from Palmetto. Belongs to the Pasternaks."

"Someone just said Lissa Pasternak was at Crab Walk."

"They're like roaches, Doll. But her parents own Looney Dunes."

Teens would get wind of it by the time they got to any house anyway, thanks to smartphones. How had Mike handled spring break? He'd made policing Edisto seem simple.

"I'll radio Thomas. In the meantime, my friend, we're headed to Walterboro. We'll go in two cars so you can head home when we get done."

"What's in Walterboro?" he asked, his cop eye targeting kids as they retreated inside the Wilkerson house.

"The courthouse," she said. "I'll fill you in on the phone en route. The short version is we're seeing who's bought or built a house on Edisto Beach since 2000."

He reared back. "You know how many people that is?"

"Yeah, but Jeb's friends saw the deceased agent watching girls. And the agent was researching a cold case, a child abduction of a little girl. We have to consider that he was killed for whatever he saw, investigated, or thought."

Raysor grunted. "May not be a high-class detective like you, but even I can see that's damn far-fetched."

"I agree, but I'm just following clues."

"And he was looking at what?"

"Who owned property out here. Maybe one of your cousins remembers him at the courthouse. Spoke to him."

"Janet Wainwright would know who bought . . . never mind," he said, dismissing the Marine real estate broker.

"Right. The fewer the better."

They wouldn't be doing this needle-in-the-haystack task if Rhoades hadn't kept illegible notes. She needed names of the addresses he'd narrowed down, because knocking on doors wasn't the way to go about this. If indeed there was a murderer on Edisto, they didn't need to see Callie coming.

Homicide had been her forte back in Boston, and she'd been good at it. Kidnapped children, not so much, and Stan had let her avoid such cases.

Callie walked Raysor to his car. "Mine's over at my house. I'll follow you."

"Wait a second," the deputy said in that long, low Southern bass voice of his. "Saw Thomas this morning."

A twinge of a scare shot through her. "And?"

"The department can't afford to lose you, Doll."

Her heart melted a little bit. Even if Stan turned his back on her, Raysor and Thomas would be there. "Appreciate it," she said.

He opened his door and got in the car. "But we'll kick your scrawny ass to the curb if any of us catches you drinking and driving again, you hear?"

She froze, sensing no right answer to what she'd assume was a rhetorical question. Thomas told Raysor and who else? And who had Raysor told?

Maybe she shouldn't have driven, but she was fine. She'd done it before, always late. Always with nobody on the road. They'd be watching her now. Which meant more staying home, more Neil, more drinks since she'd basically be confined to Chelsea Morning after dark.

But that raised another concern. Who had Kendrick, oh excuse her, Knox . . . told?

And the main concern, after all these people had discussed her, judged her, was which of them had seen fit to tell Brice LeGrand?

She'd come kicking and screaming to Edisto, paid a deep price for ultimately choosing it as her home. The saltwater ran through her veins now, and she missed sand in her shoes if she skipped a day running on the beach. It wasn't about the money, either. It was about home . . . and a badge. Losing this job would close the door on her law enforcement career.

With Jeb gone—or all but gone, her life was the beach and this job.

"See you at the courthouse," Raysor said.

Then with a quick jerk of a nod, she turned and walked to her car. She'd follow him, because she wasn't comfortable having him judge her driving all the way to Walterboro.

Chapter 13

DESPITE THE DELAY at Fantasea, Callie still managed to follow behind and park her car beside Raysor's at the Colleton County courthouse by 3:00 p.m. Nothing from Knox yet, but he'd had barely two hours. She was sure he'd have called if he hit pay dirt with the phone records, assuming he hadn't found something and pursued it on his own.

Deputy Raysor helped Callie navigate through the halls of county government. The two of them entered a back door hidden behind a camellia bush on an inside corner, and they made their way to the Register of Deeds department.

Raysor could've possibly handled this trip without assistance, and if he had to do hands-on research, he knew people. And those people knew people. And all of them were related. But Callie wasn't sure what was to be found until she found it. If she could carry something home and regroup with Knox and compare their afternoon accomplishments, then she was saving time. Time that Knox would appreciate per his blowup this afternoon.

Raysor greeted eight people before they reached the administrative office, and acted like he and Callie had never mentioned drinking.

"Don! Where you been, honey!"

"No place special, Marilyn. How you been?"

"Wonderful!" A chunky lady escaped from behind her desk and wrapped arms around Raysor's middle, their protruding torsos making the act awkward to watch. "Your momma said you haven't been to church for the last three Sundays. Aunt Sanssouci even made your favorite banana pudding last Sunday for dinner and almost cried you weren't there to eat it." She poked her belly. "But it didn't go to waste!" They laughed loud, sound echoing off the tall, turn-of-the-century plaster walls.

"*Aunt Sanssouci?*" Callie mumbled to Raysor.

"It means something royal," he whispered-grumbled back.

Callie held out her hand. "Hey, I'm Callie Morgan. Don and I—"

"Whoa, are you two dating?" The sausage-shaped woman waggled a finger from him to Callie and back again, then reared back with a gasp.

Callie's jaw dropped before she managed to say, "Um, no. I'm—"

More laughter erupted from the woman. "Honey, take a joke! Of course you're not together. There're ten women in Walterboro who'd take you out for this man." She slapped Raysor's belly with the back of her hand. "He's considered mighty eligible in these parts."

"Of course he is," Callie replied under her breath.

Resting his arm around the lady's shoulders, Raysor squeezed her to him once. "Marilyn, you about gave my boss a heart attack."

"But it's fun messing with people. So, what brings you two here?"

Raysor looked to Callie to take the lead.

"Ma'am . . ."

"Ma'am? Don told you my name's Marilyn. Use it, honey. It ain't broke."

Callie started again. "Marilyn, we need to check out deeds on Edisto Beach between the year 2000 and the end of last year."

Marilyn adjusted her gray polyester waistband. "Anyone who's bought and hasn't sold, right?"

Callie cocked her head. "Yes. I'm guessing the same information a man wanted from your records just last week."

"I thought so," she said and returned to her desk more serious and on a mission. "Don, you coulda just called me."

"Chief Morgan wanted to come by—"

"Here," Marilyn said, sliding out a manila folder about an inch and a half thick. "That man must've spent close to three days in here. I brought him chicken bog and green beans one day for lunch 'cause I felt sorry for him working so hard." She smacked her other hand on the folder. "That's when he told me to call him Pinky." With a smiley squint, Marilyn's ample cheeks pushed up to her eyes. "Is that adorable or what? Said he was coming back, but he hasn't made it yet. You want a copy of these?"

Peering back at Raysor, Callie decided to let the lady's cousin, uncle, brother, whatever Don was to her, deliver the news.

Without sensitivity, he just spilled it. "Afraid the gentleman died, Marilyn. That's part of why we're here."

Marilyn didn't miss a beat. "So, let me get this straight." If she'd been taller, she'd have looked down her nose. The effort only added to her comedic personality. "Was he a cop?"

Neither Callie nor Raysor replied.

"I knew it," Marilyn said. "What, SLED? FBI? I'd know him if he was local."

They didn't answer.

"I'll be damned," she said, unmoved at the silent rebuff. "I'm helping an investigation."

Raysor held his hand out. "How about letting me have the folder?"

Marilyn reeled it in against her chest, playfully scolding. "How about paying me $49.75 for all these copies first? And that's my family discount."

Callie extracted a credit card.

Marilyn continued to hug the file. "Prefer cash or check. Saves the county money." Guess that mattered when your family managed half the county's government.

"Fine." Callie retrieved what money she had on her and peeled off two twenties and a ten. "Keep the change."

They exchanged items, and Callie gave her thanks. But Marilyn touched Raysor's arm. "Seriously," she said, the humor gone. "Was he killed or did he just have a heart attack or something?"

Callie spoke first. "Why does it matter?"

Marilyn's expression softened. "Maybe it was more about the last day I saw him. Came to me about three in the afternoon. I asked if he found what he was hunting for, and he gave me this big ol' grin. Asked how quick I could make all these copies. I said a couple hours and offered to stay late if he wanted to wait. He said he'd get them Friday, but he didn't show. Said something about 'Mama's been waiting for this.' I'd hate to think that Mama is still waiting someplace for him to show up for dinner."

ALMOST FIVE IN THE afternoon, Raysor saluted his good-bye to Callie and headed home from the courthouse. Callie, alone without radio chatter, drove toward State Highway 64 toward Edisto and surrendered to her thoughts.

That morning she'd awoken more alive than she had in ages, other than the headache, but this evening she'd pulled somewhat of a sundowner. Crimes against children rarely ended happily, and even if saved, the child remained damaged. Television shows always got that wrong. Not that she didn't want to save a child.

Jeb was kidnapped last year, for an afternoon, but God . . . at least he'd been eighteen. The bastard drugged him, a blessing in hindsight. The kidnapper bled out like a butchered hog, cut deep across his neck.

Jeb said he remembered little of the nasty parts, but he lied. Callie still found him fixing middle of the night snacks, a weariness on him from dreams.

During Callie's rougher evenings, she dusted off the turntable to play Neil Diamond and poured a cool, tall Bombay and tonic. She bought limes by the dozen. The cashier thought Callie made pies. Callie'd even looked up a recipe once, made the damn thing, and carried it to the girl to protect the image.

But those songs. Some light and lively. Others, like "Yesterday" came with a power heavier than McCartney's. The words of "Something Blue" gave her permission to dissolve into tears. Yes, she made a mistake driving after her dinner with Knox.

Hell, she made a mistake drinking in front of Knox.

Where was Knox, anyway? Four hours since they talked, and no call. Thought the man was in a hurry?

Callie crossed back over the big bridge, an early evening's April sun flashing happy over the wide, meandering waterway. Four synchronized pelicans skimmed the water amid the scattered dips of miscreant gulls.

But then she passed the boat ramp.

Her heart hit her ribs at the memory of hunting another killer. Too sick to drive, she'd ridden with Sophie, Raysor in another car desperately radioing for Seabrook. Rain, darkness, so much confusion.

Trying to focus, Callie drove over Russell Creek, and she white-knuckled the steering wheel. Pine Landing Road lay just ahead. She pinched her shoulders forward, then butterflied them behind, seeking release.

So opposite from her trip to the courthouse earlier, when she'd been on the phone with Raysor, listening to him poke fun, in hindsight probably a distraction so when they passed Pine Landing she barely noticed.

Callie locked her gaze on the straight yellow line on the road. Pine Landing came . . . came . . . and went. She didn't dare look in her rear-view mirror until she reached the old clapboard-siding museum around the bend.

But then the Edisto Presbyterian Church sabotaged her on the left. A wadded ball of emotion filled her, rending her apart. Mike rested behind that sanctuary in the Seabrook family plot, protected by a hundred-year-old wrought-iron fence.

"Oh God," she cried, as sobs caught and her vision blurred.

They knew each other ten months, had been truly close for only weeks. Made love once. How had he meant so much to her in such a short time? She'd asked herself that over many drinks, until lying on her living room rug one night, four gins into her third Diamond album, she realized she mourned the love they hadn't had the years to build.

Her breaths . . . shallow now. The old pattern.

Face wet, chest seized almost shut, Callie skid her cruiser to a stop on Steamboat Landing Road. She fought to inhale past swollen airways, forcing herself to focus outward, angry she couldn't make out the detail of the tree leaves.

In and out. One, two, three . . .

No, you are past this. Mike took you past this.

She counted, timing the inhales, her fingers kneading her thighs. The tingling rose, pricking, numbing, but only after she quit cursing herself did the panic lessen.

One day this could be a heart attack, and she wouldn't even know it.

Soon she rocked less, her vision clear, breathing regular. A weariness settled into her muscles, and she blew out the air that told her she returned to a tired control. Last attack like this Mike had been there to walk her through it, but the thought would only rob her of control, so she stared at a young grasshopper on her car hood, its feet rubbing, unaware its life was one season long.

A big deep exhale. There.

Apparently, stepping out of her reclusive shell had stirred more than her detective skills.

Her phone rang, jump-starting her. "Yes," she answered.

"Sorry I haven't been returning your calls."

Callie lightly coughed, thrilled at Stan's voice, angry at his behavior last night. "Yeah."

"Well, retirement was easy, the divorce not so much, but both had paperwork and filings I didn't expect. Missy was quick to leave, but not so quick to sever those last financial ties."

Callie hated picturing Missy in an adversarial light. "Sorry." The Morgans and Walthams had shared a few Boston barbecues together. She didn't want to hear about that.

"I hear y'all have a case."

"Well," she said, thinking of Raysor, "guess *somebody's* calls were returned."

Stan smacked on his gum.

Disturbed that Raysor's phone calls took precedence over hers, she made a choice. "Don't worry about it," she said and cranked up the engine, sniffled, and then pulled back onto Highway 174.

"You okay, Chicklet?"

Her eyes a bit blurred, she wiped them. "Yeah. I'm fine. Fantastic."

A bristled anger climbed up her back. Raysor had to have spoken to Stan in the last twenty minutes. But she didn't blame Raysor. She blamed Stan.

Beneath the familiar gravel in his tone, she could hear the worry, feel him analyzing.

"How're you sleeping?" he asked.

"Same."

"Been to the church?"

She wanted to scream, *What damn good would it do to stand on the ground and imagine him six feet down? What the fucking good would that do? Been to the church? Seriously?*

Her blood thrummed, pulsing in her ears, deafening.

"No," she finally replied. Just no.

She heard him smack, almost smelling his cinnamon gum.

Raysor and Thomas had already warned her about her drinking. What if they saw her in a panic attack? Her instincts shouted for her to release all the toxic mental poisons pent up since Jeb found that damn body, but she feared the end result.

While Raysor cared, he'd think of Edisto first. "*. . . kick your scrawny ass to the curb.*"

She would do the same thing in his shoes.

"You're pissed," Stan said.

"Aren't you the friggin' Einstein!"

"And you're drinking again."

That she didn't respond to.

"Hmm," he answered, allowing some silence. "Well, Chicklet. Sometimes it ain't all about you."

What the f—?

"Raysor said–"

"This isn't about him," she said.

"Raysor *said*," he continued, "that you're working with some FBI agent, and he's staying at Seabrook's place."

Of course Raysor knew, because he canvassed every house every day. As Mike's friend, he'd be the first to recognize a light on at Windswept . . . be the one who'd tell Stan about her drinking.

She thought she could trust Raysor.

Stan released a grunt. "It's only a house," he said.

"And hemlock's only a weed."

"You want to talk about this, Chicklet?"

Did she?

She muted the phone and sucked in down to her toes, the trembling gone. She didn't need the scolding that would follow any honest discussion.

"Gotta go." She raised the volume on her mic as well, hit the button, the static crackling. "Callie—"

She hung up.

Chapter 14

CALLIE TUNED IN to the hum of her car tires, instead of the fact she'd just hung up on Stan. Distancing him both geographically and emotionally, she wasn't sure if she felt guilt for assuming she should be a higher priority on his list, or hurt that she no longer was.

Once in the town limits, she cruised through the Bi-Lo parking lot on her way to McConkey's. Inside, settled in her usual corner, complimentary iced tea automatically appeared before she'd even ordered carryout for her and Knox. Just had no idea where they'd meet to eat it.

People nodded, maybe saying *Chief*, but nobody was comfortable enough to sit and chat about weather, tourists, or the petty irritations that came with renting. They gave her space because she'd yet to lower that arm's-length guard.

She called Jeb. He answered on the third ring.

"Where are you?" she asked.

"Geez, what the heck, Mom?"

"Not checking up on you. I might come by the house and didn't want to interrupt anything." *That was motherly and considerate, right?*

"Sounds the same to me." A door slammed, and someone called Nolan's name, then Jeb spoke to whomever, shouting Nolan was upstairs. Callie wouldn't bring business home if Jeb's guests hung around, which, apparently, they did. "Jeb? Are you there?"

"Yeah, we ordered pizza."

She sighed, and he heard her.

"Don't get heated," he said in an undertone.

He never used to be so defensive, and she wasn't about to make things worse by ruining his party. "I'm not. Just reconfiguring plans. I need to drop in, change, then leave."

She hung up, racking her brain for locations where she and Knox could meet. Brice surveilled her office like a hawk. The library was too small with too many volunteers connected to the local gossip. Not Stan's rental . . . not anymore. Her officers lived miles off the beach. Funny, there had been an endless supply of meeting places in Boston. But not here.

Knox called. "What're we doing?" he asked. Surf sounded in the background. She pictured him on the left end of the front porch in the red double swing. She always pictured that swing.

"The courthouse gave us Rhoades's research," she said.

"Bring it over here. I have snacks."

It's just a house, Stan had said. And Knox would think her lame for not having a ready place to meet, again.

She had no choice, yet this was a choice. "I already ordered burgers at McConkey's," she said. "Be there in a few minutes."

"Works for m—"

"Yeah, see you."

She clipped his good-bye, but this would take some doing, stepping under that transom, into that foyer, past that kitchen on the left . . . the master bedroom on the right. Not to mention the police car would be out front for all to see. She had half a mind to walk.

But no. This meeting was just straightforward business. They had a stack of deeds to sift through. Sales on every block in almost every month of so many years. Slow busy work. She hoped the phone records gave them a better starting point.

A tanned teenage boy set a bag on the table. "Here you go, Chief. Two burgers. Pimento and Swiss."

From a poor family, the spirited kid had reminded Mike of himself at that age. Callie remembered the lessons Mike taught her about being the people's chief, about being aware and seeing the individuals. This was a skill Callie could maintain, and she slipped the kid the regular ten. The burger smell soon filled up her car and prompted a belly growl. She radioed Thomas for an update on the kids.

He chuckled. "Yeah, they're all right."

"What about Sammy Blackstone? He's sleeping under my roof." She wished Jeb had notified her in advance of these house guests. They weren't twenty-one but not babes, either. *Note to self: Check for condom wrappers in the trash.* She'd tear into somebody if they screwed up her septic tank with those damn things. Not to mention her furniture, her beds, *ick*, her sheets.

Then she realized *they* meant Jeb, too.

Static crackled. "Sammy was surprised I asked for him by name, but nothing on his breath and all his clothes on." Thomas chuckled at himself.

Callie reached her drive. "Tomorrow drive by periodically if you don't mind. These are kids I know."

"Poor Jeb," he replied, then signed off, laughing.

No mention of last night. Good guy. Good cop.

Good news on Sammy, too. She preferred he not be sexually promiscuous, but if he and Lissa were an item, so be it, just preferably not with alcohol. Callie tucked the girl's name in her frontal lobe, though. She wanted to compare every spring-break girl to the photos in Emma Flagg's file.

When she entered Chelsea Morning, kids chattered, but the enthusiasm went dead when the uniform walked through. Like, wet-blanket dead.

"Hey, Mom," Jeb said from the kitchen. Most ate their pizza, tea glasses all over the living room—including Callie's good Tervis cups.

"Don't mind me." She waved, entered her bedroom, closed the door, and then paused a second to listen, but they were too wise to speak loudly enough for her to hear. Short minutes later, she exited, having dug out a larger purse from the closet to carry her service weapon as well as her backup .38. No point leaving them in a house full of kids. Then she walked toward Windswept, her nerves dancing under the skin.

The day was aging, the sun headed to bed, setting northwest beyond the marsh. Windswept sat on the land side of the beach street, but like few lucky houses, its front porch faced an empty lot, opening a vista to the Atlantic. A view imprinted permanently on Callie's mind.

Knox's Toyota parked under the house, between the pylons supporting the structure. He waited in a wicker chair above, and stood as she reached the porch. "About time. I'm starved."

"The pimento's mine," she said, and took her place in another chair, a small wicker table between them.

"Be back in a sec," Knox said, his hand behind him to stop the screen door from bouncing shut. He soon returned with two bottles of water. "Sorry, no alcohol."

Was it so difficult for him to buy a six-pack?

He ripped open a chip bag and dropped it on the table, as if hosting were an effort. A few chips spilled out onto the painted wood.

She found the burger wrapper marked with a *P*, then handed him the other marked with an *S*. She glanced at the swing. No breeze tonight. No shrimp tails to toss in a bucket.

Knox followed her gaze, then focused on his sandwich. His chair creaked as he wallowed into it and placed one ankle across his knee. "You ought to live on the water." He chomped on a chip.

"Hurricanes," she replied. "Insurance. And taxes."

"What?"

"Why I don't live on the water. And Pinky worked hard at the courthouse." She pointed at the paperwork on the floor next to her chair.

"Humph," he grunted through the huge bite of burger. "Anything good?"

She folded back the paper and took a bite. "Don't know yet."

He took a swig of water. "Well, I nailed the phone records."

Was that sarcasm? *Please not now.*

Maybe two blocks back, cicadas would kick in. Here the sounds consisted of simply breakers and gulls and this acrimonious bullshit.

She watched the surf, trying to picture a sunrise. She'd seen but one from this spot, toward the end of her sick leave five months back, when she missed Seabrook so badly she drove over to huddle in a blanket on the red swing, desperately seeking the slightest sign of him, praying that in the between time of night and day she'd somehow feel him.

She hadn't, and she didn't try again.

But she couldn't stop reliving that moment now that she was here, as though her soul tried again. Her pulse throbbed hard in her neck, her hand craving the curve of a glass of something serious. God, she wasn't sure she could sit here and pretend she only thought of the job, and still deal with niceties of cooperation. She inhaled deeply, taking in salt air . . . seeking control.

While he analyzed her. "You really don't want my help, do you? Or do you need a drink that bad? That why you're so quiet?"

Dark spots danced into her vision, a ringing in her ears. *No. She couldn't do this here . . .* Faster than she hoped it looked, she gripped the chair arms and stood.

She wasn't crumbling in front of this idiot. "Um, may I use your bathroom?"

But she left before he could respond and withdrew through the front door to the hallway, almost hitting the corner when she turned for the master bath. In a rush she locked the door, spun and took a seat on the toilet, counting down.

What the hell would he think now?

Her inhalations weren't as deep, maybe because she acted the moment her lungs seized. Now how the hell was she supposed to walk out of there after what, five minutes? Twenty?

She lifted her head and studied herself in the mirror. Just a forty-year-old mom in a button-up long-sleeve shirt. She'd put back the lost weight, and nothing obviously wrong stared back at her, but something stirred her emotions horribly askew.

Pinky's case? But how the hell was she supposed to work if these episodes flared so unpredictably?

She could quit, a more frequent thought of late. But that would dump on her officers and leave them at Brice's mercy. No telling what friend of his he'd put in her place.

She almost wanted to blame Stan. And she wanted to blame Seabrook for walking out of Chelsea Morning without a vest on that evening. A grip on her pants leg, she dug into her thigh. Seated in his house, she yearned to scream at him, feeling he'd finally hear her. *Why the hell did you make such a stupid mistake?*

And scream at herself for letting him go. For not seeing the journalist for what he was. For being such a shoddy piece-of-shit detective who let everything go dismally wrong.

She dropped her head in her hands and listened. For that voice. For a hint. For consolation. For anything.

Silence.

She peered up, so tired of these thoughts.

Knox's toiletries were scattered across the counter, but his messiness wasn't what caught her attention. The towels. Then the rug. The café curtains on the window. This wasn't Mike. A whole different color scheme. Fishes on the shower curtain. Very un-Mike Seabrook and clichéd into a damn rental.

The Marine had exorcised Mike from Windswept.

Callie needed out of this room, but how was she supposed to get by Knox?

She stood. A tight grip of purpose on the handle, she opened the door, only to run into him, his fist raised to knock. "What's up?"

"I'm fine," she said, and squeezed past only to pause in the bedroom. Nothing was the same. Not a damn thing. What had been a fear of too much Seabrook had become the complete opposite. He was gone from Windswept, and it angered her as if she'd missed his departure.

She started for the porch, but Knox handed her a water. "Here. Brought everything inside. Let's move on. Go to the living room."

She accepted the water, paying an overt amount of attention to opening the cap. She was here now, across the threshold, but God help her, the experience came with a spectator—no chance to absorb and sort this out alone. Nope. She had to deal with the very curious stares of the junior G-man.

Knox opened the blinds and sat on the sofa. Not as good a view as the porch, but a piece of the Atlantic peeked back. She perched in an upholstered chair.

"My apologies about you losing your officers a few months ago," he said. "You apologized to me about Pinky, but I never thought to. . . . You sure this case isn't making you nuts?"

"I don't do *nuts*, but thanks for caring."

So the agent knew things, but some things he would have no clue of. Closing her eyes, she tried once more to find some lingering piece of her last night here. A smell, a feeling . . . nothing.

Maybe it *was* only a house.

She rubbed her chest, missing the vest. Maybe it was part of all this.

"My condolences about Mike Seabrook, too," Knox said, breaking through her introspection in an uncanny coincidence. "I remember hearing the news at the office."

Now he shows feeling? "Yeah," she said.

"Neighbor across the street came over this afternoon. We chatted."

She could imagine who, and what about. Callie drank her water, fiercely craving something more to smooth off this edge.

Then Knox raked hands through his hair. "Jesus, Chief Morgan. What are we doing here?"

She lifted her courthouse portfolio. "Looking at potential evidence."

"No," he scolded. "We're doing nothing. Getting nowhere. While I might feel crappy about your past, your cop friend, and so on, I gotta say the whole reason I took leave was so that some small-town police chief wouldn't fuck things up for Pinky. And all I've seen is a small-town bottle-sucking chief with baggage that looks like it's interfering with her ability to trail a killer. And that's in only two days. We're no better off today than the night Pinky died."

"You stupid bastard," she said under her breath.

"Pardon?" he asked, hand cupping behind his ear.

"You contemptible asswipe," Callie swore, tight, forceful, and plenty loud for him to hear. "Why don't you pack up and leave my beach?"

"No, sweetheart. We're doing this together. God help me, but I'm not leaving Pinky's legacy in the hands of the likes of you."

"Ditto." Her left-hand fingers gripping a throw pillow, again something that hadn't been Mike's, she flinched when her nail pierced the material. This wasn't working, this deal between them, but what choice did she have? She let him see her cleansing breath. "What'd you find on the phone bill?"

"I managed to get his old bills," he said, following her lead to focus on the case. "Want to see?"

She slid over to the sofa, leaving three feet between them. "So who did he speak to recently, especially the twenty-four hours before he died?" She tried to appear interested, then surprised herself that she actually was.

Knox spread papers on the cushion. "Four numbers, but two stand out. Both belonging to Amanda Flagg. Over a dozen calls in his last week, some as long as a half hour."

"The other two numbers?"

"Colleton courthouse and a burner."

Looking up to judge his take on that, she found him doing the same to her. "Yeah," he said. "Burner was used only once."

"What was the last number before he died?"

"The 0027 number belonging to Flagg. A cell," he said.

"How long before he died?"

"With the range the coroner gave us on Pinky's death, I'd say as near as an hour. My take is he felt he was on to something and needed input from the mother," Knox said.

Callie liked his logic.

"You'll also be interested in his bank account."

Kudos to the irritating fed for taking the extra step. "What?"

"Several lump sum payments from Amanda Flagg, all dated since he retired."

Finally clues.

"The mother threw money at Pinky to keep him going," he said.

Yeah, Callie thought so, too, and the mother was the closest nexus to Rhoades. The first stepping stone in this wreck of a case. The odds had just soared that the abduction and murder were connected, but Callie remained leery. She didn't want to get sidetracked by assumption. "So when are we meeting her?"

"Tomorrow. Ten a.m. You up for it?"

He wasn't asking if she wanted to go, but rather if she was going to hold it together. Callie narrowed her eyes on the Atlantic in lieu of the agent. Truth was, who wanted to meet a mom whose child was kidnapped? A mom who'd see them as new hope for finding a toddler who'd probably died about the time Callie was teaching Jeb to walk.

"Yeah. I'm up for it."

"What'd you find in the courthouse?" he asked, and for the first time he seemed to have dropped some of the attitude.

She lifted the zipped portfolio of papers. "We can read better at the table."

An hour later, Callie and Knox still studied deed information against an open map. Callie tossed aside another deed copy for a house she personally saw sold six months ago. "We're comfortable assuming Pinky wasn't wanting to buy a beach house, right?"

Knox read another deed, his pencil following a road, as he counted addresses. "Hell, where's this one? Either this map isn't accurate or—"

"Or you can't read a map," Callie said, and pointed to the right place on the paper. Their conversation remained less than warm and fuzzy, but at least it progressed to some semblance of tolerance. Neither seemed to take automatic offense.

"Maps are not my thing," he agreed. "This was the part of investigations I usually turned over to technicians."

She pulled herself up short from bashing the Bureau. Both of them had been high enough in investigative ranks to have avoided grunt work for years if they'd wanted to, but she'd never shirked the tasks. Like the cliché said, the devil often lay in the details.

Unless you had the wrong details. She leaned back in her chair. "Rhoades's demise—"

"Cold-blooded murder."

"His murder, may be hidden in here someplace, but I'm not seeing it."

Knox stretched, two fists in the air. "This place is an island, for God's sake. Why don't you just question everybody?"

"Eighty percent of the tourists leave on Saturday," she said. "I already have officers showing his picture. He did his best not to be seen."

Knox slapped another page in the stack.

Callie wouldn't upset the entire beach if she didn't have to. There was a strategy to investigations and that included consideration for the living and not scaring the guilty into the wind.

A coolness brought by the sea breeze drifted through the screen. Callie shut the door and returned to her seat, not thinking to ask Knox if it was okay.

Callie's faster fingers created a spreadsheet of dates, places, and purchases on the agent's laptop. They reduced the number to 101 bought by current owners since the year 2000. Small number out of the 2,000 houses and condos, but still more than Callie expected, or wanted.

No immediate way to tell whether people were landlords or residents. The nondescript houses with low profiles were the demographic with the most potential.

Such a damn stupid exercise of frustration.

"Why can't we just ask Janet Wainwright?" Knox asked, as if his thoughts ran on her exact track.

"Because you told her you were a famous rich guy on vacation."

"I could let her know who I really am."

Callie scoffed. "Not wise. She talks to too many of the wrong people."

"Not a fan, huh?"

"Janet has no fans, just clients."

Except for maybe Brice, self-nominated president of the Fire Callie Morgan campaign. Compatriots in the sense they protected Edisto, but they'd sell the other out in the flash of a firefly's ass. Kind of like her partnership with Knox.

Fingers snapped in front of her. "Callie? What about other realtors?"

"Won't know a fraction of what Janet does. Let's just try to decipher what we have, okay?"

Knox balanced back on two chair legs. "So the sweet and serene reputation of this place is just hype, huh?"

"No, the reputation is good. It's just that the Edisto power people deal with government and community crap with a discreet hand. We all want the beach's character preserved. And a killer is not enhancing anyone's view of Edisto."

"Sounds like your priorities are out of whack, Chief."

"Yours are, too, just in the other direction."

"He was a friend," he said.

"Was he, though?" she asked. "Funny how you know so damn little about his life, retirement habits, and mission." Plus she hadn't seen Knox's number anywhere on Pinky's phone list.

Chapter 15

THOUGH LACKING her usual stamina, Callie walked home and got into her car for her pre-bedtime drive around the beach. Sober, in her personal vehicle, her tires away from the curb, she cruised the familiar roads for an hour, too restless to go to bed.

Any one of these houses could hold the killer, and so far she'd given him forty-eight hours to design an escape plan or develop an alibi. Yet she had no clues.

In the morning she and Knox would interview Emma Flagg's mother. Hopefully a start.

A little after one she returned home, promising herself two ounces of a gin nightcap from the cooler. Callie dropped her things, locked the door, and punched the buttons of her alarm. Jeb might leave his door open at college, but here her rules applied. Rules and routine were how she got the little sleep she did.

She tried once, again, but the alarm wouldn't engage. There was a window open somewhere.

Her gut kicked into protective mode, and she went for her firearm . . . then left it in place. Leerier than she liked, she began her search, room to room. Alert but not panicked. This was her domain. She wasn't doing panic, but she'd take out someone all day long for violating her space.

First she scanned the living room, where Jeb, Nolan, and Sammy curled and sprawled across the furniture, asleep. The others gone. No windows open. She reached down and muted the television. Very still, she listened hard, then eased toward the bedrooms.

Nothing in her room, or her bath. She moved through the dining area to Jeb's room down the hall. As she opened his door, a breeze moved the blinds in the window next to his bed.

The cause for the alarm not engaging. She let out a deep breath.

In three quick moves she raised the blinds, shut the window, and dropped the cover back into place. She gave a sniff to the room for pot, cigarettes, grateful to find none. No condom wrappers in his trash. Then in a wary check of her own bedroom, she breathed relief at none there either.

Fairly sure she'd located the issue, she still checked upstairs, every window, then downstairs, every door. Finally, she set the alarm.

After checking the kitchen trash for beer cans, she returned to the living room, and appreciated the fact they pretended to be good boys. Aware of her profession, they'd relocate evidence off the premises.

Though grown men in appearance, with their chin stubble and thin patches of chest hair, the game controllers in the sleeping boys' hands hinted of their youth. She couldn't help but grin. Didn't mean she still wouldn't sniff for pot.

The television screen locked on a desolate planet, an armor-clad soldier frozen in aim at a spaceship in the distance, Callie eased the controller from her son's relaxed hands and gently jostled him. "Jeb? I need to talk to you a minute."

Eyelids heavy, he squinted. "Mom? What time is it?"

"Almost two." She took his arm. "Follow me."

Like a lanky colt, her son stumbled from the chair. She led him to his bedroom and silently shut the door.

"You left your window open. Good Lord, Jeb, have you forgotten everything I taught you about security?"

He sat on the bed's edge, blinking. "Why do you get so worked up?"

"It's a wide-open window, son!" She instinctively smelled harder, seeking purpose for the ventilation.

He grinned at her. "Sniff all you like. Nothing like your cop mother distrusting you. Why shouldn't I open a window? The chief of police has this town covered and all's right with wonderful Edisto Beach."

His bitterness angered her, and disappointed. Yet, she sat beside him, reining in an intense desire to squeeze his arm so damn tight. "You've changed," she said.

"Oh, so you think college has messed me up, too?" He snorted. "Thought you wanted me to see the world, get an education, find myself."

"I do. I did. But this," and she held her palms out, in a sweeping measure of his length. "You're a good kid, but this cynicism. . . . Where'd it come from?"

"You! All you, Mom. And you're too blind to own it."

She drew back. The message . . . so foreign from his mouth.

She'd screwed up badly coming home after those drinks with Knox.

Jeb released a peevish harrumph. "Look at you. So smart yet so lost.

You know why I finally went to college, Mom?"

Her failed promise not to drink? Sophie assured him she'd have his mother's back. Plus Stan had moved to Edisto and been her foundation since Seabrook . . . left. Not that Stan had been around much lately. "Things had settled down," she summarized.

"No, I couldn't keep putting my life on hold for you."

She sat stunned, knifed even, clueless at how deeply he meant those words. "I never wanted you to put your life on hold for me."

"But you always needed someone."

"I didn't," she argued.

"You did, Mom." This time he wasn't so harsh. "Your drinking is neon proof. Not saying you haven't been kicked around, but I was afraid—"

She stood, walked to the now-locked window, and turned. "So, you felt you could no longer help me, and you had to move on and hope I'd wake up by myself." Like an alcoholic having to hit bottom. Was that what he tried to say? "You didn't want to wake up one day and be forty and living with your mother . . . and a cop no less, who ought to be strong enough on her own."

"Yeah," he said. "In a way. I couldn't wait until you were ten-eight to decide what I wanted to do."

She wanted to smile at his use of the cop "in service/available for calls" term. A sign of some of her in him. But this wasn't a humorous moment. He'd made that clear.

What now?

To scold him would get her nowhere. To debate his logic . . . hopeless. Instead, he might prefer to be treated like an equal, like an adult. She returned to her seat on the bed. "I'm proud of you."

He let out a tired sigh. "I know that, Mom, but can we not do this tonight?"

Okay, not getting very far with that. "Hey," she said, "talk to me more about the man who followed the girls. What do the kids say about him? Did he approach anyone?"

Jeb scratched his face still puffy from sleep. "The kids only made the guy an issue because he died. Don't read more into it."

"What did they think? If they were exaggerating, be my interpreter."

He seemed to like that. "They think he was overly attentive, I'd say. I heard three different people, if you count Nolan's mouth, say the guy was seen on the beach once and in Whaley's once. And he drove by."

"What kind of car?" she asked. "Which day?"

Elbows on his knees, he messed with his disheveled hair then rubbed his eyes hard. "Maybe the day before we found the body? Lissa mentioned a green car."

The Nissan.

Edisto was like a large subdivision, with hundreds of homes, some of which she hadn't visited because they didn't demand police attention. But resident demographics skewed toward an older group. She saw hundreds of kids during tourist season, but few during the cold months . . . but they could be in college, too. "How many girls your age live out here?" she asked.

His puzzlement slid into suspicion. "Is this conversation back about keeping an eye on me?" His voice hardened. "My choice of who to date is just that . . . mine. Ms. Bianchi thinks I'm—"

"Stop it, Jeb. Forget Sophie. This is about work. How many girls your age?"

He thought. "A half dozen."

Though Callie suspected a small number, she had assumed at least double. "That's all?"

"Not that many kids live here. What's this about?"

She held up a finger, and he stopped.

Six was a good place to start. An easy number to rule out. But a uniform screamed obvious, her identity too well known. Knox would appear dubious as a grown man studying the girls, and if he flashed his credentials, it was game over.

Here was her chance. Not just to learn what the kids said outside the presence of authority figures, but to show Jeb she respected him. He could help her without feeling like such a caregiver.

She couldn't believe she was going to ask him to do this, but maybe she'd win on two fronts. "Do you know these girls' names?"

He flipped his palm up. "Sure. Lissa, Yancy, Bea, Tara, Sprite, and Kim."

"Kim?"

"Yeah, *the* Kim Smith. Lives on Yacht Club Road, you know, on the sound. In Dolphin Central, that big three-story mansion. Her parents have some kind of serious money."

Callie'd heard of that place. She'd met Yancy and Bea Wilkerson and knew Sprite. Recalled where Lissa lived, the one with the reputation. "Who's Tara?"

"Hot blonde who lives on Myrtle. She goes to Clemson so she doesn't come home until this weekend."

Guess her son had a decent working knowledge of his peers. "All the girls near nineteen?"

He frowned. "Who said anything about nineteen?"

She stood up from the bed, wanting to call Stan about her progress . . . then remembered she'd lost that link. "Okay, again, this is about work. How many kids come only periodically to use their parents' rentals?"

He grimaced. "Geez, how can anyone know that? What's going on?"

Poised in the middle of her son's bedroom, Callie studied her tall but half-grown man. If he should say the wrong thing to the wrong person . . .

"You're giving me the creepiest cop look, Mom."

She snapped to, wondering what look that was, and tried to paint on one more suited to a mother. "I'm trying to decide whether to let you in on something. You have access to certain people, and therefore information, but . . ." Yeah, a big *but.* A *but* that reminded her of too many déjà vus of him too close to too many criminals, and his aversion to her job.

"Want me to pump my friends about the dude?" he asked, not very bothered at the idea.

"Only if you want to. And something else."

He waited, and waited. "What?"

She bit her lip. "All depends on whether you can keep it secret that you work for me."

Rising off the bed, he easily rested forearms on her shoulders, their heights convenient. She missed this sort of thing between them.

"Secret, are you kidding me?" he said. "Do you think I've told the details of our insane lives to these guys? To anyone other than Sprite? I haven't even told Grandma lots of stuff."

Crap, Sprite . . . and therefore, Sophie.

"This isn't for discussion with Sprite, son. If you can't keep quiet with her, I'll pursue this on my own. Just think about it."

She patted his arm and turned to leave, but he kept a grip on her. "I won't tell Sprite," he said. "We aren't speaking anyway."

The mother in her rose front and center. "Why? What happened?"

"College," he said and flopped back on the bed. Finally they might have an old-fashioned conversation.

Though on his elbows, he awkwardly tried to shrug. "I met people. Like Ms. Bianchi halfway got right, Sprite turned pissy about who I saw, who I went to class with. The night we went out kayaking, Sprite gave me crap out on the creek, like I entered school as an excuse to study girls instead of business. I didn't date a single solitary one, but I sure will now."

He hid his disappointment with forced resolve. Callie wanted to mourn for her son's broken courtship, maybe for Sprite's tender young heart, too. Jeb's protective behavior around her when they found Rhoades's body wasn't just chivalry. He cared about her.

However, with him single maybe she *could* put him in search of an answer or two. "We think the dead guy hunted for a girl your age."

"Why? Was he really a perv?"

She debated hard how much to tell him.

He snorted. "Sorta need the details or this isn't gonna work."

With a move to his bedroom door, she opened it, peered toward the other boys, and finding them plenty comatose to suit her, she shut the door again. "Not even to your friends, you hear?"

"Nobody but you, right?"

"And Raysor as last resort if I'm unavailable. This is no game."

He nodded. "Promise."

"The man was FBI. The girl abducted."

Jeb's chin dropped. "And you think she's on Edisto?"

"May-be." Callie stretched the syllables, not eager to tell Jeb that Emma was most likely dead. One body was enough for him. "Be careful. The agent was murdered, Jeb."

His eyes widened. "That's psycho."

"It's why I always worry about you . . . all the psychos in the world."

"Well, this ought to be easy," he said, blowing off her concern. "What's she look like?"

"Therein lies the glitch."

Without naming names, Callie explained in generalities. "We only have a baby picture. Just learn more about these girls. The handful of facts you glean might be a loose thread we can follow. Not that they are the kidnapped girl, but they could be a sister, or have heard of the abduction. We don't understand yet."

"Wow, this is rich, Mom."

She couldn't stop with the warnings. "Don't go out of your way, and don't show your hand. Don't try to interrogate. Simply observe. Be a kid interested in other kids, but not too curious. Low key."

His interest was unexpected, and it scared her.

"Plenty easy," he said. "Want me to write down what I—"

"Absolutely not."

He held up his hands, resigned. "Secret. I get it."

She tilted her head. "Absolute secrecy."

Squinting, he pointed back at her. "Gotcha, Chief. Top secret, confidential, classified—"

"Jeb."

His chuckle only worried her more about her decision, but he'd lost so much of his animosity toward her. She justified this not only on a professional level but on a personal level as well. He needed to see, to know, that she was functioning and ten-eight. She prayed this wasn't too desperate a move to win him back. Not her best motherly choice.

"I see your wheels working. Go to bed, Mom. I said I got this."

She left and headed straight to her bedroom. From under some towels, she opened her cooler and took a quick draw from the bottle, then tucked her bar back into hiding. Then as she slid under the covers, she second- and third-guessed her choice to use Jeb. But also she envisioned another mother awake, unable to speak to her child. A mother with tentative, rekindled hope after seventeen long years who dared to pray that an aging, dedicated agent had finally put some pieces together.

What kind of mother would that make Callie if she didn't dog this investigation and all its tangents to an end? What kind of cop wouldn't seek the answer to Pinky's murder? What kind of mother wouldn't want her son to respect her?

Seabrook would say she was born for this case.

Sophie would call it fate's way of pulling her back into the game and handling Jeb.

Callie considered it stupid, dumb luck that all this fell into her lap.

Stan would think . . . she relaxed as sleep slid in . . . *never mind.*

Chapter 16

AN ANTIQUE PEWTER sign proclaimed Callie and Knox had reached the two-story, Gone-with-the-Wind estate of the Flagg family in Mount Pleasant. Northeast of Charleston, the smaller city's contemporary opulence competed with that of its elder sister city. Callie drove the cruiser up a quarter-mile drive with full understanding of why a kidnapper targeted this well-to-do family. From the shrubs, trees, and architectural design, the plantation home had existed long before the town exploded from a tiny gateway to secluded beaches into a metropolis of close to a hundred thousand.

The late morning sun accented everything as if freshly scrubbed and prepped for show, and Callie imagined how difficult it would be to remain in the same house where Emma once played and livened the rooms. But how much harder it would be to leave, ever waiting for the daughter's return.

They took the dozen steps to the black eight-foot double doors. "I'll start," Knox said. "I arranged this and knew Rhoades, so she'll trust the FBI more. Follow my lead."

Callie quit skimming her hand along the porch rail. When she picked him up shortly after eight, the uneasy truce of the previous night had held—barely. And now, she reluctantly agreed that he seemed the best choice for introductions. Reluctantly.

She gave him a half nod, and he rang a bell that echoed far into the house.

A middle-aged, black-and-gray-haired woman answered, her slacks and top neat but speaking nothing of money. "Mr. Kendrick? Chief Morgan?"

Guess the uniform commanded a title more than plain clothes. They acknowledged each other, and the woman smiled. "Ms. Flagg expects you."

The woman led them across a great foyer, her rubber-soled flats silent on the tiles versus their leather soles more loudly announcing their presence. Without the expected formal announcement, she slid the study open and walked away as if she had more important duties to tend to. The guests could find their way in and close their own door behind them.

Callie had always hated house help. Not the people themselves, but the way they underlined a social divide. Her mother's housekeeper only replied when spoken to, and Callie was instructed to maintain a distance. Once on her own, she never had as much as her nails done because of the caste-like division that rubbed her wrong, regardless of the tip that supposedly bridged the divide.

When the door opened, the matriarch of the noble home made no move to jump up and welcome her guests . . . even guests connected to Rhoades.

Seated rather daintily, the woman appeared fragile, underweight, and older than her fifty-five years, the too-white hair cut blunt and way too precise. Her cheeks fell on the sallow side in spite of the powder and blush. Veined hands. Though she was dressed in pleasant soft yellow slacks, here sat a soul wary of fresh news and weary of ill tidings. A lady wizened by too many false alarms.

Or ill. As she'd told Knox over the phone, the woman couldn't manage a late interview yesterday. She turned in every night by eight.

Mrs. Flagg beckoned them over with a gentle wave. "Come on in." A tray of iced tea and some sort of scones awaited them on a coffee table before a two-seater sofa, so they chose there to sit, the tea already poured.

"Which is it?" Mrs. Flagg sipped from her glass, only the slightest lilt on the second word. She stared into her drink, as if she didn't care who told her, only that they got it over with.

"Ma'am?"

Knox was supposed to make introductions, but an unspoken gracelessness hung over the room as he stopped after the one lone word. Apparently, he wasn't versed in delivering bad news. Maybe another task he gave to a technician.

Callie smoothed over his difficulty. "We're here on behalf of FBI Agent Pinkerton Rhoades."

Little reaction. Too much shock in the past maybe, but then her eyes belied a deeper, more afflicted soul. "Has he been arrested for delving into my daughter's cold case without permission?" she asked.

When neither Callie nor Knox replied, she paused, as if she answered her own thoughts, and set the tea glass awkwardly on a coaster, carefully with both hands. "He's retired, Chief Morgan. The FBI doesn't care about Emma any longer, so for you to appear so solemn, I can also assume the worst." She inhaled shakily, one hand dropped into the other. "Is he . . . dead?"

Callie leaned forward, sensing woman-to-woman worked best here. "Yes, ma'am."

Mrs. Flagg stared into her hands. "How?"

They could barely hear the word.

"He was murdered, drowned on Edisto Beach where I'm police chief." Callie noted that Knox remained mysteriously quiet. "I'm handling the case. As a friend of Agent Rhoades, Agent Kendrick felt obliged to come with me."

"Yes, ma'am," he said so gentlemanly.

"We're terribly sorry," Callie continued, an eye on him. "It's apparent from your daughter's file that Agent Rhoades was quite passionate about finding closure for you and your family."

Mrs. Flagg sighed, a small mewl of a sound, and sank deeper into the cushion, the large upholstered chair overwhelming her frame. Though shallow, the noise seemed too big for her body and pitiful to hear. "He was the last man who cared." She caught on a choke. Her chin dropped to her chest, and she fingered the damp napkin in her lap. A tear streaked slowly down her sunken cheeks.

"Are you okay?" Callie asked.

The woman shook her head. "I haven't been well, so don't mind me." Her small sob shook her. "Oh Pinky," she whispered. "I should have known when you didn't call."

Just how ill was she? While the question appeared nosy, it might matter. "What is your ailment, if you don't mind."

"Complications of rheumatoid arthritis. Runs in the family. My mother died of it at sixty. My uncle at fifty-four."

They gave her a reflective moment and waited for her to either return to the conversation or dissolve completely. Callie remained still, unsure how to behave.

Knox drank his tea, jerking as his ice cubes shifted into his face, then unexpectedly, he blurted as if a spell had been broken with the ice-cube clatter, "Mrs. Flagg, I was very close to Pinky. He trained me with the Bureau, but we didn't always work together. While I understood Emma's case was close to his heart, I had no idea he spent his retirement days working it. I wish. . . . I mean, if he'd told me I might've been there."

Amanda Flagg studied him as his words spilled out then trailed off.

"You'd lost touch with him since he retired." She reached over to a decorative box of tissues and took one, then held it to her nose. "He regretted that so much."

The mother seemed awfully informed about Agent Rhoades. Callie watched Knox dodge the woman's gaze, and tried to define whether he toyed with Mrs. Flagg or finally showed compassion.

As she dabbed under her eyes, Mrs. Flagg sniffled. "Pinky and I were close, Agent Kendrick. We met often to talk of Emma, but we spoke of many things." Words backed up, and she coughed. "A dear, sweet man. We shared so much."

More tears.

Damn. Callie'd prayed hard for a dry-eyed meet.

"Have either of you lost a child?" Mrs. Flagg asked.

Callie looked away.

Knox paused, then replied, "Not exactly."

Callie held back her surprise. She didn't want to be a part of a confessional. Almost like she feared having ammunition to use against him if he offered up secrets. Because that's how they seemed to work.

Mrs. Flagg's countenance softened. "*Not exactly.* Those are mighty deep words, Mr. Kendrick. And Chief Morgan, your silence speaks for itself."

Knox focused on a bookcase off to the side of the woman's chair.

He *wasn't* playacting.

Mrs. Flagg fingered the hem around her pastel top. "So, I assume you need me to fill in the holes of the investigation that aren't recorded somewhere. What was Pinky up to and why he still fought to find Emma."

"Yes, ma'am," Knox replied, as though relieved at the change of topic. "We hope these two cases are not connected."

Their hostess froze. "Why, I would hope the complete opposite, agent. Do you not suspect Pinky died getting close to who took Emma? Is it better he died at some random hand than in pursuit of a quest he felt strongly about?"

"Sorry," Knox said, a bit unraveled. "Not exactly what I meant."

Callie heard her, though. If Pinky died for a serious purpose, it gave meaning to his death . . . gave more meaning to Emma's case. Better to die for a cause than for no purpose at all. Callie *had* hoped the two cases weren't conjoined, and for the life of her—in the face of Mrs. Flagg's certainty—couldn't say why now except for a hope of simplicity.

Mrs. Flagg gently raised her hand. "Let's talk about Pinky for a while. Refill your tea. Would you like Agnes to prepare you something else?"

"No, ma'am," Knox replied.

Callie let the two continue with stories of the dead agent. She wasn't really part of this twosome, and she was glad. She discreetly scanned the room to distract herself during this session of communion between conjoined, fractured souls. But she still listened.

An insulated quiescence entombed the room in peace while they talked softly of Rhoades and then Emma. She could understand Mrs. Flagg cocooning herself in this place. Tasteful décor, professionally enhanced in a rich flavor that kept magazines like *Southern Living* and *Garden & Gun* in business. Thirty feet away a white marble mantel flaunted a tall porcelain clock and a dozen framed photos.

"Emma was taken at age two and a half," Mrs. Flagg said. "Right from under our noses from her bedroom. The investigators talked to the neighbors, hired help, even the pediatrician's office. Everybody who'd ever delivered to or worked on this property. There was a request for ransom. A million dollars in assorted denominations, no new bills, delivered in four different ways to four different locations on four different dates with no exact time for pickup. If we put markers with the money, they'd kill Emma. If anyone but my husband Raymond made the deliveries, they'd kill Emma. If they found a monitoring device, they'd kill Emma." Each mention of her daughter raised her voice until she reached a peak.

"More conditions, more threats to kill her if we deviated. We couldn't keep up. The FBI said they'd seen nothing like it, and there were so many agents involved that my husband and I feared they'd . . . ruin things."

Callie turned. "So y'all took care of the exchanges yourself."

"Yes, we did. Thank God we had the means." She stared at Callie with a sense of pride. "Raymond threatened to sue people and called in his political chips. We ordered the FBI out of the house. We got our way, he paid the money, but . . . we must have done something wrong."

Knox had to defend his side. "The FBI would've—"

"Ma'am," Callie interrupted. *Not the time, Knox.* "I doubt you did wrong." In her experience, ransoms never bought release, but no parent would refuse to pay for fear of being the exception to the rule. She assumed the child had been sold or killed, and considered Emma's case to be more of finding answers versus finding the child. "So what set Rhoades on fire again?"

With the question, Mrs. Flagg sat straighter, her wrinkles less noticeable. "Two things, and trust me, I was not eager to fall prey to false hope. Optimism works for only so long, and fourteen years was an ugly, difficult wait to naïvely give it another chance."

"Fourteen?" Callie asked.

Mrs. Flagg continued, steadfast in her storytelling. "Going through my husband's items, I stumbled across an old Canon camera with thirty-five-millimeter film still inside. I took it to the drugstore and almost fainted at the pictures."

Knox leaned forward.

"They were pictures of Emma at the park engaged with a little girl her age. We'd just run into the parents and their daughter and the afternoon sort of evolved. Pictures of swings, slides, a sandbox. One of Raymond with them both on his knees. It was a spring day. The sun spilled over everything, and we'd taken turns with the camera to preserve the day. Just one of those perfect days." A gentle smile. Callie caught herself mirroring it back. They'd seen some of those pictures, and they indeed reflected a perfect day.

"I called Pinky," Mrs. Flagg said. "He came over that night. I just wanted to show him how precious Emma had been, but he asked if anyone had interviewed that couple. We hadn't thought about someone we'd only met once. Who interviewed someone you met in the grocery-store line, or stood next to at the DMV? Pinky, however, searched with all his FBI tools. He was like that, you know. No stone unturned."

"Right," Knox said. "There isn't much in the file about them, though."

She sighed. "No, he worked hard to find them, but they vanished off the planet, Agent Kendrick. David and Joan Metts. He found out who they were, but after Emma disappeared, so did they. The best news I'd heard in fourteen years."

Knox might not understand, but Callie did, even before the mother gestured both arms wide and said, "It meant they might have taken Emma for personal reasons," she said, eyes glistening. "To raise her as theirs. My baby might not be in my arms, but she wasn't in the ground. She was alive, and to a mother that's like a gift from God." Tears brimmed anew. "Pinky felt it, too."

Callie rose and moved away, a catch in her own throat.

"It's okay, Chief Morgan," Mrs. Flagg said.

No, it wasn't. This lady hung a thin, fragile thread of faith on the loose research of a recently retired dead man.

Callie wasn't ready for this. Chasing clues was one thing. Juggling such emotion . . . Mike would have kept her steady. So would Stan, but they weren't around, so she had to stop excusing herself. Investigating once came so natural to her. It still could. Shame that the person she had to prove it to most was this arrogant FBI agent. Then second most, a woman too hopeful about a hopeless case.

Callie studied the wall as if she cared about pictures of Raymond Flagg with governors and real estate magnates, a Catholic cardinal, and even one with Mel Gibson when they'd filmed *The Patriot* near Rock Hill.

"Where are the photos now?" asked Knox.

"We have a few in the file," Callie said over her shoulder.

"If there are more," Knox said, "we'd certainly like to see them."

"I'll give you my copies. I still have the negatives." Mrs. Flagg reached over to hit a button beside a lamp, but it made no noise they could hear. In seconds, the housekeeper peered in. Mrs. Flagg beckoned. "Can you retrieve that stack of photos on my dresser, Agnes?"

"Yes, ma'am," she said, and retreated.

"You mentioned two things," Callie said, though a lot of conversation had passed since that moment. "Two items roused Rhoades. The new photographs and what?"

"He would've had the second," their hostess replied. "A note. Someone contacted him about a week ago, telling him to focus on Edisto Beach."

Callie glimpsed at Knox, who narrowed his gaze in return.

"Who sent it?" she asked. "How'd he get it?" *Most of all, where was it?* It wasn't in the file.

"It was plain, unsigned, and typed," the woman replied. "Completely anonymous. He told me it said *She's living on Edisto Beach*. He said for me not to get overly enthusiastic because he'd received pranks before, but this one came to him personally, after he was retired."

Callie exchanged looks with Knox again, probably with the same thought: Rhoades had been baited. So entranced was he at keeping Ms. Flagg happy—and the checks coming—or so desperate to find Emma, he took the note literally. *Living* on Edisto Beach. He went back seventeen years in the courthouse and searched for those who owned houses and lived on Edisto.

A hand on her chest, the mother smiled for once. "It's hard not to be positive about a note, isn't it? Somewhere out there could be a good Samaritan who's seen, heard, or figured something out. What are the chances?"

What are the chances, indeed?

A good Samaritan would have called the police. Or the FBI. Not sent a cryptic note. Was this a way for a kidnapper, or baby killer, to return to that moment in his life when the public made him a star? Was the note remorse? Or had Pinky actually turned enough stones to find substance, making him dangerous?

"Other than this case, can you think of anyone who might kill Pinky, Mrs. Flagg? Any personal conflicts he mentioned?" Callie asked.

But the woman shook her head.

Callie turned back toward the mantel. Among the family photos she saw baby Emma in her mother's arms, a gap-toothed toddler Emma with a boy a couple years older, who Callie assumed was the brother mentioned in the file. He had a space between his teeth as well.

Down the line, a boy posed at high school graduation with proud parents on both sides. She looked harder. She recognized this older boy with teeth straightened from braces and a light case of acne. Then she moved to the next one. "Mrs. Flagg, who is the handsome young man in these pictures?"

"Thank you. That's my son, Theodore."

The kid who'd pegged Rhoades as a girl stalker . . . the boy who slept in Callie's house for spring break. Theodore N. Flagg in Rhoades's file on Emma.

Nolan.

Chapter 17

AROUND HALF PAST noon, without the housekeeper, Mrs. Flagg walked Callie and Knox to the door. Callie carried the photos. They'd begun their visit with horrific news about Rhoades and discussing the brutal topic of Emma, yet Mrs. Flagg hugged them both with a sad sincerity. Then she requested they update her often as to what they found.

She gave Knox a second hug and patted his cheek.

It wasn't until Callie drove out of the drive that she yielded to the fact that Amanda Flagg had deftly transferred responsibility of finding Emma onto them. New bodies to take up the torch.

More importantly, though, how would she approach Nolan when she got back to Edisto?

She cut a glance at Knox. "You realize Mrs. Flagg—"

"Oh, yeah," he said, resignation thick. "We're *her* detectives now."

Knox's forehead furrowed, probably working out, if he hadn't already, where Pinky's interests lay and what that meant.

"Rhoades was way more than a detective for that woman. It's common," she said. "Don't be so quick to judge. People thrown together on cases, on the job . . . feelings happened."

Like Stan, but not like Stan . . . but so much like Mike.

"Their thing seemed more sweet than sordid," she added, filling in his silence. "Not by today's standards."

He snapped around to her. "Exactly. The Bureau . . . never mind." He caught himself but a second too late.

"The Bureau what?" she asked, but he turned deaf to her question.

Then she got it. "Did the FBI force him to retire over her?"

Knox's mashed his lips a few seconds. "He could've stayed another two years before mandatory retirement at fifty-seven, but he kept working that damn case. And that meant using resources that left trails back to him. I told him to watch his back, but somebody had nothing better to do than to dig into how he spent his hours." He let out a loud, grumpy huff. "And yes, they also found out he'd been *entertaining* Mrs.

Flagg since Mr. Flagg died."

She understood there were rules, but how juvenile of them. "It was a seventeen-year-old cold case."

"But still an *open* case," he replied.

"And Amanda Flagg felt guilty so she funded his continued search. Hmm."

Knox narrowed his eyes. "Hmm what?"

"Kinda makes you wonder who sent the note, doesn't it?"

His voice ground even harder. "Not any more than before."

"Knox," Callie said, trying not to dumb down her response. "She was a lonely woman with money."

"She didn't buy his affection."

"Not saying that. I agree money didn't drive him, she did."

But she still could've written the note.

Callie understood better how Knox had fallen under Amanda's spell back there. Showing way deeper emotion than she had seen in him since they met, he was familiar with Pinky's love life, and protective of it. In an empathetic wave of remembrance, Callie understood why.

Mike Seabrook first gravitated to her via their law-enforcement careers, with him admiring her big-city detective skills on an island faced with a murder and an inexperienced force. But their shared bereavement was the bigger bond that drew them tight.

She blinked at the recall and gripped the steering wheel.

Knox spoke up. "You aren't having one of your *moment* things, are you?"

"No!" Irritation took hold of her as he referenced her *moments* like her monthly period. Something to tolerate because she was female. God, why did a case like this have to be the one to rebaptize her into detective work? And why was she stupid enough to think he'd felt real emotions of sympathy with Amanda?

"You don't seem all right," he said. "You're tensed up like a steel cable."

"Maybe because I'm stuck in the car with you?"

"No," he said. "That's not it." Like they were playing a road-trip game and she guessed wrong.

Oh, this damn man!

"Jesus, Knox, you want me to ask about why *your* feelings spilled all over that woman's ten-thousand-dollar oriental carpet back there? Why did you turn ten shades of pale at the mention of family?"

Steam almost rose off him. His face hardened, and with compressed lips he turned his attention back on the road. "Wow, sorry I asked."

He'd spotted weakness in Callie and pounced on her. So, she pounced back, her tongue beginning to snap back just as quickly as his. That was a habit she needed to put some energy into breaking. They'd both been carrying around too much bottled-up emotion from the interview with Amanda.

"Don't shut down on me," she said. "And while you're making adjustments, cut me some slack. This case is difficult enough."

No response.

"Truth is," she continued, "I don't want to be the person to tell that mother her daughter has been dead for years. Or that we still couldn't find her. With Rhoades murdered, nobody else but us will hunt for that child again, and when we quit, it's over."

His chin rested in his hand, elbow on the armrest. "I get that fine. What I also see now is that the responsibility of solving Pinky's death goes hand in hand with Emma Flagg's abduction. He was killed hunting for her."

Okay, they agreed on something.

"But the other truth is that you drink—"

"One night," she said.

"You have spells."

"Only one," she argued. She slowed behind a semi, not attempting to pass, biting against a response that would just prompt him for a comeback.

"Then let's put that aside . . . for now. You also drag your feet," he said. "You don't want Emma's case, which equally means you don't want Pinky's murder solved. From my perspective, me, Pinky, Emma—we're inconveniences."

Son of a bitch. She couldn't deny that she'd had more than one thought and wish that the case would magically disappear, be claimed by someone else, and leave her alone.

"I'm committed," she said, defiant. "But you need to deal with your regrets if you want to make this work. None of this will bring him back . . . or change how he left the Bureau . . . or tell him that you're sorry you weren't there for him when he needed you most."

His glower all but shoved her against the door, but there, she'd said it. But instead of taking a jab back, he turned his attention to the suffocating Mount Pleasant traffic.

"Yeah, I saw your number missing on the phone bill," she said softly, finally trying not to be adversarial. They were both flawed. Now he knew she saw his flaws as clearly as he saw hers.

"Knox, what's your take on the note telling Rhoades to go to Edisto?" she asked, attempting to bring him around.

Knox shook his head and held out empty palms. "What note? Who's seen it? Where is it?"

She hit the Mark Clark Expressway to bypass all the Charleston peninsula congestion. "It makes more sense as to why he went to the beach. We're doing what Rhoades did *after* he received the note. Researching deeds. Second-guessing at which teenager might be Emma. Wish we could just check all their DNA and be done with it."

He glared at her like she had two mouths and three ears. Yeah, she got it. That DNA idea was an ambulance chaser's wet dream, a lineup of lawsuits. And what lab would process them, and who the hell would cover the cost?

"I'm very surprised he didn't stash the note with the case files in his car trunk," she said. "And that burner phone is a big unknown."

Staring down the SUV in front of them, Knox's expression remained dark. "I think we have to assume he was drawn out there to be killed."

"Probably," she said calmly. "Before he could report to anyone. But how'd he get there? How'd he plan to get back? Who else is involved? Or Rhoades's murder was purely random. I'm worried we're too wrapped up in the Emma case to give Rhoades his due."

He had no response to that.

"Well," she added, "would any of this make the FBI reconsider the case?"

"Not without the damn *note*," he exclaimed. His tone rose and hit the roof on the last word. "For all we know, Pinky told her about a note to make her feel better on a bad day."

"Or *she* sent the note to keep *him* motivated. After all, she's the only one who's mentioned it."

"We're getting nowhere."

Back to that, are we? The Ashley River passed beneath them, and Callie pulled into the slow lane of the interstate, so some high-speed semi didn't tap their bumper and spin them off the road. "Let's move past the nerve Mrs. Flagg struck in there and get back to the job."

Get over yourself is what she really wanted to tell him. Instead, she began to realize she might be all he had. Rhoades was more than a case to Knox, and he resented it wasn't the same with her.

"But before we get back to the job, want to stop someplace for coffee?"

"Where would you suggest we go and not be seen since you're so paranoid about that? I rented a house but that makes you throw up."

"I didn't throw up. Plus we're off Edisto."

They cruised in silence, took the right lane of I-526 toward their exit. She might as well tell him and get it over with, because to hide her feelings about Windswept was akin to Knox hiding his about Rhoades. "Your house isn't just a rental to me."

"Oh, news flash." He rocked his head back. "You have a past, which means you have unresolved problems, which means you wish Pinky hadn't died on your watch. . . . Yeah, how many times do you have to paint that picture for me?"

They recrossed the big bridge onto Edisto Island. Knox stayed silent. Callie took a crisp, sharp right, two hundred yards down an unpaved path to a boat ramp. The dust of the shell-and-gravel parking area clouded the air around them when she threw the car into park and turned to confront him. "Okay, Agent Knox Kendrick. Let's talk about you, then."

He thrust open the car door and got out.

She exited as well. Only one other vehicle parked in the crude lot, its trailer empty of a boat. A vivid midday sun glared off their sunglasses. A breeze teased both their hair as if trying to cool them down. Callie backhanded the air. "So you lost touch with Rhoades. And?"

He watched the water. "I missed his retirement party, which wasn't damn much from what I heard, the sorry bastards."

At least those *bastards* showed up, but she was sure Knox already told himself that. "You knew his apartment pretty well," she said, surprised she offered consolation.

He reeked bitterness. "Pinky's had that apartment for nine years. I've visited it about that many times."

"Well." She rested hands on the warm car hood between them. "You can't dwell on the what-ifs."

He pivoted. "This advice coming from you?"

She clenched arm muscles. "What, we're comparing who's the more damaged goods? I feel your pain, you idiot, but I'm not the one who deserves your wrath. The killer is."

The shoe was on the other foot now. If Knox couldn't contain his personal issues, what good was he?

Then the realization hit her like a clip behind the knees.

She stared at a mirror version of herself.

Jaw tight, Knox drummed a loose fist on the hood. "As I told Mrs. Flagg—"

"Stop," Callie said softly. "Just stop. You don't owe me any more explanation."

His confused expression made Callie peer down to study the shells. It wasn't enjoyable sorting out someone like herself. She wondered how difficult it was for those around her.

Knox overthought whether people judged him for ignoring Pinky, like Callie wondered about Edistonians. Between them, they shouldered a wealth of guilt.

She craved an icy double in hand, and the most melancholy song on a Neil Diamond album.

"I lost my brother . . ." he started.

Jesus, she didn't want to hear this.

"Pinky understood," Knox continued. "My two-year-old brother was killed by a drunk driver. I was ten."

Callie's shoulders sagged, her insides pressing against ribs already crammed with her own issues. He deserved an ear, just not hers.

"Can't handle anything to do with kids . . ."

She pressed fingertips against her temples.

"He was chunky but growing out of it. Died instantly, they said, but how can you really tell?"

Was Callie all he had to talk to?

A pitiful state of affairs, the two of them.

"And your mother?" she asked, obligated to ask a question.

"Died three years later, in another accident."

Wow, that was rough.

"Well?" he finally asked.

She blinked, back to the conversation. "Well, what?"

"Your turn. What's your story? The house, losing your men . . ."

She had pulled over for him to dump whatever sludge kept him too grumpy for her to stand, not for a *kumbaya* moment. This was not permission for him to enter her head.

Different replies came and went in her head, none fitting. She settled on short and vague, not cheating but not giving him access, either. "I lost somebody six months ago, and I'm still coping."

"Two officers. I heard, remember?"

It wasn't that simple.

Knox pressed on. "The neighbor told me quite a bit about your Mike Seabrook."

Callie hadn't even revealed the huge hole in her heart to Sophie or Stan. Now a stranger felt entitled? *Show me yours, and I'll show you mine?*

"Mike Seabrook owned your house," she began. "He was chief before me. We were seeing each other when he died." She swallowed to finish. "I killed the guy who murdered him."

"How?" he asked.

Stunned for a second, her mouth fell open. "Damn brazen of you, don't you think?"

He tried looking empathetic, or that's how she wanted to see him . . . pretending to care. "We're both law enforcement," he said. "It ought to be easier for us to do this."

"Have *you* killed anyone?" she asked, emphasis on the word *you*.

"No, never had the chance to."

She scrubbed hands across her face. "A chance? Like it's a goddamn opportunity?"

"Just trying to figure out how you see it," he said. "You have and I haven't. It's just conversation. Maybe that's why you drink, ever thought about that?"

"Six bullets to his damn torso," she said, teeth together.

"I'm glad for you."

No, that was not something to be glad about. Mike living would've been something to be glad about. "Let's go."

"What happened to the talk?"

"I'm talked out."

Callie dug a fingernail into her belt leather. She even pondered how rude she seemed, and replayed Stan's compassionate warnings about embracing life. Sophie's pleas to reenter the human race.

Wrong guy, wrong time for a clean slate.

Knox's question raked her like sandpaper, but in a stupid, callous way he'd reached across the aisle. Trouble was, her world only had room for her issues, which meant the only way she'd communicate with this bozo was solely via the case.

"I discovered something at the Flagg house," she said as she got back in the cruiser.

His grimace faded as he got into his side of the car. "What?"

"The Flagg son. Theodore," she said louder as he shut his door. "Imagine the brother living under his sister's dead shadow all these years, his mother obsessed and living for calls from a man who wasn't his dad. Can't be a happy child."

Knox frowned, trying to follow. "You make him for a killer?"

She shook her head. "No, but I bet he knows more about Pinky than we do."

"So how do we find him?"

"Leave that one up to me," she said.

She texted Jeb and asked him to meet her at home in a half hour. Then her car popped broken shells in their departure. "I recognized the kid in the photograph before Mrs. Flagg told me he was her son. Theodore N. Flagg, otherwise known as Nolan. He's on Edisto, on spring break. He's met me and misled me, because no damn way he didn't know Pinky."

Knox gripped the dash as the vehicle rocked through a rut, leaving the scrabble to asphalt. "The one who labeled Pinky as a girl ogler?"

"One and the same," she said. "I'm already busted as law enforcement, but how about we keep your identity secret for now, in case we need a trump card later?"

He released a sigh, but not quite like his old, cranky self. "Back burner again."

"You're the one who slid in here all covert. You want to pound the beach, be my guest, but I see you as our potential ace. Nolan has no idea we're looking at his sister's case. An FBI presence would scream otherwise. Stick with your first instinct."

The agent nodded. "Yeah. But I can still dig around his background and see what kind of guy Nolan Flagg really is." He looked over at her, as if seeking approval.

"Good idea," she finally said.

A need for validation was the source of much of Knox's disgruntlement. Validation that he wasn't a bad friend, a bad agent, a bad person. He was right about checking Nolan's history, but one option still hadn't been addressed. What if Rhoades was the pervert Nolan claimed he was? Who might take issue with Rhoades if that were the case?

And what if Knox knew what Pinky was like?

Nolan acted biggity, but he chose to lay his head down at night in the chief of police's home. Few had that kind of gumption, not without a whole lot of steps to a crazy plan in between. While Callie had serious doubts as to his guilt in all this, he remained a serious person of interest.

Callie needed to be strategic in how she approached Nolan, but also how she managed Knox in the process.

She missed the day when she was the good guy, and the bad guy was cut-and-dried.

Chapter 18

JEB'S TEXT ARRIVED as Callie's cruiser crossed the causeway, around two p.m. *Give me twenty more minutes.*

No worries. She didn't expect her son to leave a gaggle of kids and say he had to head home to mom. He needed to ditch buddies. Especially Theodore *Nolan* Flagg.

Tension still filled the car after the boat landing confrontation, but they'd reached a rough sort of truce with the talk about Nolan bridging them. Knox would write up their chat with Amanda Flagg and dig into Nolan's history. She'd meet Jeb, a source Knox had no need to know about. At Windswept, she still drove away quickly after dropping off Knox to avoid seeing the agent walk up those stairs.

She understood him better, not that he was a nice guy, but as much as she hated to admit it, she was probably harder for him to deal with than the other way around. Knox wanted control that neither the FBI nor Callie could give him. She'd been drunk and then had a panic attack in front of him. She got it.

Callie dropped her keys on her credenza and nosed around the kitchen for a snack. As she closed the refrigerator, a key sounded in the lock. Jeb found her eating crab salad from King's Market on a plate with captain's wafers. She needed fuel and preferred a grown-up drink, but maybe later. Once Jeb left.

"Want some?" she asked, catching a whiff of cigarettes on his clothing. His cheeks and nose showed some sun.

"Just had a burger." But he snared a cracker anyway. "Is this how a handler checks on her operative? Keeps him on this leash to be yanked in now and then?" His tone carried warning. "Feels kinda like a parent-and-kid thing."

She smiled. "Guess they do resemble each other. Where are our two houseguests, by the way?"

"At Lissa's."

She smeared crab on another cracker. "Looney Dunes, right? How much do you know about that girl? Have you met her parents?"

Jeb reached in the fridge for a water bottle. "There's something sad about her, but she likes having the gang around. Her house has a lot of porches and speakers all over the place. Two refrigerators on the ground level."

"Where the kids can keep contraband beer and flavored vodkas," Callie finished.

Concern showed in his expression. "You asked what I knew."

They had a halfway-decent mother-son balance going on here. "I'm not investigating alcohol. I'm more about kids."

"Thought you said girls. Sort of makes it less fun, if you catch my drift." He waggled his brows in jest.

"Sit down, silly." She pulled out the chair beside her.

Losing the humor, he chose the one across from her. He seemed to need space to see her and judge.

"How'd you meet Nolan?" she asked.

His easiness indicated he liked the friend. "Met in Econ 102. He's a smart guy. Funny."

"Met his parents?"

He shrugged dramatically. "There are no parents at college, Mom. Besides, I don't measure my friends by their families. And what's your deal with Nolan?"

Callie pointed with a cracker. "Did you invite him or did he ask? Just trying to connect dots."

More guarded, he thought a second. "Yancy suggested I let him stay at our place. I said no more than two, because of your. . . . I mean, I didn't want to overwhelm you."

Mixed feelings rushed in at the reference, but she kept this about him.

"Nolan and Sammy were just the first to ask," he said.

She smothered the last cracker and offered it. He declined, so she ate it, wiped her hands, and slid the dish aside. All to buy a moment to put her words in place. "Note which girls Nolan favors," she said. "Feel free to snap some pics. You don't happen to have one of Lissa, do you?"

He slid pictures under his thumb on his phone. "You think Nolan's involved?"

"I can't tell you everything, but if I felt Nolan was dangerous, I'd say so. But watch him, please."

He let out a snort. "He's not dangerous." Then he got solemn. "Not sure I'd tow him in for you, if that's where you're going."

Like she'd involve him that far. "Why?"

Defiance darkened his eyes. "Because he trusts me."

Which made her wonder if Jeb would either watch Nolan too hard or not study him hard enough. Or warn his friend if clues sent them in that direction. "Either help me or don't, son," she said, giving him an option to bail. "You're not a detective with all the facts. You're a CI feeding me data." She went to the sink to rinse her dish. Inside she regrouped, considering how to approach Nolan some other way to keep her son from choosing sides.

She turned and backed up to the sink, drying her hands. "Nolan's last name is . . ."

"Flagg," Jeb said. "I at least know their names, Mom."

"Well, that's also the last name of the missing girl."

No pretense this time. "Oh, wow. He's her . . ."

"Brother," she said, but held up a finger. "Do not ask him about her. That's for me to handle."

His befuddlement showed.

"Just find me if he mentions it. Find a picture?" she asked to lessen his concern.

He fiddled with his phone and then handed it over, showing her a picture of several people in a house she didn't know. "The redhead is Lissa."

Callie studied the girl, resizing the pic, but it didn't tell her much. Then a text came over his phone, and he snatched it back. "I gotta go or someone will wonder." But he didn't scoot right off. "Are the body and missing girl connected? I'm not real sure what I'm doing here."

Callie's urge to explain tugged so strong, but her instincts advised otherwise. Her more sober common sense also said she shouldn't have involved him to start with. A dire need for her son's respect, forgiveness, and maybe a genuine connection between them again had pushed her past the point of reason that night.

She reached over and straightened a chair. *Need to know* had always served her well. "Never make assumptions, son. Just do what I ask and don't think deeper than I tell you."

From a cop standpoint, his role as CI would be simple, but no sane mother would agree. But if Callie told him she no longer needed him, he could interpret the move as lack of trust. That also gave her a mercurial appearance, cycling things back to whether she was stable.

"Still no texts to you if I hear something?" he asked.

"Only if urgent and then keep it vague." She pointed from her to him and back. "I prefer *this* method of communication. Go on before they miss you. Don't forget to have fun."

Jeb left with a half wave, with a wariness she wished he didn't have.

Callie listened for the door lock, highly disappointed when she didn't hear it. She followed him and turned the bolt. Prior to college, Jeb never failed in his protective mode to maintain security. He'd forgotten three times on spring break. He'd lost that edge she taught him.

Edges kept people safe.

She turned to walk back into the kitchen, when an impatient fast knock rapped on the door. "Callie? Open up, girl. We need to talk."

Callie wanted to ignore Sophie, but her cruiser was in the drive. But then this might be an opportune moment. Jeb had included Sprite as one of six girls of the right age. Callie'd be remiss not to ask a question or two. While she was friends with Sophie, the friendship wasn't all that old. Police work often crossed personal lines. Now she felt like Jeb, scrutinizing his friends.

She walked to the door, a tad hesitant how to balance friend and investigator.

Knuckles vehemently on the glass. "You and these damn locks!"

"Cool down," Callie hollered and let Sophie in, grateful Jeb had missed her on his way out.

Sophie scooted in like Chelsea Morning was her house. "Has he spoken to you yet?"

"He?"

Sophie puffed disgust. "Don't blow me off, and don't act stupid."

The little hellion. "Wait, I'm honestly not sure who *he* is."

Fit as a damn fiddle, muscles tight, Sophie planted fists on her hips. "Jeb broke it off with Sprite."

"Yes, I understand they needed space." Callie wasn't surprised, and frankly, with the kids being only eighteen and nineteen, Sophie shouldn't be either. But she chose to humor her friend, in spite of the foolishness, and lead the talk to Sprite's past so Callie could check the girl off her profile list.

"Space my ass." Sophie caught herself before giving a symbolic spat on the floor.

"Listen," Callie started, hoping to take Sophie's ire down a notch. "They're babies. Children. Can't even own a car in this state. Yes, they fell in some sense of love, but you don't want them hooking up, getting married, then deciding in a few years they made a mistake, do you?"

Sophie teared. "Why does he have to hurt her?"

"Shhh." Callie reached out and hugged Sophie to her. "Because he's a kid. And she's a kid. It could have easily been the other way around, and I hope I wouldn't hold it against you."

Her buddy nodded into Callie's shirt. Their temperaments and views on life were nothing alike, but they'd hit it off as neighbors from the day Callie arrived. Sophie might be flighty, quirky, hard to understand, but she was a solid friend. A point Brice could attest to after Sophie's monologue to him at this week's town-council meeting.

Patting Sophie on the back, Callie asked, "Care for something to drink? And I have crab salad in the fridge."

"I don't do mayo," Sophie said, withdrawing. "But I'll take a water."

One day Callie needed to ask Sophie for a list of what she did eat, because the list of the do-not-eat items greatly exceeded the former. She took out a water and laid a banana beside it. Being that fit and healthy seemed way too much trouble.

"How's your ex feel about Sprite and Jeb and their breakup?" she asked.

Pursing her mouth, Sophie peeled the banana and carefully picked the strings off with manicured nails . . . manicured herself every morning, always in the same dark neon coral. "Nick leaves the kids to me. You never asked about him before."

"Just wondering how he'd react to his daughter being heartbroken."

Sophie took a bite. "He's in Italy and in love for about the fourteenth time." She mauled the banana again.

"I can see the Italian in Sprite. She's lovely. Was she born in Italy?"

Sophie gulped. "Boston."

That surprised her. "Never knew that. That would make her born right after I moved there. When did you officially move here?"

"Almost five years ago. When Nick was put out to pasture by the NFL twelve years ago . . . wow, that sounds old . . . he decided he was too old to settle down." Her head cocked. "Thought I told you all this?"

"Nope. Not this part." Callie had already heard about the NFL ex, the give-and-take between that lifestyle and family, but nothing more. "Thought you lived out here longer than that."

A leg folded under her, as was her custom, Sophie shook her head. "Wished we had." She pointed the bottle toward Callie. "Just like you probably wish you had, too."

"Yeah, for sure." Sprite came off the list, her past easy to confirm, with a semifamous father and probably a public record of Sophie's pregnancy from being in the limelight. Those facts and a thick head of black Italian hair pretty much confirmed her lineage and lack of similarity to toddler Emma. No doubt she and Jeb would make the most beautiful babies . . . but not yet.

"Soph, can I pick your brain about something?"

One carefully plucked brow rose comically high. "Honey, I suspected you needed me. Part of why I came over." She made spiral movements with her hands, into the sky. "It's what I do . . . feel things before they happen."

Callie conceded to the performance. "You have a wide array of powers."

"No." Sophie brought hands to her chest then rolled them over, as if teaching exhales to one of her classes. "Just my natural being." She took two insanely deep breaths. "Like you seem focused on Sprite at the moment."

"Yes," Callie said. "Exactly."

One more sucking of air by Sophie. "Good. I'm ready. Now ask what you seek."

"Just a sec." Callie had to turn to the sink and put a glass in it to avoid a snicker. She needed this spice and splash of rejuvenation after the tense morning with Knox and the tears with Amanda Flagg.

Quickly collected, she returned attention to her friend, her hands still up, elbows tucked against her chest as though waiting to be filled. All they needed was a crystal ball.

Callie stood before her. "Can you name any girls that Sprite went to school with who still live on Edisto?"

Her all-seeing friend didn't expect that question. "Her age?"

"Give or take one year, yes."

Sophie's structured pose fell apart, replaced with a silly perplexity. "Oh, let's see . . . there's Lissa, poor thing. Nobody knows what's up with that girl. If she'd come to one of my classes, I'm sure I could assist her in—"

"Lissa who?" Callie asked, though she had the name.

"Pasture . . . Pasteur . . . Pasterno. It's a hard name. Something ethnic."

"You mean like Bianchi?"

"Oh please."

Callie laughed. "Okay, got it. Next?"

"Tara Phillips. Tiny and blond. Zeus dated her, but she was too cerebral for his spiritual nature. They weren't right."

Callie was surprised Sophie didn't mention their astrology signs.

"Tara lives where?"

"Whiskey Beach."

That Callie could remember. "Next?"

"Kim Smith. *Everybody* knows Kim Smith. She's beauty-queen material raised by a beauty-queen momma and a daddy who spoils her rotten. Pretty on the outside, rotten on the inside. Her only friends are South of Broad in Charleston, of course. Not sure why they bother living here. She was a year ahead of Sprite. Lasted like one week in ninth grade before her parents plopped her fancy butt into private school on the peninsula." Sophie blew out in disgust. "The girl needed her elbows rubbed against more aristocratic, nose-jobbed, genteel bitches." She leaned forward, secretive. "And have you seen her house?"

Callie played the gossiper. "Who hasn't?"

Sophie patted her collarbone with dainty hummingbird fingers. "Give me another bottle of water, and I'll fill you in even more about that one. You know what she told Sprite one day after Sprite refused to share homework answers?"

"No, what?" Callie pulled another water bottle from the fridge.

"She said she'd have her father take my house. My house! Mr. NFL Bianchi would be all over their asses."

"What other girls? Come on, because I need to get back to work."

Sophie continued with three more Jeb hadn't mentioned. "They live here?"

"Used to. Just visit on occasion now." The prattle gushed out of Sophie like a broken water main, but the three additional had moved to California, France, and Maine, so not an issue.

Callie sat back down and marveled at Sophie's memory, wondering if her ludicrous diet and yoga fanaticism had merit. "You remember everyone who has a house and the ages of their kids?"

"Most of them."

"Where they go to school?"

"Yup."

Hell, who needed real estate agents? Callie'd underestimated Sophie's reach across the island. She couldn't wait to tell Knox that an Edisto database lived right next door to her. Callie handed Sophie a kitchen pad from a drawer, and the last on the list caught her attention with its underlines and stars. "What's with Yancy and Bea Wilkerson?"

"They were homeschooled," Sophie said. "Sprite used to be their third musketeer. She thought Bea had a crush on Zeus for a while, but Yancy put an end to it when Bea got her feelings hurt over some stupid disagreement. Then when Sprite took up for her brother, Yancy and Bea closed ranks and that was that." She crushed her boobs on the table, leaning over it to speak in hushed tones. "I swear those two girls can't pee without the other one helping. It's unnatural, I say."

"Just sounds like twins to me," Callie said, but they moved to the top of her list.

Parallel to Jeb's list of six—five since Callie'd already excluded Sprite. Nice. A doable size. Callie rose and wiped up the table, moving out of the kitchen and hoping Sophie would catch the hint. Sophie could be helpful in a big way, but she also laced conversation with drama, myth, and fancy. Callie'd do an in-person study of each young lady. The day grew old.

"Unh-uh." Sophie gripped the lip of the table with both hands. "I won't budge until you tell me why you just pumped me for information. I may act like a dingbat sometimes, but I read people exceptionally well. You thought you were playing me. I cooperated. Now you owe me."

"Police business," Callie said.

"I'll ask Jeb."

"He wouldn't tell you if he knew."

"Bet he told Sprite."

"He isn't with Sprite anymore, remember?"

Sophie tossed her hair. "Still not budging. And if you walk out, I'll leave your house unlocked and let all the baddies in!"

But Callie sobered instead of playing. "Someone's life may be at stake, Soph. I don't want you caught in the middle."

Sophie's contact-blue eyes turned worried. "But you asked me about Sprite."

Callie shook her head. "Sprite's fine. Zeus is fine. You're fine. Especially if I tell you nothing. Can you accept that?"

"Not easily."

"Trust me."

Running from behind the table, Sophie hugged her friend tight. Then she drew back. "Honey, do not get yourself in trouble again. You have paid a high price for this island. Don't you dare feel you owe us anything else. Promise me you won't get involved in anything risky. Please. I don't want you to lose this job."

"I promise," Callie said, endeared by the touching display of concern, noting the strength in the woman's arms. "But what makes you think I'll lose the job?"

"Brice." So matter of fact.

"What, um, makes you worried?"

Sophie gave Callie a sideways, almost sultry, glance. "When're you going to realize my reach, honey? Hate me or love me, people still talk to me. I don't even have to ask. Scandal, buzz, or scuttlebutt, it lands on my doormat."

Not good, but Callie held back asking who and when. "Um, thought that would be bad karma."

"But I turn it into good will, for people like you." Rationalization was another of Sophie's gifts. "Right now, Brice is stirring the pot, measuring the temperature of the beach. Those for and those against you."

"What's the status today?" Callie asked, like it was an ongoing poll.

"You have the edge so far. Some want to see how you handle this body thing before they commit. They ask your officers stuff, you know."

"Who?"

"Council members, and their friends."

What was Callie supposed to do about that? She'd never run for office, and that's basically what this was . . . campaigning.

Sophie deftly slid a soft hand across Callie's cheek. "You'll fill me in about the body thing, right?"

"After all is done, absolutely. And you'll call me when you hear anything about Brice."

"Agreed." Sophie moved to the front door and bounded down the stairs, doing a tsk-tsk wave.

Callie dialed Knox. "I'm about to text you a list of names and addresses. I'm pretty sure all of them jibe with our courthouse list. Use your FBI resources and see what you can find."

That hadn't been so hard.

Then Callie called Marie at the station and told her to free up her afternoon to dig up DOBs, driver's license numbers, car owners, and alternate addresses for the girls.

In a text, Callie asked Jeb where he was. He replied, *Already? I'm at Fantasea. Why?*

She typed, *Avoid Lissa's place for the rest of the afternoon, please.* She wanted as few interruptions as possible when interviewing that girl.

Jeb: *???*

Callie: *No questions.*

Rhoades got killed hunting a girl. So she'd hunt a girl and hopefully attract the attention of the murderer. Hopefully she stayed out of Brice's way. If Sophie was worried about him, Callie had a serious need to be as well.

Callie walked back to her closet, and poured herself a shot. But as it touched her lips, she thought about Brice, and whether she should . . . to hell with it. She tossed it back, licked the lip of the glass, then hid it in the cooler. Then on her way out, she grabbed a mint from the bowl on the credenza and locked up.

Chapter 19

CALLIE'S CELL PHONE rang at almost four. "Never realized the FBI was that efficient," she said and moved toward her office, device to her ear. Right after Sophie prattled off the list of names and addresses of the girls an hour earlier, Callie'd texted them to Knox.

"We're fast, but not that fast," he replied. "Working on them, though. The girls and their parents, as well as Nolan. And you'll talk to the girls when?"

"In a couple minutes I'll drop by Looney Dunes. Lissa Pasternak intrigues me the most, then the twins, but I need for my officer to get here."

Comforted about having Sophie on guard, Callie rode a small thrill at the information gained about the teens. At the office, she checked in with staff, quizzed her officers. While Knox researched in one direction, Marie ran down driver's licenses and license tags. A sense of order. Momentum, even.

"When will you check back in with me?" Knox asked.

Five girls thanks to Sophie's community knowledge. "Can't reach more than three of these addresses tonight, but I'll call you after. Before if some tidbit jumps out at me."

"You got my number."

Dang, give the man purpose, and he turned halfway civil. "Might be a stretch, Knox, but while you check backgrounds, add Sammy Blackstone. Same age and school as Nolan." She'd heard too much conversation about Sammy and Lissa, and if Lissa was Emma, and Nolan learned Sammy dated his sister. . . . She couldn't finish that connect-the-dots, but Callie'd be intrigued for any lead that might shed light on Nolan and Rhoades.

Still too coincidental that Nolan was here, while Rhoades was here. That left the possible logic that if Rhoades suspected who Emma might be, and Nolan was dogging Rhoades's footsteps to Edisto, then Nolan knew Emma might be close, too. And if he didn't, the kid ought to be pissed that the knowledge died with the agent. Unless he was at odds with Rhoades.

"Sure," Knox said. "Name added. By the way, I'm on my way to Charleston to have two of my people start on it. I'll collect what I can by seven with the rest done in the morning. If we stumble upon anything abnormal, I'll call ASAP."

All right. Knox's stock just shot up. "Fantastic."

She hung up, on the taste of a high. Knox taking anything to the FBI was a coup. Unless he operated clandestinely, but like with Rhoades, the Bureau would find out. As big a bother as Knox was, she didn't want him to risk his career. Hers on the line was plenty.

Then her high fell. The Bureau might be in on his clandestine performance on Edisto. Maybe Pinky was onto more than she thought . . . or was not such a good guy, which could embarrass the Bureau. She appreciated Knox's speed. She prayed it helped solve Rhoades's murder. But if she was being played . . .

But then why would it matter if she was? It didn't matter if Knox unearthed data that would point them in a better direction. She was curious most about Nolan. Maternally worried about him on one hand and leery about him palling around with Jeb on the other.

Callie's gut bet on Nolan and the agent being familiar with one another, and Nolan knew Pinky came to Edisto. He could've sent the note out of pure spite if he hated Pinky's relationship to his mother. But then what?

Now that Rhoades had been killed, and with Nolan flopping at Callie's, tonight, regardless how late either of them made it back to Chelsea Morning, she'd take him aside and figure out on which side of right and wrong he walked.

Only two nights had passed since Rhoades's death. The first day she was completely adrift on the case. She crossed fingers, hoping they could make some headway on this case before the day was through.

Spring break was half gone, at least for the current young-adult crew, and since this was the crew Pinky seemed intrigued with, Callie had limited time to check them out. In person, radio, and texts, she canvassed her officers for updates, but still no one had found a single soul who remembered the agent. A retired guy with thin brown hair was too mundane a description. Whether he meant to or not, Pinky had blended into the tourist scenery so well that nobody missed him when he disappeared.

Raysor had offered to stay late on the island and come with her to interrogate the young ladies, but Callie declined his generosity. A heavyset man who carried himself like he earned his badge at age eight and arrested his first gangbanger at twelve, was not the persona Callie needed to gain trust. Instead, she opted for Officer Thomas Gage, her youngest uniform, and the one most worshipped by the college babes during this season of bikinis and beer. Plus, he could use the overtime. The poor guy lived on an island and salivated at the thought of owning his own boat; he was known to volunteer to go out with anybody who'd have him as mate.

A knuckle tapped on her office door. Thomas peeked in as Callie hung up. "Ready?" she asked.

"Always," the twenty-eight-year-old replied. "But ready for what?"

"I'll fill you in once we're in the car. Care to interview some college girls?"

His smile lit up his eyes, his easy humor such a joy. "Bummer, Chief. And to think I get time and a half for this!" He tried to walk next to her casually, his sniff anything but casual.

"Not a drop, Thomas," she said, discounting the half a shot a couple hours ago.

"Didn't say a thing, Chief."

Good cop, Callie thought. *Good guy.*

IN THE MILE and a half between the station and the first beach house, Callie explained more fully the Rhoades case. A nineteen-year-old girl might be involved. They needed to learn how long these girls had lived on the beach, where the families had originally hailed from, and if they'd seen the dead guy.

"Someone bludgeoned him on the side of the head and held him under," she said.

Thomas's eyes widened. "A girl did that?"

"We don't know who did it, girl or guy, but Pinky Rhoades showed interest in who these girls were, and somebody didn't like it. Therefore, we will as well. Maybe we can stir things up. Dole out your charm and get them to talk. We'll begin with Lissa Pasternak."

"Wow," he said. "Yeah, sure."

Not nearly as comical as its name, Looney Dunes ranked above average in appraised value for the beach town, and apparently served as party central from the way a dozen kids pretended not to slink off down Osceola Street when the patrol car pulled into the drive.

Callie knocked, and six kids answered. "Hey," she said, without identification. They knew her from Fantasea's dustup the day before. After all, she was *Jeb's mom*. "Lissa home?"

Though of age to fight wars, buy cigarettes, and vote, they glanced blankly at each other as if they were twelve-year-olds in a Nickelodeon comedy spoof.

Thomas pointed at the three guys. "We can discount you, you, and you. And I'd say the other three of you as well," he said over the half a dozen heads at the girl who hugged the archway behind them. "Hey, Lissa. Can we have a word? Out here, in there, around the pool, your choice."

The kids parted like the Red Sea, eddying past Lissa into the kitchen.

"Hey, honey." Callie stepped into the house. "I'm Chief Callie Morgan."

"My dad isn't here," the girl said and tucked hair behind her ear. Her strawberry-red tresses fell almost to her waistline, her freckles attractive against the backdrop of a milk-smooth complexion. Like the freckles on Emma's age-enhanced photo.

Nolan's talk of a loose reputation had planted a different image in Callie's head. This child was beautiful.

When Lissa wouldn't choose a place to talk, Callie led her into the living room to their left and closed the French doors. Their presence sent everyone else to the back and out of sight, but Callie still had to be quick, because the nosiest would soon filter back to eavesdrop.

Decorated in adult furnishings, tasteful in beiges and maroon, the house held no party smells. No cigarettes, beer, pot. Some type of gentle berry fragrance dominated. Whether that was to hide the rowdy scents or whether Lissa and her folks managed the kids well was yet to be seen.

Seated on the far end of a love seat beside the recliner that Lissa gravitated to, Callie kept a soft voice. Thomas assumed the cushion nearest Lissa. An eagerness came easy with his youth, and Lissa tended to make more eye contact with him.

These interviews required creative handling. They'd check out the most questionable girls first in an attempt to stay ahead of the smartphones. For a second, Callie wished they'd come in plain clothes. Then in another second she admitted to herself that everyone on Edisto Beach already knew who they were.

Callie eased back and turned it over to Thomas.

"Tell me about yourself, Lissa," he asked. "Where were you born? When did you move here? For instance, I was born in Columbia and moved after high school. I love it. Don't think we've met, so you don't drag Palmetto Boulevard, I take it."

That drew a tiny grin from Lissa. "No, we've never met. I've seen you around, though. We all have."

Thomas flashed his charm and silently waited.

"Well," she started slowly. "I was born in Chicago."

"In what, 1999 or were you a 2000 baby? Always considered it cool to have *00* in a birth date."

"'98," she said.

"Oh, my bad," he replied. "So how'd a Yankee like you wind up here in paradise?"

"We came here when I was a kid. Twelve. Daddy's in restaurant supply sales. Hated the cold weather, he said. Momma came with us, but she hated being so far from her parents. Momma and Daddy divorced when I was in high school, and she moved back up there. I didn't want to leave."

"Sorry to hear that," Thomas said. "Guess you have grandparents back up north?"

"Yeah." She settled into the conversation. "But I do like Christmas up there better with the snow. My granny still makes me build a snowman in front of her picture window, especially now that she can't get around that well. She keeps an album."

"May we see it?" Callie asked.

"No, ma'am. That's Granny's. It's in Chicago. I'm sure I'll inherit it one day." The girl had brightened with Thomas. "Nothing against Edisto, but December's boring."

"I hear that," he said.

Lissa sounded believable, but Emma Flagg might have no clue she was abducted, either, which is what made these interviews difficult. It wasn't necessarily what the person believed, but how it sounded to Callie in light of the clues she gathered. A slow, sluggish collection of data.

They continued the chatter while Callie's attention split to also roam around the room. A few family pictures hung on the wall in a corner, over a credenza decorated with smaller frames and shells probably gathered nearby. All the pictures too small to see from across the room. So without comment, she rose, Thomas and Lissa occupied.

Not everyone presented baby pictures, but there, framed in pewter, was an early picture of Lissa and a couple who had to be her parents. Mother and daughter complexions were identical, pale, hair in flaming ringlets. The child no more than three.

Callie laid the picture flat on the table, used her fingers to block the hair and leave only the face. Baby Lissa grinned gently, much like now, her teeth not exposed. Those red lashes alone could rule her out as blond Emma.

"May I ask why you're here?" Lissa asked. "I'm not in trouble for a party, am I?"

Callie set the picture back up and returned to stand near the sofa. "No, we're checking with girls around your age about the guy who just died. Some people said—"

Both French doors opened. "What's going on? You all right, Lis?" Sammy Blackstone took a wide stance, shoulders back, braced for a challenge. A totally different child from the other day at Chelsea Morning. "Her dad's not present," he said, assuming the role of protector. "Is this even legal?"

"It is if she's eighteen," Thomas said and rose to meet the boy's gaze.

"Why don't you take him outside, Officer Gage. A couple more questions here, then I'll be right out."

As Thomas advanced, Sammy tried to sidestep him. "I'll stay here, if you don't mind."

"Just so happens we do mind," Thomas said, and laid a hand on Sammy's arm. "She's not in trouble. You aren't either unless you give us a hard time."

With a lingering glance back at his girl, Sammy left, Thomas behind him. Closing the glass doors, he escorted Sammy toward the front porch.

Lissa wedged both hands between her thighs, a bounce in her knees, more nervous.

Callie slid over to where Thomas had been. "It's okay, hon."

A thump sounded on the porch outside. Callie peered out the window to see Thomas standing before Sammy, who'd flopped into a rattan chair and hit the outside wall in his effort to show disgust.

She returned to Lissa. "I understand the man we found dead day before yesterday liked the girls. Is that right?"

Lissa gave a shrug, which made her long hair slide over a shoulder. "Someone pointed him out to me, and then I saw him the next day in a green car."

Callie held out Pinky's driver's license picture. "Is this the man?"

"Yes, but I didn't see anything wrong with him."

Confirmation that Pinky had driven himself at least one day. But with the car in Charleston, he came to Edisto by other means the day he died. Taxis were pricey this far out. Unless Amanda Flagg covered the cost . . . or drove him.

Lissa's knees quit with the bounces. "Feels weird to have seen him alive one day and hear he died the next. He reminded me of my grandfather back in Chicago. He runs a bar."

No help there.

Both turned at the raised voices on the porch, but Callie saw Thomas had things under control. "How well do you know Sammy?" Callie asked.

"We met in Lit class this semester. He's a good guy," she said, her voice rising, her hands freed and now massaging the recliner's arms.

"Doesn't answer my question. What makes him a good guy?" Callie asked. "What kind of childhood did he have? Where's he from?"

"He's a foster kid on scholarship," the girl said defensively. "He caught a break in high school when a guidance counselor got him money to get into C of C. Just because he doesn't have money doesn't mean he can't hang out with us, you know."

Finally, some fire to go with that hair. "Sounds like he's found a way to manage the hand he was dealt. Good for him. What landed him in foster care?"

Anguish crossed Lissa's face, and her hands went back into her lap as she withdrew into her shyness.

"Lissa?" Callie asked.

"He wouldn't want people to know, Chief Morgan."

"I understand, but I'm not just chief. I'm a mom, too. Jeb's mom." Hopefully that would help.

Lissa leaned closer and whispered, "As a kid, he was raped by his dad who went to jail for it, and after that his mom dumped him."

Jesus, no wonder the boy acted reserved . . . except for protecting his puppy love. Callie at first appreciated Jeb for inviting Sammy to stay with them. Then she wondered how deep his flaws ran from such a rough childhood. Kids who endured hardships often carried scars into adulthood.

"Did Sammy ever meet the guy who died?" Callie wished Thomas were here as a witness to this part. "Are you sure the man never approached you?"

"No, ma'am, and I see where you're going with this. Sammy's a good guy. I never met your man, and even if I had, Sammy wouldn't have hurt him. Shouted, maybe, but never kill him, and even then it would just be to protect me."

Even then, like a justified kill. But she was a kid. Callie stood. "Nobody blames Sammy. Sorry if I misled you. We're going to let you kids get back to your spring break. I appreciate it."

As she exited, Callie nodded to Thomas to follow, but Thomas had moved to the porch railing, his attention on the taillights of a car at the intersection two houses down. She moved closer to him. "What is it?"

"Brice LeGrand," he said.

Callie stared hard at the strange car, unable to see a tag. "You sure?"

"Oh yeah." The car turned left and disappeared before Thomas met Callie's gaze. "Did he seriously use someone else's car to follow us?"

Callie rolled her eyes. "Not like he caught us doing anything but our job. Let's go." She mentally listed who'd known she came here . . . Marie, Knox, Raysor . . . frankly, anyone who saw their car turn in to Looney Dunes.

She turned and shot a smile to Sammy to mend fences. "See you at the house. Y'all got sufficient to eat or do I need to make a grocery run?"

"We're fine, I think," the boy said slow, some confusion in his eyes.

Kids began to regroup and most hung around the ground level within steps of the storage room that Jeb said held the two refrigerators for refreshments. As she and Thomas opened their car doors, the group scrutinized the two cops, in unity as a force not happy with uniforms on their turf. Callie thought she saw Yancy sharing a cigarette with a boy Raysor scolded during the street fuss the day before.

Callie glanced back up to the porch, twelve feet off the ground like all the other beach houses. Sammy watched them, an arm around Lissa. While she had no reason in the world to consider him the murderer, Lissa did make her wonder something new. Would any of these testosterone-infused guys take a middle-aged gent way too seriously when he watched their girl . . . and pursue things a bit too far?

A simple loss of temper over a girl.

Most ironic to happen to a man who'd dedicated his life to finding and protecting one.

Chapter 20

MOST TOWNS SPED up at five in the afternoon, but this was Edisto Beach. Other than those in its tiny government, everyone else barely watched the clock. It was more about where the sun was than when people got home. It was after six, and getting off wasn't in Callie's cards quite yet.

She headed toward the end of the beach to the next residence, while Knox ran backgrounds on the nineteen-year-old girls, Nolan, and Sammy.

"Who next?" Thomas asked, and laughed once before his boss could answer. "This is great for my image. No longer just the young ticket cop on Palmetto Boulevard."

Callie couldn't stifle her chuckle.

"Community outreach," he said with a grin.

"Yeah, we'll call it that."

They rounded the southern curve and headed north, St. Helena Sound on their left. Regardless of the address number on this stretch of pavement, the waterfront houses ran pricey. A forty-year-old two-thousand-square-foot home started at three-quarters of a million. Drop twenty years and run a boardwalk from the house across the dunes to the water, and the price topped seven figures.

Marie said Mr. Smith worked off island and probably wouldn't be home yet, so Callie was being strategic in visiting Kim Smith now. Easier to speak to a girl she'd never seen before without the presence of what sounded like a strong, wealthy father figure. On the other hand, Callie hoped to catch the twins' parents at home.

The Smith place appeared ahead. Not ostentatious enough to overwhelm the street, but peacocky enough to announce this was a residence, not a rental, and don't stop unless invited.

A layered granite fountain with a dolphin statue posed mid-driveway. Both Confederate and Carolina jasmine roped up latticework to the first-floor porch, where the tangled vines guarded rocking chairs. The stucco home attempted homey but couldn't disguise its wealth and four thousand square feet. Nowhere else on Edisto did a wrought-iron fence wrap the property lines. An ocean-view landscape with pool further dictated the social line between the welcome and the not.

Thomas whistled low as they climbed stairs to creamy-white doors. "Should we call Kim's dad first? I mean, he has a lot of clout. Here and in Charleston."

Callie scowled. "Officer Gage, money and politics are not a consideration when we question victims, suspects, or witnesses. And she's over eighteen. Even if she weren't, she's not in custody or arrested so we're clear without the parent. Ring the doorbell."

"Yes, ma'am." He drew his arms close to his side, as if afraid to touch anything.

"Good gracious," she said. "Do I seriously need to take this one?"

"Sorta wish you would," he replied, his age overriding his training and three years' experience.

Sophie spoke of the high-handedness of this Smith child, and the wealth of the parents. Too good for the mainstream population, she said. But Callie'd gone up against a few of the well-to-do in Boston who traveled in way bigger circles than this.

She pressed the button and shook her head at the naïveté of this young man who'd saved her life six months ago . . . twice. "Follow my lead. Speak when you have a concern. They breathe the same oxygen we do, Thomas."

A petite girl with ashy brown hair answered, her age about right, a thin sarong covering a bikini that cost more than the average business suit, smaller than anything Callie ever had the guts to wear.

"Yes?" The girl possessed self-assurance in spades.

"Kim Smith?" Callie studied this girl hard for signs of Emma. Though brown haired, Miss Smith could fit the description. No freckles, but kids often outgrew those. At this rate, half the girls of a similar age *could be* Emma.

"Who's asking?" answered the young lady, totally unfazed by two uniforms on her porch, not concerned enough to bother reading the name tags over the pockets and Edisto Beach patches on the sleeves.

Callie held out her hand. "Chief Callie Morgan and Officer Thomas Gage. Glad to meet you."

The girl regarded the hand, opted not to engage, and lifted her gaze across Thomas. There it was. The slightest of grins.

"Mind if we come in?" Callie asked.

The girl debated a second, then moved back to allow them in. "We see people in the living room," she said, and waved toward the end of the hall. "Mom?" she said louder. "The police are here." As if cops were a weekly occurrence, like the yard man.

Kim turned to leave the hallway, in obvious assumption such nuisances would be handed off to her mother. Until Callie spoke. "Your mother is welcome to sit in, but we're here to see you, Kim."

The girl's mouth formed an O, then a delayed, "Well, then come this way."

A signed, numbered Anne Worsham Richardson egret greeted them behind the scroll-armed, tufted sofa, the frame as valuable as the print. Callie's mother had actually met the artist at an event. But more breathtaking, viewed through five double windows, stretched the sound, a perfect vantage to enjoy pods of dolphin. Ergo the house's name, Dolphin Central.

Where did Smith get his money? Or Mrs. Smith? A million-dollar ransom could take someone pretty far in life, establish a great basis for the future.

Callie took the sofa, surveying the girl's movements, trying to imagine her blond and snaggletoothed. If this was indeed Emma, she hadn't suffered materially, that's for sure.

"Kim," she started, preferring to snare a few answers before a mom entered. "I assume you heard about the man we found in Big Bay Creek."

Thomas sat beside Callie, away from Kim, who strategically enthroned herself in a Queen Anne upholstered chair. "I heard," she said. "Not sure what that has to do with me."

Callie nodded, and Thomas handed over the picture of Pinky. "Have you seen him?" she asked. "Did he approach you? Ask personal questions? Act inappropriately?"

The prissy scowl could've been cute if not for the arrogance. "First, I don't hang out much on the general beach, and trust me, if he'd come on to me, you'd have already received a complaint."

"But have you seen him, even from a distance? Talking to anyone?" Thomas asked.

"Well, I might've seen him with a boy my age two or three days ago. Not from here, though. Neither of them seemed happy."

A new witness. Callie scooted closer to the edge of her seat. "Kim—"

Mrs. Smith entered, a thin, nervous type, hesitant as she approached, a complete beta to Kim's alpha, and she had a phone in her hand. "Hello, I'm Natalie Smith. What's this about a man?"

"Just a moment." Callie held up her finger before reaching for her own phone. A mom like this was a handicap to an investigator. Callie sure would be if someone questioned Jeb. She prayed Marie hadn't gone home, and texted quickly for Marie to send Jeb's, Nolan's, and Sammy's driver's license photos to her phone. Cops used DL pics like mug shots.

Dramatically, Kim crumpled her nose as if experiencing a rancid smell. "You know who they're talking about, Mama. The body Sprite Bianchi found two days ago. With some boy."

"That yoga woman?" she asked absentmindedly as she hit one button on her phone, someone on speed dial.

"Her daughter," Callie said. "And my son, but that's not the point."

Natalie held the phone to her ear. "Oh, my, I hope he's not in trouble. . . . Hello? Greg?"

Out of courtesy, Callie hushed.

Natalie turned her back, as if that kept a person from hearing. "Yes, honey, the police are here speaking with Kim. Did you know?"

Everyone waited for the call to end. Kim scanned her pedicure. Uncomfortably out of place, Thomas rubbed his knees.

The mother nodded. "See you later tonight. Drive careful." And she hung up.

"Everything okay?" Callie asked, almost expecting Natalie to show them out.

Instead, with a cultivated grace, their hostess held a palm up. "All's good. Just had to let Greg know you were here."

"I understand." Unsure who Greg was, Callie could only assume him to be Mr. Smith. Guess they expected her to recognize the name.

Caring more about who Kim witnessed with Pinky, Callie continued. "Some of the kids here for spring break thought they'd seen this man, too." She held out the driver's license picture again.

Even Kim's slight shrug came across as highbrow. "No. Never met him. Saw him, like I said."

"Oh my goodness," Natalie exclaimed. "Is Kim in danger? Maybe I ought to call Greg back—"

"Ma'am," Thomas said, finally. "We just need to learn the man's whereabouts before he died, so we can put pieces together."

"Yes, ma'am." Callie gave a slight tip of her chin. "We are ever vigilant about irregularities in an effort to protect Edisto's citizens. We care about our residents."

The mother stood behind a chair instead of front and center like Kim, and the lack of physical resemblance between daughter and mother was equally apparent. Finding displayed photographs seemed odd in this type of home. One would expect a family portrait—oil painting maybe. "I'm fairly new to Edisto, Kim. You born here or did you relocate like everyone else?"

The child flipped her bangs back from her eyes. "I'm Charleston born, Chief Morgan. As were my parents. Can't say we're *Mayflower* connected, but the lineage has some considerable length and means to it."

Gracious, could this girl be any further up her own butt?

And no correction by the mom?

Then Kim released a twitter of a laugh and recrossed her bare legs, toes popping her flip-flops on her feet. "Isn't that what you wanted to hear? Something so pretentious it stank? What else do you need? This is rather entertaining."

The doorbell rang, and Natalie hopped up, expectant.

Callie began again. "At what age did you move to the beach?"

Fast and heavy steps sounded up the entryway. Brice rounded the corner. "You don't have to answer that, Kim," he said, Natalie behind him.

Thomas sat shell-shocked, but Callie stood, tired of this man's radar on her. He lived just three blocks over, but she more suspected that he'd watched from much closer. "You've interrupted us, Mr. LeGrand."

"Damn right, Chief. A man dies right up the creek here." He actually pointed in the right direction. "And you interrogate young girls. What's the logic in that?"

Thomas rose in support of his boss. "It's not interrogating. It's—"

"Shut up, Thomas," Brice ordered with an annoyed sigh.

Callie navigated around the coffee table and approached her antagonist. "That's uncalled for, Brice. We're on duty."

His cheeks held a broken-vein blush, akin to the alcoholic color of his nose. "Greg Smith called me to come over and keep an eye on his family for him." One hand fisted on his ample waist, he reached the other over to pat Natalie. "I think it's time you left, isn't that right, Mrs. Smith? How could anyone think you had something to do with a murder?"

"What?" Both hands covered Natalie's mouth. "They think we could be involved? Dear Lord, Greg will be beside himself."

"The reason he called me." Brice swept himself aside to open room for their exit. "Now I . . . we . . . think Edisto PD should get off this property."

Callie went to Natalie, and she shrank back half a step. "Mrs. Smith, shoo us away and we wonder why. We'll only come back later."

Natalie looked at Callie, then at Brice, conflicted.

The phone vibrated in Callie's pocket. She tapped her screen twice and held up a photo of Nolan. "Kim, is this the boy you saw speaking to the man? Look close."

Kim shook her head. "Never saw him before."

Callie frowned, disappointed. She returned to her screen and flipped to the next picture, Jeb. "What about this one?"

"Don't know him, but he's cute."

Then Callie showed the last.

With a limp wrist, the girl pointed at the phone. "Yes. That's him. I was driving by the marina when I saw them. No idea who he is."

Brice cut the conversation. "We're done here."

Natalie hugged his side. "I have to agree."

Seething, Callie looked to the mother, frustrated at the ignorance. "Mrs. Smith. It's important we talk to Kim."

"I said enough!" the mother screeched in a Jekyll-and-Hyde release, aquiver with the effort. "We do not want to be involved."

Callie let the shouted words fade. "Ma'am, we'll decide who's involved."

Gasping like a bass, Natalie moved farther behind Brice.

"I think that means she wants you gone, Chief Morgan," he said.

Callie flicked out a business card and handed it to Kim. "Call me if you think of anything." Then she turned and exited, with a "Thank you for seeing us."

Outside, clomping down the stairs, Thomas whispered. "Not cool, Chief. You gonna let him get away with that?"

"No, it wasn't cool, but we have to roll with some things," Callie said as they reached the drive. "Radio Marie. If she's still in, see if she can help you with the same kind of background on Kim that we got on Lissa. We're headed—"

"Hey," Brice hollered from behind them.

"Uh-oh," Thomas moaned before looking around.

Callie just turned.

Brice charged like a bull, feet pounding the drive. "Who the hell do you think you are? We never had this kind of trouble from Seabrook, or any of the chiefs before him. Never would they approach a respectable family like the Smiths and frighten them with baseless accusations. I'm calling the Pasternaks to see what harm you caused there."

"Yes, Brice," she said. "We saw you."

No telling how long he'd been tailing her, even before this case. Pinky Rhoades's demise no doubt accelerated Brice's goal to rid Edisto of Callie Jean Morgan. She half expected to find him on her porch in the mornings, though he'd already been known to sit at the PD and await her arrival.

He pounded the air with a fist, a total cliché of braggadocio. "Thank God I live around the curve and could offer Greg assistance. I swear, it's like you hunt for trouble, woman!"

Callie leaned a hip against her car, refusing to defend herself to this paramecium brain, and she wouldn't succumb to this verbal beating in Thomas's presence. "You prefer I do more normal police work? Be low-key. Write tickets and such?"

He took sunglasses out of his pocket and slid them on. "Exactly."

Brice's vehicle, or, rather, the one he'd borrowed for the day, paralleled the edge of the road. Callie donned her own dark glasses, gave the car a quick gander, and motioned to Thomas. "Got your book with you?"

After a pat to his pocket, Thomas extracted a pad. "Yes, Chief."

"What is this?" Brice growled as Thomas stopped behind the councilman's loaner and flipped page. "What the hell is this?" He reached for the officer's arm.

"Hold on, Thomas," she said. "Give Mr. LeGrand and me a moment."

"Yes, ma'am." He seemed all too eager to move out of earshot.

Callie placed herself between the two men, her back to Thomas. "The tag on this vehicle is expired, but I imagine you're used to dodging tickets, so in honor of the old guard, I'll let you off."

Brice closed the distance even more. Heat drifted off him, and he stank of old drink, as if his pores had long given up being clean. "You wouldn't have this job if you weren't a bitch. Or a Cantrell."

She stared at the councilman, making him wait to see if he'd get a rise out of her. Her blood boiled, but it was broad daylight, and surely somebody watched, at a minimum Thomas, who needed employment and couldn't afford to choose sides. So she leaned into Brice's shadow. "What can we do to end this, whatever it is, Mr. LeGrand? Seriously. Our love for this beach ought to unite us. Surely we can agree on what I want for the police force and what you wish it to provide Edisto."

Some of the hardest damn words she'd spoken in a long while.

But he remained only a foot from her, his belly the closest part. Hiding any reaction, she tried not to judge the disgustingness from his bulging nose to his wheeze, and the only way to do it was stare him in the eye.

"I want you gone," he said in a breathy release.

"I've done nothing to you," she replied, his presence an insult to her senses.

"Your parents, your gender, your need to be right. Add to that your way of bringing crime to this beach and killing Mike Seabrook. With you gone, we might return to normal."

She could do nothing about the first three, but damn him for laying Seabrook's murder on her. She did plenty of that to herself, but somehow it was easier to deny and get perspective when someone else accused her. "What exactly is normal, Brice?"

He weighed twice what she did, and he squared his shoulders, every ounce of himself playing the threat. "Pre-Cantrell. Pre-crime. Pre-bodies. Pre-anything before you arrived."

She was born a Cantrell. Her parents had forgiven each other's affairs, and for reasons that completely repulsed Callie, Beverly Cantrell and Brice LeGrand had been an item thirty-plus years ago. Thank God Callie was forty.

"Quit the force," he said in a low bass.

"Can't do that." She hated she hadn't the voice to match his.

"I will break you, then." He backed away with the sleaziest of smiles. "Agreed?" he said louder, for any possible ears. The councilman in cooperation with the chief.

With no expectation of an answer, he went to his car and left.

The dominance left Callie feeling dressed down, naked even.

"Chief?" Thomas appeared at her elbow. "He threaten you?"

She watched the expired tag disappear, headed toward Docksite Road. "Don't worry about it, Thomas."

"I got your back. We all do."

Good guy. Good cop. But she didn't want his loyalties to cost him a career.

"Next interview. It's late. Up for the overtime or need to go home?" she asked.

Thomas wiggled his brow. "Sure. Where to next?"

They headed back toward Jungle Shores.

Thomas watched his side mirror. "Who did Kim recognize back there?"

"Let me hold on to that piece of intel for a while longer, if you don't mind," she said.

"Sure, no problem." He cocked his head toward his mirror. "He's following us, you know."

Callie checked her own. "It's what he does. He has no one to impress at our next stop, so maybe he'll leave when he's not needed."

"Usually it's for other reasons, but right now I'm awfully glad I'm not you," her officer said.

"Yeah," she said. "I get that a lot."

Three nights ago, the council meeting had been juvenile, stupid banter. But the warnings to her from across the community now had substance to them.

She could say she didn't care, but with her every step being watched, she was sure to miss one. And Brice wanted to be there to record it as well as any damage done.

Chapter 21

CALLIE ROLLED INTO Yancy and Bea's gravel drive just a quarter past seven, unsettled by the uneasiness that arrived with sundown, that déjà vu time from the fire in Boston. Her head swam with more important stuff today. She again noted only the one car under the house . . . and Brice parking his vehicle across the silt road, his window down, staring.

God, he aimed to follow her every step.

"Hold on a sec," she told Thomas, and texted Jeb. *At the Wilkerson place now. Keep kids away. Where are you?*

"Still hounding your son, huh?" Thomas grinned.

"Yeah," she said. "One day you'll be the same or worse." But hopefully not because he made his child his CI on a case.

I see you, Mom, came back the text. *I'm home with Nolan.*

Sammy? Callie replied.

Lissa's.

Others? She couldn't control them all, and she didn't want to roll by every house, but she didn't want a knock on the twins' door during her interview.

Party at Crab Walk. Gtg

Gtg? Going to . . . Get the . . . Whatever.

Hopefully the twins hadn't gravitated with the crowd from Lissa's to Crab Walk.

"Let's go," she said to Thomas and exited the patrol car. But as her sidekick headed to the stairs, Callie made a path to Brice. The Chevy door opened.

She stopped, gripped the white door, and spoke as if they were old acquaintances. "Don't think about it, my friend."

The skin whitened around his lips. "I'm not your friend."

"Wow, news flash."

As he pivoted to exit, she threw his balance off with a subtle shove of the door. "Please, don't." He'd already interrupted the Kim Smith interview, arrived too late to sabotage Lissa's. With his presence here, the Wilkersons could refuse to cooperate altogether.

"Don't push me, Morgan. The least I can do is be there for these girls so you don't scare them, like you did Kim Smith."

"Brice." Callie held the door stationary to keep him in. "Somehow I think Miss Smith isn't harmed in the least. And who says there isn't a parent in there?"

"They might be naïve to police ways."

"Please. These girls *are* adults, but most of all, you're interfering with a police investigation." She had no desire to arrest him for that, because the community would explode choosing sides, but she couldn't have him popping up everywhere she went. He'd undermine all she and Knox tried to do.

"Rumor has it you're back on the bottle," he said.

"Says the walking distillery." She instinctively looked over at Thomas as she wondered where Brice got his gossip. *No. Good guy. Good cop.*

Brice yanked his door shut and pointed through the open window. "Mark your calendar, Chief. Watch your back."

Callie straightened, hands on hips, almost playing the discrimination card. Instead, she backed up and waved the dust from her eyes as he sped off.

The same cliché Janet used the day Knox checked in. Sophie'd used a version of it. How many people whispered to Brice in hope for favors? Any business owner, any town worker, any native needing a permit, or any tourist with bucks.

One thing, though. She'd have to find a liquor store off the island.

"I could write him a serious ticket for that." Thomas had wandered over as backup . . . or out of curiosity. He enjoyed his assignment, but if Kim Smith's dad, or rather his reputation, had intimidated him so easily, how readily would he give up information to Brice?

The cooler hidden in her closet called to her so damn loud right now.

Phone muted with all the activity, she checked it out of habit. She found a text from Knox. *We meeting tonight?*

She replied, *Still interviewing but we need to talk.*

He answered, *Need me there?*

Not yet, she typed. Then partly because of Brice and partly because Knox preferred being proactive, she typed, *Sorry.*

Phone tucked away, she pointed to the house to get her officer back on track. "Let's question these girls then you're done for the day. And tell me something."

"Sure, Chief."

"What does *Gtg* mean in a text?"

"Got to go." He chuckled and took the stairs.

More stairs. A dozen or more climbs like this per day, and she wouldn't have to jog. Now, however, they served as an outlet to dispel her anger for Brice's supercilious gall.

Yancy awaited them at the top. Bea peered out of a window from inside, backlit in the kitchen. Guess they weren't quite the party-hoppers the rest were.

Doing her habitual Emma comparison, Callie couldn't tell yet about either girl.

Yancy's blue hair matched the jeans with holes across the thighs and knees. Barefooted, wearing a vintage Eagles tour tee from their greatest-hits album, she watched with detachment as her guests reached the landing.

For a quick second, Callie wished she had that shirt.

"Hey." Callie held out her hand and sought some sign as to how Yancy felt about another session with Jeb's mom, *the cop*. She'd not been cordial after the teenage brouhaha in the road with Sophie but hadn't stirred a fuss, either. Yancy accepted the outstretched hand, her grip firmer than Callie expected from someone her age.

Since last they'd met, Yancy'd strung beads in two thin tresses that hung over one ear. The lone feather on the end matched the colors in her tee. "We must be high on your list," she said. "Saw you at Lissa's. Want a coke? Afraid we're all out of beer."

"Shame," Callie said. "Officer Thomas here could've used one, too."

The girl stopped midpivot and eyed the other uniform. "Hey, Officer Thomas."

"Hey yourself," he replied, humor in his eyes.

Nope, the girls didn't need Brice for protection. Yancy would've stopped him at the threshold herself. Bea slinked in from the corner and gave a wilted wave, also in jeans but dressed softer in a powder-blue peasant top, two navy braided strings dangling down from the neck to match the embroidery. Blue flip-flops. Callie wondered how she'd react if she had to wear red.

"Can we talk to you girls?" Callie asked.

"Sure." Yancy led them to the living room. She took what must have been her chair, a worn cloth recliner. Bea took a leather one across the room. Callie had almost expected them to sit on the sofa holding hands to channel their thoughts into collective answers.

Someone had burned popcorn not long ago, and Callie appreciated her windbreaker, since the room held a coolness from windows opened to get rid of the smell. Some cigarette odor. Several mostly empty plastic cups on the coffee table. Three chip bags, one empty, the other two torn wide. Soon to be stale.

In the midst of the street quarrel yesterday, Callie'd been impressed at the girls' unity, surprised at their differences. Twins were supposed to parallel. Seated in the Wilkerson house, Callie faced one with blue hair and one with soft-brown hair. One dyed and the other light enough to have been blond as a tyke.

But like any young girl, they enjoyed Thomas's company. Callie nodded for him to proceed.

"Did you ever see or meet the man we found in the creek?" he asked.

Callie handed Bea the photo of Pinky just to see if she'd make the first comment, but instead she handed it straight to her sister. Yancy shook her head. "Nope." Bea then did the same.

Okay, so they didn't have to be touching.

"What are the kids saying about him?" Thomas asked.

Yancy twisted her mouth with a half squint of her eyes. "That he was too weird in how he watched the girls. That it was pitiful how an old man drooled over young babes. I think they made too big a deal about it. We're on a beach. We wear short, tight, thin clothing over bodies old people wish they still had." She raised both hands in a *whatever* response. "It is what it is."

Überpragmatic child.

"How old are you two?" Thomas asked. "Are you twins or just close in age?"

Yancy was taller, sturdier. Bea average in structure. Though sisters, they weren't obviously akin in appearance. Callie wished she could dress the two identically, remove Yancy's makeup, and throw blond wigs on them. Force out the similarities.

"Fraternal twins," Yancy said. "Nineteen. We're Librans." She slipped a chain from inside her shirt, and Bea did the same to show matching opal birthstone necklaces.

Callie nodded. "One of the college kids thinks this guy might have had motive to do more than stare."

Yancy pooh-poohed with a loose hand wave as she drew one leg up near her bottom. "Nolan. He likes to exaggerate." The girl lounged, comfy even with cops in her house. "If there hadn't been a body, I don't think anyone would have cared."

"How long have you known Nolan?" Callie asked.

Thomas smiled over at Bea, who grinned and returned attention to her sister.

"We met in school," Yancy said. "Last year. He's a junior, I think. I . . . we didn't go until January. Freshmen. Didn't want to enroll until I had a better idea of a major, you know? These days bachelor degrees aren't worth much, and I wanted to get this right."

Callie turned to the quiet half. "What about you, Bea?"

"I started school with Yancy." She played with the long braid draped over her shoulder.

"No, I mean about Nolan. Do you think he's just seeking attention?"

"Maybe." Again a look to Yancy for reassurance. "I mean, he's funny, and he likes it when we laugh and joke back."

Doubtful that Bea joked that much. Her reserved behavior at the street scene. Her lack of makeup, the muted colors in her simple jeans and peasant top. The lesser twin didn't like drawing attention, but her natural appearance made her darling. However, Callie knew better than to underestimate the quiet ones after a situation in Boston . . . when the gentler of two brothers almost took her head off with a baseball bat.

Emma could be a girl who acted out or a girl who preferred obscurity, and if she were kidnapped into a decent environment, she could be a typical normal teen . . . if there was such a thing. One sister hid behind her hair. The other behind her plainness.

Neat house, simple lifestyle, the television wasn't even on. Better comportment than Kim Smith. Frankly, they put on a good show, but from the hairs on Callie's neck, she sensed an undercurrent of secrets beneath the manners. "What do y'all think of Sammy Blackstone?"

Yancy chuckled. "He's hot on Lissa, that's for sure."

"How well do you know him?"

"Never met him before he came to the beach this year." Yancy turned to Bea. "Am I right?"

"Lissa met him last semester," the shyer sister replied. "Remember?"

Yancy shook her head in rapid jerks. "No, I don't, but Lissa talks more to you, Bea. I think I intimidate her."

"Why would she feel that way?" Bea quipped, and they both giggled.

Twin humor.

"So," Thomas said, as though recalling he had an interview to conduct. "Tell us about yourselves. When did you move here? For instance, I was born in Columbia and moved here after high school. I love it. I've seen you around town, but don't believe you drag Palmetto Boulevard much."

Amused at Thomas's repeat of his intro to Lissa, Callie let him go with it.

Surprisingly, Bea responded first. "We're both adopted."

Thomas gave Bea a funny look at the blunt remark.

Callie gave her no reaction, however, though bells rang in her head. Adoption? Not expected at all.

"Charleston was our home," she continued, louder, like she wanted a rise out of somebody. "And Edisto has been since we were in middle school. We were *damn lucky* our parents kept us together, and we don't care *who* our biological parents were . . . are. But this has nothing to do with a dead man. You're snooping about the party again, and we already told you there is *no more beer left.*"

She jumped up and escaped to the kitchen, the frown so foreign on her face.

Thomas pursed his lips. Yancy's gaze followed her sister. "Bea?"

The sister didn't answer.

Yancy turned back to the cop duo. "Wow, not many people can make her go off like that. Does her good to escape her skin every once in a while, though. She's good."

Rather mature remark from someone not yet twenty.

Thomas seemed almost sympathetic. "Doesn't take much, does it?"

Bea suddenly reappeared. "I want to go out on the boat."

"Not now, Sweet Bea," Yancy said, like she spoke to someone much younger. "It's dark. We've talked about this."

"Whatever." Bea stomped back into the kitchen.

"She goes out and watches the dolphins," Yancy said softly, once she thought Bea couldn't hear. "One of the few activities she does without me. She reads the tide and predicts when they'll be in the sound for breeding."

Callie could name a dozen people on the island like that. St. Helena Sound, especially at dusk or dawn, when eight or ten boats would search for dolphin pods.

"Guess water soothes her?" Callie asked.

"I guess. It's why she wears blue, too. She gets embarrassed, though." Yancy spoke with a parental sort of nonchalance. "Been trying to break her of that."

Thomas acted stumped. "Embarrassed of what?"

"Our adoption, for one thing. Doesn't bother me, but it sure does her."

"But why?" Callie'd never met adopted twins before, but adoption was a good thing.

"She thinks people will consider us discarded, you know, flawed."

"I don't think so," Thomas said.

Yancy shrugged.

Another opposite between the twins. Callie scanned the room for ID material. No photos, no sign of dad things, a tad too much dust on the furniture, no magazines on the coffee table. No indication that anyone other than teens lived here. "When were you adopted?"

"At birth. It was an arranged thing."

"And where are your parents?"

"They had to run visit our grandmother in Charlotte," Yancy said.

"Last minute?" Callie added concern. "I hope your grandmother's okay. Is it anything serious?"

Bea stepped back in from around the kitchen island, not quite fully in the room. "What about Grandma?"

"Just telling them about Mom and Dad going to see her in Charlotte." Yancy nodded toward Callie and Thomas.

"Oh," and Bea returned to the kitchen.

The house had an open floor plan with a counter/bar between the kitchen and family room. Bea stared out the window over the sink, tending dishes, which Callie and Thomas must've interrupted by coming in.

Callie rose and walked over.

"She might not want to talk to you now," Yancy warned and stood.

Well, she'd have to.

But there were no dishes in the sink. Bea scrubbed the sink itself almost hard enough to remove the enamel finish.

"Bea?" Callie rested against the cabinet a few feet away from the quiet twin. "Where are your parents?"

Bea shut off the water and leaned heavy on the sink's edge. "In Charlotte. Like she said."

"We'd appreciate it if you didn't blab our business around the beach," Yancy said from nearby.

"Not what we do," Callie said.

"Okay, we're done. While it's been fun, we have things to do." Arm out, Yancy motioned toward the entryway.

"Hey, give us a few minutes more," Thomas said, not taking Miss Blue Hair's request seriously. "Everything is confidential, and we still have questions."

But Yancy strode to the door, drew it open, and waited. "Good for you, Officer, but we're fresh out of answers. I believe we *can* ask you to leave, right?"

"You can," Callie replied, "but if we have reason, we can resist. Can you think of any reason why we need to be concerned?"

While Bea glimpsed over, nervous, hands still in the sink, Yancy remained poised and assertive. "Can't think of a thing. So please leave, and have a good night."

"We'd like your parents' phone numbers before we go," Callie said. "We have some questions for them as well."

"Sorry, but we don't give out their numbers. Give them a couple weeks, and they'll be back."

Callie paused, noting Thomas's stunned expression, avoiding looking the same. "Thanks. I take note of your level of cooperation, Yancy. Makes me wonder about your motivation. But that's okay. We'll talk again." She motioned for Thomas to leave, then turned. "You have a nice night as well."

This cursory interview was suitable, but not palatable . . . for now. Better to leave them on friendly terms now and save the more serious meeting for when Callie had more details.

She and Thomas exited to the porch, and the door closed neatly behind them . . . then locked. Guess someone other than Callie did lock their doors on Edisto. It was just before nine. The sun going down. One of the sisters turned off the porch light, leaving the two cops totally in the gloom that made footing tricky.

Thomas pulled out a tiny Maglite and shined it down at their feet. "That was odd."

Callie took the stairs, one hand firm on the railing. "Certainly was. What teen has that level of hubris with a cop?" Then she stopped. "Wait, listen." Inside the house, a pair of voices escalated, an argument lobbing back and forth, the words unintelligible since they'd obviously moved from the kitchen to a room more distant.

"Should we go back?" Thomas caught himself before he shined the light back up at the kitchen window.

"If you want to." She turned back around and took a few steps down. She needed Nolan and Sammy, not dueling sisters.

A muted screech of teenage angst wafted down toward her. No words understood, but the ill tempers traveled distinctly. A window slammed shut, and Callie could no longer hear.

Callie stepped into the dark beyond his Maglite beam. "Thomas? Either come on or go talk to them."

"We might have another body in the morning," he said.

"Well, we'll know who did it, won't we? Besides, sisters like to leave their victims alive to torture for the rest of their lives."

At the base of the stairs, Callie's foot touched gravel. A *psst* sounded from the blackness beside the house.

Thomas heard it, too, but Callie held down his arm when he started to shine the light in the general direction of the noise.

"Chief Morgan," came the whisper.

"Yes?"

"It's Parker Bender, from next door. We need to talk." But she didn't come out.

The two cops moved toward the heavy shroud of bushes. Callie whispered in keeping with the neighbor's secretive behavior. "Everything okay?"

Her signature bookstore ball cap atop her head, the neighborhood do-gooder and peacemaker peered out as Callie reached her. "Chief," she said with a breathlessness. "So glad you're here!"

Callie scanned the area for something threatening. "What is it?"

"I've watched those girls for ages, and I'm so grateful you checked in on them. Finally."

Callie relaxed. "What do you mean, Ms. Bender?"

"Those girls are fluky."

Fluky? "You'll have to explain a little better than that, ma'am."

Clasping her hands in a semi-prayer position, the neighbor's fingers kneaded against each other. "Not sure what they're up to, but those parents have vanished," she said.

"Ms. Bender." Thomas moved closer so she could see his pleasant, we-will-fix-this smile doled out so often to tourists. "Their parents are in Charlotte. Visiting a relative."

"The hell they are," the woman replied. "I've lived next door to them for over ten years. They came, they went, mostly remained inside, but they never tried to assimilate. I can count on one hand"—she held it up, fingers splayed—"the number of times we held a conversation consisting of more than *hello*."

Unusual, yes, but the couple might have avoided this neighbor and her, um, chattiness. "How often did you see the girls?" Callie asked.

"Oh, I'd see *them* regular enough. Yancy always experimented with that hair, her clothes. A pretty girl if she wouldn't be so radical. Bea did whatever Yancy wanted, until the last couple of years. Poor thing decided to become a hippie Pentecostal, if you ask me."

Somehow Ms. Bender had made those two words work in Bea's description.

"This may sound odd, but were either of them blond?" Callie asked.

"Why?"

Scratching her ear, where some of the first buzzing no-see-ums decided to taste flesh, Callie went with the standard excuse. "Can't comment on police business."

"Yeah, well, both of them were blond at one time or another," the woman replied, "but what's more important is they're alone, on their own! Can you call Social Services?"

Callie appreciated the concern, but this bordered on meddling. "They're nineteen. Legally adults."

The fluffily-built woman waved her hands like wings. "But . . . but that's not right. Those people left a year and a half ago."

"What?" Thomas glanced back over the bushes to the Wilkerson house.

"Wait," Callie said. "If they left that long ago, why'd you wait so long to speak up? Why didn't you call Social Services?"

Ms. Bender shook her head, patted her chest, and huffed. "I don't know. I kept thinking they were, like you said, visiting someone. Taking vacations. Going on business trips, though I have no earthly idea what they do for a living. The girls went to college so I excused the parents as taking advantage of their freedom. But look." She pointed up toward the house. "It's spring break and no parents. Last Christmas the girls came home . . . no parents. They're just babies, Chief. Can't you do anything?"

Thomas gave her a mild frown. "If you were worried, why didn't you ask them?"

"Are you kidding? They dodge me. Once they even ran when I called out, high-tailing it to their car and locking the doors. Poor dears are abandoned, I say."

Callie slowly swiveled the woman around to head toward her home. "Thanks, Ms. Bender. We'll be sure and check on them. You did a noble thing calling us over."

"One last question, though," Thomas said.

Having received the desired accolades, the neighbor seemed to settle down, her animation almost tranquilized. "Yes?"

"Why are you hiding?"

"Oh, I don't want the girls to learn I told anyone."

"But why?" Thomas asked.

"Because there's obviously a secret, Officer, and I don't have all the facts. Now that I've delegated to you, I can sleep easier." She hurried over and hugged Thomas. "Thanks so much for all you do for us." Then she repeated the gesture with Callie, but paused to whisper, "Don't let Brice get to you. I'm in your court, honey."

Then she scurried into the shrubbery, and they watched as she climbed her stairs and went inside.

"What'd she say?" Funny how Thomas still whispered.

"A woman-to-woman thing," she said. And all the more proof the entire beach was aware and audience to Brice's pursuit of her.

"Oh, yeah, I get it." Though he wouldn't. "You putting any weight in what she said?"

"Not sure." But Callie thought she might understand some of Ms. Bender's logic. Weird that anyone's parents remained invisible and unavailable. Yancy and Bea were recognized on sight by kids and neighbors, but not the couple who raised them.

But somehow these girls attended school and paid the utilities and taxes. No. Those parents hadn't abandoned those kids. And even if they had, they'd left them financially safe.

There was certainly something to investigate here, but it could be no more than another tangent taking them further away from Pinky's murder. But on the other hand, any new piece of information could be the next step in solving this case. She hated the conflicting priorities of evidence.

Chapter 22

PARKER BENDER'S news about the twins would take some digestion, but not now. A few night birds tweeted sleepy goodnights in the palmettos and across the water into the mossy oak woods. Callie and Thomas had completed their planned interviews. Callie, however, would pursue Nolan and Sammy on her own, regardless of the hour. She toyed with whether to involve Knox.

Thomas cocked his head toward Ms. Bender's house. "What do you make of her?"

"She's all right."

He scratched his head. "Maybe, but I'm sort of confused, Chief. What are we doing? Our dead guy sounds weird. Maybe we ought to look harder at *him*."

Callie's phone lit up in the blackness as she checked quickly for texts. "We *are* looking at him, just right now via the living."

But Thomas had a right to his confusion. He saw no direction without all the information. Callie struggled with it, too, even with the loose array of facts in her grasp. Knox maybe deserved to be a little upset at her, too. She'd spun in circles since she fished Pinky out of the creek.

She could call SLED, but if that wasn't a career breaker at this point, nothing else was.

Or was that her fear of Brice talking?

Sammy spoke to Rhoades, and Nolan might've brought Rhoades to Edisto. Then there was the mysterious note. Lots of loose leads.

And, God help her, she might be mad at Stan, but she missed his guidance. He'd been eerily quiet since she hung up on him. But she couldn't think about that. She had Knox, but what the hell did that mean?

With the sun gone, a moist April chill snaked its way from the marsh that Fantasea fronted, each neighboring residence about thirty yards apart, separated by trees and tall shrubs that thrived in the jungle climate. Even with the windbreaker, Callie felt a chill roll over her as she contemplated whether to interview Nolan or Sammy next. Tomorrow she and Knox would repeat visits to Kim Smith, Lissa Pasternak, and most definitely the twins. Backup interviews served to solidify facts and root out lies, especially after the interviewer had already pegged a baseline of how each person would react based on the first meet. Callie predicted attorneys maybe getting involved at the Smiths after Brice's disruption. She didn't see that second attempt going well at all.

On their way to the car, movement from the silted roadway caught her attention. She froze, just moving her eyes, Thomas doing the same. But the male form strode over without discretion, cutting behind the patrol car. "What'd the girls say?" he asked.

Callie hid her surprise at Nolan's appearance and donned a smile. "Nolan. Thought you'd be back home."

"Heard you met with them, and Lissa, too."

A thump sounded from inside Fantasea. Something fallen . . . or thrown. "Thomas? Go check on them."

The officer surveyed Nolan, the gloom giving the boy a devious bearing. "You sure, Chief?"

"Hurry." She waited for him to climb the stairs. Then she ushered Nolan toward her cruiser, moving him to the side opposite the house, where neither Wilkerson girl could see him when the front door opened, or in case the porch light came on. Between a row of tea olives and the car, the darkness and lack of streetlight, she and Nolan had privacy.

But Nolan wasn't trying to be clandestine. "Sammy said Deputy Sidekick up there dragged him outside and practically cuffed him to a chair." The boy's usual flippancy was replaced by an edge.

No mention of Kim from him or Sammy. Guess she really wasn't in the thick of the college beach set, meaning the kids knew less of her than all the others.

Callie's phone vibrated. Caller ID said Jeb. He was supposed to talk to her only in person unless it was pretty damn serious. "Yes," she answered professionally, hoping he'd catch the drift, and that this better be important.

"Nolan slipped out," Jeb said, speaking freely. "He saw you at Fantasea and got weird."

"Sorry, but I'm in the middle of something, sir."

"Oh, is he there with you?"

"Yes, sir. I'll get back with you later on that. Thanks for your help." She hung up. Jeb was really taking this CI to heart. *Good boy. No, good man. She'd give him his due.*

"What's your interest in the girls?" Callie asked Nolan, then smiled.

"Besides the obvious."

Hands in his pockets, his T-shirt and cargo shorts insufficient for the cool evening, he shook his head. "Trust me, not my type. But they love drama, and I want to know if that includes me."

If this was about gossip, Callie would ordinarily move on, but this was Nolan. "I'm not in the habit of sharing police business, Nolan. But I am interested to know why you're so bothered you had the nerve to approach two uniforms and demand to know what *they* were up to?"

"Heard you're making the rounds and got tired of waiting for you to corner me." He smirked and dipped his shoulder. "Kind of like stepping into a punch to cripple the blow."

She was rather sure he stole that line from a movie, because no way this affluent, soft-handed boy understood fists.

Two feet, maybe less, separated them as they stood beside the cruiser. "You knew Pinkerton Rhoades," she said.

His upper body twitched. "Yeah, and what of it?"

"You lied to me about that."

"Yeah."

Admission. She wished she could study his intricate facial movements with more clarity. She stared through the grayness. Nolan's clipped responses spoke defensively yet he confronted her. Made no move to leave.

"You first talked like he was a stranger," she said. "But I've met your mother and been to your home. Agent Rhoades knew you for seventeen years. What were you, four or five when your sister disappeared?"

"Two months short of five." His voice flat-lined. "Made for a helluva birthday, or so they tell me. I just remember strangers in my house and my mother crying every day."

"I can't imagine." The kidnapping would have ruled the Flagg household, even after the FBI left and the Flaggs heard nothing after the ransom delivery. Then after losing his father, after thinking life had distilled down to him and his mother, Nolan learns Mom and the aging agent kept the quest, and a relationship, alive. Did Nolan hate or respect the man?

"I have questions," she said.

Thomas strolled up. "Chief, the girls are fine."

"Did you check in yet?"

"Chief?"

After an eye roll that she realized he wouldn't see, she sighed deep, hoping he'd follow. "Weren't you supposed to meet that witness about now? Don't let him slip off again."

"Oh," he said, then tried to control his surprise with a smaller *oh*. "Dang, you're right. Back at the station."

Callie heard Nolan's feet in the gravel, side-to-side steps. She needed to get this kid talking fast, while she had him. He hadn't run her down for nothing.

She reached for her keys. "I need to get Thomas back, but care to ride with us? We can talk on the way home."

"Um, sure."

She held open the backseat passenger door, but when Nolan looked in, he hesitated. "There's a cage in there."

She patted his shoulder. "Three can't ride in the front. Don't worry, both Thomas and I have ridden back there a time or two."

Thomas laughed on cue.

Nolan stooped and got in antsy, afraid to touch much. Callie stopped herself from laying a hand on his head to avoid his hitting the car.

The two-mile ride to the station sped by. All three remained silent, accepting that what was to be said would happen without Thomas, Callie hoping it gave Nolan a few seconds to put his thoughts together. After dropping off Thomas, Callie pulled onto the asphalt from the parking lot. He waved a two-finger salute as she left, waiting for them get out of sight so he could just go home.

Callie took the long way home down Palmetto. "Why did you tell me Pinkerton Rhoades was a pervert? Was he?"

"I doubt it," he said, then grumbled, "Not with teenage girls anyway."

That made for a decent segue. "You weren't too delighted about his relationship with your mother, were you?"

His sarcasm carried an edge. "You've seen pictures of my dad, right?"

The autographed photos with celebrities had hung regal in the mansion study. "Sure. He socialized with some serious names." And was quite the handsome gent. Nolan held some resemblance.

"Compare *that*," he said, a smug sort of admiration woven in, "to Senior Special Agent Pinkerton Rhoades. A big step down, wouldn't you say?"

The occasional streetlight illuminated the boy's disgust in her mirror.

"Not my place to compare," she replied. "Rhoades seemed to care about finding your sister, though."

Nolan quietly touched the cage divider. "My sister was his gravy train to my family's money."

An angle they would consider. One of the many theories stacking up.

Too small to travel for long, Edisto Beach had few hidden streets and no alleys. So she turned left onto Portia Street and took it all the way down to the marsh, where a private entrance cut across the water to a private island. She did a three-point turn and parked on the edge, tucking the cruiser sufficiently among the myrtles. Unless someone needed to head out to the island, she'd be good for a while. Throwing her arm over the seat back, she bumped the cage. "Now we can talk."

Enough moon shone along with ambient lighting from the street corner for her to catch his bewilderment. "Here?"

"We couldn't outside of the Wilkerson house. Not many folks enjoy the station, and Jeb and Sammy are at the house. You ran me down, remember? And you still haven't answered my question. Why did you mislead me about Agent Rhoades?"

"I didn't like him."

Callie sucked once through her teeth. "Imagine that. Did you kill him?"

He gripped the cage, his tension now panic. "What the fuck?"

Callie could feel his energy. Borne of anger and confusion, and fear. Callie could smell that. "You've lied about him and flashed serious hate issues. How'd you lure him out here?"

"Jesus," he whispered, then with his right and left hand searching for escape, he repeated himself. "That's not how this happened. Jesus Christ, are you arresting me?"

She winced. "Depends. Did you bring Rhoades to Edisto?"

His hesitation only made her doubt him more, but then, he was a kid, lacking much reason.

"Why would I bring him?"

"Somebody did."

"Maybe he drove."

"His car's at his apartment."

Nolan's flop back in the seat made him kick the base of his confinement, and crossing his arms told Callie he was warning himself to be careful in his words. She'd seen the pattern.

"Well?" The lilt in her tone was meant to tell him he could answer here or be taken elsewhere. Surely he'd seen enough Netflix to deduce that.

"He came to me first." Now he couldn't be still, his movements taking him to the edge of his seat, then back. "He wanted me to drive him. Said if a lead panned out I'd thank him, and my mother would add years to her life." He shrugged. "But he was forever saying things like that."

This was definitely not the story Jeb told her. "I thought Yancy suggested you come to Edisto, then directed you to Jeb. It's how you wound up at my place."

"Yeah, after I kinda hinted I'd like to come. Rhoades told me to find a reason to be here, since he'd been seen in his Nissan. I dropped him off around the marina, worked myself into the college crowd, and waited for his call to take him home. He wanted me to snoop around."

"To look for what?"

"My sister."

That had her attention. "And how serious did you take this assignment?"

Giving her a snort, he stared out the side window. "Not very. I only did it because of Mom, not that he told her what we were doing . . . what he was doing. It was 'our secret'"—he drew air quotes with fingers—"he said. Like we bonded or something."

Callie tried to sort his truth from his hyperbole, but the kid had married the two for a lot of years, making it hard to tell one from the other. "Why should I believe you?" she asked.

He huffed.

"Did he mention about meeting anyone?"

"Said he didn't want to tell me until he confirmed some things."

"Why that particular day?" she asked.

"Don't know."

Humidity began to build inside the car. Callie didn't want to lower the windows and allow their voices to carry. "What else, because right now you have the only motive for killing Rhoades."

"Wait, what motive would I have?" His voice rose, shrill.

"Why didn't you call the police when he didn't call you?" she asked. "But more importantly, why didn't you come forward when you heard he was dead?"

His voice cracked, but it was no longer tremulous, his eyes no longer as frantic. "It just freaked me out." He waited for her to respond, as if to measure his effectiveness, to see if he was telling the story right.

Her pupils finally dilated, accustomed to the evening at last. What had been a black shape outlined by a different shade of black now took form as a young man backed into a corner.

"He tells me he has leads to Emma," Nolan continued. "I just thought it was his way of padding a story. He told me not to tell my mom and get her hopes up, like I had a choice. Shit, she's a shell of what she used to be, so I'd be a pure ass telling her I was helping Rhoades on yet another breadcrumb trail to where the big bad wolf stashed Emma. When he didn't text or answer, I didn't know who the hell to tell. I mean, he was friggin' FBI. So I figured maybe he found a ride back. Then I heard the kids talking . . ." Hands animated, head shaking, eyes wide. "You can't tell me it wouldn't look fishy for me to pop up and say I delivered him here only for him to get whacked. Who'd believe I wasn't guilty?"

The tale had legs, but the thick resentment he harbored hindered her judgment of him.

He seemed eager to keep her goodwill, seeking validation that he in some way did the right thing.

"He waited outside of my classes at school," he said. "He had a wild theory that Emma might be a student, and he asked me questions about girls on campus. 'They may lie about their age,' he said. 'They may dye their hair.' Sometimes I felt sorry for the guy and we did dinner. The old man couldn't let go. Sad . . . and sick." He jerked his head in a hard nod on the last word. "I couldn't look at a girl without seeing Emma thanks to that old bastard. Do you know how sick that makes me?"

"What about the note?" she asked.

His brow met in the middle. "What note?"

"Don't lie to me."

"All he told me was he had an appointment. I didn't ask how he made it."

So there was another player. "Do you have any idea who else might have killed Rhoades?"

"God, no!" His words reverberated off the car interior, then the car fell silent except for his breathing.

Callie waited. Waiting has its own magic with frustrated witnesses . . . and targets. Now the front windows began to fog.

"How's my mom?" he asked more softly. "I assume you told her he was dead."

"She's sad but handling it," she replied. "She's tougher than you think. I'm surprised she didn't call you."

His form wilted. "She did."

So his mother had confirmed Rhoades's death to him as more than hearsay and community gossip. The kid danced in and out of lies, but he wasn't adept at it, explaining why he turned anxious, how he realized the cops were looking. He seemed over his head.

Then Callie asked the question she could only ask him, because she couldn't ask Rhoades. "Do you feel Emma is alive?"

He gnawed on a lip, hard. "Nobody's ever asked me that," he finally said.

"Doesn't mean you haven't thought about it."

Callie's phone gave a hum, another text, but she remained still, and would remain still until Nolan answered.

"I guess I don't think she's alive," he said. "Actually, I hope she's not."

Callie tried not to react. "You hope she's dead?"

His reply choked. "No. I think I'd like my sister back, but she wouldn't be Emma. That Emma's dead." He coughed. "My mom wouldn't cope with that." Some seconds lapsed. "I just think everyone ought to move on."

Either a superb performance, or the kid meant it. "Hard for some people to do, Nolan. A mother would never give up. An agent would feel responsible for the unsolved case. A brother . . ." Their gaze met, him waiting to hear what she had to say about him. "A young brother, with the world before him, would be caught between missing his sister and wanting to move on with his life."

She left off *resenting the sister for ruining his childhood* or *hating himself for not being taken instead.* He didn't need to hear from her what he already thought.

Cranking up the engine, Callie left the conversation there. As soon as she dropped off Nolan, she'd find Knox. The kid sank back into his seat, as if realizing they were done.

Rhoades sounded mildly obsessed, if she believed Nolan. Hell, if she believed anything she'd gathered thus far. Callie's success back in Boston had relied heavily upon her ability to recognize the gullible in the guilty, the guilt in the innocent, the monsters in the angels, and the angels crashed to earth.

The perpetrator in the victim.

She used to be better at it than this.

Callie pulled up at Chelsea Morning and dropped off Nolan. Before the kid reached the top of the stairs, Jeb appeared on the porch, puzzled.

She'd let Nolan give whatever story he liked about being brought home in a patrol car.

However, she dropped her son a text. *Don't push him. Go stay next door with the Bianchis. Text me as needed. Sammy back?*

No, at Lissa's, he replied, and she welcomed the fact he didn't question going to Sprite's house. Nolan had no place to go except Chelsea Morning, and she damn sure didn't want Jeb isolated with the kid without her there. Not until she understood more.

He added. *You?*

With the FBI at Windswept, she typed. *Back in an hour.*

Then she texted Knox she'd be right over . . . to Windswept. She could do this.

Chapter 23

CALLIE PULLED INTO the Windswept drive, and Knox waited inside with Cokes. She sucked down half of hers, dry mouthed, suddenly aware it had been forever since she'd had something to drink, and fighting the small panic in the pit of her stomach from standing in Seabrook's kitchen.

Knox must've noticed, because after Callie wiped her mouth, he threw a potato-chip bag on the kitchen counter, opened the fridge, and returned with a store-bought plastic container of chicken salad and a spoon. "I can cook something," he said. "Or open a window. Just don't puke in my house."

She grabbed the chicken salad. "Stick to the case, Knox. Your people skills suck."

The open front door gave her a sense of relief, and the screen door allowed in the cool night tidal breezes straight off the Atlantic. The slight chill suited her. She took her seat at the dinette table where Knox had already sat down, and after a few fast bites, she stood the spoon up in the tub and nudged it aside. "I need to update you about Nolan. And Sammy. The twins and Kim Smith, but first, what have you found on everyone's background, because we need to get busy and knock on a couple more doors."

When they did, Brice might knock on *her* door before tomorrow afternoon, but his threat to end her career, while serious, wasn't more important than solving this murder. She'd come so far. And she had to live on this island. They both loved this community, but he clearly didn't want her among its government elite.

However, if he, and everyone on this beach, couldn't understand the urgency of this case, then maybe she'd let them have their way once she'd done all she could to solve Pinky's murder. If she lost the battle, best to finish her short tenure on her best effort.

Knox waited for direction. "Where do you want to start? Girls or guys?"

"A girl," she said. "Start with Lissa. Sammy Blackstone is her *true love*, and Kim Smith witnessed a negative exchange between Sammy and Pinky the day he died. This could be no more than a kid who overheated and overreacted about an old man with eyes on his girl."

Knox sifted through his notes. "Here. Lissa Marie Pasternak. Nineteen. Born in Chicago. Pretty clean. Parents check out. No police record. Honor student." He rattled off more dates, details, people, and places, in sync with Callie's info from earlier in the day. Enough to deduce she wasn't Emma.

"You didn't by chance check birth certificates on parents, did you?"

He gave her a *WTF* stare. "We never discussed the parents."

"My bad." She shook her head. "I thought you'd connect the dots. If any kid has a forged birth certificate, the parent might be hiding their identities as well." He ought to know better after fifteen years as a fed.

"Hell, I'll get on it tomorrow."

"Great. Now, what about Sammy?" She wanted to compare facts to Lissa's description of her beau's hard childhood.

Knox didn't even have to find the right paper. "Helluva life, that one. One parent in jail after raping the poor guy and the other dumped him into the foster system. On scholarship at College of Charleston, though. No criminal record, which amazes me. Can't tell you the number of times I've seen such kids flunk out of society."

Nothing about a temper that got him into trouble.

"Go to Kim Smith." Callie unmuted her phone and set it on the table in case Jeb texted.

The agent watched carefully. "You're certainly buzzing. But you're not drinking. What happened?"

Tiny feelers happened. Like the poison ivy on the zillion oaks in the Lowcountry jungle, tiny little roots happened. Individually weak, but together climbing a seventy-foot tree to take charge. Every name in this mess knew little about the big picture, but their collective knowledge might create a reason that Pinky died.

Callie was keener than she'd been in ages. All pistons firing. There was something about these little clues that had engaged her again. Ironic, considering her investigative days might be limited.

"Too many people know we're digging around about Pinky," she said. She thought of not only the kids and the force, but also Brice. His stubbornness, along with that of his snoops, could impede progress, and without a doubt he'd pin a failed investigation on Callie, regardless of his hand in the effort. "We're on a clock and don't have a lot of time to dick around." She threw another potato chip in her mouth and pulverized it.

"I sent my son next door, but he's watching Nolan best he can via social media. Didn't want him physically with Nolan at this moment."

She tapped on the table. "Kim Smith. We'll get to Nolan in a minute. Then I want to talk about the twins."

He blew out, whispered "Okay," and lifted a paper. "Her father's been in bankruptcy. One domestic violence on record with Charleston PD but wife dropped charges. Otherwise birth certificate and all else appears legit."

"I worry about that one," she said. "Now, Nolan."

"Born and raised in the area. Pretty solid."

"He's a Flagg. Surely you dug deeper than that."

Knox squinted, a warning he could dole snark right back at her. "Our charmed boy has been arrested six times. Money bailed him out of each one. He entered college via the family name, because he barely passed high school."

Wadding up the chip bag, Callie threw it in the open garbage can. "Again, sort of expected. He's had a messed-up life. What types of arrests?"

"Keyed a neighbor's car. Stole a car. Threatened a high school teacher. Defaced school property. That sort of thing."

Callie held out her hands. "Surprise! Guess Pinky kept all that to himself. And I wish Jeb vetted his friends better."

"Well, sorry, Chief. Guess Pinky didn't see his murder coming or he'd have documented better." He pushed back his chair. "For someone who came in itching for details, you're sure dosing out a lot of inner Satan toward someone trying to help."

Closing her eyes, she rubbed the bridge between them. She could tone it down, but she was eager . . . and eager about being eager, which meant observation and confrontation at whatever level deemed necessary. "My inner Satan is solely aimed at obstacles right now, Knox. The kids, maybe even Amanda Flagg. But I'm also torn about someone else."

"Give me his name, and I'll put somebody on it right now."

There he went, delegating some technician to do his work. Well, not in this case. "I can't," she said.

"Why?"

"Because it's you."

A silence hung between them. Part of their conflict and sandpaper words came from a weight on both sets of shoulders. Neither could trust the other. No doubt he had checked her out with his deep pockets of resources and staff, but she hadn't had the time, or the assets.

She rested crossed arms on the table. "I'm trying to figure out if your participation is nothing more than regret for missing Pinky's retirement party."

"What?" His mouth dropped open. He glowered. Then he banged the table with a slow, tight fist. "I cared for that man."

"Not lately you hadn't."

Redness climbed up his neck from under his collar. "Oh, you . . ."

"What, bitch? Say it. When the Bureau blew you off, in essence blowing Pinky off, you came to me, and all that wrath and regret and burn for revenge got dumped on my head. You blamed me for everything they wouldn't do . . . everything you hadn't done. I didn't deserve that."

His fist still rose and fell once, thumping the table.

"You don't think clearly making restitution. You have to keep your head open to more than doing right by Pinky so you feel better. Frankly, Knox, you're the wrong man for this case, if you're just trying to absolve your guilt and make yourself feel better. And you know it." She let him ponder all that.

"*Bitch* doesn't begin to describe you," he said.

She released a hard breath, for him to hear. "Maybe not, but it needed airing. Your guilt is no different than my drinking. It's part of who you are. You feel you need to regulate me, well, I feel a need to regulate you. Don't let anything in this investigation get caught up in what Pinky would think. It's just about finding out who did what and when. Nothing more and nothing less. When emotion crawls in the middle of things, we run the risk of missing something obvious."

He'd loosened his fists, but he seemed mixed on what else to say.

A text pinged on Callie's phone from Jeb. *Nolan is texting me. Might be leaving.*

Callie frowned. *Going where?*

The answer came quickly. *Not sure.*

Still at our place?

Jeb: *Yeah.*

Callie: *Sammy there?*

Jeb: *Don't think so.*

Stay at the Bianchi's, she typed. *Until I say otherwise.*

"What's up?" Knox asked, gruffer than normal, but his indignation seemed watered down, the interruption opportune.

"It's Nolan." She explained the emotional conversation that occurred earlier in her patrol car, and how she'd left him at her place.

"Hey, before we jump back to him," she said, hating to go off topic, but Brice's remark at the Wilkerson place indicated a mole, and she prayed it wasn't in the PD. "Did you report my drinking?"

Out of the myriad people who could've told Brice, Knox held the least allegiance to her. And made the most sense.

"Unfortunately, yes," he said. "The next morning after our dinner." His gaze slid off her. "I was directed to a man named LeGrand."

"Directed by whom?"

His sigh came from a deep place. His silence puzzling.

Was he ashamed? Knox could have simply denied her allegation, a very expected response. Callie certainly didn't expect sincerity.

"Would rather not say who I told," he said. "Not anyone in your station, because I assumed they'd cover for you."

She lowered her forehead to her hands, not hiding her disappointment. She'd hated the feeb, but she thought they worked together for a common cause—Pinky. And he'd done to her precisely what the FBI did to his beloved Pinky, discarded him for a private indiscretion.

And she'd thought she couldn't feel any more alone.

How were they supposed to work together now?

Leaning back in his chair, Knox stared at the papers still in his hand. "I really wish I hadn't."

"Yeah, well, that horse is miles out of the barn, isn't it?"

"No, I mean it. You've . . . surprised me," he said.

"Trust me," she said so damn firm. "You've surprised me, too."

Brice must be orgasmic. Next council meeting would be his crowning achievement, assuming there wasn't a special meeting before.

Knox reached over, his hand out to her. "I still want to help," he said.

"I would assume so," she said, but refused to accept his gesture. "We still have to deal with Pinky, the guy you—"

She started to say, *the guy you let down. The guy who trained you, and you forgot about. The guy the FBI screwed over and you didn't fight for.* But barbs were more Knox's forte. Not that he didn't deserve to hear every damn word.

Remorse shone in his expression, with a willingness to take whatever she threw at him. "I meant to help you, not just the case."

"Not sure I can afford your kind of help, but the case won't solve itself," she finally said.

She almost ordered him to find her a drink somewhere, out of spite. What did it matter anymore? Instead, she went to the kitchen, settling for more caffeine, and poured another Coke. Didn't offer him one.

His gaze followed her there and back. "Now," she said, "I need your take on some things. I'm on the fence about Pinky after talking to Nolan."

Knox didn't react to her Pinky remark, because he owed her. For a change, she might even get him to focus on facts better, to think like a real detective.

"Was Pinky so plagued with Emma he made things up?" she asked. "Nolan thinks so. He's scarred by the kidnapping, but he knew Pinky maybe better than you."

Knox didn't react. He seemed uncertain how to.

Callie swiped crumbs off the table and let them drop to Knox's floor. "I'm not even sure there was a note. If the man wanted to impress Amanda Flagg and hand her some fresh sense of support—"

Knox blurted, "There *was* a note."

Knox had taken the bait. Time to learn what else he hadn't told her. Seemed to be a lot of unsaid coming out tonight. "Did you see it?"

He shook his head. "I brushed him off when he called me and mentioned it."

"For God's sake, why?"

He paced to the sink and faced the window. "Because he'd slept with Amanda Flagg for at least a year, a rather unprofessional move." He turned, his eyes deep with regret. "He asked me to come with him to Edisto that day. I told him to quit chasing ghosts."

"The day he got the note?" she asked. "Or the day he died?"

The agony sank deeper into the creases around his eyes. "That's harsh."

"Oh, you don't get to say that to me tonight, Knox." Only one solitary mission left before her, and that was Pinky. Agent Kendrick should've told her about the note sooner, and she cared little about how far down his guilt traveled into his soul. "Why did I have to learn about the note from Amanda Flagg?"

"Because I . . . hell, I don't know."

She scoffed. "Damn shitty answer."

His voice rose, defensive. "I had him describe the note. It was nothing. Honestly." Then his voice fell. "I considered it a ploy to make me respect him since he retired. I didn't expect Amanda Flagg to mention it, trust me. That's when I realized it might've been real."

She couldn't bring herself to state the obvious.

Callie's last few years held more than a few wrong decisions and ill timing. A small piece of her wanted to forgive Knox for a misjudgment that led to his mentor's death. But more of her wanted to smack the man to the moon and back.

And they'd wasted too much time on bad decisions.

"Let's talk with Nolan again," she said. "You and me. I want your take on Sammy, too." Then she added, "You owe it to Pinky."

He flexed his shoulders as if he came to the conclusion himself.

"And I need your take on the sisters," she said. "Nolan's too interested in them, and the neighbor told me—"

"I'll interview every kid between here and Charleston, Callie. I'm not taking this lightly. I'm taking down whoever killed him."

"Beautiful words there, Supervisory Special Agent, Sir." She held back reminding him he'd already betrayed and taken *her* down. Chairs pushed under the table. She studied Knox's rush of heated allegiance. "Whose case is this, again?" she asked.

"Yours. Though the FBI—"

"This isn't about the FBI, just like it isn't about you. It's not about turf. It's not about regret. Compartmentalize, Knox. It's the only way to stay sane when it gets personal. It's about Pinky." She came around the table. "Get that straight or you're not coming with me."

He gave a slow nod.

"Now," she said. "Did you find anything on Yancy and Bea?"

A heavy-handed knock sounded on the screen door. "Kendrick?"

Brice. He had to have seen her cruiser in the drive. Next he'd demand a police-frequency radio.

Knox walked to the door. "It's a bit late, isn't it, Mr. LeGrand?" He left Brice on the porch, speaking through the screen, not inviting him in.

"Need an update. Today I watched Ms. Morgan grasp at straws all over the beach, without you, I might add. I had to intercede at a couple places, which might not have been necessary if you'd policed her like you promised."

Knox, you ass. Callie's heart crashed into her gut. She'd seen herself as a better cop than this. If Knox had reported her for drinking, he'd probably agreed to keep the devil informed of any further transgressions.

She gave Brice more credit at being the more honest person. He damn sure didn't hide his goal of ousting her and showed some serious diligence, his mind on his mission.

"She didn't need me," Knox said firmly. "And we had our respective tasks. Thanks for asking, but it's premature to expect law enforcement to issue a report."

Brice tried to peer around Knox. "Not what you said before."

Callie leaned over and met Brice's gaze.

He feigned surprise, but he also had the look of a man rewarded. Brice flaunted the fact he thought he'd caught her. She flaunted the fact she no longer cared.

"Rather late for a guest." Brice made a show of scanning the place. "Wasn't this Seabrook's house?"

Of course, the moron knew it was.

Knox acted stymied. "Have no idea. I'm just a renter."

"Yeah, our chief's had her skirts lifted a time or two over here. Sure that's not what's going on, Agent?"

Knox couldn't help but glance back at her and wince. But then he straightened, and stepped in the man's view of her. "You owe Chief Morgan an apology, Mr. LeGrand."

"For the truth? Don't think so," Brice said. "On the contrary, she'll owe the council an apology in a couple weeks when we convene a special meeting."

Knox reached for the wood door. "Excuse us, but we're in the middle of work."

Brice reached for the screen door handle, and without apology, Knox connected the simple hook lock. "Good evening, Councilman." Then he closed the wooden door.

For a moment, Knox kept his back to Callie.

"So much for the brotherhood of blue," she said slowly.

"I'm at a loss right now."

"New experience for you, I imagine."

He didn't answer.

When he didn't come back to the table, she reached over for the papers he'd been reading from earlier. They were too far into this. But they were back to being strangers, or worse, back to being two people forced to work together with nil for trust.

"So," she said in an awkward segue. "Appears the Wilkersons adopted a set of twins, born in October, in Charleston. No criminal records. The only real estate they own is that house here at the beach. Information's rather scarce on the parents."

He lifted his head. "Right. The girls attend the College of Charleston. Yancy's major is pre-law and Bea's is English lit." In slow, easy steps, he returned and took his seat, at her mercy.

Callie recalled their opal necklaces. Being Librans. "You pulled birth certificates?"

"On the girls. Not for the parents. Tomorrow, I'll—"

"Driver's licenses?"

Slightly puzzled, he replied, "Of course. On them and the parents, thank you. All current."

But if Parker Bender was correct, the Wilkersons hadn't been around for over a year.

"They're clean, Callie."

No, the trust issue reared its head again. Not in his truthfulness but in his ability to connect dots.

"I need a copy of the parents' driver's license pictures. And I'd like to see their birth certificates as much or more than the others."

She stood, adding the twins to the top of her to-do list in the morning, regardless what he thought. "Gotta go see Sammy. You able to see the Wilkerson girls tomorrow morning?"

"Whatever you need, Chief."

"Thought my name was Callie."

He rose. "Wasn't sure that invitation was still open."

She snorted. "We're just solving a case now, Knox. That's the only thing on our plate. But we're doing it right, assuming you're willing to give that notion a try."

"I deserve that."

She scoffed again. "Right now it's about seeing Sammy. Let's go."

And it wouldn't be long before Edisto PD wasn't about her anymore, either. Her insides twisted, and suddenly keeping her badge mattered more than ever.

Chapter 24

THEY LOCKED UP Windswept, and got into her cruiser. Callie drove, rehearsing her interview. Knox spoke little, not even questioning why they were continuing their efforts this late at night. She didn't care why, and she didn't have to explain why, and she couldn't verbalize it if he asked other than to say she had momentum, she had Brice ready to clip her wings at every turn, and she had a bad feeling about Nolan.

Well after eleven, muggy. A few clouds had crawled in, making the beach community seem darker than just an hour ago. Rollers growled in from the ocean and dug at the hard sand, as if judging how loud to make their white noise as people tried to go to bed.

Knox seemed a hollow individual to her now, his use limited to ideas about Pinky, hopefully attached to a glimmer of his Quantico training. Common conversation? No. She'd been simply a tool.

Four short blocks to Looney Dunes, Lissa's house. Callie wondered if Nolan knew Sammy had seen Pinky. And what he would think about that.

Nolan remained at Chelsea Morning per Jeb's texts, and Callie had no qualms about waking Nolan up once she got home, later, but right now she wanted Sammy. What had been Pinky's mind-set when they met? What had been Sammy's? What had Sammy learned? Why hadn't Sammy told her he'd seen the dead agent?

Knox's information showed that Sammy's record confirmed what Lissa had said. A violent childhood, giving him the propensity to carry that history into adulthood.

Callie eased her cruiser onto the shoulder of the opposite side of the road, along the grass, not wanting to make a lot of racket on the gravel drive this late. After softly shutting their doors, they crossed Osceola and climbed the stairs to Looney Dunes. If Sammy wasn't at Chelsea Morning, he was here. Knox hung back and let Callie take lead for once.

Few lights on inside. The porch lights were out. Callie raised her hand to the doorbell.

"Don't ring the bell," came a delicate female whisper, hushed, making Callie wonder if she'd heard it. Knox looked over, too, so she must have.

The porch was dark, but movement, the clank of chain, and Callie's adjusting eyes made out two bodies on a double swing on the end of the porch. Lissa stood first and shifted her long loose blouse into place, hair disheveled. "Daddy's asleep. Don't wake him, please." She slipped a hairband from her wrist, reached around and contained her long hair into a ponytail as if that made her appear less compromised.

Sammy appeared behind her, unabashed at his bare chest, but testy about the interruption from the tense lines around his mouth. "Just because I'm at your house doesn't make you my mother, Chief Morgan. Lissa and I are adults."

"Not interested in your sex life, Sammy. We only want to ask a few questions."

A stronger, cooler breeze blew the length of the porch, the beach perpendicular to the house and a block and a half away. Goose bumps crept up Callie's arms, and Sammy returned to the swing and retrieved his shirt after sorting through the throw blanket to find it.

"Do we talk right here? In the house? Or go to the station?" Callie asked.

Trying to appear ominous in bare feet, Sammy stiffened all six foot tall and lanky, and studied the more broad-shouldered Knox. "Who are you?"

Knox pulled out his credentials. Even in the dark, the gold shield made a statement. "The FBI, son."

"Oh." Lissa took a step back.

Guess Knox had given up justifying the covert angle. Guess Callie'd roll with it, the man's inconsistencies becoming the most consistent thing about him.

Sammy fought to keep his offense intact, but it dissolved when he couldn't think what to say.

"Nobody's in trouble," Callie said. Unless Sammy spilled more than she expected. If he sounded too suspicious, he'd be staying with Knox tonight, a safe distance from Nolan and Jeb. Or locked up.

"Talk out here." Sammy stepped back to the swing.

Lissa sat beside him, and he threw the blanket over her, keeping his shirt unbottoned as if that emphasized his manliness.

Seated in a rattan chair to their left, Callie rested forearms on her knees. Knox remained standing.

"It's late, y'all," she said. "So let's get on with it. Sammy, you were seen talking with a Mr. Pinkerton Rhoades at the marina on the day we found his body. What was that conversation about?"

Lissa jumped up, the throw puddling on the plank floor. "Oh no, I *am* getting Daddy now." Bolting past them, she ran in the house.

Callie pursued the questions before anyone new made it complicated. "The truth is simple, Sammy. You might be the last person to have seen him alive."

"That makes me the prime suspect, doesn't it?" he asked, as meek as the day she met him when he was almost too shy to speak.

"No," Knox said. "We said *might* be the last person. He could've seen ten others before he died. So help us piece together his day."

The boy's posture went rigid as he weighed what to say, and probably how to say it. "I saw him near Bay Creek Park and called him out, wanting him to explain why he liked the girls. That's all."

"Had you seen him watching girls?" Knox asked.

"No," Sammy replied. "But Nolan and the others said he had."

"And his response?" Callie replied.

He reared back enough to rock the swing. "Gave some stupid excuse about hunting for his niece who'd run away from home. Lame, right?"

"Questionable for sure," Knox answered.

Sammy lightened up, feeling credible.

Thumps sounded in the house. Callie'd have to hustle. "Did he say why the marina, though?"

The kid shook his head. "No. He headed toward the boats once I let him go, but he could've also been getting something to eat at that restaurant there, too."

"Did you ask his name?" Knox asked.

"Um, no."

"Did he show you ID?"

Sammy shook his head again.

"Did you ask who his niece was?"

"Yeah, but I think he gave me some bogus name."

"You wouldn't know that. Was it Emma, by any chance?" Knox asked.

The boy planted his feet on the floor and stopped the swing's rock. "I didn't care who his niece was."

The house door opened. A middle-aged man came out in jeans, slippers, undershirt, and a windbreaker open in the front. Lissa's dad, from the resemblance. "Kind of late for the police, isn't it? What's the emergency?"

"No emergency, Mr. Pasternak." Callie stood and held out her hand. "I'm Chief Callie Morgan. We're researching a man's disappearance on the island, and Sammy may be able to help."

"Well," he said, his voice deeper. "Don't you think the boy needs his parents for that?"

Lissa tugged at her father. "He has no parents, Daddy."

"Then where's he staying?"

Callie patted her chest. "Actually, with me for spring break, at Chelsea Morning."

At an impasse at the fact the closest responsible adult for the kid happened to be the one in uniform, the dad shifted his attention to the blanket on the swing . . . then to Sammy's chest.

Be glad his pants were on, dad. Callie motioned to Sammy. "Come on. You can ride with us." Callie shook the dad's hand, Knox likewise, and they took the stairs to the road.

The boy stumbled behind, sneakers in hand. "You're not the boss of me."

"Rescued your butt from Lissa's angry father, in case you didn't notice. But you should've shot straight with me earlier today." She turned on him. "Ever thought whoever killed Rhoades might want to likewise deal with those who came in contact with him? You're on that list now, son."

Sammy stopped in the middle of the road. "This is some shock thing you're doing, right?"

Knox held open the back door. "No, it's fact. Get in."

"Wait, that's where you put arrested people."

"No, it's where we put people when there's no room in the front seat," Callie said. "Get in."

"Now," Knox ordered, still holding open the door.

"I told you everything," the kid said, scanning the seat as if something would stick to him. He finally got in.

"Yeah, we know." But Callie didn't believe anybody these days. Knox shut the door, and she started the car. "Sammy, after you spoke to Rhoades, I bet you didn't just walk off. You watched him leave. Waited to see where he was going. Who he might meet."

Via her mirror, she watched Sammy rethink that day.

"I watched him," he said. "He knew I knew he was lying, so I hid and watched."

"Where'd he go?" Callie asked.

"To the dock. For probably five minutes I waited from behind the fence, but he just waited. After ten minutes, I figured he was an old man with nothing better to do."

Callie glanced over at Knox. He stared ahead, but he listened.

She doubted Pinky stood there enjoying Big Bay Creek. He waited for someone. Maybe Nolan. Maybe someone else. But shortly thereafter, he wound up in someone's boat.

Callie took a couple extra blocks in a roundabout way to drive back to Chelsea Morning. Sammy didn't ask why, though he would certainly recognize the delay.

Knox spoke over his shoulder. "You see Rhoades speak to anyone else? Not just at the marina but anywhere?" Lights flickered into the car every few houses they passed.

"No."

Callie tried to bring the talk around to something more personal, to open him up. "Did Rhoades ever speak specifically to Lissa?"

"Told you," he said. "I went off what Nolan said."

Hmm. "What about Kim?"

Sammy quit studying the passing scenery and looked into the rear-view mirror at her. "Kim who?"

Just like Nolan. "How about Yancy or Bea?" she asked.

"No and no. Doesn't matter how many names you throw at me, the answer is the same. God, I wish Nolan had kept his mouth shut about the dick."

Knox's fist hit the dash. Callie jumped, the explosion piercing her mental preparation for seeing Nolan again. "Agent Ken–"

"A man died, you little shit. Murdered!" Jerking around, he leered through the wire mesh.

Instinctively, Callie checked her mirror for the damage done by Knox's heavy-handed delivery. Eyes large and fearful, Sammy sat statue still.

"Yeah, you better be worried," Knox said and twisted around more, his lips all but eating the cage. "The side of his head was bashed in, Mr. Blackstone. Bone crushed. Then someone held him under to drown." He ended the rant with a small grunt of frustration.

Callie prayed the agent was done, wished he hadn't revealed so much about the murder, but before she could defuse the situation, Knox socked the screen. She jumped. Sammy jumped, both hands grasping for something in the seat for stability.

"Chill, Kendrick," she said low.

But the agent paid her no mind. "Someone killed this guy while he tried to find and save a girl. Save, Goddamn it! Not gawk, gape, or drool over." He took a hungry breath. "Does that put it more into perspective, Mr. Blackstone?"

The kid didn't speak, but his wide green eyes sure registered.

Her own blood pumped a bit harder. Cops were trained to raise their voices in appropriate situations, but the agent was running the risk of shutting Sammy down. If this was a ploy to put the fear of God in the boy . . . She drove past three more houses and pulled to the curb. "Here you go, Agent Kendrick."

Knox stared out his side window, as if trying to make sense of why they stopped.

Callie dipped her chin for emphasis. "Let you out here, right?"

"But we're not done," he said.

Callie threw the transmission into park. "Jesus, not in the car, Kendrick."

"Then let's take it outside." He slung open his door, slamming it shut. She exited with firm control.

His back to the boy, Knox lowered his voice. "You sure you don't need me any more tonight?"

She had to consider the question, which effectively answered it. "Sammy and I need to get home. How about giving me a head's up when you play bad cop."

"Whatever." Then he gave her a knowing wink. "See you in the morning."

She pivoted crisply and donned a look of disapproval for Sammy's eyes. The next steps were hers. Time to be the good cop.

In the mirror as the car pulled away, she watched Knox on the sidewalk eyeing her taillights. She never saw the drama coming, and it took her a sec to recognize his play. To speak in a manner to elicit the proper response. Police academy 101.

"Sorry about that," she said to her passenger, but when she glanced at the mirror, Sammy's attention was in his lap, on his phone. "This case is tough," she added.

She interpreted by his attention to his phone that there was no residual damage.

"Sammy, with this man brutally murdered, we're concerned about the safety of the rest of you."

"Don't see why," he mumbled, texting.

Either his past misery left him calloused, or he figured Pinky's death wasn't his problem. Either mind-set seemed chilly to her.

"Nolan pointed you in Rhoades's direction, Sammy. Nolan concerns us." She glanced toward the backseat for a read.

He still stared in his lap. "I can see that," he mumbled.

She grew impatient at this kid's lack of attention, lack of interest, and if she hadn't just lectured Knox on taking things personally . . . she'd take it personal that Knox drew a higher rise out of the kid. Maybe she'd underestimated him. The boy wasn't so shaken by the FBI agent that he couldn't spread his gossip. "Who're you texting?"

Sammy's fingers tapped more briskly. He paused a nanosecond, apparently for a response, then typed again.

Callie gave a little swerve to the car. "Hey. You're still locked in my cruiser and still the last person I'm aware of who spoke to Rhoades. Now answer me. Who're you texting?"

"Lissa."

Stopping the vehicle, she exited, and opened the back door. Sammy reared back into his seat, no place to go. In a slick move, Callie snatched the phone, then shut the door, locking him in.

With the palm of his hand, Sammy banged on his window after realizing he couldn't open the door. "Hey. You can't take my phone like that!"

Callie scrolled. She couldn't help herself, even if the action negated her ability to admit what she found into evidence. A text to Lissa. Some emojis from her showing exclamation, then another blowing a kiss. Hitting a back button, Callie found what she suspected. A text to Nolan. *They're asking about you, man.*

Who? Saying what? Nolan texted back.

Sammy: *About you and the dead dude. Shit, man. . . . Hear what happened to him?*

Nolan: *Drowned?*

Sammy: *Head caved in. Damn. An FBI guy went off on me. Hard. Shit.*

Nolan: *Bluffing to get you to talk, idiot. Don't without a lawyer. FBI?*

Sammy: *Guy in a golf shirt. Riding with Jeb's mom. Sounded legit. Why do I need a lawyer?*

Nolan: *Golf shirt?*

Crap. Callie pocketed Sammy's phone and leaped back in the car, heading toward Chelsea Morning. No detours. No extra blocks. Just a beeline to Nolan . . . Sammy fussing about his civil and constitutional rights en route.

Nolan was pivotal here. He'd been warned by Sammy that she had her eye on him. Somehow she didn't expect him to roll over and go to bed, and while he was agitated, she'd see what she could get out of him. Her night was never going to end.

She had half a mind to make Sammy spend the night in the back of her car.

Faster than usual, she entered the carport and positioned the patrol car between pillars. She released Sammy and handed him his phone.

After peering at the cell front and back, as though Callie compromised it somehow, he looked her in the eye. "I didn't deserve all that."

"Neither did Rhoades. And if you had all the facts you'd better understand." But he had no right to understand. And since a murderer running loose didn't even faze this kid, why give him more to text his peers?

Sammy headed for the closest stairs, to the back door. Callie followed, prepared to address Nolan, despite it being past midnight.

Callie stopped short.

Sprite sat huddled, blocking the stairs.

Chapter 25

CALLIE WASN'T SURE it was Sprite at first, the closest streetlight one house down, an oak blocking part of its effect. But in low cut bell-bottomed jeans, Sprite rose all cute and ambrosial, her raven cork-screw curls peeking out from under a crocheted hoodie. Sophie's progeny without a doubt. But she twisted the edges of her sleeves, apprehensive and skittish. "Ms. Morgan, I need to talk to you."

Sammy stopped to listen.

Callie pointed up the stairs. "Go on. This is none of your business."

She waited until he climbed to the top of the stairs.

"Sorry, Sprite, but I really can't talk. Where's Jeb? Does your mother realize you're out this late?" Ordinarily, she would've enjoyed visiting with the child, might've tried to explain Jeb's flummoxed feelings about her.

"Jeb was at my house, texting his friend Nolan—"

"Ms. Morgan?" Sammy hollered down. "The door's locked."

"About time Jeb remembered," she mumbled, then raised her voice. "Knock harder. Maybe they're upstairs." She smiled at Sprite.

Hands grasped in front of her, the girl hunched her shoulders, chilled. "They aren't here, and I need to tell you something." Sprite fingered a curl out of her face. "Jeb texted you but you didn't respond, but he's at Fantasea with Nolan. He asked me to wait and tell you since your phone might be off."

Callie had muted her cell, ever able to tell when her phone vibrated in lieu of a ring. Counting back, she guessed Jeb texted while she was outside the patrol car with Knox. She pulled out her phone to see, but Sprite grabbed her arm, shivering from waiting outside, craving to be heard.

"They argued a lot, I mean, texting. That's what Jeb said. I tried to go with him, you know, to fit in? My mom said my jealousy was childish, and that I ought to accept Jeb's world more since I'd be in college this fall." Her voice cracked. "Jeb told me I couldn't come with him. What kind of boyfriend is that, Ms. Morgan? I thought Jeb liked me. You know he likes me, right?"

"Sprite, slow down." The girl didn't understand, but Callie did. Jeb didn't dump Sprite, he protected her. "How long ago?" *Before or after Sammy texted Nolan?*

Scared at Callie's reaction, Sprite half whispered, "It's been a while."

Callie found the text. *Nolan left. I'm following. Will text in 30 minutes.*

A deep dread spilled into her, leaving no room for a discussion with Sprite about puppy love.

Callie rubbed the girl's back, grateful Sprite had been left out of the equation, but her heart thumped about Jeb. He assumed he owed his mother an obligation to tail Nolan.

Damn it all, she shouldn't have involved him.

"I'm the one who knows the twins. We were tight until my stupid brother and his crush on Bea. I ought to—"

"Not now, Sprite."

"But Ms. Morgan . . ."

"Did Jeb tell you anything else?" Callie asked.

"Yes, ma'am. He said *Tell my mom*, and that's why I waited on the steps. Wh . . . what's wrong?" Sniffling, she rubbed a sleeve across a red-cheeked face.

Now Callie shivered. The thirty minutes Jeb had promised had come and gone.

Sprite stared down the silt road. "I still don't understand why he had to go over there. I could've fit in," she repeated.

"Do the girls really not have parents?" Callie asked, praying adults were down there.

"Haven't seen the Wilkersons, like, in forever." Sophie and clan did live one house closer to Fantasea than Callie.

"Did your mother know?" Callie asked, disappointed Sophie didn't tell her the other day.

"She never said." Sprite gave a small twitch of her shoulders. "Sort of felt like a secret among the kids. Besides, they're usually in college, so what does it matter?"

"Text Jeb," Callie said. "Tell him I'm home and want him here immediately." As Sprite typed, Callie did the same. Screens lighting their faces, they waited for a response. Callie caught herself waiting for that teeny little notice that said a text had been seen. Nothing.

Crap. Think. Raysor lived forty miles too far. She didn't want to bring one of the new uniforms up to speed. So she called Knox. This could be no more than a teenage reality show, but Knox knew more about these kids right now than anyone else out here besides her.

"What is it?" he answered with urgency.

"Meet me at Fantasea," she said, praying Nolan was only being nosy, and Jeb the same. "My son followed Nolan over there. I could be wrong, but I don't like it." It was too late for a casual visit, and Nolan had been overly curious as to why she and Thomas were there earlier. She could not explain the sick feeling in her belly.

"Done." He hung up.

Knox hopefully felt the same indescribable creepy foreboding Callie did. She missed a few pieces here, but some were trying to fall into place. Nolan and the girls. That was somehow key.

She turned Sprite toward the base of the stairs. "Go on home. Jeb will call you in the morning."

"Is anything wrong?" she asked.

"Just go."

Sprite did as she was told, but glanced back, then hunched into her hoodie and proceeded home.

Callie climbed the stairs, and Sammy again typed on his phone. "What are you telling Nolan?"

He put the phone safely in his pants pocket this time. "I'm not."

"Then what *did* you tell Nolan?"

"I, um, you saw what I said in the car—"

She unlocked the back door but stood in his way, holding out her hand. He withdrew the phone against his opposite side, under his arm.

Lowering her tone, leaning into his space, she almost ground the words between her teeth. "Don't make me take it."

He passed her the phone outstretched on the tips of his fingers. She scrolled past the earlier messages to two minutes ago.

Sammy: *What the hell? Chief is on the f'in warpath with Jeb's old girl.*

Nolan: *Keep lady fuzz occupied.*

Sammy: *Not my game, dude.*

Nolan: *Make it your game. You owe me.*

Sammy: *Go F yourself.* Then, *She's coming.*

Callie looked up. "Owe him?"

Sammy's voice oozed with annoyance with no phone to pour it into. He went from uncomfortable to defiant, maximizing his height to glare down on her. "Lissa told you where I come from. Nolan got me a bed here at your place so I could see her."

"What else?"

"Loaned me some money so her dad wouldn't think I was such a bum."

She didn't see Nolan as a generous guy, particularly with no strings attached. "What exactly did he pay you to do?"

"Follow that old guy and keep Nolan informed where he was."

Callie glared. "Why did Nolan want to keep up with him?"

"Said he wanted to see what the guy was up to. Who he talked to."

"Such as?" Her voice flashed her aggravation.

But Sammy yelled back. "How the hell should I know? And I don't care!"

Dead end.

"Any texts on there to Jeb?"

"Why would I text Jeb?" he asked.

Why indeed. Only because he'd invited them to his home and introduced them around the island. But then Jeb would've told Callie things, and she could see the kids being wary of a cop's son. He'd been played.

Nolan had kept his friends close and his potential enemies closer.

Callie kept Sammy's phone and let him in the house. "Lock the door and do not let him in this house. I swear I'll arrest you if you ignore my instructions."

His glower told her she had a yes.

She withdrew a card from her pocket. "And if he contacts you, you contact me."

"How am I supposed to do that? You have my phone."

"There's a landline in the house. Learn how to use it."

Running out the back door, she made her way to the bottom of the stairs. After snaring her flashlight from her car, she trotted across the road to the opposite side. With the flashlight off, she skirted the three-house distance to the Wilkerson home, having a complete déjà vu about the Russian when he left Chelsea Morning with a gun to Jeb's back.

Sprite didn't mention anything threatening, but Callie wasn't relying on a high school senior to dictate her level of alert.

But Sammy's half knowledge scared her. What if Nolan had played Rhoades, too, and the agent, probably sensitive to the boy's bruised life in the shade of his sister, let Nolan in on way too much intel. Then paid dearly for it.

Then Jeb had caught a scent of something wrong. Maybe walked in on whatever Nolan was up to. Sometimes she hated knowing how quickly coincidence became so much more sinister.

Chapter 26

KNOX ROLLED UP to Fantasea with headlights off, and parked under an overhang of oaks and against a thickly woven fence of jasmine outside Parker Bender's house. Callie reached the house seconds after.

"I called Thomas," she whispered. "He lives off the beach, so it'll take him a few minutes to get here. Two officers on duty to call if needed. This could be a fluke or teen drama, Knox, but with my son involved—"

Even in the dark she saw him raise his palms up. "We shook stuff up. So what do you want to do? Just knock? You know your kid better than I do."

She peered through the overgrowth to Bender's house, relieved to see no parted blinds. "Yes, we just knock on the door."

Knox went first. Noting the Glock 19 clipped to his belt, Callie took her steps with stealth and the balls of her feet. Easy and slow, they climbed the stairs. No lights on the porch, but a distant glow showed through the kitchen window. At the top, she peeked in that window, and Knox slipped to the other end of the porch and glimpsed inside.

Then he returned to the door. She nodded. He rang the bell.

She scanned through the window inside for movement. Nobody. A physical sense of quickening rose in her chest at seeing the overturned coffee table.

"It's open." Knox let the wooden door swing in, his Glock gripped and aimed. He entered. Callie drew her own sidearm and followed.

"Jeb?" she hollered as she and Knox reached the living room. A lone beer bottle had toppled and spilled on the rug. Hadn't been there earlier. So much for the girls saying they were out of beer. The slight whiff of alcohol drew her in, a reminder of how long it'd been since she drank. But she forgot about booze when she noted the back door partially open. Jumping over Bea's scattered pink flip-flops, Callie ran to the exit, regretting not having checked outside sooner.

Dark, no movement. She barely made out the moored Sea Pro at the dock fifty yards out. No lights or movement there either.

She returned inside, nudging the door shut with her shoe.

"Nolan," yelled Knox from the closest bedroom. Then he moved into the bath.

Then as she returned to the living room, Callie froze. Blood on the throw rug. Not a lot, but plenty to indicate a struggle around the splintered coffee table. A cut hand, a busted nose maybe.

Knox came in and holstered his weapon. "Appears it all happened in this room. Is that blood?" He hurried to her side, but relaxed upon examination. "Nothing serious here, Callie. Glad you called me, though. I mean, better safe than sorry."

She straightened, taking in the details once again, in a slower study, in greater depth. The edge of a phone peered back from the creases of Yancy's recliner. Donning gloves, Callie pried it out. Locked code. Callie searched the other chair. "Look for more phones."

"Because you found one?" he asked.

She had a scary buzz about all this. "They had to have just left, Knox. Within minutes. I saw their texts just moments ago."

Callie looked in places Knox didn't think of and found Jeb's phone atop a folded pizza box in the kitchen trash. Beneath it, they found another. She hit the button to light up the screen. The last text from Sammy, *She's coming.*

Nolan's phone.

"Knox? Remember the last number on Pinky's phone bill?"

"One of Amanda Flagg's. I think so, why?"

"Call it," she said.

He tapped across the phone quickly and waited.

Nolan's phone rang in Callie's hand.

Pinky's last caller before he died.

And undoubtedly, Emma's case and Pinky's were conjoined, with Nolan being the glue.

The kids' disappearance mattered even more now.

"They bolted when Sammy told them I was coming," she said. "Look for the burner."

It didn't take long for Knox to find a fourth phone on what appeared to be Bea's nightstand. Hers, but no burner. Or no others.

Knox laid all four out on the kitchen counter. All inaccessible without passcodes. "This makes no damn sense."

Callie stood beside him, testing codes on Jeb's phone. He'd changed his since she last knew it.

"What teenager goes anywhere without a phone?" he asked.

She continued with passwords. "The bigger question is why throw them in the trash?"

"After a few beers, probably didn't know what they were doing."

She tried another code. "Jeb doesn't drink." She hit her mic. "Thomas? Where are you?"

"Almost there, Chief."

Knox cocked his head to the side as she clicked off. "What're you thinking?"

"Nolan was already worried about my discussion with the twins, so when Sammy texted Nolan, Nolan got concerned and came here."

"But why?"

"Nolan paid Sammy to tail Rhoades the day he died."

Knox got stern, suddenly more aware of the seriousness of the night.

"Because he'd been keeping eyes on Nolan for me, Jeb came with him but had no idea what was actually going on." This much Callie knew for sure, but she'd figured out little else, her logic trying to make too large a leap with ideas she didn't want to think about.

The agent remained silent when he could've asked more questions, and in those seconds that he gave her the unchallenged time to sort through the options, Callie respected him more. Minimal comfort at the moment, though.

Jeb wasn't involved with Nolan, she told herself. He just followed his roommate to Fantasea, then all of them disappeared for no damn reason she could define other than to get away from her. *Thank you, Sammy.*

But Jeb would've texted her at the thirty-minute mark, as promised. Motherly belief in her son had her distraught the most.

Had one or two of them forced the others? To where? And why? Hell, how?

"The car's still under the house," Knox said.

"Jeb's and Nolan's are at mine," she said, but a flash of light outside caught her attention, and she ran to the back door again. The partial moon reflected the water and small white caps that kicked up beyond the dock . . . and lights bobbed at the far side of Yacht Basin. "Shit, the boat's gone."

Knox peered out. "You sure they have one?"

"Damn straight I'm sure. It's a Sea Pro fishing boat, twenty-two foot center console. Noticed it this afternoon, and damn it, I checked not ten minutes ago. It was here. No lights. No movement. Goddamn it, they were on the boat, hiding, and the tide's now high enough to go anywhere they want."

Callie reached for her mic on her way out the back door. "Chief Morgan here. Be on the lookout for four young adults, ages nineteen to twenty-one, two girls and two boys. One girl with blue hair, I repeat, blue hair. The other with brown hair in a long braid. Boys in cargo shorts and jeans, both blond. Uncertain whether in distress . . . or dangerous."

She sprinted the remaining yards to the dock, Knox on her heels.

Seabrook would've gone out and checked the boat, not assumed it was empty like she did. Surprised at how his memory ambushed her, she also suddenly realized how long it'd been since she missed him.

Knox caught up with her. Thomas parked in the drive.

"Thomas! At the water," she shouted, and stopped short at the wooden steps.

There was no light, but Callie found the ground too matted with grass and weeds for prints anyway. However, the mooring lines were wet. She peered off in the distance as the navigation lights on a suitable-sized boat moved toward Scott Creek. It drove slowly out of the basin, the only possible destination being Big Bay Creek, or farther to St. Helena Sound. Or God forbid, the Atlantic.

But Scott Creek wasn't wide, which was one reason it was frequented by kayakers intimidated by the more open water, and even as it blended into Big Bay, regardless the name, the water's width was small. Residents could look out their windows and watch the teens go by, and still make out deer on the other side.

Callie needed to head them off before they hit deeper water. While they could be easily corralled.

She ran back off the dock, with a leap past the three steps to the ground. "Thomas? Meet us at the marina. Call Bobby Yeargin and get the Zodiac ready."

Thomas jumped into his dated two-door Ranger pickup and took off toward the marina. Callie mounted the stairs two at a time, locked the back door as she ran in and the front door going out, to preserve evidence; Knox waited with his rental Toyota at the base of the stairs. He approached seventy speeding them west toward the marina.

The marina sat at the union of Big Bay Creek and St. Helena Sound. The Sea Pro navigated narrower, shallower water that grew wider with distance, deeper nearer to the marina. Unless they veered right where Big Bay forked off.

That route, however, would snake past the park interpretive center, the Neck subdivision, and a couple of old plantations until it exited on St. Pierre Creek. Made no sense, because they could still be caught from the other end, or by a faster boat.

"Please just be stupid kids," she mumbled, gripping the door handle as Knox cut a sharp right into the parking lot at Bay Creek Park. "I'm positive, Jeb would not go along with a joyride this late at night."

"And?" Knox asked.

"And Nolan is hiding something big."

Knox skidded into the gravel drive where Sammy supposedly confronted Pinky that day.

Callie jumped out and ran toward the water. Suddenly, she couldn't hear Knox and turned back. At the car, trunk open, he rummaged through the contents.

"Knox, come on!" she yelled.

He slammed the trunk, shotgun gripped in one hand.

"No, the hell you don't," she said. Who brought a Remington on a boat . . . to meet kids? "Put it back."

He hesitated.

"Now!" she ordered. Her son was in the thick of something she didn't understand, and she had half a mind to leave Knox on the dock.

Sweat on her forehead in spite of the coolness, Callie suddenly caught herself breathless. Pressure in her chest. *No, no.* Think. Focus.

If this wasn't a damn joyride, maybe Nolan had flipped out. He'd grown up listening to Rhoades, and she could pray he absorbed a smidgen of the agent's ethics, thought processes, maybe even regret after the agent turned up dead. The same kind of guilt Knox had from not believing in the note.

Think, Callie. She rapidly covered the asphalt to the steps, then the wooden planks past the restaurant.

The kids took a damn boat. Why? *Why were teenagers so damn unpredictable?*

Their shoes echoed as they pounded past a seafood joint now empty and lifeless. The police department's slip with the Zodiac was farther down.

A few lamps lit the docks and slips, and eerie shadows gave strange dimensions from one section to another. Buildings loomed austere and ghostlike without tourists and shop owners. This late the moon retreated smaller, its illumination limited.

Thomas had already arrived, untied the moorings, and now cranked the engine.

"Where's Yeargin? Thought he drove this thing," she shouted.

"I didn't even bother with him, Chief. Not on this short notice," Thomas bellowed, then threw her a smile. "You know I've been dying to drive this baby."

Callie and Knox leaped into the boat. Callie managed to fall into the seat in front of the console before Thomas peeled out, the other boats rolling in their slips from his wake.

The cool wind cut through Callie, the salt spray giving it an even bigger bite. They had barely a mile to the fork, and by now the kids had less than that. "We need to get to Scott Creek before they get off it," she yelled over the wind.

Gripping belts on the seat, Callie turned to locate Knox and winced as the Zodiac's spotlights came on in her eyes. Spinning around toward the bow, she stared up the creek, across the marsh. It wouldn't take long to catch a glimpse of the kids' boat.

Callie squinted through the spray and the dark and replayed the evening. The girls had been in for the night. Jeb with Sprite. Not until Nolan headed to Fantasea did any of this happen.

She flipped damp hair out of her vision and sniffled, the humidity filling her sinuses with brine. Disturbed by the unexpected engine, two cormorants rose fast and clumsy from their slumber on a dock, their squawks left behind the boat only for those in their creek-front homes to hear.

Callie spotted the boat about the time Knox yelled at her to look. The kids approached from the east, the Zodiac from the west, with the creek's fork behind the historic Indian Shell Mound.

The kids' boat slowed.

As the Zodiac eased to a stop, engine in a low rumble, Callie stood. Water lapped the sides of the boat, bobbing it as the wake caught up and the disturbed creek tried to settle down. Knox approached the bow. One hand on the helm, Thomas shined a spot in the Sea Pro's direction.

Jeb drove. Relief spread across his face, but a fear still showed as well.

Bea sat behind Jeb, Yancy in the front. Nolan to Bea's left and shielded by Jeb standing.

Callie held out her hand. "Pass me the mic, Thomas. And keep that light on them." Before she keyed the mic, she leaned over to Knox. "Don't let them see a firearm, you hear? This might be a simple talk down, and nobody appears dangerous."

The kids reacted with arms up to block the glare as Thomas repositioned the spot. Except Jeb. Callie's adrenaline shot up at the way his hands remained clenched on the controls. Tied? Threatened if he let go? An unseen weapon trained on him?

"The four of you hold it right there." Callie's voice rebounded off the shell mound and the dense jungle behind it. "Shut off the engine, Jeb."

"No, he won't," Nolan shouted. "We're adults. You have no right to stop us."

"Afraid you're wrong there, Nolan." Callie tried to read each child. Yancy seemed wary, but way less afraid than Callie would've thought. Bea sat still, just her hand up to protect her eyes. Unemotional.

The only one terrified was Jeb, whose rigid stance and wide eyes belied whatever role Nolan wanted him to play. "I'm pulling alongside so Jeb can come with me," Callie said.

Nolan nudged Jeb, who said, "I'm good, Mom. The girls wanted a boat ride." He gave her a quick smile . . . that said everything was far from okay.

Only Callie would be able to read the slightest tremor in his voice that betrayed he didn't come willfully. Jeb had stumbled into the middle of something. His fear said they weren't letting him walk away.

"It's really just a pleasure ride, Ms. Morgan," Yancy hollered. "A double date with Jeb being mine, but he's not exactly a hell-raiser. Sort of a downer."

Callie welcomed the conversation. "I'd have paired you more with Nolan," she said, the distance being about fifteen yards now. "You two seem to have a lot more in common." They most certainly did. She strutted, like him. Their resemblance was showing, their behaviors too parallel.

She was Emma. Callie'd bet her badge on it.

"We need to talk about Rhoades."

"What?" Nolan yelled, but both girls gave surprised reactions that showed they heard Callie fine, their eyes wide. Even seated at opposite ends of the boat, they mirrored reflexive responses.

With his feet braced for more balance, Nolan seemed to be physically and mentally taking a stand. "I did not kill him, Chief Morgan. And you can put away your gun, Mr. FBI, along with that other guy." Nolan laughed, with a nonchalant wave toward Thomas. "He's just Edisto's meter maid anyway."

Knox shouted, "You sent the note, kid."

Nolan shoved Jeb aside to see better. "No, I didn't! Rhoades got a damn hard-on because of that note. But I—never—saw—a—note."

"Follow us on in," Callie shouted.

Nolan shook his head. "Ain't happening."

Bea sat Mona Lisa-like, benign . . . so unnatural that Callie began to wonder about her mental stability.

"Okay. I'm coming aboard to you."

Then Jeb screamed. "Bea has a gun, Mom."

"Shut up!" Yancy shouted. Then to the Zodiac, she yelled, "There is no gun, so nobody lose their mind."

"Knox?" Callie uttered. "If Jeb says there's a gun—"

"Yeah, I heard."

Thomas released the thumb break on his holster.

"Jeb?" Callie hollered, but he remained glued to the helm, too terrified to speak.

What the hell skittered through their half-developed, juvenile minds?

"Show me the weapon!" she shouted. "And show me your hands."

All four held up empty hands. "See? No gun," yelled Yancy.

But the weapon could be on a seat, tucked under a leg.

Helplessness. The sensation threatened to choke Callie, fueled by a heart that pounded blood way too hard for her to think clearly. If Nolan was indeed armed, too, if he at any second felt he'd run out of options, he could easily hit all three targets before Callie and her guys could make a move. A law enforcer's nightmare: a guy shielded by hostages. The darkness, distance, and movement of boats . . . the immediate proximity of the gunman to the others.

Callie held the mic against her chest. If Nolan decided to shoot, it was best he start with her. "Thomas, move in and prepare to board. Knox? You ready?"

He stared, jaw tight. "Sure thing, Chief."

"Weapons ready, then. And don't either of you bloody shoot my son."

Chapter 27

AT CALLIE'S DIRECTION, Thomas eased over to the Sea Pro. He held the light in place to compromise the kids' vision.

Near the bow, Callie surveyed each teen, anxious, hoping none of them decided to make some stupid sudden move. Jeb had ventured with Nolan down to Fantasea because of her. This kid—her kid, the one who'd hated law enforcement since it killed his father, turned her to drink, and took Seabrook, was now caught in the middle of a demented, dysfunctional family also affected by the law. Yeah, family, because one of these girls was Emma Flagg. Callie'd bet her career on it. She'd already bet her son.

Yancy was the first to shift her gaze off Callie and into the beyond, and if the others hadn't followed suit, she would've read the twin as deceptive.

"Vessel approaching," Thomas said. "We might have help."

Callie turned. Lights bobbed. Another boat. If they weren't law enforcement, they'd be a hazard.

"I didn't call for another boat to be out here," Thomas said.

And this was not a heavily trafficked area, especially this late.

Knox swiveled his attention between the Sea Pro and the oncoming boat. "Can you raise them on the radio?" The boat got louder.

"They'll be here before they answer." Thomas stiffened, taller. "They aren't slowing down much, either."

Though the night was pitch, the half-moon outlined the craft by its white color, its speed by the plumes of the parted water. With a hard stare, Callie tried to identify any marking, any shape to tell her friend or foe. Her first thought was Sammy; her second one of her officers.

But an officer would have radioed.

And where would a landlubber like Sammy find a boat this quick, at this time? Much less know how to drive it and navigate at night?

"Swing the light around," she yelled over the motors.

Thomas flipped it quick to reflect on the boat that bore down on them.

A bullet zinged past Callie's shoulder from the kids' direction. A handle on the Zodiac exploded, shredded. "Gun!" She grabbed Knox by the shirtfront and yanked him to his knees, then down onto the nonskid bottom.

"They're coming close. Grab ahold of something!" Thomas shouted.

Callie scrambled to a crouch, groped for new holds, and expected to have to dive, the muscles in her thighs tight, primed, and ready to spring one way or another. However, the thirty-foot boat veered right before coming close enough to spray, then in an S maneuver, turned toward the kids.

Callie shoved herself to the other side to see. Unable to scream *jump*, Callie watched numb in what seemed a harrowing, slow-motion action scene.

"All right!" screamed Jeb, a smile exploding across his face. Then he twisted around and dove off the boat.

The larger boat banked left then right, and smacked across the Sea Pro's engine and starboard quarter, barely more than a spank for the larger, more rugged Grady-White vessel. The half collision, half scrub tipped the Sea Pro in a slow heave onto its port side, the incapacitating crack loud and sharp.

Nolan pitched back then forward, his shift throwing him hard against the gunwale before he took a half flip into the water.

Bouncing off the gunwale nearest her almost kept Yancy in the boat, until another counter heave took her backward over the side opposite that of the boys.

Callie couldn't see Yancy, and Nolan seemed stunned, his face bobbing in and out of the water. Where the hell was Jeb?

She dropped her belt and dove shallow into the dark water, the cool temperature stealing her breath. April was spring, the water not the tepid warm that came with the end of May. As she broke the surface, she hoped to see Jeb ten or so yards from her based on where he went in. Instead, the Grady-White puttered up, and a girl leaned over the side.

"Jeb! Grab the ring!" Sprite tossed the life preserver ring from what had to be her brother's charter fishing boat. Callie'd never seen the boat Sophie's ex bought their son, but she damn sure would remember it now.

"Callie!" Knox shouted and pointed. "To your right. Get Nolan. I'll throw you a ring!"

Nolan floated awake but stunned. He instinctively swept at the water to stay afloat but made no effort to find safety.

With a half dozen good strokes, she reached the boy from the rear in case he decided to panic. The preserver hit the water a yard from her. With eight inches of height and sixty pounds of weight on her, Nolan could take her down, intentionally or otherwise. After all, not five minutes ago, someone had shot at her. As she shoved the float in front of him, she shouted, "Nolan! Grab it."

He didn't respond, so she reached around and splashed water in his face, to which he flinched. Then from behind, she shoved him, and he took the preserver. Knox hauled in the rope, hand over fist. "Anyone see the girls?" he shouted.

Thomas shined his light around. Bea's backside showed her effort to lean over the boat rail and recover her sister. "I see Bea."

Treading water, Callie turned to see Jeb safely in Sprite's craft. Knox hauled Nolan in, handcuffs at the ready. Waves still stirred the area, gas in the water from the hit, and Callie took an unexpected, nasty mouthful of the mixture.

Callie reached her boat and clung onto the looped nautical rope along the side of her boat; she coughed once, then spit some more. "Did Yancy get out okay?"

Knox leaned over, gave her both hands, and effortlessly lifted her short frame into the boat. "Bea got her," he said. "She appears fine, but we'll see in a second."

As she slicked her hair back, Callie tried to peer through the dark and confusion and still take head count regardless of what the men said.

"You familiar with the crazy captain of this other boat?" Knox asked. "Your son appears to be."

She peered over to the Grady-White to catch Jeb planting a hell of a kiss on Sprite. "Yeah, I'm familiar with her."

Callie accepted Thomas's windbreaker, the breeze prompting shivers as the cool air cut through her dripping, even colder clothes. She wasn't sure whether to praise Sprite or whip her ass, but without a doubt, she'd driven her brother's boat enough over the years to be pretty damn good at maneuvering the vessel. "Thomas, we still need to board and find the damn gun that about took my head off."

Nolan appeared more collected now, safe in the bow of the Zodiac. No blood or apparent broken bones, which was all Callie cared to know at the moment. While Callie wanted to understand the idiocy in Nolan's mind, her son and that gun took priority.

"Jeb," she hollered. "You okay?"

He held Sprite against him, in the crook of his arm. "Yes, ma'am."

They drew alongside the damaged craft so Callie could clamber on board. Bea clung to her sister. Callie searched them and found nothing.

Knox canvassed the listing boat. "Can't find the gun," he said, his balance challenged as he turned seat cushions.

Callie sat, her leg against Yancy's in the confines of the boat. "Which one of you is Emma?"

As the twins peered at each other in that ingrained habit of theirs, they seemed to mentally weigh their words.

Callie touched Yancy's chin firmly and made her look at her. "It's not that difficult a question, young lady."

"Yes, it is," Yancy said. "We protect each other."

"Meaning you take shots at people?"

"Nolan did that," Bea replied.

Doubtful. Why the hell would he? "Yancy, you ride back with me in the big boat. Bea, you go with Agent Kendrick in the Zodiac."

Bea shook her head in little tiny movements, jittery. Reaching over, Yancy slid wet bangs out of her sister's face. "It's just for a little way, honey."

"Unh-uh. No."

Yancy reached up for a fist bump, and Bea turned away.

"Come on, Sweet Bea. Give it up."

Reluctantly, Bea gently fist-bumped her back. "Just a ride to the dock," Yancy said, and stood.

Moving toward Knox, Callie waved at the incapacitated boat. "Thomas will radio back, and we'll send someone to come get this thing, hopefully before it goes down. You take Bea . . . and watch her."

She preferred Yancy on her boat, apart from her sister. This saccharin, cooperative side of her playing out at the moment wasn't one Callie trusted easily.

It took a few minutes to place everyone before Thomas gazed up at Callie, and she gave him the wave to proceed to the dock. Slow and easy. Upon arrival, however, there'd be no changing clothes and catching shut-eye. Dawn would come and go before Callie let any of these souls rest. She had at least four interviews to deal with if she didn't count Sammy. Long complicated ones, and the more stubborn the participants, the more likely Marie would be ordering breakfast, lunch, and even dinner for all parties concerned. Stress, adrenaline, and lack of sleep made for the best interrogation opportunity.

With a tug on Jeb's sleeve, Callie pulled him apart from Sprite.

Yancy sat alone on the port side, watching her sister on the other boat. The Zodiac crept a half boat length ahead and to the left, luckily easy to monitor, because Callie wanted to keep an eye on its newest occupants.

She leaned into Jeb. "We've got little more than seconds here, so talk to me."

"I'm sorry I didn't call—"

She yanked his sleeve again. "Later about that. Who shot at me?"

"Bea," he said up close to her ear. "She had the gun the whole time."

"Where'd she get it?" she asked, also up close, wondering if the firearm had belonged to Rhoades.

Jeb shrugged.

"What caliber, Jeb? You can tell the difference."

"Nine millimeter," he said. "Like your service weapon."

Callie hid her reaction and instead cut a glance over at Yancy. "And what happened at Fantasea to make y'all get on the boat?"

"They didn't expect Nolan, much less me. Nolan didn't want me there at first, but then he asked if I'd be a witness to his questions to them, and I said sure. He'd gotten awful mad after Sammy's texts and wanted to hear what the twins told you. Nolan and Sammy had some sort of secret between them, Mom. Nolan kept saying he had something to prove. I figured you'd want whatever intel I could get, plus it was just too weird to leave."

Ahead of them, Callie noticed Nolan alert, still seated in the bow, dueling words with Bea, who sat in the seat Callie had, in front of the helm. Maybe six feet between them. He yelled, slinging barbs at the girl, and she yipped back. Knox fussed at them, stepping up to be heard, a hand on Bea's shoulder at one point. "What were they arguing about at the house?" she asked, her ear on Jeb, eyes on the other boat.

"They're related, Mom."

Yeah, she figured. "How?"

"He's their brother but don't ask me how. Bea told Yancy they needed to take the argument to the boat, or she couldn't do this. That's the way she said it . . . *do this*. I asked *do what*, and they wouldn't say. When I tried to leave, they wouldn't let me."

"Nolan or the girls?" Callie asked.

"All of them. He was mad and wanted me as wingman. They were just . . . mad. At him, at me for just being there. He said he knew stuff, and they said he didn't. Nolan said he saw them, and they denied it. They spoke in code, Mom, probably because I was there."

"So why didn't you just walk out?"

"Because of Bea's gun."

With that comment, she stared at her son. "She held a gun on you?"

"No, she never pointed it. Listen to me!" He was confused, still stunned, some residual shock about his friends.

"I am listening," Callie said, but grew impatient, anxious at the danger she learned he'd been in. She wanted to shake every piece of the night's experience out of him.

"I didn't want to get involved, but when I tried to leave, Bea showed her gun more. Yancy tried to take it from her, but Bea wouldn't let her."

A gun now overboard. Sounded like going out in the boat wasn't a consideration until Jeb became a witness they couldn't afford.

"What about your phone?"

"Nolan and I were told to throw them in the trash," he said.

She returned attention to the other boat as Nolan stood, Bea back on her feet. Knox yelled at them, probably to shut up and sit down.

"Knox!" Callie shouted, unheard over the engines, having learned that Bea needed cuffs as much or more than Nolan. She fumbled for her phone. Swiftly, Bea reached around to the side of the helm and came out with a fire extinguisher in hand. In two steps, she covered the distance to Nolan and drew the red canister back like a baseball bat.

Compromised by his cuffs, Nolan leaned right, ducking behind his bound arms.

Bea brought the can down, landing square on Nolan's forearm.

Knox snared both the girl's arms, the canister dropping as he twisted her hands behind her back. She yelled, crying, writhing. Then once he lowered her onto the floor, his knee in her back, Knox hollered at Thomas, who threw his cuffs to the agent. Nolan nursed what had to be a broken bone against his chest.

"Bea!" Yancy yelled.

Though she couldn't hear over the boats, Callie saw Bea scream the same word repeatedly. *Yancy.*

The marina showed more lights than when they left. Everyone's departure activity had stirred one or two people, which raised eight or ten more. Both of Callie's on-duty officers, the new ones, awaited them. One assisted mooring the Zodiac, while Thomas filled them in on what happened. The other gingerly escorted Nolan up the dock toward land.

"Take that one to the hospital," she directed, "but don't let him out of your sight."

Sprite brought in her boat close enough for Callie to climb down.

She ran over to where Knox had lifted Bea out of the boat and onto the dock. "Your office at the station?" he asked.

"You're a mind reader," she said.

Yancy hollered from behind them. "I'm coming with her. She's my sister. You can't—"

But Thomas stopped her.

Callie pointed at the new officer. "Ike, you finish with the boat. Thomas, bring Yancy in your truck," Callie said. "And sit with her in the lobby until I get done with her sister."

"You can't do that!" Yancy yelled. "She needs me. Don't talk, Bea. Don't tell them a thing."

Which told Callie exactly how she needed to treat Bea.

Chapter 28

JUST MINUTES AFTER mooring the boats, Callie stood in her office while Knox placed Bea in a seat before her desk. He rolled a chair to the side for himself. Though not invited, he intended on staying for the interview. No problem. Callie wanted him to. He'd earned the right to see this damn thing through.

She tossed him a notepad and shivered once, her damp underwear keeping her chilled. She hadn't a dry uniform, and not wanting to interrogate in civvies, she was stuck in clammy clothes. But then she recalled an old coat, a permanent fixture on a coat rack in the lobby, long left by an unknown owner. She exited her office to retrieve it. Bea could wait and stew.

Though the coat swallowed her, the quilted interior was warm. But it wasn't until she shifted her much smaller shoulders to adjust the excess material, that she slowed . . . and caught the woodsy scent of Seabrook.

Her eyes closed. *Oh, dear Jesus.* Another breath. Damn, how she missed him.

Not that he'd been a great cop, but damn, she'd have welcomed him. His calm. She inhaled again . . . his scent.

The pneumatic glass door gave its signature whoosh. Callie expected to see Mike's six-foot frame, the gentle welcome of his smile.

Instead, a glowering Thomas arrived with Yancy.

Callie waved to the lobby chairs. "Sit with her right there." Even tired, Callie still pumped adrenaline, and she'd need that and more to carry her through this. She was incensed at these girls, and Nolan wasn't off the hook. Even Jeb would have to be questioned.

Yancy wore a blanket but seemed anything but tired. Her gaze darted around the station in search of Bea. Yancy's facial muscles drew tight as Callie turned to leave. "Chief Morgan?" Her demanding voice rang out, the type A personality unaccepting of limitations.

But Callie returned to her office without a backward glance and left the blue-haired sister wanting. Bea held the limelight for a change, and

Callie was eager to play her role.

"So let's get started, Miss Bea Wilkerson," Callie said, as she shut her door and moved behind her desk. She set up the recorder, identified those present, and began by reading off Bea's Miranda rights. "Do you understand these rights as I have explained them to you?"

Bea pinched her brows in silence.

"Yes or no, Bea."

The girl pasted her attention on plaques behind Callie's head. "Yes."

"Okay." Callie straightened papers and waited for Bea to ask for an attorney. During the silence, she studied the girl who bonded with dolphins and wondered if her entire wardrobe was actually all blue, like Yancy indicated.

Nothing from Bea, and lots of ground to cover, so Callie continued. "Why did you try to shoot me?"

Bea jerked, not expecting such directness, nor did she remember her sister's advice to remain silent. "It went off accidentally. I was scared with that boat coming so fast, and I guess the gun dropped in the water. Daddy takes us shooting, and we kept it for protection after they . . . whenever they go out of town."

"Bullshit," Callie replied, not a fan of the Pollyanna behavior. "Your parents have been gone for well over a year, and you aimed at me."

She mumbled her reply. "I was nervous. You scared me."

Even the NRA would want to deny this girl a weapon.

"What type of gun was it?"

"I . . . um, it was . . ."

"A .45? A .22? If your father taught you how to shoot, he at least told you what you were shooting."

"I'm not sure."

"Right." Callie looked at her, dubious. "Well, the divers will retrieve it, which makes this night about more than a joyride and a misfired gun, doesn't it?"

The firearm was most likely Pinky's, and Yancy's interview would further clarify. Knox started to speak, but without taking her eyes off her subject, she discreetly showed him her palm to stop any interruption. This was not a good cop / bad cop situation, and Callie believed a woman would capture Bea's attention better than a man.

From the way the child scanned the tiny room and stared at the door handle to her right, she craved an outlet. Trapped, she would soon turn to her accusers and hope to make them understand. The question was how long it would take to make her reach that point.

Callie'd pretend they were of like minds, for a while.

"What did you and Nolan argue about at the house?" Callie continued.

Bea regarded the chief like she ought to understand better. "That was Yancy."

She let Bea have that one. "I see. What did they argue about?"

"Just stupid stuff."

A sigh of distrust. "After I speak to you, I interview Yancy. Then Nolan. Then Jeb. I'll get the story, hon. But we'll also soon have the gun, and we're damn good at piecing half-truths together. You can talk, or let us take you down with evidence. That scenario will have more dire consequences for you, unfortunately."

Bea dropped her focus to the long braid in her lap, where her fingers adeptly unwound the last few inches of strands. A few hairs came out, and she wriggled her fingers to let them loose to drop to the floor.

"What was Nolan bothered about?" Callie asked.

Nolan had hired Sammy to tail Pinky. That much Callie understood. Sammy confronted Pinky, watched him go to the marina, then left. Or so he said. But as aptly as these kids used phones, Sammy would've texted Nolan before he left the marina, to earn his money.

How could Nolan not have driven down there? How could he not want to see who Pinky was so thrilled to meet?

Bea repeatedly picked at a patched hole in the leg of her jeans like it was a bug that wouldn't die. "He saw me."

"Who saw you?" Callie needed Bea to say it aloud for the transcript. Knox nodded. Bea seemed not to even notice him in the room.

"Nolan."

"Did Nolan ask you to pick up the agent in your boat?"

The girl looked up surprised. "No. Why would he do that?"

"So, we agree you picked up the agent." Callie avoided using the name for the moment, in hopes the girl could mentally distance herself enough to speak more openly. "You took him out on your boat. To see dolphins? Isn't that why you go out in your boat?"

That drew a hint of a grin from Bea. "Most people don't understand dolphins."

"Yes, I've seen that, and it's a shame," Callie said. "The agent didn't understand you either, did he?"

Bea's fingers climbed into her hair, then back down, playing allegro like Callie used to do on a clarinet her mother forced upon her.

Callie held a warm smile until Bea peered up. The girl let the corners of her mouth turn up a bit, too. Good, settling back down.

"You've been a good sister to Yancy. Everyone saw y'all have that special twin thing going, which I have to say has always dumbfounded me. Very ESP-ish."

Bea's posture loosened upon hearing what she could easily accept . . . and was proud of.

"Can you really read her mind?" Callie asked.

A shrug. "That's not really how it works, but we're close."

"So, if you didn't tell her about the agent, she wouldn't automatically know?"

"We just follow each other's lead."

"Okay, explain it to me," Callie said, as if trying to get it.

And Bea fed off that. Her shoulders went back, and her voice took on a touch of self-worth. "What we don't understand at first, we accept. Yancy is strong and smart, but she needs *me* to be whole. People think she runs us both." Bea shook her head. "But behind the scenes she relies on me. It's why I'm always at her side. We click."

Not exactly an absolution of Yancy, and Callie wasn't sure about that last part, where Yancy relied on Bea. Bea had a deep dependency on Yancy, but apparently, she held on to an even deeper emotional need to protect her blue-haired sister. There was an even deeper strength to her than she showed.

Callie slid back into the substance of the interview. "Shame Yancy wasn't with you at the meet, huh, because the agent didn't take you seriously, did he?"

She shook her head in quick, tiny jerks.

Time to determine if there'd been a collaboration with the girls. "What did Yancy think?"

No answer.

"Guess we have to bring in Yancy."

Bea perked up. "Yes, go get her. She'll make it sound right. I'm not good with words."

Meaning Yancy could lie better. Rubbing her chin, Callie stared pitifully. "Oh, not together, honey. We interrogate *her*—alone. Most likely we'll pin something on her, because everyone knows she's the mastermind of your duo." She rolled her chair back. "Agent Kendrick? See if there's a room at the fire station to lock up Bea and then bring in her sister."

Bea's expression tightened, fear in her eyes. "But she didn't do anything."

"Sure she did, and she's going to jail for it." Then to Knox, she said, "Agent Kendrick, take her."

"No!" Bea moaned, stretched the word out, gripping the sides of her seat like she couldn't be pried loose.

"Then tell me how you contacted Rhoades," Callie said.

When Bea released the seat, her gaze pleading with Callie, Knox lowered himself back down.

"I sent a note," Bea said.

That was fast. Eerily normal.

"What kind of note?" Callie asked.

"Typed. Said Emma was on Edisto and gave a phone number."

Yes, headway. "We have your phone, by the way, so we'll find—"

"No, you won't."

With a glimpse at Knox, Callie tried to read if he understood her certainty, because she sure as hell didn't. At first, like her, he seemed unable to decipher Bea, but then the wrinkles smoothed from his forehead . . . about the moment she got it, too. Bea meant the call wasn't on her phone. It was on the burner cell. The burner cell on Pinky's phone record. The last call before Nolan's.

Her pulse quickened at another step.

"Why meet then?" Callie thought she understood why use the marina. The needed comfort of the boat and a desire to avoid her sister.

"Spring break, high tide, and the dolphins would be out."

Funny how the dolphins factored in. "Sounded like a plan," Callie said. "Was he nice?"

The girl scrutinized the back wall, to remember the moment. "Yeah." She slid out the word slowly. "I guess he was."

A slight sting showed in Knox's expression, but he blinked back.

"Did you introduce yourself to him?" Callie asked.

"Yes, told him I was Emma."

Knox slowly sank back against his chair.

Callie's next question flew out of her head. She'd have sworn Emma was Yancy. She studied this girl addicted to blue clothes and tried to picture her as the tyke in the photo with gapped teeth. Blond wavy curls.

"How did you even find him, Bea?" she finally asked with sincere marvel in her voice.

The girl beamed, proud. "Yancy is so smart, Ms. Morgan. Ever since our parents told us about Emma on our eighteenth birthday, my sister searched for history." Odd how she spoke like Emma was a third person. "Yancy found so much information about that kidnapping and it didn't take long to find him."

"Or Nolan, I imagine."

She shook her head, nose scrunched, like their sleuthing had been a piece of cake. "He's why we went to College of Charleston. So we could watch him."

"Why?"

"Why not? Wouldn't you be curious? We could watch him on our terms. Why would we want to stake our claim without educating ourselves first, or deciding if the family was worth going back to?"

"But . . ." Callie stopped herself from going down the rabbit hole of the old kidnapping. The agent's case came first. The Emma situation would come out in the wash when Callie asked the questions that begged the asking. Who stole Emma? And why, if they intended to return her later?

Callie pointed at a case of bottled water in the corner behind Knox's chair. He pulled out three and passed them around. For once, Callie preferred wetting her tongue with the water in lieu of the single barrel in her bottom right drawer.

"Okay," she began again. "Let's talk about you and the agent in the boat. Did you show him the dolphins first or tell him you were Emma?"

She poised herself in her chair like a marionette doll, sitting tall and posed just so. "Dolphins. Not the best show, though. And then I told him who I was."

"Was he surprised?"

Another light shrug. "He took it in stride. Seemed more to enjoy the ride."

"But then you went up Big Bay Creek, right? What happened then?"

Bea's hands toyed with each other. "I told him Emma liked where she was. He could go home. She wasn't going back to that *other* family." She dipped her chin, like it was a conclusion anyone ought to come to.

"Makes sense," Callie said.

"You'd think so," she replied. "But he said no, he had to tell the Flaggs and the FBI. That meant nothing would be the same." Her eyes grew moist. "I begged him, Ms. Morgan. I cried, and he hugged me, but still, he said it was how it had to be." But then a darker child seemed to come forward. "Yancy and I were already happy as things were, but he wouldn't listen."

"What then?" Callie asked softly, just sufficient for recording.

"I don't remember," Bea mumbled.

"Then let's go over it again, and maybe you'll remember more."

The girl shook her head and returned attention to her hair.

"Hey, it's okay. I'll go through it with you."

Still nothing.

Callie had to bring this girl around and get her to completely repeat the events . . . without memory losses. Readjusting the front of the coat, Callie drank in its scent. This was a pivotal moment. She needed all the support she could get, and if a whiff of Seabrook would help, so be it.

Little tremors emanated off Bea. If Callie'd learned anything from the evening, it was this dolphin-loving girl wasn't 100 percent together.

Some would define the next steps in the interview as harsh. Seabrook might have, with his bedside manner too deeply ingrained. Stan wouldn't, his goal being the truth. But they weren't here. This was her game. Her mission to solve this case . . . these cases.

And it was time to quit being Bea's friend. "Let's start on Yancy—"

"No!"

Callie went for the gold. "What did you use to hit Rhoades?"

In a snap, Bea resorted to tears, her crying a crescendo of alto sobs. On like a spigot.

Knox stood, ready to address a physical reaction.

Callie held her hand out for him not to interrupt, then raised her voice. "Did you hit Rhoades in the head? Answer me."

Bea cried louder, and Yancy's scream could be vaguely heard from the waiting area. "Bea!"

"What did you hit him with?" Callie commanded.

"A fire extinguisher."

"Thank you," Callie replied, stern. "Now, did you hold him underwater?"

Bea wept into her braid. "Yancy didn't need a brother. And that mother wasn't mine."

Wait. . . . Bea wasn't Emma after all. Yancy was.

But as hard as Callie wanted to launch down that trail, Emma's identity wasn't the focus at this exact second. "Did you drown Agent Rhoades?"

Bea groaned from behind clenched teeth, with her eyes shut. As if she were running in place, her knees rose and fell, bare feet smacking the linoleum, energy flying out with no place to go. Then she stopped and nimbly undid her hair again, tresses flying like a mane.

"Bea?" Callie said in a commanding tone. "Did you hold him underwater?"

With a growl, Bea dug both hands into the loosened mane and stretched her arms out taut, gritting, straining. The strain grew, her forearms shaking. If she didn't stop, she'd—In a scrambled leap from her seat, Callie rounded the desk. Knox jumped up. But neither prevented the small chunk of bloody hair that tore loose, entangled in Bea's tortured fingers. Tiny droplets of blood rained across Knox's chest before he pinned Bea's wrist and took her to the floor. They trapped her in a double-arm bar restraint, arms behind her, then while Knox contained the squirming girl, Callie fastened cuffs.

Bea screamed until her throat went hoarse. "I couldn't let him tell people." Then she wept. And they let her.

Once she'd settled into a quieter round of tears, Callie opened her door. "Thomas, bring some towels. We've had a little accident in here."

"Bea?" yelled Yancy, then tried to rush through the swinging gate that kept the lobby's citizens from the staff. The lock jerked her to a stop. "What's wrong with my sister?" Yancy cried, anguished, stretching over the gate as though the extra inches would help her see or hear more.

Callie made sure Knox had Bea contained and in her chair, then walked out. "Frankly, Bea got upset and spilled her bottle of water, Yancy. Don't worry, we're almost done." Then like before, she turned and left, leaving Yancy eager to talk, with nobody to talk to.

Thomas arrived with the towel in a rush, quick to check on his charge.

"Are you okay now?" Callie asked Bea as she shut the door. "Can we calm down and finish?"

Cheeks blotchy, Bea hunched on the edge of her seat, arms fastened behind her, Knox remaining at her back now. "Finish what?" Bea replied, sounding pitiful.

Behind the desk again, Callie checked the recorder, ensuring it remained on. For the record, they'd efficiently and humanely contained a suspect disturbed over the direction of her future.

"You busted the man in the head," Callie said. "Where's the fire extinguisher you used?"

Bea really should've requested an attorney.

The sniffling and couple of coughs took a second. "Threw it in the creek."

Not around where they found Pinky. "What about the burner phone?"

"Different part of the creek."

"So," Callie began, "did Rhoades fall in the water when you hit him?"

Bea nodded.

"Out loud, please."

A sigh. "Yes."

Bea couldn't see Knox from his guarded stance behind her, and she wouldn't want to judging by the way he gripped the back of her chair, learning how his mentor spent his last moments.

"Did he try to get back in the boat?" Callie spoke faster and raised her tone. "How loudly did he beg for help, Bea? Could he speak, or was it coarse, inaudible? We'll impound that boat and check it for proof of how hard he tried to live."

"He couldn't talk," she said almost inaudible herself. "He never woke up."

Callie glanced with warning at Knox before delivering the next question. "When you stepped between his shoulder blades, how did you decide how long to hold him under?"

The glare shot like a laser from the girl.

"It's not a hard question. When did you determine he was dead, and you could leave and go on about your business? Bubbles? Or did you recognize that his instinct to breathe, even unconscious, stopped when he ceased twitching?" She gave Bea only seconds, then barked, "Answer!"

"Both? I don't remember. I just knew."

His complexion paled, and Callie studied Knox a bit to ensure he was stable. He gave her a nod.

"Now," Callie said, "when and why'd you take his gun?"

Tears rolled down Bea's cheeks. Hunching farther over her lap, the girl shrugged.

"Tell me the words, Ms. Wilkerson."

The deep breath ended with a mewl of a moan. "Didn't know he had a gun until his coat rode up in the water. All I could think of was what if someone stole it."

There was a deeper *messed up* to this shy young girl with the blue hippie clothes than Callie would've thought. "So . . . you did all this on your own, to include murder, to prevent Rhoades from telling Emma's real family she was alive and well. Yancy ask you to do this? Did she set it up or prepare the note for you?"

"No," she pleaded. "Yancy didn't help. I didn't even plan to kill him. He just wouldn't listen to me about what was important to Emma." More tears now, flowing more freely. The wet face having succumbed to its former innocence after the release of such a burden.

Knox came around to take stock of her, misery etched in wrinkles Callie didn't remember. "You murdered a good man over this? Yancy's nineteen. No one could force her to go anywhere."

"You don't understand," she sobbed. "My parents saved Yancy when they took her. That family did bad things to her. How could anyone send her back to that?"

"Bad things?"

"What else do you call being raped by your dad?"

Chapter 29

CALLIE NEVER SAW that coming. Knox appeared just as stunned. Yancy molested as a toddler, and a shrewd couple stealing her to save her from the abuse. How would they have called that? How was anyone able to even prove that? Nolan was too young. Yancy, too. The dad was dead. At the end of the day, though, the Wilkersons were still kidnappers.

God, was Nolan molested, too?

Far-fetched, but what if any of it was true?

"Cooperate with us, Bea," Callie said, "and we'll protect Yancy from being incriminated."

"But Yancy was a victim!"

"Absolutely. Your parents stole her from her warm bed at the tender age of two."

"No, you can't make the Flaggs the innocents here. Her father molested her!" Bea said, seething. "She di-didn't need to g-go back there."

But *was* Yancy abused? Or was abuse the story that two parents used on the girls to justify their nabbing a playmate for their daughter? It was irrelevant anyway. Kidnapping was a crime, period.

Callie scoffed. "You two weren't pissed off to have been lied to all that time?"

Glaring, Bea tried to push forward on her seat, but Knox detained her. "She was grateful, you hear me? Extremely grateful she didn't remember being raped. Grateful someone risked their lives to save her. Don't spin this into something it's not."

"And let's not overlook the fact your parents stole her, possibly without all the facts. A lot of selfishness falls into this mix. But let's leave the history and return to the present. What did Yancy plan to do to Nolan and Jeb?"

Quite the puzzlement on Bea's face. "Yancy?"

"Yeah, Yancy."

"She didn't have a plan. She'd have told me."

Callie relaxed in her seat a moment, to let Bea see she could do the same. Callie was beginning to think the kids just took off with no plan, extemporaneous in their actions. Their first thought was to simply run when they felt the police chief was on her way. Knox stepped over and scribbled on Callie's notepad. *Make her resent her sister.* Then he returned to stand behind Bea. They weren't taking another chance at her flying off again.

"But then Nolan arrived," Callie continued. "How did that make you feel, Bea? Did you like not being Yancy's only sibling anymore? Here walks in her blood brother, leaving you the fake."

It hurt to watch Bea's eyes fill with agony, false memories, and veiled history. Trying to compartmentalize seventeen years of having a sister, belonging to a family unit that felt so right, only to discover it a lie. A child already struggling in her identity.

A cold-blooded killer who held a man underwater until his last breath.

Callie decided to push the girl's button. "Did you ask if you were stolen, too?"

Bea jumped up. Knox gripped her shoulders, taking a degree of effort to sit her back down. "I was not kidnapped."

"But how do you know?"

"My birth certificate!"

Callie looked at Knox. "Tell her."

"Your birth certificates are counterfeit. Both of them," he said. "I'm with the FBI. Agent Rhoades was FBI. Using what he dug up, and updating it with our programs, I believe we'll find that your parents aren't even named Wilkerson."

Her complexion paled to almost white. "I'm . . . kidnapped?"

He came around for her to see him. "We'll be digging pretty deep to ensure everyone's past is confirmed and identity clarified, but the FBI will keep watch on both of you, hoping you lead them to your parents. Sooner or later they'll read the papers and try to connect. Once caught, they'll go away for life. Not sure how long you'll get."

"The Flaggs are wealthy," Callie said. "Yancy will want her inheritance. Maybe not now, but somewhere downstream those dollars would call her name. She'd be the only one getting money out of this, Bea."

"Money isn't important," she replied.

Offering a mild laugh, Callie retained a smile of pity. "Tell that to someone worth millions."

Bea looked away.

Press harder. "Why did your parents get tired of you two and leave?"

An angry shake of her head. "They didn't—"

"How did it feel waking up one morning to find their closet empty?"

"No," Bea demanded. "They weren't like that."

"Sounds like it to me." Callie snapped her fingers. "Poof, and they're gone."

"We had a candlelight dinner the night before."

Callie gave her a *whatever* sneer. "You expect me to believe that?"

"Maybe not, but we did. Mom cooked us each our favorite dish. Four different dinners with lots of leftovers so we wouldn't go hungry."

With all the tension in the room, such an evening rang nonsensical to Callie. And she sniggered. Extra leftovers.

"Stop it," Bea yelled.

"Sorry." Callie rested fingers over her smile. "But I can't picture that. Kidnappers cooking their own farewell dinner, kissing their daughters' asses good-bye with, what, pizza and burgers? A cake with Bon Voyage for dessert?" She chuckled again.

"They loved us! They cried!" Bea screamed.

With a skeptical brow, Callie stared at her.

"They did." Bea's voice choked. "They had to so Yancy could step forward and claim what was hers without them being in the way."

"Not get caught, you mean," Callie said. "They'd be waiting in the wings, waiting for their compensation for raising you two."

Sweet plan, actually. Long, but not bad. This couple had already proven they could change identities and get away with it.

"That's not exactly right," Bea said, but the uncertainty in the voice told Callie she was close enough.

"Where are your parents?"

"I . . . don't know."

"What if they moved on?" Callie quickly tacked on.

"They wouldn't do that."

Again. "But what if they did?"

A nervous frown twitched, and Bea mashed her lips to stop it. "I'd have Yancy. She would take care of me."

"One could only hope, but then her new family might not appreciate a stranger." Callie let that one sink into the girl's fragile psyche. "But why was Yancy waiting? What made her wait to tell the world who she was?"

Bea dissolved into tears. "She wasn't sure which person she wanted to be." Bending her forehead to her knees, hands still cuffed behind her, she cried beneath the long hair that collected around her. "I kept telling her to wait . . . because I might be left alone."

Exhausted, Callie figured she'd dug up just about all she cared to from this child for now. Her throat tightened at the pitiful sounds of her target's mewling. A mere child thrust into a world not of her choosing, but she'd gone too far. A girl making adult decisions and not knowing how . . . and getting it oh so wrong.

Callie opened her office door.

"Chief?" Thomas was standing, stretching to appear taller while keeping close to his prisoner. "Mr. LeGrand is—"

"I'll announce myself, if you don't mind!" Hair still amiss from being in bed, his shirt loose over crumpled khakis, Brice went to reach over the counter gate and unlatch it. To head back to Callie's office.

"Stay right there, Brice," Callie ordered. "We're too busy for you right now."

"As head of town council, I have the right to—" But he stopped when Callie moved the few steps to meet him head-on.

She got to the gate, reached over, and pulled his shirt to bring him closer. After two jerks, he pulled loose.

Callie leaned over and whispered through her teeth. "Get your ass out of my station. We cannot afford for you to screw this up. Get out or I'll cuff you to a bathroom stall until we're done sometime tomorrow and then book you for impeding an investigation. Is that understood?"

"You don't have the balls," he growled.

"Don't need them," she replied and reached around her back for her cuffs, stunned a second after realizing they were already in use.

But Brice recognized the motive.

Staring daggers, he glanced toward Callie's office at Knox in the doorway, then back at Thomas next to Yancy, as he analyzed the strength behind his adversary.

Both held stoic expressions saved for perps and crowds that needed to disperse. No give in their demeanor at all.

"I'll be in touch, Chief." And he spun and stomped out the door.

Callie inhaled and didn't care who heard her blow it out. "All right, guys. Swap girls."

Knox retrieved Bea, then he and Thomas exchanged prisoners, the young officer taken aback at Bea's cuffs and the clotted blood on the side of her scalp.

"Bea?" Yancy reached for her sister, but Knox gripped her arm and kept her moving toward the back office.

"Chief?" Thomas asked, going through the motions with his charge, but a bit awestruck.

"Just keep her comfortable, Thomas. We won't be long."

Yancy took her seat without coercion, but could hardly take her attention off Knox's blood-speckled shirt. "What did you do to my sister?" she asked with forced authority.

"Nothing," Callie replied, then turned on the recorder for a new interview and a fresh repetition of Miranda rights. Yancy said she understood her rights, with some nerve twitching going on in her body.

Callie asked a handful of small talk, common questions that wouldn't threaten the girl and would determine her microexpressions and behavior when telling the truth. Yancy was Emma, and the rest shouldn't be hard to put together. The Miranda rights were in case Yancy advised Bea before or after Pinky's death, which Callie gave fifty-fifty odds.

"Did you help Bea kill Pinkerton Rhoades? We already have her confession."

Simple. To the point. Nothing gray about the answer, either. She did or she didn't.

But Yancy fought not to crumble while irregular shakes traveled the length of her. "No, I didn't." Not as strong as she behaved in the thick of her peers.

"When did Bea confess to you?" Not so black-and-white.

Yancy just shook her head, protecting her rights. Yeah, this child would be cagier, but she wasn't as robust as she pretended. And Callie'd been down this road before. "Did you try to stop her?"

One could always read the eyes, and the blue-haired sister's seemed to contain a deep gravity of—what—regret?

"Bea wouldn't listen when you tried to stop her?"

Instant frown reaction. No, Yancy didn't have that discussion, but she remained silent, unwilling to condemn Bea.

"You didn't know what she did until after, did you?"

Yancy lightly chewed the inside of her lip, then seemed to catch herself.

"Did Nolan know before you?"

Ah, a surprise question from the opened eyes, then a straight look past Callie. A sign of recalling a memory. She wasn't sure.

"Did you decide to take the boat?"

"Did Nolan force you?"

"Did Bea hold a gun on you?"

"Were you going to kill Jeb?"

"Did you tell Nolan who you were?"

Peppered with questions, Yancy's defenses weakened. Then . . . "Do you remember being molested as a child?"

Yancy went white. "Bea told you? Why would she?"

"Part of her confession," Callie said. "Do you remember any of that?"

She shook her head.

"What if it was just words to justify the abduction, Yancy?"

With tear-rimmed eyes, Yancy stared at her inquisitor. "Who am I supposed to believe?"

Callie wished she could tell her.

A lot of questions resulted in mostly silence from Yancy, but by the end of the hour, Callie determined that Yancy had been unable to protect her sister because she never appreciated she had to. She was cognizant of too little, her facial expressions stating too much. But the few remarks she gave were concerning her abduction, mostly obtained from headlines and the stories her *parents* deemed important. All she understood about the Flaggs, she'd gathered on her own.

It was almost five. Dawn would soon rise over the Atlantic, returning the gray waves to blue green, and gulls would swoop in and out of the spray, snaring breakfast.

But they couldn't rest yet. Nolan and Jeb needed to be interviewed that day. She'd let Knox take care of Jeb, with she and Raysor in the room. Amanda Flagg would most assuredly dictate the presence of an attorney for Nolan, and all of this would hopefully occur before the FBI decided these were cases suddenly worthy of their attention after all.

She'd place a call to Amanda Flagg midmorning. While in-person was preferable, the course of events negated that chance, but a face-to-face would absolutely happen within the next forty-eight hours. The mother deserved that much. Callie's concern was whether any of Emma still existed, and if Yancy would give a damn about the woman who birthed her.

It didn't take long to piece together that Bea was the little girl Yancy played with on the playground seventeen years ago. Likenesses in the old photos made more sense. The new and old driver's licenses of the Wilkersons and Metts as well. The Wilkersons weren't total crazed scumbags. They were a mother and father desperate to find a partner for their daughter left isolated by the death of her twin. Yancy'd been raised well, a million-to-one exception to child-kidnapping odds.

Not that the Wilkersons were altruistic in any shape or form. *Selfish* more defined them. If they could disappear and adopt a different identity once, they most likely did it again. Their income since the kidnapping? Who knew. Ransom took them part of the way. They'd played long-term odds and almost cleared the table by setting up Yancy to return and claim her inheritance.

Lavender and soft rose began to show in the sky, giving a touch of color to the view outside the station. Knox escorted Yancy into the lobby. She broke away, and he let her. Rushing to the chair beside her cuffed sister, she cried, "We don't need parents, Bea-Bea. We have each other." Rubbing her sister's back, she shifted closer against her twin, and cooed phrases inaudibly into her sister's hair.

Chapter 30

IT HAD BEEN TEN days since Bea's confession. It had taken three days to define how much Yancy and Nolan had been involved in Pinky's death. The murder belonged to Callie, the kidnapping still to the FBI, and the logistics involved a bit of chest thumping. The weight of the expected public opinion about a poor kidnapped girl returned home safe after seventeen years factored in big-time, so Yancy walked free. At least that's what Knox's take on the situation had been.

Once again, Callie drove past the antique-looking pewter sign declaring the entrance to the Flagg's Mount Pleasant estate, on a final mission she never dreamed she'd make. The radio off, the silence between her and Knox felt needed, to respect the moment. Yancy followed, driving herself in her own car.

Callie's blood ran cold at the thought of what might've happened if she hadn't stopped them on Big Bay Creek. And who would've been left standing.

Callie had expected Yancy to be a collaborator with her adopted twin. But though Yancy served as the leader of the pair, Bea could self-govern, willing to literally kill to save her lifestyle and sister. A death certificate quickly proved Bea's original last name was Metts.

There'd been no grandmother visit, and the girls had no idea where the parents were. Smart move on their part, though how long they'd wait in the dark with their daughter arrested for murder remained to be seen.

There'd been a rush put on Yancy's DNA to ID her as the abducted toddler with the gap-toothed smile.

Funny how the FBI owned the cold case now.

Callie called Amanda Flagg the day she'd interviewed the sisters, and dutifully offered to watch over Yancy until a formal meet would take place. Like she really needed to. Yancy'd already proven she could make her own way in this world.

Nolan went home from the hospital, arm in a cast, his mother hovering, so technically Nolan broke the news to her first. Callie interviewed him at the Flagg residence the night after questioning Yancy, with an attorney and the FBI in the mix. The revelation of Nolan's resentment of Pinky had stunned his mother.

By the end of the questioning, Nolan was a puddled mess in his mother's arms. He'd not believed Pinky, but hired Sammy to see just what Pinky was up to. Sammy needed the money, and Nolan had it to spend. Why not? But Nolan had seen Bea meet Pinky at the marina, and in his anger, guilt, and curiosity, confronted Bea at Fantasea, with Jeb as his witness. He hadn't confronted the girls earlier, knowing the cops were looking, holding on to a residual fear that he would be considered part of the murder. Sammy's text that Callie was coming to Fantasea that night sent them all to the boat.

"God, what an intense butterfly effect because a one-year-old twin died," Callie said, approaching the driveway.

Knox sighed. "I do and don't want to be here."

"I wouldn't miss it for the world," Callie uttered.

Wheels silent on the concrete circular drive, her heart thumped harder than when she met here to report Pinky's death. Rubbing her chest, Callie tried to stand in the mother's shoes, welcoming her once-thought-dead daughter, just years older.

God, if only.

Her Bonnie would've been almost five, and if someone told her a mistake had been made, and all she'd lost was time? Callie'd take that all day long and twice on Sunday.

The weather gentle, the noonday sun bright, April chose to shine in lieu of showing its rainy, windy side. Amanda and Nolan stood on the landing before those huge, black, eight-foot double doors. The mother gripped the wrought-iron railing, the son holding his mother's shoulder with his good arm.

Both cars parked. Yancy exited first, sweet in a spring dress that hugged her then swung out easy to her knees. Soft blue flats on her feet, complementing the blue in her hair, today minus the beads and feathers.

Always the blue.

Knox and Callie held back. He laid a hand on her shoulder. She watched and prayed.

Yancy took the first six steps of the dozen with a meekness contrary to her personality, and stared down at her shoes for a second, a heave of her shoulders to collect herself. Then she stood tall and took the rest steady and sure.

As she reached her mother, Amanda released a soft yelp of happiness with open arms, beckoning with moving fingers for her child to come in for a hug and the love she'd saved for seventeen years. Six inches taller than her mother, Yancy let herself fall into the embrace, stiff. She looked over to Nolan for support, and he weakly smiled, uncomfortable. Then slowly, Yancy hugged Amanda back.

After ample hugs and holding a rigid Emma back to drink her in, Amanda gestured to the two law-enforcement officials in the background. "You two," she said, the energy in her voice volumes louder than their last visit in the study. "Come in, come in."

Callie climbed first, eyes moist, but when Amanda wrapped arms around her, a few tears fell.

"Thank you, thank you, Chief Morgan," Amanda whispered, then embraced her again. "God bless you for bringing my Emma home."

She released Callie and expressed the same gratitude to Knox.

"You are welcome . . . from Pinky," he said.

Amanda peered into Knox's face. "Yes. From Pinky."

Everyone moved into the foyer, the scene becoming an awkward family reunion. Having imagined how difficult it would be for the mother to remain in the same house where Emma once played and livened the rooms, Callie better understood now as she stood in the entry way. Amanda could retain old memories and build new ones in the same geography, where the past and present could mend the in-between.

They entered the dining room. What Southern family didn't bond over food? The luncheon served was unconditionally worthy of the heady homecoming. A ham covered in pineapple and cloves. Scalloped potatoes, deviled eggs, and spring asparagus, and lemon icebox pie. The spread flaunted itself atop a creamy tablecloth draped across a cherry dining table that seated twelve.

Silverware clinked on Spode everyday china, napkins properly across laps, but it wasn't until the pie plates were taken away and coffee offered that anyone felt inclined to speak of more than the flavors in the meal.

Food just made for easier conversation.

Amanda sat between her children instead of at the head, occasionally touching one or the other. Callie and Knox sat opposite them. So weird. Both children acted like they preferred to be anyplace other than there.

Yancy wiped her mouth and set her napkin on the table. "I'll break the ice. I don't really recall anything, Ms. Flagg . . . um, M—" But she couldn't bring herself to call the lady *mother*.

"Honey," Amanda said, not saccharin because this wasn't a child, but matronly because the girl needed some motherhood. "You were a baby. Of course, you don't." Then Amanda set her napkin on the table, a seriousness in her eyes. "The Metts lost one of their twins to a horrid cancer, leaving the remaining daughter distressed. Very reserved. The poor dear crawled up inside herself and tried to disappear." She glanced over at Callie. "Y'all told her about the Metts, right? I wanted y'all here so you could answer any questions Emma had that I couldn't address."

Awkward, but that's why Callie suspected she received the invitation . . . to play moderator, the person with answers, or rather the person who could explain the answers easier. "Yanc . . . Emma, knows what we know, ma'am. Everything in the file. Everything we discovered."

Yancy still held a stiffness about her. "I don't recall any of that. And Bea didn't know any of that either." She looked at Callie. "Did you tell Ms. Flagg why my parents said I was kidnapped?"

Resting crossed arms on the table, Callie tried to lessen the formality. "Yes, I did."

"Nobody molested you, sweetheart," Amanda said, no longer brushing Yancy's sleeve, as if the topic warranted space. "You could not have been happier in this house. Your father died brokenhearted, and he would've been devastated hearing you'd been told he hurt you. Nothing could be further from the truth."

Kudos to Amanda. Nolan had said she was made of some stern stuff. No longer the fragile, pale woman who'd sat empty and spent with them in the study that day.

"And please," She touched Yancy's arm again. "It's Mom, Momma, Mother, whatever you decide. You take all the time you need to figure that out."

Nolan remained quiet, had remained silent throughout the meal. Callie noted he'd barely eaten.

As if prodded, Amanda turned to her son. "I'm so sorry you couldn't talk to me. I'll kick myself for years to come about this rift between us."

"It wasn't a rift, I told you." Nolan's tone bordered childish.

Amanda pivoted in her seat. "We talked about this."

He peered at Callie and then Knox, as if they could release him from this torture.

Knox held up his phone. "I need to take this." And he left the room.

Damn him. Callie wished she'd used the phone excuse before he did. And no wine with lunch, either.

Taking both his hands in hers, Amanda stared into her son's face. "Emma's kidnapping didn't mean you were worth less." She glanced back at the daughter. "And you not being here didn't mean you were worth less either, Emma. Life handed us this . . . this crap." They all lightly grinned at her use of slang. "Now we make the most of what we're reclaiming as ours."

Callie wiped her eye backhanded. Knox reentered the room. Suddenly nobody had a thing to say.

Then Yancy cleared her throat. "I can't just overnight become this new girl, y'all."

Each person nodded or mumbled agreement in some way, Amanda making the firmer point with, "Of course, honey."

"And I have a sister, and regardless what you think about her, we're still twins."

Glances darted, each uncertain as to the proper thing to say to that. Amanda refolded her napkin.

Yancy continued, "I'm supposed to say I'm grateful to everyone, but that's so unnatural for me. My life was just destroyed. Twice, I guess you could say." She turned to her mother. "Nothing against you, please understand that."

A hesitating nod. "I understand."

Elbow on the table, Callie studied these chipped and fractured souls. "I think there's room for a Yancy in this house, too."

"Absolutely," Amanda said.

Yancy allowed a small smile, though not completely relaxed. "And can she be *called* Yancy?"

The pause didn't last long, but it was noticeable, and nerves seemed to rise to the surface on everyone. But Amanda lifted her spoon from the table, tapped her water glass, and stood. "Here's a warm welcome to Yancy Emma Flagg, heretofore referred to as Yancy. And we couldn't love her more."

The release worked, and for an hour, the conversation having carried over into the study, the family and the cops shared questions, some drawing halting consternation, but none left hanging when 3:00 p.m. rolled around. Callie nudged Knox and stood. "We need to go."

Hands shook and hugs doled out, Callie and Knox headed to the study's doorway. Yancy followed. "You don't have to leave because we are," Callie said. "Stay."

"That's okay." Yancy glanced over her shoulder. "I told them I'd walk you to the car and come back."

Amanda just smiled. Nolan had pulled out his phone.

Yancy escorted them to the landing outside. "Heard anything about Bea?" she asked.

"She's being closely watched," Knox said. "And they've assigned her a psychiatrist. Give the detention center a call. I'm pretty sure you can see her now. A damn fine Charleston defense attorney stepped in to take her case, but you probably heard."

Yancy nodded. "Amanda, um, my mother hired him, out of respect for me."

"So y'all communicated before today," Callie said, only slightly surprised.

"I told Amanda that Bea and I were a package," Yancy said. "And the best thing I can do for my sister is use my newfound financial means to provide her the best defense. She thought she was saving me. It's the least I can do."

Callie was unsure how to read that proud smile. "She didn't have to kill the man, Yancy. Bea needs help as well as incarceration."

Despite the contrary words, Miss Blue Hair's nod was loose. "Oh, no doubt. But I'll stand by her, regardless."

"What happens when your parents come hunting you two?" Knox asked. "Assuming you really don't have a clue where they are."

Yancy regarded the agent with a haughty gaze.

"Do you *have* their location?" Callie asked.

"No," Yancy answered, but Callie wasn't sure she believed her.

"Remember? My major is pre-law," Yancy said. "I may not see my parents ever again, but just in case they do appear, I intend to secure them a good defense. When they informed Bea and me of . . . things . . . when we turned eighteen, law just seemed the smart way to go. I love those people, and they'll need a good attorney." She grinned. "And I intend to ace law school."

A touch of ire crept up inside Callie. "Your mother, and I mean your *real* mother, never stopped searching for you. That's loyalty, too."

"Again, no doubt," Yancy said.

Normal to keep Amanda Flagg at arm's length. Expected to still love the parents who raised her, but Callie sensed a darkness in this deal. She leaned in with not so much a threat as a warning. "Don't you hurt her, Yancy. Don't you steal from her, and don't you overwhelm her with any theatrics that rob her of even one day she has left in this world. Your return has given her a new lease on life. I will not see you kick dirt in her face."

"And you won't see it, Chief Morgan."

Which way did she mean that?

From over Callie's shoulder, Knox challenged as well. "Until the Metts are apprehended, the FBI still has an open case on your kidnapping. With you and Bea in their sights, you'll be questioned and watched, then questioned again. Cases may get cold"—he stared down his nose at her—"but they're still open cases, and we all know how those situations can heat up and come back to life."

Again with the nodding, as though Yancy had already measured these thoughts. "And that's fine." Taller than Callie, Yancy looked down. "Three people took care of me for what I thought was my entire life. Nineteen years. Now I learn it's been, what, two years less than that?" Her arms went out on either side of her, like a set of scales. "Ten percent Flaggs . . . ninety percent Wilkersons?"

"Metts," Callie corrected.

Yancy lightly shrugged. "Same same."

"Yancy . . ." Knox started.

The girl laughed. "Lighten up, Mr. FBI. I'm seriously grateful. You two did a great job, but I'll take it from here." She held out a hand to Knox, who took the shake with reservation. Then she reached out to Callie, who gripped Yancy's palm with a firmness she hoped the ex-twin understood.

As they hooked their seat belts to leave, Callie and Knox glanced back at Yancy, one foot in the front door, waving good-bye. Then before Callie put the car in drive, Miss Yancy Emma Flagg entered her new mansion and closed the door.

"Wow," Knox said.

"Yeah." Suddenly Callie really felt sorry for Nolan.

Chapter 31

AT TWO IN THE afternoon, Callie walked along the water barefoot, her Bermudas worn for the first time this season. A healthy wind off the water kept her loose blouse flapping behind her. It had been a while since she had simply walked the sand, in lieu of pounding it to get in her miles. The slower solitude gave her moments to sort and sift things, with the surf undulating in and out, long overdue.

Moments that took her closer to Seabrook than sitting on that red porch swing.

Closer to John than if her steps walked Boston streets.

Regardless of her future, this was her beach.

A fit, flat-abbed twentysomething ran by, looking back with a Solo cup in his hand, his slim girl pretending to chase. Funny how she could catch the promise of alcohol, even over the sea breeze. Clemson students, along with a few from small schools like Charleston Southern and Presbyterian College, enjoyed the last day of fun in their spring break sun. The College of Charleston crew had long returned to class.

But Callie wasn't out here to police kids, and no point ruining their fun. She'd taken the day off, against the advice of Marie, who felt Callie ought to be front and center meting out justice every minute of this particular day. Brice had scheduled a special town-council meeting for five thirty, refreshments afterward for those worried about missing dinner. Food also attracted more attention.

By now, though, it was what it was.

For the last week, Sophie canvassed the beach and approached neighbors on Callie's behalf like this was an election campaign. Guess it resembled one, since public opinion factored into what the council would do this evening. Callie had solved a murder and a cold-case abduction, but according to Brice, none of that seemed to matter as much as her evening disruptions of a few of kids in their affluent homes.

Spring sun shone on the beach softer than in July or August, but she still wore shades. But even through them, in spite of reflection off the water, she watched a heavyset man enter the beach ahead on Access 11, a stark contrast to the other beachcombers. Especially in his uniform.

He almost waddled, taking the uneven sand in awkward steps. “Hey, Doll,” Raysor said. “Thought you’d like some company.”

She smiled in spite of her need to be alone. He meant well.

They walked a few yards. “You just coming in to work?” she asked.

“Had errands this morning, but hey”—he nudged her—“you’re off duty, so you aren’t supposed to know.”

She lifted her chin in a *gotcha* move, and smiled again.

She started to ask him about Stan. If he’d heard from him lately . . . if he was ever moving back to Edisto. Like when she almost slept with her old boss, she’d sort of burned a bridge with Stan, again. But he wasn’t here, and the meeting this evening deserved her attention at present.

“Worried?” Raysor asked.

Callie studied her feet. They’d reached a heavily shelled area, and she stepped carefully. “Maybe a little.”

“Yeah, well . . .” But he couldn’t complete the sentence. Instead, his big hand patted her back, and they returned to their reveries. They walked past four more beach accesses, the water’s roar and gulls’ playful screams filling their heads with white noise.

“Listen,” she said, and he looked exceptionally more interested than he needed to. Raysor wasn’t a walker, and she guessed he’d endured more than his comfortable share of exercise. “I probably need to get back unless you want to walk some more, Don.”

“Oh no,” he said. “Don’t let me hold you up, plus Marie’s probably hunting me.”

Not like he wasn’t wearing a mic.

“But, Doll.” His mouth moved all around, his weight shifting in the thick sand as he seemed uncomfortable in his words. “I’ll be there for you. My man Thomas will, too. Can’t speak so much for those new twits, but I’ll give them an earful.”

Callie patted his bulky arm. “I appreciate it, Don.” And she turned and headed back from whence she came. She didn’t know where Raysor had parked, but he was giving her space—and taking the opportunity to walk over to the easier sidewalk to make his way back to his car.

Not a man of many words, but the few he managed always mattered.

Five accesses back, she detoured across Palmetto then a quick zigzag of blocks to Chelsea Morning. Jeb’s Jeep parked in the drive. Rather odd and unexpected.

She took two steps at a time to the porch and grabbed the door handle . . . and it was locked. And then he opened it from the inside. She grinned. "You finally locked the door." She entered. "What are you doing home?"

"Sprite's school is out for a teacher's workday, so I cut my two classes."

"Jeb," Callie warned, though she cared little since he carried As and Bs.

He shrugged. "It's too nice a weekend to stay away from the beach."

She hugged him anyway. "Good. Maybe we can go out to eat later."

"Sprite and I . . ."

Her eyes rolled. "Yeah, I know." She hugged him again. "Well, then I'll enjoy you from afar, but you owe me at least one formal meal this weekend."

With a click of his tongue he turned and wandered to the side porch, phone to his ear. "Hey," she heard him say. "What you doing?" Had to be Sprite.

Most girls love a white knight. But Sprite playing the heroine that night on Big Bay Creek had turned Jeb's head back in the right direction. Not that Callie wanted Sophie's daughter involved, or enjoyed watching her crash into another boat, especially containing Jeb, but it was quite evident that after many a summer day on the Grady-White with Zeus and Jeb, Sprite could captain a boat.

Three thirty. Her heart thumped a bit checking the clock. Guess she'd shower.

She couldn't help the what-ifs in her head as water beat it hot and steaming. With hands on the shower wall, she moved so the jets hit her back. A rough case and no scars to show for it. She almost wished she had one to show the ignorant at this meeting that she'd fought hard against the crime on their beach. Sure, the killer wasn't a big brute with knives and guns, clubs and grenades, but the teenager was a killer nonetheless. Of a good man who'd been abandoned by the Bureau after thirty years of service, and thanks to his diligence and big heart, died after only six months of retirement.

That was the saddest part of all of this. Not Bea, not Yancy, not even Amanda Flagg, though there was plenty of sadness to go around. Callie'd righted some wrong, and she felt some sense of pride about that, but everyone's world was changed.

Crap, she'd taken too long in the shower. It was five till four, and she wanted to appear in full uniform. Impressive as hell. Impression was everything to a lot of these people.

She reached for the cooler . . . only to remember it was gone. Ice dumped, the gin given to Sophie once she heard about the special council meeting. No matter.

"You don't need it," she whispered.

Collar, insignia, belt, shoes, makeup clean but not too feminine. She'd even had her hair cut yesterday, taking her cap so the hairdresser got it right.

"Jeb?" she hollered, exiting her bedroom. Nothing. Had to be with Sprite.

She paused in front of the hall mirror, satisfied with the reflection, then she set the alarm and left the house, alone.

One and a half miles to the administrative building that housed all of Edisto's government, to include the PD. Cars backed up alongside the avenue leading in half a block before she reached the complex. Thank goodness she had a reserved spot, but then maybe not.

She analyzed the cars, happy at seeing some, cringing at others. Brice's, of course. Each of the council people. Mayor Talbot. Oh God, was that . . . no, of all people to attend this meeting, Beverly Cantrell was the last person Callie needed. A show of support, she guessed, but how embarrassing to be hung out to dry in front of your mother.

Beverly's presence would only fuel Brice, giving him yet another one-up on his old girlfriend as he dismantled Callie to the utmost of his ability.

People strolled into the complex, but nobody noticed her behind the old oak. She laid her head on her steering wheel. At the last special meeting, she'd been sworn in as police chief, Seabrook beaming, standing at the back of the room. Her mayoral mother had competed with the Edisto mayor for media attention.

Oh crap. Media.

Jerking erect, she scanned the lot for a particular set of letters . . . and there they were—WLSC, aka Alex Hanson, granddaughter of an Edisto native and reporter for the Charleston news station. They were congenial with each other, having shared a strangling fear of a night coping with the Edisto Jinx, but the twenty-five-year-old was a reporter, and everyone knew what their priorities were.

She checked herself in the rearview mirror once more, collected her hat off the seat, and exited. Deep breath. This could actually go her way, she kept telling herself. Not everyone loved Brice. Frankly, nobody loved Brice, but he could make you fear going against his grain.

As she entered the complex, Sophie met her in the hall. "You got this, honey," she whispered.

"We can only hope," Callie said. "Let me go get this over with."

So I can have a drink was almost her silent response.

She hadn't had a drink in five days. It had been her best friend through some damn hard times, and she missed it, and hoped hard that not drinking was worth these jitters of abstinence. Not just in her gut, but unexpectedly in her hands. Today was better, but the last three nights had been hell to get any rest. She'd used extra makeup under her eyes this morning to disguise the shadows she hadn't seen before.

In front of her, someone she didn't recognize held the door open for her. Great, strangers were here for the show. How many tourists were here?

Staring straight, she made her way to the front. A seat had been reserved for her on the front row, facing the line of chairs in front. Two of those chairs, however, remained empty, but she heard their owners, Brice and Mayor Talbot, capitalizing on the group to make nice and shake hands to prove their worth. The clock said 5:27.

"Brice?" said a council woman. "It's about time."

He walked toward the front, his double take recognizing Callie, his sneer so happy at her presence. Her reserved seat on the audience's front row sat strategically in front of him, and so stood a podium. God, she hoped she wouldn't have to stand there and be scrutinized.

"Let's call this special meeting of the Edisto Beach Town Council to order," he said, then reiterated it with a gavel. "Since this is a special meeting concerning the Edisto Police Department, in particular, Police Chief Callie Jean Morgan, let's get down to business. We've planned this evening to allow the public and any interested party to speak their mind, pro and con, regarding Chief Morgan."

A few mumbles rolled around the room behind Callie, but she couldn't make out the identities of anyone in particular. And she didn't dare look around.

Though she had a speech prepared, the paper rolled up in her hand, she was uncertain whether it was the right speech. Marie helped her with statistics and dates, savings and accomplishments, but without an understanding of the exact flavor of the meeting, she wasn't sure she'd nailed the proper tone. She gripped the paper tighter, controlling. Her hands were *not* going to shake.

I should've had a shot. Just one.

A hand rested on her shoulder and patted. A man's hand. She didn't dare turn to identify its owner, so she reached up and patted it back in thanks.

Mayor Talbot asked to speak next, his oration more factual about how Callie came to Edisto, her background and qualifications. Covering his own butt as to why he hired her. Some general verbiage about the challenges she'd faced. As straight a fence-line stance as anyone could take.

"Good, good, thank you, Mayor Talbot," Brice said. He was loving this.

"Now, would anyone else like to come forward? Chief Morgan? Would you care to express yourself to everyone?"

Heat rushed up her neck. To open the discussion would give fodder to those against her, using her words against her. To refuse demonstrated weakness.

"I'll start," came a familiar voice a couple rows behind Callie.

Knox strode up the aisle, a small briefcase in hand, decked out in a charcoal suit, the epitome of a federal agent. The lavender tie softened the overall aura of him, but it looked good, as if it made him approachable and not all Joe Friday.

"Yes, Senior Special Agent Knox Kendrick of the FBI. Let's give him a welcome, Edisto."

The room politely applauded.

Callie stiffened as the feeb reached the podium. The same man who'd reported her to Brice for drinking and offered to feed Brice details about her progress on Pinky's case.

He set his briefcase on the floor. "Mr. Mayor," Knox said, tipping his head. "And Edisto Beach Town Council. Thank you for hearing me."

The room went silent.

Callie's heart beat like hell behind her badge.

But then Knox stepped to the side, analyzing the podium. "Does this thing have wheels?"

Someone several seats down from Callie jumped up and offered to assist. Between the two of them, they unlocked its wheels, and at Knox's direction, they moved it to the side.

Callie held her breath.

"Thank you," Knox said to the volunteer, then stood solo before the audience. "This is an amazing turnout. Of course, I'm not one of you, and my experience with the Edisto Police Department, in particular

Chief Morgan, has been limited." He glanced at Callie. "But what we lacked in experience, we made up for in intensity, didn't we, Chief?"

She was forced to smile and nod back.

"And I've had conversation with Brice LeGrand, your head of Town Council. Thank you, Mr. LeGrand," he said, turning to see Brice who nodded regally.

A small sense of restlessness circled the room. Shifting in seats, the brush of clothing, feet moving as attendees wondered what to expect.

"Well, since we worked a joint case with the Chief less than three weeks ago, I've been asked to represent the FBI in this inquiry into the Chief's abilities."

Loud mumbles rolled at the first mention of a trial of sorts. Clicks sounded from the side, cameras saving the moment.

Knox raised his voice. "Let me do this so this meeting doesn't take too long. I'm sure you folks have better places to be, so if you'll give me your attention," and he reached down into the briefcase, withdrawing a plain brown cardboard box. He reached his hand out to Callie. "Chief Morgan, would you come up, please."

Pulse hammering in her ears, Callie rose and moved to the agent, and Knox motioned for her to face the crowd.

Those present stole her breath away. Every one of her officers decked out in full dress. The fire department as well. Several from the Colleton County Sheriff's Department and a couple guys from SLED. With respect for etiquette, they stood around the room to save the seating for Sophie, Sprite, Zeus, Jeb, and all the civilians. Beverly was adorned in her most striking suit, Janet Wainwright decked out in one of her red dress jackets over a gold top, ever the Marine.

"Chief Morgan?" Knox slid the box away from its contents. "On behalf of the FBI, we would like to honor you with this plaque of appreciation for not only solving the death of one our own, but also the seventeen-year-old Emma Flagg abduction. Any one of those cases would be landmark for any agent, but you managed both, with minimal support and manpower." He handed the plaque over with his left hand, and reached out with his right.

The room erupted in applause. She slid her hand into his, stymied, stunned . . . suddenly awed at what this man was doing for her. He winked, and she couldn't help but be grateful for this idiot, self-righteous agent, regardless of his initial strategy.

The clapping turned into a standing ovation. Her throat grew thick with gratification. She blinked back the moistness. From the looks of the room, Callie sensed this whole event a clandestinely planned celebration by all, until she glanced back at the town council. Brice remained seated, flushed, and the glare that met her could've melted rock. To his right, one council woman clapped slowly, making no noise, unable to stand fully behind Brice, afraid not to follow the crowd. The other three were on their feet.

"The least I could do, Callie," Knox said, leaning down to be heard over the noise.

She let loose the handshake and reached up to hug him, the plaque between them. "I was hoping there was a good guy in there someplace," she said. And as he squeezed her back, she had to wonder if she really deserved all this . . . if maybe Knox had supported her just enough through the drink and the self-doubt for her to stumble, rally, and get these cases right.

They separated, and she looked over the room. It took two or three minutes for the room to settle, everyone enjoying a happy moment, but as they sat, except for the uniforms lining the walls, she spotted a large man slide into the door. With no place to sit, he noted those present and wedged himself next to Raysor, reaching over to shake Thomas's hand before he crossed his own in parade rest. Every bit the cop as the uniforms around him.

Stan.

A gavel sounded, and the room quieted.

She made eye contact with Stan, whose stare softened with a grin.

Knox held out his arm for her to return to her seat, as he followed. She took her place.

Stan hadn't texted or called about his return, but then she'd sort of cut him off, too. So confusing, especially in this moment of extreme confusion. She couldn't analyze Stan now, but she allowed herself a moment to run her hand over the commendation and drink it in.

"Well, that was . . . impressive," Brice said, earning a few chuckles from around the room. What *could* he say? His allies surely expected a different flavor of public appraisal.

Those not in Brice's pocket would think what a genius stunt to convince so many to participate in proclaiming that tiny Edisto Beach had a woman chief who flat knew her stuff.

Brice cleared his throat. "Our FBI friends can sure steal the show, can't they?"

Light laughter traveled the room.

"But we're overjoyed at this surprise recognition. Glad we could coordinate this evening with our federal friends. But, the goal of this session was also to give the public a chance to offer feedback, too. Anyone else have anything to say about our own Chief Morgan?"

"Sure. I'll go next." A representative from Colleton County Sheriff's Office came forward, and sang her praises. Then a guy from SLED. Even Ike, one of her new officers, though she smelled some mighty fine BS in his appreciative words, as though he needed to earn some credit. But in the end, eight people rose and proclaimed Callie more than fit for duty and much beloved.

The point was made.

None of this changed the fact that Brice wished her gone, but it changed his fantasy that he could snap his fingers and accomplish it.

"Well, Chief Morgan, the people have spoken. Congratulations. Now, I smell shrimp down the hall, so this meeting is adjourned." No sooner did his gavel hit the wooden block than people jumped up and vacated the meeting room.

Whaley's catered the event. Before it closed, Bo-Pig held the honor for the last special council meeting like this, when she was presented her badge, but the feeling was just as invigorating, and the sense of community intoxicating.

But as she was about to enter the open fire-station bay area, someone tapped her on the shoulder. With a tiny thrill in her belly, she turned with a smile, hoping to see Stan . . . only to face Brice.

"What, no booze, Chief?"

Callie didn't answer, and she no longer smiled, except briefly to a gift-shop owner who gave her a thumbs-up as she passed by.

Brice leaned in, a half smirk in place. "I'm doubling down, missy," he grumbled. "You won't see me coming."

"Hey, Chief, nice surprise, huh?" Thomas held out his hand to Callie for a shake, and Brice slid off to one of his waiting buddies.

Callie gave his grip a hard shake. "What the hell would I do without you, Officer Gage?"

"I don't rightly know, ma'am, but I could always use a raise." And the corner of his mouth curled up to the side as he left for the food.

The shrimp and all the rest of the fixin's were half eaten by the time Callie finished shaking hands and speaking to attendees.

"Told you I'd save your ass," Sophie said in her ear, whisking by.

Arms enveloped her from behind as Jeb gave her a big squeeze. "Not mad I cut school now, are you?"

"Humph, congratulations, Chief," Wainwright stated, her grip almost breaking bones.

But after Callie dropped her paper plate into the trash bin, her hand achy from the best wishes, she scanned the fire-station bay area.

She hadn't seen Stan.

Chapter 32

CALLIE OFFERED to help clean the fire-engine bay of paper tablecloths and cups, but the Whaley's staff wouldn't hear of it.

Relieved? Oh, yeah, she was relieved big-time at the meeting, and she should feel more a part of these people than ever before. But she couldn't patch a hole where she used to keep someone close.

She walked to her parking spot. Almost eight, wow. The evening had flown, ending at the saddest part of her day.

And she was a little worried she'd get home to a welcoming party.

Maybe that's what she needed, though. These folks loved her, especially those she'd expect to appear at the house, and they deserved a celebration. Plus, Jeb would be there, silly boy. Fibbing to her that he was having dinner with Sprite.

As she reached the car, almost alone in the lot, a white piece of paper flapped from under the windshield wiper. *Give me five minutes at Seabrook's place.*

Very familiar handwriting.

Not a mile from the station, Windswept wasn't rented right now. Hadn't been rented since Knox left it, because she checked each evening.

But why would Stan ask to meet her there? He appreciated the meaning of the place to her. He also owed her a damn explanation for staying gone so long, for ignoring her calls, for leaving her so alone.

Shells and gravel popping under her tires, she parked in the drive and gazed up. Stan sat on the red swing in an easy rock . . . on Seabrook's porch . . . and she had no idea what to feel, or how to express it.

Regret for hanging up on him? Anger at his refusal to return her calls, her texts? Sorrow that he'd chosen to speak to Raysor over her since he'd left Edisto for Boston?

Or nothing, because this was Stan coming down to say he belonged back in Boston? Regardless of her grudge, that one scared her the most.

The coach light was on, alive with swirling bugs already eager for summer. "Hey," she said as she reached the top of the stairs, a weakness in her knees, a mild shake in her hands.

"Hey, yourself." He slid over and patted the swing.

She hesitated, then saw no wrong in such a simple act. She sat and eased all the way back in the swing, her feet leaving the floor, and to prove she had her act together, she slipped off her shoes so she could tuck one leg under her.

"Heard you had a hard time," he said, and threw an arm over the slatted back.

Miffed, she stared back. "How would you know?" They always looked at each other in a discussion. None of this staring in the distance, paying attention to cuticles, doodling. While awkward, they were forthright with each other. No tippy toeing around. She missed this about him probably more than anything else, other than his trust. And he'd cracked that foundation.

"Raysor told me," he said. "Care to talk now without all the emotional bullshit?"

"Not until you tell me whether you're still married, and whether you're back in Boston for good. We need some groundwork laid here." He sounded like the old Stan, but the old Stan wouldn't have abandoned her.

He gave a deep sigh, one you'd imagine from some mighty king in a cartoon, or a huge, friendly dragon who could fry you with one blast, but wouldn't because he made sense of his power. "Well, Chicklet, sometimes it ain't—"

"About you. Yeah, so you keep saying, but sometimes it is, Stan. Today was all about me, and I'm damn exhausted from everything that led to it."

He nodded. "I bet you are. It's why I came."

Goose bumps ran down her arms. "Are you returning to Boston?"

That low gravelly chuckle. Oh, how she missed it. "No, Callie. I'm done in Boston. It's been damn hard for me as well."

And guilt draped over her. Retirement from Boston PD. Divorce after a twenty-five-year marriage. He did have his hands full. "But you said two weeks," she said. "It's been six. I started wondering if you missed the old days. In some selfish way, I guess I made it about me, but I needed to know. That was cruel only talking to Raysor and leaving me in the dark right smack in the middle of a murder investigation."

She realized she'd been rambling and sighed. "I really could've used your help."

His sigh sounded forced, edged with a groan, and the weighty sound of a message coming. She'd heard it so many times before.

"Chicklet . . ."

Always a good sign using her nickname.

"Leaving here was difficult. Not necessarily because of what awaited me in Boston, selling the town house, signing the final divorce papers, seeing and saying good-bye to people I'd known for decades, but because I left you here in a bad, bad way."

She looked toward the horizon, the endless water morphing into its grays and federal blues, the sand taking on a golder cast. "So my sadness made you stay gone longer? Not feeling the love there, Stan."

"Look at me, Callie."

She did. She had to. He was using her real name. It's how they'd always played this game.

"You were stuck deep in that rut, honey. And you had no desire to crawl out. Never saw you drink so much."

"I know," she said low.

"Not that I expected a body to float up in your backyard, but that was probably a good thing for you."

She didn't like him talking about Pinky that way, but she understood what he was saying.

"You . . . not me, not Raysor, not anyone else . . . had to handle that situation. You had to exercise different brain cells, dust off your skills, put someone else's concerns before your own."

Her eyes narrowed. "I was selfish?"

"No, honey, you were grieving."

She turned back to the Atlantic.

"Take this house, for instance."

"Windswept," she reminded him. "Convenient you picked here instead of your place."

"Yeah, isn't it? You treated this place like it had a soul . . . and still harbored Seabrook's soul. Now," he gave a backhanded wave at the porch, "you're sitting here without the first sign of a panic attack."

"I had a couple of those, by the way. And you weren't—"

"Chicklet, you have no idea how damn hard that was for me not to be here for you. God, you have to see that." He was no longer so relaxed, and the swing had stopped. "But you needed to have those attacks, and have nobody here to pick you up. Don't you see? Until you picked yourself back up, you were not going to get better."

Tears trickled down her cheeks. She couldn't argue with him. She was better. Not in a huge way, but in the right direction. Not that life was cotton-candy wonderful, but it was a hell-of-a-sight better than the day Jeb called her from Big Bay Creek. Rather symbolic, the difference between the town-council meeting of that day and the one today. She felt more alive this evening, with more depth to her. But like a frostbite limb turned numb, with the revitalization came prickling, agonizing pain.

"I did not wish all this on you, Chicklet."

Stan, her voice of reason. "But why did you call Raysor instead of me?"

"He reported to me, and he wasn't oblivious to you hurting, by the way. I wanted to throw a glass against the wall each time I didn't answer you." He paused. "I'm sure he did, too."

In her mind's eye, she recalled the deputy offering to interview the girls and escort her to the Colleton County courthouse. How he chastised her for driving drunk. A more redneck effort to replace Stan.

Stan waved at her to slide over. She did without question. They fought to remain platonic, the two of them, but he hugged her. This time, he hugged her hard and planted a kiss on her head.

She closed her eyes, tears spilling. That's what Seabrook used to do.

"You want me to go to the church with you?" he gently said.

"No. That's not in me yet, Stan. Let me cope with one issue at a time."

No point putting a name on that issue. They both understood she drank. Tomorrow maybe she'd think about being an alcoholic . . . or not.

With a push, Stan put the swing back to rocking. His big beefy arm drew her harder against him, his palm petting and patting her arm.

They swung for a while.

"It's been longer than five minutes," she said. "Are there people at my house waiting?"

"Yeah." He stopped the rocking and straightened. "We better get you over there. And we don't need people talking about you cuddling some old bear in public."

It was almost dark. She reached down and retrieved her shoes. "Stan, today's the day people can say anything they like, because, frankly, I think I got this."

The End

Acknowledgments

Every book has a personality of its own. Each has different trials as well as sweet spots when the words gush onto the page. This one started from a dark place after Callie's loss in *Echoes of Edisto*, and I struggled for months to pull her out of her abyss while telling a story worthy of the series. I have several people I would be remiss not to embrace and thank for enduring, assisting, and understanding me through the tough times.

Blessings to those readers fresh and longtime who help me continue to believe in Edisto and Callie. Trust me . . . every review, email, Tweet, and Facebook post thrills me to my core. You keep me on this course, and I'm addicted to your enthusiasm.

Sidney Blake, Margaret Telsch-Williams, Lynn Chandler Willis, and Lee Kelsall . . . as my beta readers, y'all helped me beat this book back to life as well as endured my doldrums and mini-tantrums when I worried my talent was dry.

My new editor, Debra Dixon, sensed my frustrations and proved a most remarkable cheerleader. What I wouldn't give to have the essence of her bottled in an atomizer next to my computer, to use as needed.

To Debbie Parker-Bednar, steadfast fan, who in a roundabout way, through a friend of a friend, convinced me to name a character after her. I had a ball weaving her essence into Parker Bender.

To my son Nanu, thanks for coming up with the simplest, wisest, most obvious title for this book.

To my grandchildren, Jack and Duke, bless you for yanking me out of my dark writing cave every few days to make me enjoy what true joy is and to understand that life is about more than deadlines.

Of course, my hubby is the most remarkable, patient, loving man for tending to my needs while under pressure . . . and is a pure gem for accepting the title of Uncompensated Executive Personal Assistant with such grace and dedication.

And finally, to my parents, who will not read this book because of their journey through the halls of Alzheimer's. At one time, no one could pass them on the street without them bragging about their writing daughter.

About the Author

C. Hope Clark holds a fascination with the mystery genre and is author of the Carolina Slade Mystery Series as well as the Edisto Island Series, both set in her home state of South Carolina. In her previous federal life, she performed administrative investigations and married the agent she met on a bribery investigation. She enjoys nothing more than editing her books on the back porch with him, overlooking the lake with bourbons in hand. She can be found either on the banks of Lake Murray or Edisto Beach with one or two dachshunds in her lap. Hope is also editor of the award-winning FundsforWriters.com.

C. Hope Clark

Website: chopeclark.com

Twitter: twitter.com/hopeclark

Facebook: facebook.com/chopeclark

Goodreads: goodreads.com/hopeclark

Editor, FundsforWriters: fundsforwriters.com

95754017R00162

Made in the USA
Columbia, SC
15 May 2018